The day Dallas will never forget

DESTINY IN DALLAS

by Shirley Seifert

On April 3, 1858, Alexander Cockrell rode
into Dallas early in the morning, in advance
of his wagons. He had been on a trading ex-
pedition. His wife, Sarah, was waiting for him
with their four children. Will Toomy, his con-
struction foreman, was waiting for him.
Charley John, the Cherokee Indian who had
befriended him in boyhood, was waiting for
him. The whole town of Dallas was waiting
for him, because, at thirty-eight, Alec Cockrell was its first citizen. And, among all the
rest, Andrew Moore was waiting—the town
marshal, who owed Alec money and therefore hated him.

Alec had left his Missouri home as a boy of
fourteen, on his own and ready for anything.
He could neither read nor write, but he was
destined for success. He made Texas his land
and Dallas his town; and he courted gray-
eyed, level-eyed Sarah Horton, the "Methody" woman who didn't hold with dancing or
drinking, but who was ready to go with Alec
to the ends of the earth. Their marriage was
darkened by tragedy and illumined by love,
and their story culminates in one dramatic
day of destiny, April 3.

Here is Dallas in embryo, Texas in the raw.
With its roots in historical reality and based
on painstaking research, *Destiny in Dallas* is
an accurate, absorbing portrayal of a signifi-
cant segment in America's story. And of all
Shirley Seifert's twelve historical novels, its
drama is most concentrated, and its impact
most effective.

Jacket design by Paul Laune

$3.95

By Shirley Seifert

●

DESTINY IN
Dallas

By Shirley Seifert

✝

J. B. LIPPINCOTT COMPANY   /   *Philadelphia & New York*

To my friends, the Cockrells of Texas, and to
Monroe Cockrell in particular, chief polisher of
the family escutcheon and keeper of the records

Of all the Cherokee wizards or witches, the most to be dreaded are the Raven Mockers, they who rob a dying man of life.——JAMES MOONEY: *Myths of the Cherokee*

DESTINY IN DALLAS

chapter **one**

Spirits of evil...

ALONG THE UPPER Trinity and its three forks, a new day was beginning. So far, it was no more than a promise, a knife edge of light at the eastern horizon, cutting the darkness. Overhead, near this edge of light, stars paled slowly; but, nearer the river, where a huddle and a scattering of low houses marked in 1858 a small town called Dallas, night still ruled. There, in the way of folk likely to run themselves out each day of get-up-and-go, everyone— almost everyone—slept heavily, unaware of change or cleavage.

A deep hush held all. The river flowed sluggishly, without a whisper of sound. The town, what there was of it, stood up and away on the gentle rise of the east bank, separated from the stream and almost hidden by a stand of timber, thinned now by considerable cutting, but still thick enough to be a screen. Trees grew in even denser profusion on the low bottom land of the west bank, so that, altogether, water level made the blackest part of the before-dawn darkness. Not a twig moved in the trees, not a bird fluttered; and yet, day was coming. Water, even muddy water, reflects light. By degrees but finally with sharp suddenness, individual trees stood out here and there, then an opening and the shadowy outline of a low, covered wooden bridge. The bridge, a one-room log cabin hard up against the town end of it, a narrow road of trampled earth leading up toward the town, and, to the right of the road as one looked from the bridge, a house.

It was such a house as one might not have been surprised to see in the town above, on one of the newer would-be streets fanning out from the courthouse square, but hardly to be expected in this

11

low spot, so near to the river as to be endangered by a sudden rise, so near to the bridge as not to miss man, animal or wagon that crossed by it. A two-story, double chimney house, sleekly sheathed in clapboarding, standing out boldly, even defiantly against deep shadow surrounding it. But this house, too, was held still under the spell of night, its windows tightly shuttered, as if hoarding the dark, except two at the corner of the lower floor, looking out on the road and the bridge. There, panes of glass caught the first faint increase of light and were like two eyes watching.

In the room behind those windows two people slept—a woman alone on a broad bed and, close beside her on a low trundle bed, a young child. The light, gathered on the windowpanes, may have fallen across the woman's eyes. For some reason she stirred in her sleep and spoke a name:

"Alec?"

It was a low, questing cry, hardly audible, drawn from the deepest depth of unconsciousness, such a sound as a bird, aware of many perils but none in particular, might make, gently fretting; but the unease of it communicated itself to the child, who roused and whimpered.

"Sh!" the mother said, still softly, still not wakening, spreading her care over the child as naturally as a hen might spread a wing. Her eyes remained closed, as did the child's. Another second, and both slept soundly, as before.

Up in town, where the light, now softly brighter, was still barely enough to separate buildings, in a one-room cabin adjacent to the jailhouse, a man slept with even greater unease on a hard bunk bed. The jail, also on Commerce Street, but east of the courthouse square, was in itself a stout structure, sixteen feet each way, with double walls of oak logs set on foundation posts of cedar driven deep into the ground, with a ponderous, nail-studded door and a single window barred both ways with iron. It suggested a blockhouse and in a crisis could have been used for such. Had it been occupied, as it often was, by the most desperate characters of the locality, iron bolts and bars and padlocks would have held them securely captive without much other precaution and, on this night just ending, it stood empty; so, there was no good reason for the town Marshal to occupy the warden's cabin. Andrew Moore, a carpenter by trade and reputed a good one, had a more comfortable bed in his own house elsewhere. Sworn into office only two days before, he was, perhaps, overzealous in discharging his duties; or he may have had personal reasons for sleeping in town.

However that was, his sleep was not easy. The cabin was small and bare of comfort, intended to house a guard when needed, but chiefly someone who would see to it that the creature needs of the tenants next door were supplied. The crude bunk attached to one wall indicated that sleep was not generally expected, and Andrew Moore fulfilled that expectation.

Going to bed, he had not bothered to remove more of his clothing than his boots and his armor. The boots stood on the floor, handy to his feet. The armor was on a stool at the head of the bed—a vest with the bright badge of his office and a belt with a sheathed knife and a holstered Colt's revolver, loaded. A double-barreled shotgun, also loaded, leaned against the near-by wall. It might be excessive protection or it might not be. Either way, Andrew Moore slept uneasily, his hands now and again clenched into fists, a muttering of broken speech on his lips. A man with a grudge, one might have guessed, watching him. Yes. Also—and this was worse—a little afraid.

A few miles to the north of the darkened town, just above where the Jefferson Road from the Louisiana border joined the so-called Central National Highway from Preston Bend on the Red River, another man, one with a sense of time born in him; who in a covert of trees edging a stream known as White Rock Creek had slept more quietly than these others, had caught, however, the first promise of light in the sky and was now immediately and purposefully awake. With catlike smoothness of movement, making no more noise than a light breeze stirring the leaves, he rolled out of his blanket and stood erect. The next minute, which was all he needed for examining the waking world around him, he was as motionless as before. South of the Red River, in Texas, an Indian, no matter how peaceful his record and behavior, had always to justify his presence. That could take time, and Charley John of the Cherokee Nation had no time right now to spare. He had an appointment, not with man, but with Fate or Destiny or whatever the white man called the power that ruled the world and life, and he was late to the meeting. A day or some hours? He did not know. Simply, a deep urgency possessed him to move on without further delay or interruption. He should not, he knew, have wasted the night hours in sleep; and he would not have done so, except that in the evening his pony, wearier than he, having been ridden hard all day, had stumbled and given warning that there must be rest for both of them or the journey would not be completed.

An Indian, Charley John, by his coarse black hair, by the jutting bones of his brown face, by his utter oneness with the earth, the trees, the sky, even the dark, he was in other ways disguised by the faded cotton shirt and jeans pants of a white man of humble station. He wore these homely garments, not naturally, only with passive tolerance. They were husks around him as he stood motionless, against the trees, listening. All he heard was a rustle and a snuffling sigh, indicating the whereabouts of his hobbled pony. Reassured, he came to life again, shucked off shirt, pants, moccasins, and, naked as Adam before his fall, made for the bank of the creek. All Indian now, not young, a man well past maturity, but spare and wonderfully sinewed, he stood there, straight and dark and still, facing the spreading light in the east. Then, slowly his right arm came up in a gesture of reverence or prayer or both. That pose, too, he held rigid for another minute, then smoothly and swiftly dived into the running water.

He came up, gasping at the chill, laughed at himself, his teeth white against his dark skin, faced the light in the east as before, and dived again. Seven times he went under in rapid succession, then swam briskly for the shore. On the bank he shook himself like a dog, did a few running steps in place, swept his wet hair back on his head, and, with no further drying, took up his clothes. Once more he listened for his pony, located him and brought him out into the open glade. The ashes of a fire he had made the evening before were dead, but still warm. He did not kindle another. He had eaten bread and meat when he made his camp and that must carry him now. He scattered the ashes, covered them with dust and forest litter, rolled his blanket, strapped the roll to the pony's saddle, tightened the girth, mounted and rode off.

Southward and westward. The light on his left was advancing now. Too rapidly. Anxiety pricked Charley John as he rode. Not for himself. The road he followed was a wide strip through grass and brush, well marked by wagon ruts; but at the immediate moment there was no sign of any other traveler on it. If he smelled smoke or caught other evidence of a settlement, he had need for caution, but not now. The anxiety that pricked him was for another.

"Patience," he said under his breath, in Cherokee. "Patience, Little Older Brother. Charley John does not forget. Not the day or the hour or the season. He comes . . . as always."

Speech, even this much, evaporated into nothing. He leaned forward on the pony, ears straining to catch a sound far ahead. Hoofbeats, he was certain, and not the echo of his pony's unwilling advance. There went a horse of nobler breed and swiftness, ridden by one whose wish or need to go forward was greater than his. A bold rider, knowing no caution, reckless in pursuit of what he sought.

A light, brighter than that of the sun, just showing now at the horizon, broke over Charley John's dark features. He kicked his pony into a trot.

chapter **two**

...there is no sure way
to know one.

WHEN IT CAME right down to it, only one kind of man built the
state of Texas. He could be a preacher, bent on saving souls; he
could be a homesick settler, imported all the way from France or
Germany or, maybe, only from Tennessee; he could be a drifter,
a bum, a poverty-whipped castoff or a rich man's son looking for
high adventure, a bullwhacker or a planter; but, if in the end he
became a Texan, most of him was rawhide. That had to be. He
lived hard, most of the time he lived lean, and he never turned
his back on a fight.

Alexander Cockrell was a Texan. Never mind where he had
been born. Most Texans came from somewhere else. He was a
Texan now. If twelve years, up and down, good and bad, had not
proved this, why, it was possible that today might. He had known
when he rode off at the beginning of the week that trouble was
brewing, that it would be waiting for him when he came back.
Business had taken him away, business of first importance to him;
but now that was done and he was on the homeward trail.

You knew I would be back, Andy, didn't you? Sure you did.
You must have known.

Rawhide. A lean, extra-long stretch of man. Standing, he
topped six feet; and most of that was hard bone and muscle. A
lean face, ruddy, weathered, hollow-cheeked, almost ascetic, but
that quickly given the lie by a ring of newly grown dark chin
whiskers. He would have liked them to bristle, but they remained

16

stubbornly soft and young. The whiskers were his fancy, though Sarah, his wife, did not favor them. Too black, she said. Naturally, his hair being the color of a crow's feathers. The whiskers, Sarah said, gave her a turn every time she looked at him. Reminded her of a settlement of religious folk she and her family had passed through, coming west from Virginia. All the menfolk had such whiskers, though she recollected none as black as Alec Cockrell's. Made him look like Satan, she said. He liked that. Maybe people who had known him too long for what he was would turn now and give him a second glance.

The whiskers were not satanic. They just didn't suit the gaunt leanness of his face generally. But he fancied them. Rawhide, and he indulged in fancy? Afraid so. Unexpectedly a corner of his thin-lipped mouth would turn up; and everything hard, determined, tough on his face would soften into a near grin—boyish, mischievous, wistful, secret. His eyes—they were a startling blue, considering his black, black hair—would soften and glow. But why? Hard to know what he was thinking about, Sarah said, or what he would be up to next, though she gave the matter much study. Alec? No wonder she cried out his name in her sleep.

Thinking of her or the little ones, he could have told her. Looking out over the wide land, taking proper shape now as daylight came on, thinking what a hold he had on it now and what a hold it had had on him since he first laid eyes on it, an aimless, drifting, out-at-the-elbow, out-of-pocket vagabond. The beautiful, wide, free land—his kingdom on earth, heaven being something no man could be sure of, though some pretended.

The beautiful land. Some didn't look at it that way. Called it deserted, desolate, said it gave them the lonelies. He had been born to loneliness. Maybe that was why he loved it. He could close his eyes now and paint the whole picture; but he still liked to ride out early in the morning and take a fresh look at it. The wide prairie land, seeming empty, but teeming with life really, if it was only critters—green at the opening of April, patched with flowers, flat as your hand for a stretch, then swelling to a gentle rise or dipping to the deeper green of a watercourse. A solitary tree here, a mesquite thicket there or oak maybe or cedar. Mostly the timber grew near water—oak, walnut, pecan, cedar—magnificent cedar. At his sawmill below Dallas he could cut cedar logs that would span a river. He had done so.

His sawmill. His town, for that matter. By right of purchase, if for no other reason, though there were other reasons—plenty of them. His town. Let nobody try to rob him of that now. But some would try. That being human nature. O'nery folk, made up in equal parts of shiftlessness, meanness and pure, cussed spite. Andrew Moore, for example. Now, who would have thought that a man like that could make trouble for Alec Cockrell? Well, Alec Cockrell should have known; and, maybe, he did, but too late. As far off and as near as last November he had smelled smoke.

November. Late November. Leaves off the trees, prairies dry and brown, grass burned out on the courthouse square, dust in the road. Dust in the bare room above Peak's drugstore on Houston Street, across from the public square, where James N. Smith, Justice of the Peace for Dallas County, Texas, Precinct Number One, which was the town of Dallas, held his court.

Case of Alexander Cockrell, Plaintiff, versus Andrew Moore, Defendant. John McCoy, Alec's lawyer, stated the case.

"Your Honor, better than two years ago, the month of June, 1855, the Defendant, Andrew Moore, a carpenter by trade, residing in this town of Dallas, Texas, came to the lumberyard and sawmill owned and operated by the Plaintiff, Alexander Cockrell, likewise a citizen residing in this town of Dallas, Texas, to purchase building materials to complete a contract which said Defendant then had in hand. Stating that he was at the time out of funds and showing the contract, he asked for and obtained credit to the amount of the purchase. A bill of sales was executed as a promissory note on the spot, namely the Plaintiff's sawmill, and signed by the Defendant. The understanding was the customary one, and clear to both parties. Payment was due when the building contract was completed.

"Your Honor, said contract was completed that same year, 1855. Since then Mr. Moore has been gainfully occupied elsewhere, but has never paid a penny of his debt to Mr. Cockrell. He has evidenced no intent to pay. Rather, he has consistently refused to countenance any approach made by the Plaintiff, requesting payment. Two years having now gone by, said Plaintiff, Mr. Cockrell, who manifestly cannot continue to do business at such a rate with any profit, has no other recourse but to sue in a court of law for money long overdue.

"Therefore, Alexander Cockrell, a resident citizen of the town of Dallas, Texas, complaining of Andrew Moore, who resides in the same town and state, respectfully represents to the Honorable Court that the foregoing is a true statement of fact and prays for a judgment in his favor, requiring the Defendant under law to pay the amount of the aforesaid promissory note—to wit, thirty-nine dollars and sixty-two cents, principal and interest, together with the costs of this trial."

A neat statement, Mr. McCoy, and true as far as it goes; but you left out considerable, didn't you? What about the names Andy Moore threw at me when I "approached" him about the money? Remember what he said when I told him I'd sue? "You do, and I'll get you." Threatened me with my life and you had a name for his goings on—"malicious malingerer," that's what you called him. Seems to me you left out the best of it, John.

"Told you I would, Alick. Suing a man for debt in Texas is never a popular thing to do, even if it's right and justified. We've got the law on our side, anyhow. We can afford to be polite. If Moore wants to deal in abuse, let him. So much the better for us."

A good lawyer, John McCoy. Before settling in Dallas he had practised in courts over most of the United States—Missouri, New York, Massachusetts, down the coast, around to New Orleans and Galveston, from there here. Where he would stay henceforth, weary now of traipsing about. Weary in body, maybe; but he had stored a sight of knowing in his fine, large head.

"Your Honor, we rest our case on the evidence of this note in hand."

With that, he laid a piece of paper, hardly bigger than his hand, on the bar before the Justice. Justice squinted at it and pursed his mouth.

"Do you have witnesses to verify this note?"

"If Your Honor please, I should like to call the Plaintiff."

So now he, Alec Cockrell, stood up before the bar and swore to tell the truth, so help me God; and the only thing wrong with that was that he had to turn his back for a few minutes on Andrew Moore. When a man defaults on an honest debt, he's not to be trusted even that much. As it happened, even with his back turned, he could see Moore only too clearly.

Came to the trial in his work clothes—coarse, cotton shirt, jeans britches, and stout-soled shoes—as if the Marshal with his summons, which had been served weeks in advance, had caught him just this morning in the middle of a job he could hardly bear to leave. He was good at putting up a false front, whether it was to a store building or himself. A big fellow, almost as tall as Cockrell, stouter built, and a good seven or eight years younger. Supple-muscled and strong. Black-browed, of Irish mixture—mostly mixture. An ugly mouth, big and loose-lipped, not improved any by the sneer it wore at present. Very sure of himself, Andy Moore was that day.

"Alexander Cockrell, do you recognize this paper?" McCoy put the question.

"I do."

Don't worry, John, he wanted to add, for McCoy's comfort. I know every pen-scratched line by heart. They won't catch me there. And I can put my finger squarely on the signed name at the bottom. Couldn't miss that.

"Do you swear that the circumstances and the sum of money as stated are correct?"

"I do."

"Does the defense wish to question the witness?" Justice speaking now.

Moore had a lawyer. Nobody Alec had ever seen before, but that was no sign. Lawyers, doctors, missionaries blew into Texas these days on every high wind. A rusty-coated man; and he would be rustier if he tried to live on such practice. But, maybe, he had collected money in advance. He had a paper of his own in hand.

"No questions," he said, offhand; and the Justice told Alec he could sit down again.

"Does the defense wish to argue?" Justice asked then.

Moore's lawyer stood up, one pants leg catching on the top of a boot and a-hanging there. He cut a poor figure, but he was smart enough.

"Your Honor, defense sees only one way to argue. Defense moves that the case be dismissed."

Now, what in thunder? Justice was dumbfounded. Moore grinned. Alec felt an odd squirming inside. Law was a devious process. Now, wasn't it? But McCoy only hoisted an eyebrow and waited.

"As Your Honor must know," the lawyer's voice, when he raised it, whined a little, like a fiddle bow needing rosin, "the Plaintiff is a man totally ignorant—"

"Your Honor, I object." McCoy could move fast enough when he had to. "The extent of the Plaintiff's schooling has no bearing on the validity of the note in hand, which is all that is on trial here."

"Objection sustained," Justice said. "Defense will speak only about the note. Does the defense admit or deny the validity of said note?"

"Defense admits or denies nothing, Your Honor, the case being outside the proper jurisdiction of this Court."

"What?" Maybe Justice saw a fee blowing out the window. Maybe he just didn't care for the stranger's kind of smartness. "On what grounds do you base this pree-posterous claim?"

"This note," the stranger whined, "being only part and parcel of a larger transaction, which, if taken, as it should be, as a whole . . ."

McCoy was on his feet again.

"Does my opponent wish to base his defense on the plea that his client owes the Plaintiff other sums of money?"

Which Moore did—a lot more. This suit was only the first flick of the whip.

"Your Honor, the word 'owe' is not part of the present argument." Not if this timber lawyer could cover it up. "Defense wishes to point out that a fragment, and a fragment only, of a disputed contract has been made the subject of this suit. If it is irrelevant that in this instance we have only the sworn word of one man against the oath of another, it still remains true that said contract—a single transaction, I repeat, though it can, by finagling, be broken into small pieces—if treated as a whole, as it should be, can be reviewed only by a higher court. Therefore . . ."

The lawyer was right, up to a point. That summer of '55, when Alec Cockrell had made the mistake of trusting Andy Moore, he had sold the fellow three lots of lumber on credit. He had, therefore, in hand three notes, not one, each coming to less than one hundred dollars, but all, lumped, counting up to a little over two hundred. McCoy had pointed out to him that he could sue for the entire debt in District Court, or he could take one note—the first, since he knew which one was first—and sue before a justice of the peace. Since there was no denying, without perjury, the validity of the notes, he would obtain judgment either way; but the process was quicker and easier in the lower court. If he brought suit before the District Judge, he must wait for the next term of court and there would most surely be other delays—a full docket, jury trouble, unexpected evasions—and it could be another year before he got his verdict.

"Hell," Alec said, "I won't give the coyote that much time."

He could skip town. Anything could happen. McCoy thought Alec was right. On the evidence of the note, the Justice of the Peace would render judgment. Moore then must pay up and have no defense on the remainder of the debt.

"Therefore," the rusty lawyer whined, springing his knees as he spoke, "defense moves again that this case be dismissed, as belonging properly in a higher court."

McCoy was still on his feet.

"Your Honor, this whole thing smells of conniving."

"You're out of order, John," Justice said, "but . . . you're right." Then he stood up. A justice, being a one-year man, was usually not looked upon with too much respect, but he could be smart enough. Justice Smith didn't like being whipped around by this stranger. "The Court," he said, "finds for the plaintiff, and there's an end to it. Plaintiff will collect from Defendant the sum of thirty-nine dollars and sixty-two cents and two dollars and seventy-five cents, the cost of this suit. Mr. Moore, you are now bound under law . . ."

"We'll see about that," Moore said suddenly, and he wasn't grinning now.

"We will, indeed," Justice snapped.

"Defense will appeal," the rusty lawyer whined.

"Your privilege—if you can work it so," Justice told him.

And then the case went, all at once, back to where it was before the lawyers took hold—man against man. Andy Moore turned on Alec Cockrell, fists doubled, his eyes pale and mean under their black brows.

"I said I'd get you if you tried this," he growled, "and I will. You wait . . ."

Alec met his glower with eyes steadier than Moore's could be, under brows even blacker, though never as bushy; and he felt his face harden and everything inside him chill and set like a frozen pond.

"You threatening me, Andy?"

Not once, but time and again, openly and in secret. That was what it was to be a "malicious malingerer"—a man who would beat the devil around the town rather than take a straight road to what was right. In the four and more months that had passed since that November morning court, Moore had paid no money on his debt, but he had been busy every other way. He held up the court judgment against him by taking an appeal to the District Court. That was January. In February, Nat Burford, the District Judge, said he would grant the appeal, meaning he'd review the case in the next term of court, provided Moore could produce sureties, meaning bondsmen, to cover the cost of the trial.

"He's just working for time, Alick," McCoy insisted; but others disagreed.

"He's laying for you, Alick. That's for sure."

"Get along, Sinful!"

The black horse tossed his head, picking his way at his own gait over the uneven road. Grim-faced, Alec Cockrell looked out over the smiling prairie, coming slowly awake as daylight warmed the sky. Grim-faced until a solitary chimney rose up suddenly against the far green of trees and then he felt better. Why? Because he knew the folks who lived in that house. He had cut the timber for it, helped them to settle in. In a place like this a man had to trust his fellow man—only, of course, until he found out he was wrong to do so.

A few minutes later there were several chimneys, closer together.

Not too close. People who settled in Texas did not like to feel crowded. He could name the folks in this settlement, too, tell whose cattle pastured near by, whose colts frisked about. It hadn't been like that twelve, thirteen years ago, when he first laid eyes on these prairies. A man-built chimney then would have made him jump with its suddenness. Jump and pull off the trail until he knew what was what. Mostly then the land was really empty, far as the eye could see; but the very emptiness had soothed a young heart that hardly understood its own achings. It had been spring then, too, he remembered, a young sun stealing through his patched britches and his thin shirt to warm his bones.

"He's laying for you, Alick."

"Just working for time," McCoy insisted. "Give him no notice."

That was what Alec had done, mostly. He was traveling too fast these days to stop and look at every pebble he kicked out of the road; and that was all Andrew Moore had been—until just lately. Lately, the pebble seemed a more sizable stone. Everywhere Alec turned, Andrew Moore with his loose talk and his swaggering threats seemed to rise up in his way, trying to block the road. He still shoved the fellow aside, gave him no notice, but the thing was getting to be a nuisance and could be a hindrance.

He had no mind to be stopped or even delayed by a hindrance. Never reckoned on any such thing in making his plans; and he had plans, great plans. The smiling prairie, the settlers' cabins brought them all to mind. People sleeping in those cabins didn't know. Folks asleep in Dallas, still a couple of miles away, didn't know. He hadn't even told Sarah. A man with big ideas, really big, which might take a number of years to show up real, had little wind to waste in talk. He kept most of what he wanted tight under his own breastbone.

Someday . . . he checked his horse now, held him deliberately to a walk and looked out over the prairie—both ways. Alternately his eyes narrowed, then glowed. His face set itself into hard, stubborn lines, then lost all hardness in a radiance that was a fair match for the rising sun.

Someday these scattered chimneys would be one alongside the next—neighbors. The scattered small settlements—Farmer's

Branch, Cedar Springs, all of them, would be part of a greater Dallas—a Dallas that would reach out and take in a thousand acres of prairie in a careless handful. Prairie and timber, farmsteads and sparkling water courses—a growing town would need water, for drinking, for mills, for everything. The big spring at the foot of Elm Street, which furnished abundance of pure water now, would seem hardly a pailful then.

Someday . . . there! That was why he didn't talk. Why he never told anybody, even Sarah, all that he had in mind. Few people would look that far ahead—or could, for that matter. Most wouldn't believe him. They'd call him a fool or worse. They'd point out that from where he sat now he couldn't even see that town he was building so fast. Well, he didn't want to hear it. No wind to waste in talk. No strength to waste in argument. He knew all that was against him. Better than anybody could tell him. The biggest thing others might not think of or venture to mention. Time might run out. A man's life could be too short . . . well, damn!

"He's laying for you, Alick . . . laying for you. . . ."

Sinful's hoofs beat out the refrain in the soft dust of the road.

"Just working for time," McCoy now. "Give him no notice. You're not afraid of his threats surely."

Hell, no. If he, Alec, could have been stopped by a threat or a hindrance, he would have been stopped before he'd ever got well started. Back yonder, when he was a boy, before he'd ever laid eyes on Texas.

A boy . . . Alexander Cockrell, aged thirty-eight, riding over the wide prairie toward the little town of Dallas this April morning— silver spurs on his hand-sewed boots, silver rings making a pleasant jingle on his horse's bridle, a silver cord knotted about his broad, black felt hat—seventy per cent rawhide and the rest, he thought, cool, hard sense, ducked his head and grinned. Half in shame. A boy . . .

A boy, a lean, weedy fourteen-year-old, grown too fast for his strength to match his inches, his head even then filled with big ideas, his heart bursting big one minute, and the next, flopping about like a fish on a hook. A boy mounted on a young bay horse, bred of the best western and Kentucky stock. Sitting on this horse, which he himself had broken to the saddle and his father had given him for his own, looking out over his father's broad acres on Missouri's western border, turning his head stubbornly away, closing his eyes and his heart to a lush and gentle richness, saying good-bye.

His father's image blurred, compared to the sharp image of the boy, but was clear enough. A tallish man, with a stoop. A strong man, who seemed, however, tired, even early in the morning. Thinning black hair, turning gray. Deep furrows in his cheeks, where solid, round flesh had gone, leaving the skin slack. A kind man, loved and respected, gentle as his sunny acres. Never raised a rumpus about anything, good or bad. Saved his strength for what he had to do. He closed a stout, barred gate behind the boy, not arguing, just talking easylike; and the boy heard everything the older man said, though he wasn't listening. He must have heard, because, the farther he got away from that morning in time or distance, the better he remembered.

"You've got your head set to go; and I won't urge you not to. When you set your head, no mule can be o'nerier. I don't know what the trouble is, so I can't do anything about that. You ain't said, and you probably won't. Likely it don't much matter."

Not to anyone but the boy himself; and he wouldn't let on, the matter being deep and personal.

"You can't hold a grudge against your stepma or the young'uns growing up around you. There's plenty now for all; and I've said time and again you'd come into your share of all I've got, with, maybe, some extra. On account of things not being so good when you was a little shaver back on Troublesome Creek, in Kentucky. And for a while after that."

The old man fretted gently.

"How're you going to make out? Sure, I know you can ride. You can drive cattle, too. Going to miss you here that way. Maybe you won't starve, but living ain't going to be easy. You'll be up against strangers. Say you fall among thieves? Say you don't. Say you make out all right. How are you going to get on? You ain't had a mite of schooling. Never seemed time for it or the right place up to now. You can't spell out your own name. Can you now?"

No, he could not. Couldn't to this day. Alexander Cockrell, his mark. That was what that timber lawyer in the Dallas court-room meant by calling him a man totally ignorant. At fourteen, when he could have done something about that, he thought he was too big. Later he knew he was. At fourteen, ignorance was most of his reason for leaving home. As his father said, there had been no time for school before that. They had been too busy finding a place to locate and settle down. Now it was different. High class people were taking up land in Johnson County, Missouri. Educated folk, who wanted schooling for their children. His father's people had been that sort. His dead mother's folks, too. His stepma had schooling. There was to be a school. He, Alec Cockrell, aged fourteen, was to go to it—along with his little stepbrothers and sisters. And he was afraid. Afraid of the show he'd make, a boy with a man's growth riding a bench alongside six-year-olds, fretting with a bit of sharpened soapstone on a slate, his hand, maybe, so shaped to other, larger matters that it would be clumsy at forming letters and numbers. And the six-year-olds would pass him by and he be shamed before them. The thought of it turned his stomach.

The small fry at the stretched-out and still stretchable Missouri farmhouse, a piece of the way up the wagon track from where he and his father said their good-byes, thought their big brother Alec was quite a fellow—the way things were. Because he could ride and shoot and build a brush fire, and trap a beaver or a fox, and cure its hide. A boy with near a man's growth had to be looked up to. He couldn't bear to have it any other way.

Not that he wanted to leave home. The fair Missouri land spread warm and full of promise all around him. Ahead, on his lonesome own—he didn't know. Who could? If he gave his mind to risk and danger, he could be plenty afraid. But it didn't turn him sick. He couldn't figure any other way out. South and west, there were still miles of land, unclaimed, wild, where a man could make a place for himself, using such wits and strength as he was sure then he had and would have, no matter what—without cramping himself too late in a schoolhouse.

"How are we going to hear from you? How will we know?"

His father's eyes were moist. His dark, furrowed face worked with feeling.

"I'll send you word," Alec promised.

He never did. Time he reached the point where he would have or could have sent word, time he heard again from the family in Missouri, his father was long gone. Too late then to be sorry. Too late to ask who had taken over the old man's chores, with son Alec gone beyond the reach of hailing. Dead. Dead at the age of thirty-eight. Exactly Alexander Cockrell's age this very morning.

"Whoa, Sinful!"

He swore at his black horse for stumbling. Swore at himself for sinking in a bog of remembering. Doggone! If there was one way better than another to waste time, this was it. Looked like the older a man got, the more remembering he did, until he ended finally sitting slack on a doorstep all day, thinking backward instead of forward. Here he was now, time pressing, and his horse taking advantage of a slack rein to drop down to a crawl rather than a walk. Another minute and he'd be grazing. You, Sinful! He nudged the horse back to a trot; but it was no use, so far as remembering or forgetting went. The fourteen-year-old went away; but that brash young tramp wasn't a circumstance to the piece of carrion that trudged along in the dust beside the black horse now.

Sorry carrion. Too lean for a buzzard to take a second look at him. "Say you fall among thieves," his father had warned. Well, he had. Made out all right the first summer and the winter after that; then it happened. Lost his horse first, then his gun. Too far away at the time to turn back home and he wouldn't, anyhow. His clothes in rags, his moccasins in holes, fever and chills by turns burning him to a cinder and shaking his teeth loose.

One wet night, not knowing where on earth he was, not caring, he crawled into a cave on the side of a rocky hill, just to be out of the rain. Didn't know what other critter might have claimed the hole ahead of him. Didn't care. It was hardly big enough for bear. A fox den, could be. If the vixen herself with pups, or a catamount had been inside waiting, it would have made no difference. He never expected to come out of the cave alive.

The cave smelled of earth and animal and litter, but it was empty. And warm. And dry. A shiver took him, just because of the sudden comfort. Chill after chill racked him from head to foot, but slowly the dry warmth soaked through to his bones. Finally he slept.

It was the Little People who watched over him that night, Charley John said afterward. The Little People who live in the hills and the mountains and watch over straying children and other helpless wanderers. They showed him the cave and put the deep sleep on him. The Little People. The Cherokee believed things like that. Many a night after this, young Alec Cockrell had fed chips and sticks to a fire and listened to the tales old men told as they sat in a circle about it—aye, and daytimes he had listened some to the old women; and he had never come to the end of the stories, which went back to the beginnings of their people. Without doubt it was the Little People who sent him to that cave, and in the morning brought Charley John to find him.

It was full day when the sick boy awoke. He could see brightness at the end of the cave. He smelled wood smoke. Green wood mixed with dry. He smelled—no, he must be wrong about that—meat, the salty juices of cured meat trying out over flames. This was a cruel dream that haunted him often. He would be back home in Missouri. It would be early morning and he had already been to the barn. He would have stopped off at the summer kitchen behind the house; and a Negress, broad and shapeless as an elephant, would be cooking salt pork and fresh corncake, grumbling and never stopping while she did so.

"Mist' Alec, you hollow to yore toes. Cain't git you filled up. Nobody else goin' to git a bite o' brekkus dis rate."

He closed his eyes, opened them again. He wasn't dreaming. He was not back in Missouri. He was in this old cave and the odor of wood fire and cooking persisted. Curious, but wary—all his life henceforth he would be wary on awakening—he moved slightly, to see better; but, for all his caution, the dry litter under him rustled. For a long minute everything was still, inside and outside the cave. Then . . .

"You, inside there! You awake now? You hungry?"

A man's voice, deep in the throat. Not hostile. Friendly, or so it sounded. The man moved. The fire crackled. A tin lid was lifted and set back. Coffee added its fragrance to other smells. "You come out now? Yes?"

It was an invitation, but Alec held back another minute. The cave was snug and safe. Still . . . those smells! After his long sleep he was painfully hollow. When he turned and began a slow crawl forward, he shook again, but not from chill. Just weak. Cold sweat broke out all over him. He swore, to keep from blubbering.

He made it to the mouth of the cave. On a narrow shelf of level, open ground, carefully swept clear of fallen leaves, a man in faded gingham shirt and jeans minded a small fire. Right now he examined what looked to be a slab of corncake, baking on the blade of a short-handled spade. His hair was as black and straight as Alec's own. His hands were brown. He turned—a thieving Indian!

If he had been able, Alec would have scurried back into his cave; but he wasn't able. And in that short interval of helplessness, he knew he was wrong. The brown face turned to him was as open and friendly as any he had ever seen. The eyes, searching him, filled with pity.

"You pore, sick feller?" the Indian said. "Yes?"

Yes. With desperate effort, Alec tried to stand. He couldn't make it. His knees buckled and, except for the Indian, he would have fallen into the fire.

When he came to, the Indian was sponging him off with cold water from a near-by spring. No doubt he needed washing; and, one way, the water felt good. At the same time he was so sore, so battered by all he had endured that every touch of the wet rag was a bruise.

"Ouch!" he said.

The Indian stayed his hand, regarding Alec soberly. Then, perhaps because he had uncovered enough of Alec's face to take a reading, he smiled. Weakly Alec smiled back. At that the Indian laughed, and Alec with him, helplessly. And they were friends. Forever after. If he lived a hundred years, Alexander Cockrell knew, he would never have a better friend than Charley John, the Cherokee. If he lived . . .

Charley John was a full-blooded Cherokee Indian. He had a farm place not far from the hill where he and Alec met. With some cattle on it. Alec was in the Indian Nation, then, but well to the south, near Arkansas, getting along toward the Red River.

A farm place, with cattle. Some of the cows had strayed and Charley John was out rounding them up when he saw the signs that told him somebody was in the cave. The Little People, he said, led him there. The Little People? Well, maybe. Charley John let his lost cattle alone that day while he cared for a stranger. Washed him, fed him a little bread and meat and hot coffee, loaded him on his pony and led him home.

Home. To this day the years he had spent among Charley John's people had for Alec Cockrell the elemental dry warmth and security of that cave. He made a nest for himself in Charley John's peaceful valley. Miseries were forgotten. Scars healed. He learned to live day by day. He learned new ways, a new speech. He acquired a new name. Charley John, twice his age when they met, called him Little Older Brother. Because he knew about cattle and had now a wary sharpness in trading, which passed for wisdom. Now, long, long afterward, Alexander Cockrell, rich and prospering, knew tim   when he wished he could go back to that way of living, knowing he never would. There were times when he wondered why he had ever gone away. Knowing the reason for that, too. It had to be that way.

He still had not learned his letters. Here there had been no need. Trading was trading in the Indian Nation—a matter of barter usually. He talked Cherokee as easily as he did English, maybe better. He knew what the old women said over their cooking pots or as they beat out their wash on the edge of a stream. He learned from them the names and legends of the birds and the beasts, and the seasons for planting and harvesting, as they had learned them from their grandmothers, who had them in turn from their grandmothers.

There were other sources of wisdom. Sitting a long night through in a circle of wise old men, feeding chips and sticks to a sacred fire, listening to the tales the old men told as they had heard them from men older, hearing the shaman say his spells and prophecies, a young fellow was likely to pick up something besides a new language. The Cherokee were strong believers in destiny. What was to be would be, and there was little a man could do about it but be ready. Maybe it was the only way they could take their own history—the long wanderings from one lost home to a new one. Maybe this valley was it now, they said. Maybe here some day their sun would rise, if not for them, then for their children.

There was one such night he would have liked to forget, but never could. He was a man full grown then, strong with the unknown strength of young manhood. He had come in from a week of driving cattle with other young men of the tribe. After a hot bath and seven purifying dips in cold, running water, it was good to laze in the *asi*, the council house, and idly watch Charley John's young sons now feed chips to the fire. He drowsed as the shaman droned on and on, then came all awake as a screech broke the spell of sleep. At first he thought it was the shaman who had cried out. Then it came again, and he knew the sound was outside the hut.

"A raven," he muttered to Charley John. "Smells a storm and don't want to be caught out in it."

Charley John blinked and moved his head a little toward the old priest, who stood stiff and straight, the fingers of his hands spread, commanding silence as he listened. He turned now toward Alec, and the fire made his old eyes glitter.

"A raven," he said, "but he does not smell a storm." The cry came again and close by. "He smells death—death in this house." Again the cry, but now the bird had gone on. "It is not tonight," the shaman said. "The time is not yet. He returns to the Darkening Land—to wait; but he will come again. He will come again."

Then, from around the room you could hear the question, spoken or not, on the lips of everybody: "Who?" At the same time all thought of the shaman, who was a very old man; but the shaman said no.

"The raven mocker does not want the heart of an old man. I have no years to give him. He seeks the heart of a young man and many years."

That was the story. The raven ate the heart of a young man, dying, took over the years death stole, and added them to his own. So, if he had success in his hunting, he came finally to be an old, old bird of prey—and mean in proportion. The shaman turned a full circle, fixing his bright eyes on each man in turn, making them all shiver. The fire went down, untended. In its last glow the priest thrust his withered arm out at Alec Cockrell.

"You! Son of a white father, beware the raven mockers in the spring of the year. The time is not yet, but it is not far away. Beware. . . ."

Darkness fell on the *asi*, and the hoarse cry of the raven was swallowed by the night.

Bunkum! It might be that the old priest, with his long memory of hardships at the hands of white men, suddenly did not care for Alec Cockrell's pale face at the sacred fire. However that was, the next morning Alec said good-bye to Charley John and rode away southward—no richer and no poorer, but ten years older than when he had left Missouri. A horse, a gun, powder and shot to last him a while, a blanket, a length of rope, a sack of meal, a smaller one of coffee. There was good land beyond the Red River, Charley John said. He had in mind one spot in particular, where three rivers came together to make one. Years before this, his people, some of them, had camped there; but the white man would not let them stay.

He crossed the Red River at Preston Bend, and Texas opened before him. The beautiful, smiling land. Here I am, Alec Cockrell, waiting. Been here all along, waiting for you. You've been a time coming. Where have you been? And he had answered in kind. Not fooling. Been held up. That's all. Heading this way from the first. Heard of Texas way back in Missouri. Now here I am.

A dozen years and more had passed since then. He had done right well for himself and for Texas in that time. Very well. And he would have forgotten the old witch doctor's spell and warning except for one thing. Every year about this time, old Charley John roped a pony and rode south to see how his Little Older Brother was faring. Knowing where to find him because he had sent him there—to the Three Forks of the Trinity. Rode south and carried a loaded gun, his business being to shoot the feathers off any raven, crow or other black bird that lit within a mile of where his friend and brother had his house.

"Whoa, Sinful!"

He pulled up his horse. On a whisper of morning breeze he thought he'd heard the sound of hoofs, padded by dust, coming down the road behind him. The next minute he was urging Sinful on again and swearing at himself for his foolishness. The whisper of breeze and the sound were gone. Hearing spooks, that was all. Spooks—you had to go a far piece in a roundabout way to connect Charley John and his ravens with that black-browed son-of-a-gun, Andrew Moore. But was it so far, after all?

"He's just working for time, Alick," McCoy said. "He knows that, on the evidence, he can't win; but he wants time."

Maybe that was it, maybe it wasn't. Maybe he knew he couldn't win through the law or somebody told him. Maybe he thought of a shorter cut, or maybe somebody put him up to it. Town elections were just over. Andy Moore came out for the post of Marshal; and, big, strapping fellow that he was, he'd been elected. Well, what of it? Just this. A marshal could arrest out of hand anybody who overstepped a town ordinance—and in a few years time there had come to be a maze of those. Also, where other citizens went, unarmed, about their peaceful business, he carried a gun.

"He's laying for you, Alick! Watch out!"

Alexander Cockrell tightened his mouth to its thinnest line and his eyes struck fire from some bit of unseen flint. With word and knee he pushed his horse into a fast lope.

"You, Sinful! Get along now. We're wasting our time. We top this next rise, and we'll see home, but we ain't there yet and I'm hollow hungry."

chapter **three**

Often they take the shape of birds...

Iᴛ ᴡᴀs ᴀ ʙɪʀᴅ striking, thud, against a window light that brought
Sarah Cockrell awake finally. At first she hardly believed what her
eyes had seen, it came and went so quickly. But she had seen it.
As clearly as she had ever seen anything. The window was vacant
now, the room filling with daylight; but the shape of the bird was
as plain as if she were still looking at it.

A large bird, black. The lunging body, the head, the neck,
one wing spread out flat, showed against the glass; then it was
gone. She lay in bed, studying the thing in her mind. What was
it? What did it mean?

Well, nothing, of course. It could have happened. Once, as a
child, she had found a bird dead in the grass near her home in
Virginia. Abingdon was where her people, the Hortons, lived
then. The bird didn't show a sign of hurt except a spot of blood
on its gray poll. That was it, her father, Enoch Horton, said.
Birds didn't see as well as a person might think. Sometimes they
couldn't tell the difference between window glass and open space
and they tried to fly through. Killed them usually, there was such
power and speed in their wings. God's poor innocents.

But that had been a Phoebe bird. This bird was as big as a
crow, though she didn't think it was a crow. Its neck was too
long. She looked at the window steadily. Still surprised her to
see it empty. The bird was so clear in her mind that it seemed
the shape of it must be printed on the glass. She didn't believe it

35

had struck the window flying directly against it, though some
sound had wakened her. There was that one outstretched wing.
The creature might be flapping around helplessly outside now.
She ought to step outside, to see. If it was there, she'd be sure
she had seen it against the window. Pshaw! She was sure. She
could and did dream some at night, sleeping, but never with her
eyes wide open. She would get up right this minute and prove it.

No, not this minute exactly. Not in her nightgown. Scandalize
Barry over at the tollhouse and anybody else passing by? If they
had still lived at the ranch, she could have thrown a shawl about
her shoulders, slipped her feet into her shoes and gone out like
that. But not here—in town.

Commerce Street, City of Dallas. That was the way it read on
deeds of sale and on the survey map in the town records, a copy
of which, with other papers, she had in her keeping in a small
wooden trunk, seldom farther from her than the foot of her bed.
Commerce Street; and there were, besides, Main and Elm and
Water Street and Broadway and Houston and a handful more, all
fair, straight lines on the map, and a few staked out on the ground,
so that building lots should keep their places as planned. In actual
fact, the streets were, so far, but wagon tracks, heaped with dust
in dry weather, axle-deep in mud when it rained. A creek ran the
length of Main Street to the river. A body had to believe strongly
in dreams and in lines on paper when he set out to build a town.

Nevertheless, Commerce Street, if it did look like nothing but
the way to the bridge, was Commerce Street; and she had no mind
to betray its future or her own position by personal looseness of
behavior. Furthermore, it was now broad daylight of a Saturday
morning. The house should be astir, and it was not. It would
not be until she stirred it. At that thought she laid back the
covers of the bed, then lay still another minute. If, she thought,
by keeping real quiet, a body could hold time and everything else
just where it was . . . but, pshaw! nobody could; and a good thing,
no doubt, if life in general was to go on. Everybody would be
choosing a different minute to hold.

*Lazy Miss Sally, will you get up? Will you get up, will you get
up?* . . .

Chiding herself as if she had been one of her own young ones, she slipped from the bed, then dropped to her knees beside it. It was her habit each morning to thank God for a new day and, all in the same breath, ask for strength with which to meet it. Now no words came—at least, not the usual ones.

"Our Father, I had such a dream. I was walking along a path— I don't know where. It was a clear path, firm under foot, and flowers and green grass grew beside it. Suddenly it ended. There was nothing beyond. I fell. Into black dark, all empty. I fell and I fell and I fell. I hollered out. . . ."

She dropped her head against the bed, shamed. She knew right well she had not cried to God Almighty to help her.

"Father, forgive me. And send him back safe and keep him, too, this day. . . ."

It was the best she could do. Lightened a little of the night's burden—it was a wonder that bird hadn't scared her witless—she rose, and stepped quickly across the room to open the hall door and see whether she was right about the quiet in the house.

She was. Not a stir of life anywhere. Only, through some opening at the rear, drifted the smell of salt pork in a fry pan. Good! Hannah, the cook, was awake and had breakfast under way in the summer kitchen. Sarah closed the door and came back into the room to begin her preparations for dressing. The child in the low bed, thank goodness, still slept.

Walking away in her long, straight nightgown, with two brown braids swinging down her back, Sarah Cockrell looked not more than half her years, which, she would have said frankly, were the same as her husband's—thirty-eight. And she would reach thirty-nine before he did. But she didn't look it. Not even when seen full front. This was due to no lack of maturity or to any illusion created by vanity. It was just the way she was made. Slender, slab-sided, and, except for the rounded swell of her bosom, almost boyish in her slim erectness. Not until she tied a petticoat over the shapelessness of a chemise, drawing the waistline tightly about her middle, did femininity assert itself. Charmingly of a sudden, the braids still swinging. She gave sober thought now to the matter of petticoats. Should she or should she not add to two starched cambric ones a short flannel "modesty" for certain comfort? How warm was it likely to be by midday? Back in Virginia, folks kept to flannels until mid-April. This would be pretty uncomfortable in Texas. However, she decided in favor of the modesty. She could rid herself of an unwanted petticoat more easily than she could add one in case she misjudged the weather.

That issue settled, she was ready to wash her face and hands and put up her hair. Her movements at the washstand—a person was bound to rattle china against china—roused the child on the trundle bed. A cheerful gurgle announced the awakening. Sarah, studying the gurgle, wondering how much of her morning toilet she might hope to complete before the temper of the awakening changed, raised her eyes thoughtfully to the small mirror over the stand. Grave, gray eyes, with greenish lights, set deep in the sockets, well-marked brows curving above them, near to meeting at the nose, drawn well down at the temples, framing the eyes, calling attention to their gravity, their clear honesty, the unusual directness of their outlook. Above the eyes, a high, broad, unlined forehead, and dark hair, parted in the middle and drawn down without a suspicion of crimp or frizz to the beginning of the braids—smooth, keeping a smoothness even after a night's sleep. Below the eyes, a nose that didn't matter one way or another and a mouth, remarkably sweet, considering the firm chin under it.

Not a pretty face. Long ago, at an age when girls begin to think about such things, she had learned that and it had worried her then and for a long time afterward. Girls wanting more than anything else in the world to be pretty and to be noticed. Only once in a while did someone, who, seeing her just once, had passed her by, turn and look again. Hers was that kind of face. Being her own, she could not know that it had an arresting quality. It was a face that an artist might have liked to carve. That was why at thirty-eight she kept the freshness of her maiden days. Some of that she might keep always, such beauty being less destructible than the prettiness she had missed. Raising her hands to her hair, she thought this morning, I won't have time to brush it properly and do it up right. She almost never did in the early morning have time to shake it loose and comb it properly. The child in the small bed began to fret. Swiftly she smoothed the top hair with a brush, caught the swinging braids next, coiled each into a round bun, fastened the buns securely at the back of her head, and the thing was done—neatly enough to all outward appearance. Only she knew better. But she turned from the glass cheerfully enough. No good to quarrel with what had to be.

"Now, then, young man!" She stooped to the level of the bed. "Mister Alec!"

And knew why she kept this one still close beside her at night and would for a time to come, though he was near two years old now, ready to sleep with the others and he'd be a baby until the change was made. To be able to say aloud and naturally a name that was so constantly on her mind that more than this one night she had called it out in her sleep.

"You marry a man like that Alick Cockrell," her father—and others—had warned a time ago, "and you'll never know peace your whole life long."

They were right. No peace. Little tranquility. Like being wedded to a hive of bees.

"Wild as a colt," they said. "No proper raising."

Wild. A young man in a gaudy calico shirt, tail out over his britches, a wide piece of red calico tied in a sash around his flat waist, holding a long snakelike whip in his hand. A square of the same red tied in a headband, Indian style, below a shock of black hair. Eyes hot and blue as the Texas sky. Moccasins on his feet. Hup! Ho! He drove a span of oxen through the brush. She heard him before she saw him, and still was unprepared for the sudden brightness that broke out of cover with him. Then she knew. Something inside fluttered and cried out: Here he is at last, Sarah Horton! Take a good look, now you've seen him. There will be no other. He is the only one.

"A vagrant," her father said.

Two years older, in the red shirt of a Texas Ranger, he led her away from the candlelight and curious eyes of a house into the moonlit dark, halted then, but in the next minute blurted out a question he was compelled to put to her. Was she spoken for, promised to any other? And she, without thinking, answered just as directly that she was not, then began to shake so that she could hardly hear what followed. Dear Lord, he meant marriage. How, then, should she hold back her heart's cry: But that is what I want, too. All I ever want now.

He talked of taking land, of settling down.

"He never will, to stay," her father said. "A vagrant never takes root."

"He's never been married before," she answered. "Never had loving hands to hold him. He will stay now."

He built her a house, the first one. A rough house, on wild, high ground rising from a busy little stream called Mountain Creek. He saw for himself how rough the house was, and in a fury mixed a barrel of whitewash and laid it on the walls inside and out. In sunshine it stood out whiter and brighter than a chalk hill.

"Mr. Cockrell, it is just beautiful!"

Mr. Cockrell—had nobody ever called him so before? Mighty few, he said.

"But the evil ways of misspent youth are there," her father insisted, still doubtful. "Bad habits keep their hold on a man."

Yes. Texas was a hot and a wild land, a dry and thirsty land, a stubborn land. A man sometimes lost his grip on it and needed extra strength and took it where he found it soonest.

There came a day—they had been five years wed then—when he rode up the hill, whooping and hollering and waving a paper, and she thought, her heart failing her, that it had surely happened again. He was drunk or well on the way to it, and that was a fact; only it wasn't whiskey that boiled in him that day. He dropped off his horse and came bringing her the paper.

"Mr. Cockrell, where have you been?"

"Been buying a town," he said. "Mrs. Cockrell, may I present you with a town?"

"What town?" she asked, not making head nor tail to his raving.

He roared at the question. There was only one town to him—that huddle of cabins around a log courthouse on the far bank of the Trinity River. A man named John Neely Bryan had claimed the land years before and laid out a town on it. Since then it hadn't grown any more than a scrub oak; but Mr. Bryan, too, thought it was one of the world's wonders. He would hardly sell his headrights . . . but he had sold them. To Alec Cockrell.

"But how?" Sarah asked. "How did you . . . ?"

"Hell, woman," Alec stormed. "What do you want me to do

with all that money we've made from cattle and hauling freight? Bury it in a cookpot in the ground? Think it will sprout that way —like potatoes?"

Town. They would be leaving the ranch. Sarah thought she couldn't. How could she? So many things had happened by then. Then she knew she must go, if Alec wanted it so, and he would have it no other way.

Town. They lived in a borrowed house at first, trading with the Bryans, until Alec built this one lower on Commerce Street, close to the river. This stout, square, two-story house of cedar wood boarded over. Five rooms in it. A center hall, with a stairway. A parlor to one side of the hall and a bedroom, with a small office opening off it on the other side. Two more bedrooms upstairs— a mansion.

Town. Neighbors. Meeting every Sunday in the Methody mission church. People coming and going. A hustle and a bustle. Alec set up a sawmill on the river's edge. He was building a bridge. He finished the bridge. He moved the sawmill downriver then to the mouth of a creek and had a lumberyard. He had a brickyard. He built this house for his own family. He built houses for other folks to live in. The town grew now. Men came with trades and without—hunters, trappers, plain tramps. He put them all to work. There was one—a hefty, black-browed young man who called himself a carpenter.

"That's what he is," Alec said. "None better. Carpenters don't grow on bramble bushes, Sarah Horton."

Andrew Moore. A master hand with tools, but Sarah didn't like him. And now she was writing out a bill for lumber which he was to sign, making it a promise to pay. He was building a house— not for Alec, for another.

"You don't know much about Andrew Moore, do you?" she asked.

"No, I don't," Alec admitted. "No more than I know about some others I have to take a chance on."

"Suppose he defaults, Mr. Cockrell?"

"He'd better not. I'll take it out of his hide if he tries. You write out the bill. I'll do the collecting."

But he had defaulted. Andrew Moore, master carpenter, liar,

cheat—and what, besides? Her eyes swept the room. The bird haunt was still at the window. Her dream was still heavy on her heart, but she made out to smile at her youngest as she reached to lift him from his bed.

"Now, then, Mister Alec!"

"Three sons," she had said at this one's birth—the first birth in this house at the river's edge, "and none to carry your name forward, Mr. Cockrell?"

Alec Cockrell stood beside the bed, looking down at the fuzzy-headed little thing in the crook of her arm; and, like always, much of what he had to say was in the twist of his mouth and the shine of his eyes.

"You think," he said, dry as dust, "it is a name now that a young man would want to carry?"

"I never thought anything else," she said, "and I never will."

Three sons. There could have been four; but . . . no, she would not dwell on that now. On births and deaths and wicked men who hated Alec Cockrell, or bird haunts or . . .

"Now, then, Mister Alec!"

But you don't look any like him, she thought. None of you do. Sister's the nearest, because she is dark; but she has Horton ways, not much Cockrell. A spark of willfulness and odd fancies now and again, but mostly a gentle child. Land sakes, Alec's folks could have been gentle. The mother who had died too soon for him to have a clear memory of her. The father, though he, too, had been a restless, wandering man and had died too soon to prove that he could stay settled for long on the green prairie lands he had found and claimed for his own in Missouri.

Too soon. In the wooden trunk at the foot of her bed she had the letter that had come down through the Indian Nation into Texas, seeking young Alec, telling him his father was dead. Aged thirty-eight. Her age now—Alec's. Her hands, reaching for her son, were still. She went quiet and cold through and through. Her eyes looked over the low bed at the wall and saw a window and a black bird flat against it. Some old tale she had heard, some anxiety that was never far away haunted her. The bird image seemed part of it. What did it mean? Why, nothing, probably. Certainly nothing. Again she reached for the child.

But in those few minutes of distraction, he, too, had remembered that he was two years old and a baby no longer, had squirmed beyond her reach and was now letting himself down to the floor unaided. But not unimpeded. His nightgown was long, to allow for growing, and his feet were pretty well tied by it.

"You, Alec!" Sarah warned, too late.

The boy yanked himself free temporarily, got safely to a stand, and, with a shout of triumph, started across the room. A short flight. The gown tripped him and he fell, cruelly hard. Sarah was up and after him on the instant, ready to kiss away tears and hurt; but there was no outcry. Instead, the baby face darkened in a scowl, small hands beat at the floor and tore at the treacherous gown; and her youngest, her baby, yelled, but only in anger, when she tried to pick him up. Yelled at her; and she had thought there was no resemblance. Well, she'd deal with that before the young man was an hour older.

"Alec!" she said firmly. "You stop that!"

For a wonder, he did stop. Yelling, that is. Then, his lower lip still in a big pout, he rolled his blue eyes up at her in such a way . . . she could have died where she stood, laughing and crying. But again circumstance diverted her. A firm knock on the door was followed by its opening. In the space stood Hannah, the cook.

"What goin' on yere?" she demanded. "Yellin' an' carryin' on, nobuddy dressed yit. Mist' Cockrill come ridin' down de road, an' company mebbe."

Hannah—sovereign ruler of all the help about the place. Black as they came, her woolly hair covered by a clean bandanna, a clean apron over her not so immaculate wrapper. Men's Congress gaiters for shoes, well stretched to accommodate the spread of her feet. Glasses on her nose. Alec Cockrell had bought them for her at Hirsch and Shirek's store uptown when she complained of gnats getting in her eyes when she hung out wet wash. She had worn them constantly ever since, and had bound master and mistress to see that she was buried with them in place. She entered the room with respect, but also with assurance, swooped down on the angry boy, and gathered him up before he knew what had him.

"Kin take on one mo', I reckon," she said. "Dese yere his cloes? I'll take dem, too. Miss Sally, you git yoreself dressed now."

"I won't be a minute," Sarah promised. "Are the others down?"

"Boys is. Miss 'Relie ain'. She upstairs yit, watchin' Miss Polly primp. Miss Polly makin' what she call her gran' toilet, and Miss 'Relie don' aim to miss a turn. I got de boys out back wid me an' my Willie."

"Are you sure?" Sarah asked.

"No'm, I ain'. I lef' 'em dere, bofe hands full, but I better go see now. I'll jes' take dese cloes an' . . ." in the door she turned back to give Sarah a searching look through her spectacles. "Miss Sally, you sleep all right?"

"Yes. I always do." An untruth, and Hannah saw through it.

"Miss Sally, you got worries? You needn'. Any man, any man at all, tries any shines wid Mist' Cockrill, Mist' Cockrill squash him wid one han'."

He would try, certainly; and he might well win the argument. But there could come a time. . . . Sarah twitched impatiently.

"Hannah," she said edgily, for her, "go on back to your kitchen. Don't talk foolishness, and don't listen to any. Go on. I'll be out in a minute. We ladies will take our breakfast in the house, as usual."

In the small room behind this one—Mr. Cockrell's office, though she worked there more than he did. For reasons that needn't be gone into. Under any circumstances a man with as many affairs to look after as Mr. Cockrell had would have to be out seeing to them, and would need a clerk to keep his accounts. She was that clerk. That was all.

"Yas'm," Hannah said, not relishing even a hint of reprimand. Faithful creature, obviously she had heard something she would have liked to take up with Sarah. "You do like you say, too, den. Don' stop to redd up dis room. Somebody will git aroun' to it. It's Satiddy mo'nin', remembah. You goin' to be kotched sho'."

Saturday. As the Negress closed the door behind herself and the boy, Sarah turned to her wardrobe to take out a dress. Saturday. Alec had gone out early in the week to meet a train of wagons coming from Shreveport. His wagons and mostly his goods. Finish lumber from the pineries in East Texas, to be worked up at his mill, print paper for Wake Latimer's *Weekly Herald,* sugar and molasses from New Orleans, whiskey from Kentucky—Temperance societies were doing what they could but thirst still prevailed—shoes, hats, piece goods and miscellanies for the stores uptown—she and Sister Polly must pay Hirsch and Shirek a visit Monday, before the new things were picked over—bottled medicine and raw drugs and books for Peak's drugstore . . . good land, business would halt in Dallas if the wagons didn't get through. And Alec was never sure they would if he didn't go out to crack a whip over them on the last stage of their journey.

He had set out over the Jefferson Road on Monday, expecting to meet the wagons at Black Jack Grove. Ordinarily he pulled them out of that pool of iniquity with dispatch, then set out for Dallas alone, riding faster than he did going away. He had his best horse this time, too. Sarah had listened for him for two days now. Mr. Cockrell, have you any idea how my heart rides with you every step of the way?

She listened for him this morning, and heard only a light scuffle upstairs and a child's merry laughing. Aurelia, their eldest, their one girl child, teasing Sister Polly. Probably had her ruffles again. Poor Sister Polly! It was a wicked caution the way the children tormented her, but she brought it on herself really. She was as good as gold to all of them and they loved her, but she was an awful fool some ways. Trust young folk to find that out. Her weakness was vanity. Ten years older than Sarah, and a childless widow, she clung pitifully to a memory of earlier charms. In her day she really had been pretty. At Aurelia's age, Sarah had marveled at her big sister's sunny curls and pink and white skin. Poor Sister Polly! Curls were now the result of crimping pins. Gone was the pink and white skin, and the graceful slenderness; but she primped more than ever. Flat as a board, lean and stringy, she padded herself to a suggestion of curves in every sort of way, ruffles on a tape that she tied around her under her arms being a favorite device. And that wicked rascal, Aurelia, would snatch them and run off—she must speak to Aurelia, try to make her understand.

Mr. Cockrell, Alec, where are you? I wish . . . what did she wish? How could one woman call another a fool? Impatient with herself, with time, she fastened the full skirt of her dress securely about her waist, then, more complacently, buttoned over it and over her own well-rounded bosom, the simple, close-fitting bodice.

As vain as the next one, when you came right down to it, and for very little reason. The dress, a calico print, white flowers with yellow eyes scattered over a dark green ground, looked good because it had been sewed by a Frenchwoman up in town, a poor unfortunate from a settlement of her people that hadn't been able to make its way. It kept its pretty color and crispness because Hannah, besides everything else, was a good laundress. Friends from both sides of the river sent their girls to learn from her about soapmaking and clear starching. All this talk about freeing slaves that one read in the papers. It was the Christian way to look at it, no doubt; but what would she do without Hannah?

She fastened her dress at the throat with a pin, an oval of fretted gold with an amethyst stone at the center. It came from a New Orleans jewelry shop. Alec had bought it for her on a freighting trip to Shreveport. Any trip he made he usually brought back a pretty or two for her. He had rare taste in such things. Sometimes it wasn't a pretty. It might be a surprise—like buying Dallas. He liked to work up a move like that in secret and hand it to her all done beyond recall. With a shout of triumph.

Alec, Mr. Cockrell, where are you? I'll not be easy until I hear you at the door. You'd no call to go this time . . . now, what a thing to say or even think! What a state she was in—because of a dream and a bird flying at her window. If Alec should come now and find her like this—if it should happen that there was really nothing wrong uptown, what would he think?

With a great effort of will, she steadied herself. Giving her hair a last lick with the brush, she went over, as calm as you please, to the window where she had seen that bird shadow, raised the sash, put a prop under it, and looked out. Didn't see much. Trampled earth, bare of grass. Some sticks left by the boys, playing soldier. Her boys and a half-dozen others. She would admire to have a pretty garden place someday, but not now. The river near by, crawdads, and do as you please kept her brood closer to home than a fenced-in plot could ever do. But a fence wouldn't be bad. With a wide gate. Chickens and pigs would get through or under, but they would be their own. Not a sign out there of any big, black bird. Maybe she had dreamed that part, after all; but she knew she had not. A mist rising above the low scrub along the water. Going to be a warm day, she thought. Summer right on us. And she took out the prop to let the window down. If birds could fly, so could other winged things.

It was then that she heard a horse coming down the road from the direction of town. She let down the window and hurried to the front door. Then, as she stood on the block of cedar that made the step, her heart dropped so fast and so far that she thought she must go down with it. She recognized at once the man in the shapeless hat on the droop-headed, spotted pony.

That's all I needed, she thought—a spook bird and that Indian!

chapter **four**

...but they may take other forms.

THIS EARLY MORNING, about the time Charley John slid off his pony in the Cockrell dooryard, Alec Cockrell sat on his horse up on Main Street opposite the town square. He might easily have reached his home ahead of the Indian, except that he could never ride through his town without stopping to look it over. Was he away only overnight, when he got back he had to see for himself if everything was just the way it was when he left.

It was still very early in the morning. From the rear of the Crutchfield House, just ahead, on the near side of Main Street, the first smell of sizzling fat rose on the still air to torment his empty stomach, but it took more than that to move him when he wanted to stand still. He had mail in his saddlebags to drop off at the tavern, which in 1858 served as the Dallas post office; but the mail could wait. Let a man snatch a minute to look and think, now that I'm here, can't you?

Across the rutted strip of Main Street, the Dallas County courthouse reared up proudly on its patch of green. And Alec Cockrell, studying it, sat up just as proudly. A person might have thought, to see him, that he had laid up the walls himself, brick by brick. Well, that person, he would have said, wouldn't have been too far wrong. Those four walls, two stories high, he thought fondly, the first whopping order from my brickyard. Had everybody sweating, from clay pit to kiln. Look at those windows. Count them. Sixteen, upstairs and down, any way you face. Hauled every piece of that glass on my wagons. Didn't break but two panes out of all. Look at the doors. A door opening to every street—Main, Jeffer-

48

son, Commerce, Houston. Cut the oak where it grew, sawed it and dressed it at my mill. Hauled the finish lumber, too, and dressed it.

Look at that hitch rail. Who stood up to the aldermen and said right out to them, "You got a courthouse now nobody can make small of. Nobody can say Dallas ain't fit to be the county seat if a judge don't have a place to hold court except an empty store or, maybe, a saloon. You want to keep it looking proud? Want a green square to frame it? Then you'd best build a fence on all four sides—a fence without a break in it. Folks with business in the courthouse can climb a stile. Set a stile in the middle of the hitch rail against all four streets, lay walks up to the doors, and maybe grass will have a chance. Won't if you don't do something like that."

Look at that hitch rail now, he thought. Straight and true as the day the posts were set. Not a fence to strain dogs or cats or even pigs, maybe; but it did keep out cows and horses—and people. Those who grumbled when it was set roosted on it now and held their confabs and liked it fine. Look at that grass. By heaven, he thought, I could lay down on it myself right now and roll like a dusty mule. If I had the time. Didn't any of it look like this when I first saw it back in '46—no, must have been '45. Don't much matter. What I do remember . . .

Hell! There he was—at it again. Seemed like this was a day sure enough when a man couldn't separate what had been from what was or might be.

That spring morning long ago he had sat on his pony just about in this very spot. The Crutchfield House was there then. An ordinary double cabin with a loft, but it was all the town needed in the way of a tavern. Since then, Old Man Crutchfield—in Texas, when you hit forty, if you had grown sons, you were Old Man So-and-So—had added to the cabin and lifted the roof to make more room. His hotel had grown with the town and, up to now, was still the only hotel there. Up to now. A smile, the secret smile that made Alec Cockrell's friends sit up and take notice— his enemies, too, if they knew him—curled his thin lips. Time's short, Mr. Crutchfield. One of these days—the smile faded.

From the Crutchfield House, then as now, you picked your way across Main Street, jumped the creek, and you were looking down Houston and not much to see—that first view he had of it. To the left was a plot of ground, bare or grown to weeds, with another log cabin in the middle of it, a single cabin, but bigger than ordinary, about sixteen feet each way. The bare plot of ground was the public square and the cabin was the courthouse. It was also the trading store of John Neely Bryan, and the business done at one end of the cabin never crowded any going on at the other end.

East of the square, behind the log courthouse, on Jefferson Street, Alec could see—that April long ago—a couple of smaller cabins, matching a couple on Houston, right in front of him. In one of those on Houston, Wake Latimer printed a single-sheet, weekly newspaper. Called it *The Cedar Snag*, to show what he thought of it. The other cabin on Houston was a general store. You looked down Houston, past these two runty cabins, and came to another street, running the same way as Main Street, and that was Commerce. All the streets had names, but that was the most you could say for them. On the far side of Commerce was the rest of the town—two more cabins, a small, peaked-roof one, which was Adam Haught's dramshop, and a large double one, which John Neely Bryan had built for his family, he being then sole owner as well as founder—of what? A settlement, doing poorly.

Young Alec didn't think much of it. Had half a mind to ride on through, but he didn't. While he was waiting on the second half of his mind to catch up with the first, the door of the little cabin facing him opened and a man came out, to look around. He saw Alec on his pony, let out a whoop and came loping down Houston Street to greet him. A big man in hunter's buckskins, whiskey on his breath that you could smell a hundred feet away, but his face smiling wide and his hand open.

"Howdy, stranger. Welcome! Welcome to the city of Dallas!"

Welcome—now how did John Neely Bryan know? He didn't. He just hoped. Used to sit a good part of each day with Adam Haught in that dramshop, a demijohn of whiskey between the two of them, and he asking Adam—or, maybe, it was the demijohn—why nobody but him saw the possibilities of the likeliest townsite in North Texas. The very likeliest. Main north-south road ran right through it, meeting an east-west road just below. Good timber for building. Good, deep soil. Good spring. That was how John Neely Bryan kept hope alive. With the help of a demijohn. Every so often he'd step to the door; and, if he saw a stranger. . . . Lord, he was so deep in the demijohn the day Alec Cockrell went through that he couldn't tell a tramp from a real prospect; but that made no difference in his welcome.

Welcome. Who bothered today? Alec Cockrell sat on his blooded horse this third day of April, 1858, thirteen years later, and looked out over a town five or six times the size of that stalled settlement; and it seemed to him suddenly that the town looked back at him pretty blankly. Shucks! Probably just the first light of the sun on the courthouse windows. It was still that early. Not a critter moved anywhere—yes, there was one. Old Man Crutchfield, whose business now gave him short hours for sleeping, stood outside his inn, looking over the road; but, when Alec rode over with the mail, he was scant in his thanks.

"Thought you might have some," he grumbled. "Halfway wish you didn't. Folks hear about it and they'll trample everybody to see whether they got a piece. This a Saturday, besides."

Grumpily he loosened the string on the packet of mail and began sorting it.

"Might be something for you," he said, in explanation. "Or did you look?"

Alec said he hadn't. When he got to Black Jack, postmaster there had this package waiting, all tied up and labeled: "Dallas." He'd brought it just that way.

"Ha!" Halfway through the sorting, the innkeeper had stopped. "Well, you got something all right. You'd never guess from who."

No, and Alec didn't mean to try. Crutchfield knew he couldn't read.

"Never in this world," the innkeeper repeated. He had separated the letter now from the rest of the mail and held it by itself in one hand while he studied the writing on it.

"John Neely Bryan," he read out. Alec wanted to snatch the letter and wondered why he didn't. "Where do you think the old geezer's turned up now? 'Jamestown, Cal-i-for-ni-a.' That's a long way from the Creek Nation, where the last letter come from. Hm!

So, he did make his way to the gold diggings finally. At that rate we can't be looking for him home yet a while. Unless he struck it lucky out yonder. Ain't likely. John never had the luck of some folks."

The innkeeper turned the letter over.

"Shouldn't have left town in the first place," he said. "Man he shot wasn't worth it. Should a-waited at least to see whether the feller died." Crutchfield threw a quick look at Alec. "You ever let John know the man didn't die?"

"He knows," Alec said grimly; and now he did reach out and pull the letter from Crutchfield's hold. "Got to be getting on," he said.

As he turned in the saddle to thrust the letter into his open saddlebag, the smell of cooking from the outdoor kitchen behind the Crutchfield House hit him another blow in the stomach. Morning was on the move now.

"What's your hurry?" Crutchfield fumed. "Would a-liked to know how John's faring."

"Tell you later," Alec promised.

Maybe he would, maybe he wouldn't. All depended on what the letter said. Hell! Did Crutchfield think he'd sit here all day chinning about the troubles of the first and best friend he'd ever had in this place? Let nobody ever say that he, Alexander Cockrell, began the town of Dallas. He knew, better than anybody, that whatever he built here he built on another man's foundations. Didn't know John Neely Bryan from any other hunter or trader when they met and John Bryan knew no more about him. Yet, in a way, both had known.

The smell of sizzling fat pursued him across Main Street and down Houston, past the fine new printshop of Latimer's *Weekly Herald*, past Peak's drugstore, but it couldn't tempt him now. He was back once more in that other April of thirteen years ago, sitting before the Bryan fire, corncake and sorghum molasses and hot sweet potato and acorn-fed pork pleasantly heavy on his stomach. Stout vittles. There were folk, he'd heard tell, who made mock of such food. Thin-blooded folk they must be, with their noses turned up too high to smell properly. He'd never ask for better food anywhere. It put life back into him that day. Maybe it wasn't just the vittles. Might a-been the bright-eyed woman who stepped from the fire to the table and back again. Margaret Bryan, John's wife. It had been a weary time since anyone like her had set food before Alec Cockrell.

Toward evening, as he drowsed before their fire, the Bryans were bold enough to ask him a few questions. His name was one, and where he had come from. Why, Margaret said, when he told them who he was, there were folks of the same name ranching out on Mountain Creek, west of the river; and nothing would stop her from sending word to them that same evening. The next morning here came a man, say five to six years older than Alec, name of Wesley Cockrell, who declared he was Alec's own blood cousin. And Alec couldn't disbelieve him. He had the same coal-black hair and bright blue eyes and a soft way of speaking that Alec remembered of his father.

Wes Cockrell, his own cousin. The only thing bad about his coming was that he brought with him a letter he had kept for years written to Alec by his family in Missouri. It was the letter telling how Alec's father had died. Sitting in that comfortable house, stuffed full and feeling good, wondering if his luck had turned now, the letter took Alec like a blow in the chest. Knocked the wind and the manhood right out of him. Not wishing to make a show of himself before strangers, he rushed out of the house, finally, to do his bawling. Bawled like a calf for he didn't know how long. Next he knew, Wes Cockrell had his pony ready and was pushing him into the saddle. Going to take him out to the ranch, Wes said. Fresh air, riding herd on a bunch of cattle, good sleeping and regular eating would heal him of his hurt. The way he spoke, he knew the hurt was deep.

It all happened much that way, but what Alec remembered best about riding off that day, what he remembered now, was John Bryan standing beside his pony and saying, calm and sure:

"You'll be back?"

He must have known. Both of them must have known right then. Seven years later Alec sat on one side of a table in the trading end of the log courthouse and Bryan sat on the other, and a deed of sale was waiting to be signed by the two of them. The property involved was the town of Dallas—all of it, except the square and a few lots Bryan had managed to sell to other settlers. Very few of those. Bryan's face was seamed a little deeper than when Alec had first known him, and what he was thinking Alec could only guess at. Appeared just as friendly and honest and kind as always, but he was cold sober. Hardly ever was after that, but he was sober that day.

"Seven thousand dollars," he said, "is a sight of money, Alec. You're sure you'll get it back? Hell, of course, you will. You got push and you're young. Thought I had the push once, but it's gone now. Or maybe I leaned too hard the wrong way. You'll make it where I didn't. May not be easy. There'll be times . . . but you'll make it one way or another. That's what I want to see happen."

Alec himself was pretty tightly tuned up that day. Feeling good over the sale, more sure of himself than Bryan was, but something blocked his windpipe.

"You sure you want to go through with it, John?" he asked.

"Dead sure. Ten years ago, when I married Margaret Beeman, I promised her a fortune if she'd take a chance on me. Ten years she's stood by me, watching the chance fade to nothing—until you came. Here you are with a draft in your hand for that fortune. I've got to take it."

"What will you do?" Alec asked, his windpipe still choked up.

"I don't know—exactly. California, maybe." This was 1852. "I like your idea about swapping houses. Margaret and I and the young'uns will move out to your ranch and you can have our house meantime. Give us all a chance to know what we want to do—permanent."

"I want to bring Sarah to town," Alec said, "soon as I can. I've got my reasons."

"I know," Bryan said, and he did know. No use going into that now.

That was in '52. Three years later John Bryan set out for California, but Margaret didn't go with him. The Cockrells were living then in the house close to the river and the Bryans had moved back to town. Might have known they would. Neither one could let go of the place merely on account of a deed of sale.

It was just after dark. Alec was at home, thinking about going to bed. Sarah was upstairs telling the children good night—little Alec hadn't been born then. All of a sudden the front door opened and their black boy, George, came busting in, looking for Mist' Alec. Mr. Bryan, he said, was in trouble and had sent him to find Mist' Alec. Quick. Well, if John Bryan was in such trouble that he hollered for help, he needed it right then. Alec pushed George ahead of him getting out of the house, not stopping to ask why or where; but George told him.

"Not thataway, Mist' Alec. He's waitin' at de bridge. He say don' stop to make a light and don' tell nobuddy—fo' Gawd's sake."

The covered bridge was a black tunnel at that hour. Barry Derritt, solid, quiet, dependable, stood outside his toll cabin. Alec told George to stay with Barry and both of them to keep still till he knew what all this was. Then he went into the tunnel. Hadn't taken two steps before Bryan grabbed him.

"Alec? Thank God. Alec, you've got to help me." Well, sure, but why? "Alec, I've killed a man."

At first Alec wouldn't believe him. But it seemed it was so. Then Alec hoped . . . but no, it wasn't Andrew Moore. It was another no-account, with a loose lip.

"He called Margaret—no, I won't say it," Bryan said. "Seemed to me I had to shoot him. I . . . what else could I do?"

Nothing, to be sure. Only, it didn't seem like John Neely Bryan to raise his gun against a fellow man; and Bryan said it wasn't like him.

"I've killed many a critter in my day," he said—the big man was trembling—"but never a human. Alec, I'm leaving. Now. Tonight."

Nothing could persuade him not to. Said he should have left long before, while he had something to carry with him. And maybe he was right about that, but he hadn't done so. So, he was leaving now. He would not stop to tell his wife or children good-bye. All he was waiting for was to make arrangements for somebody to take care of them. That meant Alec Cockrell. Who else was there?

Alec tried to tell him then that he might be mistaken about killing the man. There was no commotion that he could hear when he left his house. None now. Bryan said it happened around the corner from Haught's and maybe they hadn't found the corpse, but they would; and he'd no mind to hang or face trial—not where Margaret must look on, not in the City of Dallas, once his hope and his pride. He was leaving.

"Can you send for John McCoy?" he said. "I want it down in writing."

Stuck to that, too. A man crazy with guilt and fear and what-not. Alec sent Barry Derritt uptown for McCoy, and sent George home to saddle a horse. McCoy, out of breath from hurrying, his broad forehead creased with anxious lines, came, with Barry, both saying Adam Haught's place was dark and nobody around; but McCoy said John ought to know what had happened and they could investigate later. He was of the mind that Bryan should clear out while he could.

So, by lantern light in Barry's cabin, McCoy wrote out guardian-ship papers and—hell, that was no matter. What mattered was the muffled hoofs of the horse carrying John Neely Bryan into banishment. Three years he'd been gone now, wandering over the face of the earth, gathering years and hard knocks, wanting only to come home but not willing to do so in a state of misery. A hell of a finish for a man who . . . hell, no kind of a finish for a man.

Time McCoy got back uptown after seeing Bryan off, the man Bryan had wounded with his revolver was conscious and groaning and somebody with a lantern was out investigating. But all that made no real difference except that Bryan was to know too late that he wasn't a murderer. He didn't come home even after the news reached him. He wrote a letter from the Indian Nation, an-other from Colorado and now there was this one—all of them to Alec. All of them using hopeful words but the only hope really was his wife's, Margaret's. She still lived in their house. She said John would come home some day and Alec thought maybe she was right. He'd come home to die, if not sooner. Why that? No reason. Just seemed he would, that's all.

"Jamestown, California." Here, he, Alec Cockrell, was, riding down Houston Street toward Commerce, that letter burning his coattails. Nothing would save him from passing the Bryan house on the way home. If Margaret was up—he had an idea she slept lightly—and she saw him, like as not she'd stop him. Sometimes she'd ask if he had a letter for her. Usually he didn't have, but now! Well, he wouldn't stop. That was all of it. Watch her read the letter, see life dreen out of her face as she did so? No, sir! Sinful, smelling his home stable, was stepping right along. He'd give him his head now. . . .

"Hy-ya, Alick!"

Hell and damn! He had forgotten, though he knew it well enough, that he'd pass Adam Haught's dramshop before he came to the Bryan house. Adam himself stood in the door now, rinsing yesterday's dregs from a tin cup. His face was crisscrossed with lines like a patch of dried mud, but friendly; his eyes, narrowed by sun squint, were bright and searching; and his hail had the volume of a steamboat whistle. There was nothing Alec could do but stop and give the old man howdy.

"Alick, you're here. Finally. Doggone, you had some of us wonderin'. But here you are. Uh . . . how's business?"

"Thriving," Alec said, knowing well what Adam was driving at, but not meaning to help him.

"Wagons on the way? Hope so. Hope they're loaded. Well's running dry back yonder." Adam jerked his head toward the cabin interior.

"Clear dry?" Alec jibed.

"Pretty near. A few leavings o' this and that. Mostly country stuff. O'neriest backwoodsman they is, if he's got a ten-cent piece in his jeans, calls for Bourbon or Monongahela these days. Had a mess of soldiers yestiddy, patrol out Fort Worth, and their loo-tenant. Lootenant was the thirstiest of the lot. Alick, will you light for an eye-opener?"

Alec tried to shake him off, but had no luck.

"You got a minute to spare, I reckon," Adam insisted. "Alick, I want to talk to you."

From his tone, Alec could guess what he had to say and he didn't want to hear it; but now reinforcements for the saloon-keeper appeared—young Jeff Peak, come to open the family drug-store. Jefferson Peak, Senior, had brought his family down from Kentucky the year after Alec bought out John Bryan. He opened a general store first—most everybody did—but when he turned the business over to his sons—he had a row of sons—two of them, Worth and Jeff, the younger, settled on drugs. Did a thriving business, too. Alec was proud to call the young men and their father his friends.

This morning Jeff's long, lean face was as solemn as Adam Haught's. A man might brush past one, but not the two of them. Alec alighted.

Compared to the freshness of the morning, the interior of Haught's cabin was dark and sourish. A pity a house couldn't be rinsed like a tin cup. But Adam had out on his counter presently the choicest of his leavings and was pouring three measures of whiskey as mellow as sunshine and about as fiery. No doubt about it, whiskey gave a man heart even if he hadn't felt the need of it.

"Sure cuts the dust," Alec said, and handed back his cup for more.

"Alick," Jeff Peak said suddenly and sharply, "are you really as ca'm as you make out?"

"No," Alec said bluntly. "Would you be?"

Jeff shook his head.

"Alick," Adam Haught said then, "we're sorry as hell about the 'lection. If we'd a-had any warning of what was likely to happen, we might a-done something."

"What?" Alec asked. Why talk about the election now? It was over—forty-five votes for Andrew Moore, thirty-five for the other fellow, a quiet man, too much so for the job, maybe. Not many men would want to take on the job of being Marshal. Andy Moore did want it. So, now he had it.

"The feller's got backing, looks like," Adam fretted.

Yes. Some ways that was more a worry than Andy was—if a man wanted to worry.

"Alick," Jeff Peak put in now, "I want you to know that all the Peaks who were of age to do so voted against Moore."

"Well, I thank you, one and all," Alec said dryly. "More families that settle here should be the size of yours."

"Alick," Adam said, the seams on his face deeper than before, "you got friends, plenty of them. Trouble is, most of 'em couldn't vote—not this time. Hadn't lived here long enough. Another year, maybe . . ."

"Now is now and then is then," Alec said and set his tin cup on the bar, bottom up. "Look, you two sour-faced idjuts. I think I know what you're driving at, but leave it be, will you?"

"Alick," Jeff Peak said, "all we want to say is—be careful, will you?"

"No. Don't know that I will," Alec said stubbornly; and anger flamed in him then. The fire of Adam's whiskey had hit the pit of his stomach. "Hell, what do you want me to do—run? Hide out somewhere, like I was in the wrong? Well, I ain't, and I won't. You wouldn't, either. Adam, you remember what the town looked like when I came here. Jeff, you've seen most of the changes come about. Hell, it makes no difference who owns the townsite. It's a free town in a free country. Andy Moore is our new Marshal —and that's a sour joke, I'll grant you; but there it is. He's been sworn to enforce the laws; and, if he does just that, there won't be any trouble. Like I said, it's a free town and it's where I live and go about my business, which I intend to do and pay him no attention, which is more than he's worth. . . ."

"Alick," Adam said sorrowfully, "you just got here. You ain't had time to talk to your building boss."

Anger cooled, but it didn't go away. What was this now?

"Will Toomy can tell you better than we can," Adam said. "You'll maybe listen to him."

"I'll send for Toomy soon as I get home," Alec promised, "so, don't hold me here any longer. Adam, I thank you for the eye-opener. Jeff, there's two boxes of stuff from St. Louis for you and Worth on the wagons, with bills of lading. If you can spare time Monday, Sarah will check them with you and you can see what it all comes to."

It was good then to be out in the early morning sunlight once more, free of the sourness of the dramshop, worry churning in his empty stomach all right now, along with some mad and Adam's whiskey. What had that double-dyed good-for-nothing Moore done in the two days he'd held office? Should have made Jeff or Adam tell him.

Couldn't see much from where he was, looking up Houston

Street from Commerce now instead of the other way around. On the corner directly across from him, one of the original log buildings, after that Peak's drugstore, with the Justice of the Peace Court upstairs, where he had first locked horns properly with Andy Moore, next to that the *Herald's* printshop . . . whoa! His eyes came back to the corner.

"Feller's got backing, looks like."

Smith's general store. Uncle Jack Smith, no kin to James Smith, Justice of the Peace. Store used to be Smith and Patterson; but Patterson was County Judge now and Smith ran it alone. Neither Smith nor Patterson had ever thought much of Alec Cockrell. They were always watching for him to overreach himself and fall—and kind of hoping. Especially Smith didn't like him. Not since he had put up a fine brick store on the one remaining corner of the crossing, looking at the square one way and just across Houston from Haught's place, and rented it to outsiders.

Hirsch and Shirek's Mercantile Emporium. Now there was a store building. As Alec watched, a little man in a black sack suit came out of its doors, to open the shutters and hook them against the wall. He bowed to Alec Cockrell on his black horse. Bowed.

"Alick, you got friends, plenty of them. Trouble is most of 'em couldn't vote."

Abraham Shirek. Little Jew fellow. Came to town after Alec had finished his house at the foot of Commerce, and moved his sawmill to Mill Creek. Came to town bent double under a peddler's pack, and no wonder, seeing what the pack held. Bright buttons, silk thread, braid, laces, silk stockings—one woman cried when she saw them—perfume, hairpins and combs, little paint pots for pale cheeks. Opened the pack on the square, and the women swarmed like bees. By late afternoon the weight on the peddler's back was less, but his pockets dragged with money. He asked permission to rest on the Cockrell doorstep.

"Is a good land," he sighed. "People buy with a free hand, but they are too few; and it is far for me to come. I am no longer real young. I have a cough. . . ."

He rubbed his lean shanks wearily, but his eyes were bright as new money from the Philadelphia Mint.

"You'll lose the cough if you stay here," Alec told him, his own eyes bright with an idea just forming. "Maybe you can. I've got a piece of empty land up a way on Commerce. A corner lot, handy to the square. Thought of building on it. Just right for a store. Like it to be a brick building." He grinned. "Own a brickyard. Windows to make it light inside and to show something of the goods, maybe. Two stories high—don't want it to be crowded. . . ."

That was how he dreamed it and there it was now. Best store short of the city of Houston. Shirek brought in a partner. They paid twenty-five dollars a month rent on the store building and the warehouse behind it. Never missed. Shirek said the luckiest day of his life was the one that took him to Dallas and gave him Alec Cockrell for a friend—and his good wife—bless them both.

"Alick, you sinner! Ride right past my place and never stop. You know I depend on you for my foreign news. How can I put out a paper without it?"

You got friends . . .

Wake Latimer, now, from his newspaper office on Houston. Ink on his shirt front already, or maybe he hadn't changed since yesterday. His broad face pink and shiny from sideburn to sideburn. Alec's spirits, which had lifted a notch over the Shirek store, went up still more.

"Ain't been where news happens," he told Latimer. "No further than Black Jack this time."

"You've seen people, heard talk," Latimer insisted. "Out with some of it now. What's the latest on railroads? Or Washington?"

"You know as much as I do," Alec said. "Railroads still surveying—east to west, south to north. Washington's as far away as ever, and maybe it's just as well. Speaking of railroads, and how long it takes to build one, St. Louis is starting a stage route to California this summer. The Overland Mail, they call it. Man named Butterfield's running it. Plans to run regular—summer and winter. Got his road all mapped out. On account of weather and mountains, he aims to dip south into Texas, going west."

"You don't say!" Then Latimer's eyes sharpened. "Wouldn't come as far south as Dallas, I don't suppose. Or would he, Alick?"

"No, of course not." But Alec was feeling better and better. "Sherman, I hear tell. But it wouldn't call for much enterprise to connect with the stage line there."

"No," Latimer agreed—softly. "Only a little road building and a couple of stages." Alec waved aside the obstacles. "You mean it, Alick! Can I print it? 'Alexander Cockrell, who in the half dozen years since he took up residence in our city . . .'"

"Whoa!" Alec said. "Idea just crossed my mind. Haven't mentioned it to anybody—even Sarah. Got a few other projects on hand that I ought to finish first. There's the hotel, for one." The hotel . . . a sharp stab cut through his consciousness. He tightened rein on Sinful. "Come on, Wake. Let's take a look at it —now!"

"Whoa yourself!" Latimer said in his turn. "Look at it from right where you are, Alick. Nothing's happened to it while you were away. It's all there, and growing. Alick?" He stopped. Alec wasn't hearing him.

For a fact, Alec wasn't. He sat on his horse right in front of the Bryan house, and never gave a thought now to the woman who might be watching him from one of her windows. The hotel— his hotel—the big, fine hotel that was going to make Dallas famous up and down Texas.

"Alick, you just got here. You ain't had time to talk to your building boss. . . .

"Toomy will tell you . . ."

He would have stopped in any case on his way home to take a look at the hotel, to see how work had progressed while he was away; but now he sat, frozen still, studying it from across the street, studying it inch by inch, those hot and cold feelings churning again in his stomach. By heavens, if a way had been found to halt the building . . .

His hotel. When it was finished it would take up the whole block across from the Bryan house. He'd have to find a way to pry Uncle Jack Smith out of his lousy cabin at the corner, and he would find it. Some of the windows must look right on the square. His hotel. Four unfinished walls now, the second story just shaping up. There'd be three stories when the work was done. Pillared doorframes marked the entrances from the street. One was wide enough to take a carriage. No proper carriages had yet been seen in Dallas, but there would be carriages—some day. So far, all right. His eyes traveled up the walls. Window frames set now in the second story. High, proud windows, he had specified, and plenty of them. Two to every room. "Two windows to a room, Alick," folks asked, "and you plan to rent one room to a customer?" Whoever heard tell of the like? At the Crutchfield House, they slept four to a bed, four beds to a room.

Not here. His eyes studied the window frames, the brickwork around them. He drew a sharp, quick breath.

"They're short a day's work," he said.

"Now, Alick!" Latimer objected. "How do you know? D'you count the bricks?"

"I know," Alec said. "What happened?"

"Nothing. Forget it, Alick. Toomy took care of everything. You've got a fine building boss."

"I know; but what happened?"

"Forget it, I say."

"No."

"Alick, you're too big a man to be stopped by any trifling. . . . Alick, as a newspaper publisher, I'm not supposed to take part in any town differences. Get Toomy to tell you about it. Just take my word for it, it's all right now. Go on! The hotel's fine. One of these days . . . Alick, it's a whopper. Some folks say you'll never fill it. What do you think?"

Alec looked at him, scornfully, the scorn for those folks. He'd filled that hotel in his mind a hundred times over. Right now he could look at the skeleton yonder and see it complete and occupied. Glass in those upstairs windows. Fancy blinds behind them to keep out the midday sun. Lace curtains, maybe. Pretty ladies resting in rocking chairs behind the windows. In the public room downstairs broad-chested men lolling back in stouter chairs or steadying themselves against a bar. An elegant bar, with a mirror. No rough wood counter. In the street, carriages coming and going—carriages with matched horses—well, matched mules, maybe, right at first, and light wagons, family style, but carriages finally.

"Still think you'll run her up the full three floors?" Latimer asked, watching him. "Disregarding what the first norther may do to your roof and chimneys?"

"Three stories high," Alec told him. "Ought to be starting the third story now, and thinking about the roof and those chimneys. Well, we ain't that far, or anyway near. That's how I know we lost a day."

"Alick," Latimer's hand rested now on the horn of the saddle, "forget it—if you can. Keep being sure that your hotel's going on up to the roof. I want to be there at the opening. I'm all for you, Alick—hotel, stage line, railroad or whatever you do next. Don't let anybody stop you; but go easy. You've got others to think about, remember. That's all. Those my newspapers back of you? I swear . . ." He stepped back to untie the bundle. "New Orleans, St. Louis," he read. "You son-of-a-gun, you'd have ridden off without giving them to me. Well, get on home now and . . . give my regards to Mrs. Cockrell." He slapped Sinful's rump, but cautiously.

"Obliged," Alec said, steadying Sinful; but it was he, rather than the horse, that snorted as they went on their way now, down Commerce Street toward home.

You've got others to think about, remember. When had he forgotten . . . what did Latimer suppose a man built courthouses and hotels and store buildings for—his own pomposity? A man thought, he planned, he worked, he built; and then . . . the snort went out of him and he slowed Sinful. He could still feel the hand of Wake Latimer on his saddle. It was a staying hand. He saw the homely face of Adam Haught, seamed with years and knowing all kinds of people and happenings, the young, anxious face of Jefferson Peak. The letter of John Neely Bryan in his saddlebag added its warning: "Be careful, Alick. He's a mean one."

Well, I won't. Anger welled up in him afresh as he rode on. He was leaving the Bryan house now. Margaret Bryan, if she saw him, had not come out to add her pinched face to those others. He crossed a rutted lane named Broadway and had now one more block to go before reaching his house. On his left was a blacksmith shop, which Henry, a hired-out Negro, ran for him. When the hotel was finished, the livery stable would stand there.

He passed the blacksmith shop. The low, covered wooden bridge was in sight at last. Ha! The same folks who made mock of his fine hotel had said he couldn't build that bridge. Not where it was. Said the whole thing would sink of its own weight in the black waxy. Bound to. Feeling just about as balked then as he did now, he'd set out to show they were wrong. He'd cut giant cedars, peeled the trunks down to heartwood, hewed them square, thrust them deep into the banks, bound them with cross ties, filled the space between with rock; and there, on both sides of the muddy little river, were his abutments, ready for the bridge timbers. Four years ago the first wagon had rattled across, the owner complaining bitterly over the thirty-cent toll. He had given Sarah the three silver dimes to keep. Someday, say when the railroads came, he'd have to build a better bridge, higher, stronger, but he would bet anything that, when that day came, those cedar abutments would still be there, and holding.

Someday . . . his eyes left the road to seek out his house. That, too, was nowhere near as fine as he meant to build for Sarah someday. Just a step up from the ranch to better things, but, like the bridge, a solidly built house, four square, lifted out of the mud on cedar chunks.

But he didn't get as far as the house. Not this time. Three hindrances stopped him, rooted him to the middle of the road. They were, in quick succession, a spotted pony, the jeans-clad Indian, and Sarah. His first shock was over Charley John. So, he had heard, with the day just dawning, a horse following him down the road, too far behind to be seen. Doggone! He had squirmed then and he squirmed now, almost as much as he had that night in the *asi* when the old shaman pointed his skinny arm at him.

Then Charley John and the shaman didn't matter except as they mattered to Sarah. Her back was to the road, but it seemed to Alec that she held herself pretty tight and stiff, even for her. She wasn't afraid of Charley John. She couldn't be. And he'd never told her about the old shaman and his prophecy. Still he could have sworn, looking at her, that she was afraid of something. His mouth softened as he watched her, then hardened, then somehow managed to be both soft and hard. Doggone! All his world, all his dreams, all his fight centered in that neat, tight little woman body standing there, fresh as the day in her starched calico.

chapter **five**

Having the power to render
themselves invisible...

IF HE LIVED to be a hundred, which he knew he wouldn't, and kept his senses, Alec Cockrell would never forget the first time he saw Sarah Horton. He had been living with Wes Cockrell at his ranch a full year then, had halfway settled down there. It was a rough sort of life, but easygoing. Wes had a Kentucky wife, as easy in her ways as her husband, and a mere handful of young ones so far. He had come to own considerable cattle; so Alec, who knew how to drive cows better than he knew anything else, was welcome to a place at his table and a bed in the loft of the house. He might have done worse; but he had a sneaking notion that, also, he could do better. Every now and again he would ride over to Dallas, to hobnob with John Neely Bryan and hear from him what the town could be, and see for himself what it was not. At least, so far.

It wasn't long before he began to haul, for hire. Built himself up quite a business, borrowing a team and wagon at first. Drove the mules or oxen himself. Chiefly oxen. Their split hoofs pulled out of the mud easier. Now—this was summer, 1846—he had bought his first span. And roaring proud he was of them, too.

"Think you'd never owned anything before," Wes mocked at him.

It seemed to Alec he never had—outright.

So, that was how, early of a September morning, he was on his way to deliver a load of crockery from Smith and Patterson's store

66

to some new people who had just come to Dallas County from Virginia—name of Horton. Alec had heard Wes mention them. It seemed in Virginia they were neighbors to what was left of the Cockrells back there. So, when they came to Texas, they took a farm place close to Wes Cockrell's ranch. Because Enoch Horton, who got the notion of moving west from the land agents of Peters' Colony, a kind of company hired to settle Texas, had written to Wes before tearing up in Virginia. Was the land as healthy as folks said, he wanted to know. Mrs. Horton was ailing, and he thought the damp of eastern winters might be to blame. And Wes had written back that climate and cheap land were two sure things about Texas, and there was a farm place going to waste right next to him that they might get if they came on. It took a couple of years for the letters to pass back and forth and for the Hortons to sell out in Virginia; but here they were now—Enoch Horton and wife, two, three daughters, a parcel of sons, and several hands, to help work the place. Quite a houseful for a log cabin even with loft and lean-to, but two of the sons were talking about setting up for themselves elsewhere; so, Wes figured they'd manage. He seemed right glad to have the Hortons for neighbors again, talked about them considerable, but Alec didn't give much attention to what he said, nor to Mr. Patterson's comments now.

"Genteel," Patterson informed Alec. "Used to fixings. Two of the women come in here to look around. One of them kind of twittery, the older one; the younger one was quietlike, and did most of the deciding. Bought a couple a dress patterns of calico and every dish, crock and pot I had. Washstand set for every room with a bed in it, though I pointed out that the outdoors was close, and handy to all but the old and ailin'. China plates and cups and saucers to match for table and cupboard. You ever hear tell o' the like?"

Somewhere, in the dim past, Alec had.

"Had their own knives and forks and spoons, they said; but they hadn't ventured to carry many breakables with them and had lost much of what they did take. I pointed out that folks around here got along mostly with tin plates and cups, and gourds for drinking water. They said a tin cup or a gourd was all right for the wash-bench at the back door, but not for meals in the house. Well, so it's breakables in them barrels, young feller. I promised I'd git it to them safe—so you stay sober and don't overturn, hear me? They won't relish cracked or chipped pieces, let alone what you'd smash outright."

"If I upset," Alec told him, "I'll have more to worry about than chinaware." Not owning the wagon then, just borrowing it.

"Better spare some worry for the china," Patterson advised. "I'll hold you for every piece."

It was easier to upset a wagon than not, Alec knew. Just getting down the slippery near side of the Trinity to Bryan's ferry and up the even slipperier west side was a test. Beyond that no proper road across the bottoms—just tracks. He could have said he wouldn't take the job at Patterson's terms and was minded to do so; but he didn't refuse it. Why? Because Patterson said first that it was tough. Then Alec had to prove he could handle it.

So he started out. In high spirits and they got higher with every mile he covered. Do a thing or don't was his motto, but don't fret over which. Where the going was easy he sang; when it was hard to impossible, he roared, and cracked his long bull-whip. Anybody to hear him would have thought he was flaying the skin off the backs of his beasts. He never touched them, just flung out the whip, to hear the crack of it. Between cracks he bellowed. Before coming to Texas he had learned all there was to mule language. Now he'd added words suitable for oxen. They expected it, went right low-spirited if their driver kept quiet.

The last hundred yards was the worst. Coming out of the bottoms, folks naturally set their houses on rising ground if they could find some. Wes Cockrell lived on what was called Chalk Hill, and the house the Hortons had taken was on a low ridge, known in this flat country as Oak Cliff. Took its name from a patch of timber that covered the rise—mostly scrub oak, with some cedar. The cart track here was pure murder. It wouldn't have surprised Alec at any minute to see one of those danged barrels break loose and go tumbling bottom over top down the slope. So he yelled twice as loud, to hold the barrels and keep the oxen pulling. Time he broke into the clearing where the house was, his holiest thought was: Well, God damn! I made it.

And there she stood.

Just a woman body in dark calico—a green, viny pattern on a black ground. She hadn't had much to choose from, she said afterward. And a slat sunbonnet. Pulled well forward, because, if you had to wear such a thing, you'd want the good of it. How he, Alec Cockrell, recognized in her, in such a get-up, something special, he could never explain, even to himself; but he did. Must have been the way she stood there, facing him. Not much thicker through the middle than his arm. Figured he could just about span her waist with his two hands, and wanted like thunder to try it. But steady and sturdy. And quiet. Her hands crossed before her, her shoulders back, her eyes gravely watching him.

When he saw her face more clearly under that bonnet, it wasn't the prettiest he had ever seen. Far from it. But it caught his fancy where prettiness wouldn't. Clear skin, not pasty white, not pink like a flower, more like milk, but warmer than that. God knew a slat bonnet made no woman beautiful, but she was right to wear one. Then he met her eyes.

"Whoever set your eyes in your face," he told her afterward, "must have used a measuring stick, to get them so straight."

Never, in man or woman, had he met a look so level as that she gave him. Level, without being hard. Just thoughtful. They were gray eyes, near as he could make out, with a hint of hazel. The clearing, the woods below, went fearfully quiet. The oxen dropped their heads. Hot as Tophet, noon coming on.

He spoke first.

"Mis' Horton? Got some stuff here for you all. From town. Crockery mostly."

"I've been expecting you," she said. "I heard you coming."

She didn't smile, not exactly. Her eyes brightened. Her mouth softened. He took special notice of her mouth now. Not too large, not too small, ripe, sweet, making peace between a straight nose and a rather narrow chin. All the while those level eyes kept command, asking him now what he was staring at.

"Seems to me," he stammered, "I know you. Seems I must have knowed you—somewheres."

She shook her head.

"I don't think so. You wouldn't recall Virginia." He had never seen Virginia. "Somebody that favored me, maybe. Some of my folks that moved over into Kentucky? My folks and your folks were good friends from 'way back."

Now, why did she say that? My folks, your folks—your folks, mine. If she'd hunted for it, she couldn't have found more surely the place in him that was sorest. He didn't know he could still hurt like that.

"I got no folks," he said fiercely, daring her to deny it.

The level, gray eyes widened.

"Everybody has folks," she said. "How else . . ."

She meant, without folks how had he come to be? That was true enough, but hardly the sort of thing a young woman of proper raising would say to a young man and a stranger. She broke off, stammering; and, for the first time since their meeting, he had the upper hand. She blushed; and, when Sarah Horton blushed, it was something to see. Warm color spread over or under the healthy smoothness of her skin. He widened his eyes now, and suddenly sparks flew.

"You!" she cried, outdone with herself, but blaming him. "You!"

And she turned and ran for the house.

Now, having just come up with her, Alec had no mind to let her go like that; but he didn't know just what to do about it. He looked down, and there was the bullwhip in his hand. Without his hardly willing it, the cracker snaked out into the air and exploded. Profanity rushed from his throat to follow. By God, he'd give her something to blush for, burn that damnation bonnet right off her high-born ears.

"You Baldy! Broad! Git to hell on with you. Got a load of goddam crockery here, brought it the whole goddam way from town."

The door of the house banged to in his face, was barred and bolted.

"Aim to deliver the putrid lot of it, shut door or no."

He never swore better. In two languages, Spanish and English, which was all he knew, except Injun. And he couldn't recollect any swear words in Cherokee. There being none that he'd ever heard.

He was still bellowing at the top of his lungs, when a man came around the corner of the house and hushed him. A tall man, maybe twice Alec's age.

"What is all the noise about?" he demanded. "Are you aware, sir, that there are ladies in my household?"

Sure enough, Alec was aware. That was why he hollered. And he wouldn't have hushed, except that the man reminded him of his father, sort of. Not quite so gentle. A little fiercer. But they'd had the same kind of raising.

"Have you business here, or are you trespassing?"

Angrily Alec told him about the four barrels of crockery from Smith and Patterson's store in town.

"Very good. Drive around in back. My son will help you unload."

Son was named Jim. Patterned after his old man. Gentle-spoken, but livelier, with a sense of fun. Hoisted himself into Alec's wagon and laid large, powerful hands on a barrel.

"What did you say to Sis?" he asked. "Scared her into a near fit."

It was the truth. Sarah Cockrell, born Sarah Horton, fifth child of Enoch and Martha Horton of Abingdon, Virginia, and their third daughter, would also remember this day as long as she lived. She leaned against the door she had barred and didn't know whether to laugh or cry or pray. So, she did a little of all three.

Dear Lord, she thought, this is a terrible land, the people—some of them, near savages. I never saw, I never heard the like. That man out there—that young man—if he is a Cockrell, he's got none of their ways. I never saw, I never heard . . . something stopped her short of denunciation.

He favors them some, she admitted. Could be right handsome. He was handsome, if she would tell herself the truth. Hair as black as an Indian's, blazing blue eyes, tall, slim as a sapling and as tough and supple, with a look of lean hunger upon him as if he had never yet eaten his fill. That was absurd, she knew. He might have gone hungry once or twice, but that hadn't been always or even lately. The lack was something different. What? Why did he flare up when she mentioned folks? *"I got no folks."* What a thing to say! As she had told him, everybody had folks. Was that his lack and his hunger?

At that, another yell of defiance came through the log walls. She turned faint and leaned once more against the barred door. How could she call him handsome? A savage, even in his dress. A long-tailed hunting shirt of calico—he'd never bought that gaudy blue and red piece at that store in Dallas—a red sash around his middle. Moccasins on his feet. A handkerchief, red, tied around his head. She'd seen drawings of Indians, wearing such. He was an Indian. He . . . dear Lord, this terrible land. It was nothing like Virginia. Why had they left Virginia? It had been a dreadful uprooting. A dreadful journey. Would they ever know peace again? And safety? Here? The land had her by the throat now, shaking her.

Another wild yell from outside, then her father's strong voice taking command and in another minute calling for Jim. Her long-legged brother let himself down from the loft, where he had been setting beds, making things as comfortable as he could here for all, before he and brother Enoch moved over to a place called Eagle Ford, where they were taking over a gristmill.

Eagle Ford. Places had wild names. Wild . . .

"What ails you, Sis?" Jim stopped to ask.

And she couldn't answer. She turned and ran, to hide her burning face in a pillow until she could find an answer for herself, if there was one.

That evening Mr. Wesley Cockrell came over, as he often did, to sit with her pa and talk about Texas and Virginia, making out that Texas was the better, as it was in some ways, Ma being better of her cough already; but, oh, it was still a wild, a terrifying land. Sarah believed now the tales she had heard of courage, of looking death in the face and not quailing, whether death came with the wild howl of Comanches or from a firing squad of Spaniards. Only a Texan, who took hazard—from Indians to rattlesnakes, from chaparral to bog mud—as part of living, could be that tough.

This evening, however, Wesley Cockrell asked for her. She was minded still to hide; but she was minded stronger not to; so she smoothed her hair, wiped a tear out of her eye and went to hear what he had to say to her.

"What did you do or say to Alick this morning?"

That was it, and she was minded again to run, but did not.

"Nothing," she declared, and, after a tussle, "Why?"

"Figured it was you," Mr. Cockrell said. "He didn't say so. Hardly got a word out of him, except generally where he was going." Going? "I went over to town after he left." Going—he was gone. "Patterson told me he'd been out here. He got back to town shortly after noon, swollen to burst with mad, took a drink— or several—turned in his wagon, and sold his oxen. Asked if he was quitting the town, he said he sure as hell was doing just that. Couldn't stand some of the folk who were coming in. He was still boiling when he got back to the ranch. Washed up, wouldn't stop to eat, rolled a blanket with his buckskin hunting shirt and some cold bread and meat inside, loaded his gun, saddled one of my best horses, and took off for the border."

"Oh, no!" Sarah said.

"That's what he said. Still fighting down there, I hear; and, when it comes to that, if he's bound to shoot somebody, I'd liefer it would be a Mex than one of us. We ain't got hardly enough settlers in this whole county to make one sure enough, solid township. If you sassed him or in any way spoke rough to him, I ain't blaming you, ma'am. Alick's all right inside, but he's wild. Ain't ever been gentled properly."

She could have died, she hurt so bad.

Excuse me, Mr. Cockrell, I hear Ma calling: the words were right there, but she didn't speak them.

"Tell me about him, Mr. Cockrell," that's what she said. "Will you, please?"

"Tell you what I know," he answered. "Ain't much."

It was enough. She cried that night as she hadn't since she was a young thing grieving because she hadn't been born pretty.

"For heaven's sake," Sister Polly asked, "what ails you now—besides Texas?"

"Nothing," she answered, womanwise. Everything ailed her, really.

Born to be an old maid, she thought. First man, first halfway suitable man, who ever looked at me that way and I slammed the door on him. The shut door was a loving joke between her and Alexander Cockrell forever after. Any time the subject came up —any time Alec brought it up, for she wouldn't—any time he would look at her with a sly, teasing smile, as Baby Alec had this very morning—Sarah would feel a jerk and a hurt inside, remembering. Did he feel that way about it, too? She often wondered.

Sure as hell did, Alec could have told her thinking back to it this very morning. That blankety door burned him all the way to Monterrey and back again. Why he rode in that direction he had no idea, unless it was because a woman had made him look small in his own eyes and he was bound he'd change her estimate. Like a boy who can't get any notice walking ordinary on his feet, so he walks on his hands, upside down. Bound he'd prove himself a hero, even if, on an outside chance, he didn't live to enjoy the glory. "Now, look what you done!" he could say to Miss Gray Eyes in that case . . . or, could he?

Things didn't work out just the way he meant them to do. There was a Colonel McCullough down on the border, commanding a troop of Rangers. They were anybody's idea of wild men, and Alec wished to join up with them. At Austin he learned of their whereabouts. Monterrey, with Zach Taylor's army. He rode hard, but it wasn't hard enough. Time he reached the encampment, the shell-torn town was smoking, as were some of the forts roundabout, but the fighting was over.

"Hell and damn!" he said to the Colonel. "I started too late."

"Sure did," the Colonel agreed. "If you'd got here three days sooner, you could have found room in a burying ditch. Maybe. We contributed to those ceremonies as well as others. Considerable. Can you ride?"

Colonel knew that was a ridiculous question. Soon as he put it. So, there still being some duties connected with burning out a town and routing a hostile force, he put Alec on the rolls and gave him dispatches to carry. That was how he spent his time before Monterrey, riding back and forth and around from one officer's tent to another. Seeing where all the fighting had been, hearing about it, but getting not one nick in his own hide.

He fell heir to a Ranger's outfit. It suited him to a "T"—fire-red workshirt, any sort of breeches—his own, as it happened—held by a broad leather belt—the leaner the belt line the better—then tucked into the tops of his boots. He acquired a taste for

Spanish leather, worked soft and supple in the curing, and patiently and delicately stitched in fanciful patterns. A Bowie knife and a Colt's revolver. A broad hat to shade him and a braided lariat on the front of his saddle, good for hanging or roping, about finished the picture. A blanket roll behind, if he could keep a blanket in this nest of thieves. He did.

This was the outfit he wore when he started home. Some time later. McCullough's Rangers, having fought as bloody as any, were mustered out the end of September; but Alec, having come this far, stayed behind to look things over. It was not until the first hot breath of the coming summer struck him that he decided he'd as well drift northward.

He looked a sight bigger, somehow, than when he had left. Felt it his own self. Riding into Wes Cockrell's clearing, he was met by his kinsman with an admiring whoop:

"God's sake, it's Alick! Hey! You don't aim to herd cattle in sech a shirt, I hope. Run 'em clean off the range, if you do."

"After this," he informed Wesley, "when I herd cattle, they'll be my own, and I'll answer for 'em to myself."

That was what being around folks and seeing new places had done for him. That and gray eyes meeting him every which way he turned. Looking at things with him, judging their value. Looking at him. He wished he could see Sarah Horton now. He wished she could see him. Maybe she wasn't anywhere around. Her folks might have given up and gone back to Virginia. He wanted to ask Wes Cockrell about them. It should have been easy. "Those folks making out all right on the next farm?" he could have said, careless-like; but he didn't, though here was all his reason for coming back. Just in the nick of time then, before he went into a crazy rage at himself and all else, Wes saved him.

"Seems to me," Wes said, "we could do some celebrating. Ain't had a merrymaking in this house since we moved in. We got neighbors now that like to get together. If it's only to sing hymns. There's the Hortons and the Overtons—new folk, Alick, and they're from Missouri."

Alec was not interested in strangers. He'd heard what he needed to know. For the time being. The Hortons had stuck it out. They were still here. He left Wesley Cockrell talking at a gallop. God's sake, the rest of what he wanted to know he'd not know until he saw Sarah Horton with his own eyes, until he spoke to her and heard her speak in answer.

It was a big party. Nobody troubled to send out invitations, but word got around. The weather was fine, the roads were dry, the fighting was over. Texas was freer than ever and bigger, the Rio Grande marking it off for all time from Mexico to the south, the United States surrounding it on the three other sides—east, north and a new stretch to the west. Everybody who could catch a horse or ride a wagon came, the men to talk politics and cattle and this new idea of raising cotton instead of corn, the young things to dance, and the women to visit and see that nobody went hungry. Most of the women, soon as they lighted, went right around the house to the kitchen with their crocks and baskets.

That way Alec missed her. Looking and feeling big in his red Ranger shirt, and leather belt over new breeches, and his Spanish boots, he stood with Wesley Cockrell near the house door to make folks welcome. Unwillingly he had left off his Bowie knife and Colt's revolver. People came and came. Names he didn't know a minute before and knew less a minute later. Cochran, Hord, Miller, Overton—had they all moved in while he was away? Finally a brace of Hortons, the big, pleasant one named Jim, who had helped him unload crockery on that memorable day, and a brother folks called 'Nock after his pa. They gave their parents' excuses. Ma was ailing again and Pa wouldn't leave her. The girls were there, but temporarily busy in the kitchen. Ennerine had baked a cake, her first; and Polly and Sally were standing by to catch her if it should have fallen in coming over and she should faint. Ennerine, Alec thought. Now, if the one he remembered had been called Ennerine—but of course, she wouldn't be. If this was Ennerine's first cake, she must be a younger sister—real young. He swallowed hard and waited for the dancing.

And still she wasn't there. The place was full of Ennerines and such; but no slim touch-me-not with grave gray eyes looked out at him from the rustle and the twitter. No. She was older, what you might call responsible. That was part of her dignity, the quality that marked her as special. He must look for her if he would find her. In the kitchen, probably. Bravely he started around the house, and stopped. In a spot of light from a window she stood alone, looking up at the stars as if they would give her what it was she wanted. God's sake, he thought, she is more wonderful than I remembered.

No slat bonnet, you see, it being night. Her hair sleek and shining and plain and proud on her small, proud head, her face looking paler than it was in the near dark, and earnest. That was a thing about Sarah Horton. Even when she smiled, she looked thoughtful. Her dress was some light stuff. Either Smith and Patterson had got in some new bolts, or she had gone farther for the material. But plain. All her life she would be sparing with ornament—a simple pin to finish off the collar of her dress, a plain gold chain. His gifts to her later gave her pleasure, but often only just to hold in her hand.

She looked thinner, slighter than he recalled. He thought again, I could close my hands about her waist, and, I could crush her between my hands like a bug, but I would rather die than harm her. I would be proud to be the dust of the road she walks on. I would be prouder than that to be the one to march ahead of her down that road, and she following, of her own will. God, what must a man do or be to have that befall him?

Why, nothing, seeing how folks are made. She wasn't looking at the stars now, but at him, taking him in, too, red shirt and all. Shaking like a leaf in the wind, if he had only known. Again, he spoke first.

"Well, I come back."

"I'm glad," she said, cool and prim; but he knew she meant it.

Through the window near them came the screeching of a fiddle and the stamping of feet.

"Are you spoken for?" he asked. "I mean, for this dance?"

"Don't you know?" she answered. "We are Methodist folk. Methodists don't hold with dancing."

A Methody woman. That was a facer, but here she was.

"Don't you like to dance?"

"Yes," she said honestly—never known to speak otherwise. "I do."

He held out his hand.

"To pleasure me—this once?"

And, after a small tussle with herself, she gave in. A small hand inside his, slim like the rest of her, a little twitchy right now, but warm and strong. He held fast to her until he had her on the dance floor and . . . she was right about one thing. If she wanted to be a stout Methodist, she should stay away from the screech of fiddles. As light as a bit of tumbleweed, pointing her toe with the best of them, into his arms and then out again before he knew he had her. Maybe it was his own lightness as much as hers. The wonder was that his feet stayed down and his head up. Before he knew it, he was singing:

> "Dinah got a meatskin laid away,
> To grease that wooden leg, so they say . . .
> Shake that wooden leg, Dinah, oh . . ."

When it was over, everybody breathless, the cool, oval face he had dreamed about was flushed and he himself was plain on fire. They went out into the dark again, to cool down if they could.

"Call that sinful?" he teased.

"Maybe it is," she answered.

"Feel like running away?"

"Yes . . . I do."

"Why don't you?"

"Maybe because I've lived in Texas a while now and am more used to it."

"Maybe," he agreed. "How do you like us?"

"I don't know—for sure."

But she had been giving the matter thought, he took it; and then somebody came after her. Her sister Polly, it turned out, as flighty as Ennerine, flightier, because she was old enough to have some sense.

"So, that's where you have run to," Polly twittered. "What do you mean, Mr. Cockrell, by carrying off the best hand we have in the kitchen? I could have been spared better."

Hell and damn! He didn't say it—for but one reason. He took himself off before it came out. No more shut doors for him now, not if he could help it. He stamped off into the house, cut out Ennerine from the herd, and danced with her. She was all right when you got to know her better. Silly, green young, rattle-pated, but not a clear fool.

"Why are you so quiet, Mr. Cockrell? I saw you dancing with Sarah. You weren't quiet then. Are you wishing I was Sarah?" Exactly what he was wishing. Tongue-tied with wishing. "Sally is the best of all of us, we know; but sometimes other people don't. The mainstay of our family, Ma says."

Yes? Then they'd better get some other support. He was about to steal the prop they counted on. The next time he asked Sarah Horton was she spoken for, he was not inviting her to dance and she knew it.

"No," she said, open and honest, to his question.

"Folks troubled with poor eyesight back in Virginia?"

She shook her head.

"No more so than here."

"You're wrong," he crowed. "We look sharp hereabouts—have to." And then, "I'm back in the business of hauling. I've hauled twice from Shreveport already and am leaving for Houston for a load tomorrow."

"I heard," she said; and he had to tease her a little, being almost as much of a tremble over what he was leading up to as she was.

"You don't mean it," he said pretending that she was speaking of the noise he made, driving his wagons. "Been trying lately not to let go anywhere near where people live."

"You!" she said to that.

"Thinking of taking land further up on Mountain Creek. Got a place in mind. Good grazing and fine water. Wes allows I can claim about twenty head of cattle bunched with his now. That would be a starter. Cattle for meat will pay for the small trouble it is to herd them. They'll pay better when we have better roads. Know places right now where folks prize beef almost as much as pork to eat. It's a likely spot I have in mind—a little hill for a house, and, like I said, good grazing. Right now I can take up three hundred twenty acres free. Could have headrights to twice as much—if I was a married man."

He waited to hear what she thought of that.

"It is worth considering," she allowed.

"Ma'am, I been considering it," he shouted. "Long and lonesome—every which way." Then, before her level, though kindly eyes, confusion fell upon him again. "Sound big—don't I? Well, I'm not. I know damn well—excuse me, ma'am—how little I amount to. There's things I ought to tell you—things you ought to know."

"I do know," she said. "Mr. Wesley Cockrell told me."

He was furious at that—scared mostly.

"The old busybody," he fumed.

"No," she said. "I asked him."

The fire went out of Alec at that, leaving him plain dumb for a stretch. But he figured finally that, unless he wanted to go raving crazy with not knowing, he'd as well take an answer that would settle things once and for all.

"Then," he said, meek as a bleating lamb, "will you? Will you have me, Sarah?"

"Yes," she said.

A woman who could always speak her mind, but never used too many words doing so. That's why he remembered them all. Every separate one, he was sure.

But there was one thing, it appeared, that Wes Cockrell had failed to tell Sarah. It came out when they went to sign the papers for the ranch land on Mountain Creek. At the log courthouse on the Dallas square, before Lawyer John McCoy, who was acting as the local land agent for Peters' Colony. Mr. McCoy had the papers all made out and ready. He pointed to the place where Alec was to sign; and Alec shut his mouth tight, took the pen and made his cross. John Bryan, who knew how things were and stood by to act as witness, took the pen from him, meaning to fill in the name; but Sarah was ahead of him.

"Please," she said, "let me."

The letters of *Alexander* wobbled some to the left of the x, steadied on the *Cockrell* to the far side; and her hand was well under control when she signed her name below; but there was a blot on the lower leg of Alec's mark when she straightened up, reaching blindly with her left hand for Alec's, which she held to after that as if afraid of drowning.

"You cried," Alec charged later, bristling still if she had any rebuke to offer. "You let a teardrop fall on the paper right there."

"No," she said, talking a lot for her. "The pen caught and sort of sputtered. Why make a fuss over a little thing like that? It wasn't your fault."

No? Whose fault was it, then? If he had had a rope long enough to go around the world, he would have drawn it tight, knotted it, and handed the whole globe to her right that minute.

chapter six

Few can know them.

"**M**Y REGARDS TO MRS. COCKRELL."

They were married that same summer and went to the ranch to live before Alec had the house clear finished.

"Lonesome living for a woman used to family and neighbors," Sarah's father complained. "Nobody within call. Now, is there?"

No. Nobody that close; but, somehow, it seemed all right for two people starting a new life, with a lot to learn about each other. Sarah took a girl from the Horton place with her. Name of Pokey, and suitable. She didn't have much in her head but her back was strong. She could carry water and scrub and make lye soap. She was about as much care as she was help, but she was company. As for Alec, he had more help than he wanted. As busy as if he was settling a tribe into a new village, but he had his own ideas of how he wanted things done. He appreciated and needed extra arms to help raise the walls of the house and set the roof timbers, but he could have done without the advice that came with the help.

"You aim to fort up in this place?" Jim Horton groaned one day, weary with hoisting and straining. "You got logs here stout enough for a stockade."

"Don't aim to have the house blow down or buckle," Alec said, with not too much breath to spare, himself. Presently he added, "Where I been lately, folks make their walls thick." It was how you told a *hacienda* from a *jacal*, a peon's hut. "Keeps the place snug in cold weather and holds out the heat in summer. Some of it."

Yes, and he had picked up another idea down on the Rio Grande. When the house was finished, he mixed lime with water and whitewashed everything, outside as well as in. Forever after, the place had a name: Whitehouse Ranch. Sarah's eyes shone when she saw it. Then her nose caught the sharp, clean smell and she made a long speech—for her.

"Mr. Cockrell, it is just beautiful."

Well, maybe that was claiming too much. Just one room, though a large one, with a loft and a lean-to; but it had a good floor, puncheon, and a stone chimney, not mud and sticks. Furniture was mostly plain, the bed built fast against one wall, which gave it firm support. A table with a pine top, because that scrubbed white. A dish cupboard to match the table, and chairs of hickory with rawhide seats. Sarah brought with her a couple of more elegant chairs, of dark carved wood and with cushioned bottoms; but these she kept against a wall, except for special company. She had also her own washstand and chest of wild cherry wood, all these refinements from the home in Virginia. And that was about all. The clothes they were not wearing hung from pegs in a corner handy to the bed, with a calico curtain to hide them—and keep off the dust. Alec hung his gun on pegs above the fire, and on the wall across from that they had a painted picture.

Fact. Smith and Patterson gave it to them when Alec bought the chinaware for the house. They could afford to throw in a framed picture, considering what Alec laid out in that purchase. He was bound Sarah should not lack for proper crockery. He bought a complete set for her washstand—white earthenware overrun with blue vines and flowers, and china for the table with a pink moss rose on every dish, top, side or bottom. This was wanton extravagance. He could have bought several head of cattle for the same money, but it pleased Sarah more than anything else could have and so it was worth it. She could even spare a pitcher from one set or the other to stick a posy in and set on the pine table, and did so the year round, if it was only a bunch of wild seeds or a sprig of cedar.

That was how they came by the picture.

"It's Columbus discovering America," Sarah said.

Was it now? How did she know? Mr. Patterson hadn't said.

A dark man in odd clothes—looked like plush—kneeling on the ground holding to a cross, with a flag floating above him. Indians standing around with feathers on their heads and spears in their hands. A foreign-looking man and a foreign flag, and Alec said so.

"The flag of Spain," Sarah said.

"You don't mean it," Alec marveled. "So, there was where trouble began."

"You!" Sarah said. It was her way of expressing her opinion, meaning he was her own true love, her wedded husband, an amusing ignoramus, the cockle-burr in her blanket and all the rest of it. "You! That's where we began."

"Don't believe it," Alec maintained, liking to see her warm up. "Don't see a sign of us. Just them—those foreign monkeys."

But he drove a nail in the wall, anyhow, and hung the picture, and would have shot the hand off anybody who tried to take it down. It added to the room, that was a fact.

That night, in their quiet time sitting before their own fire, Sarah told him about the settling of people in America—the Spaniards first, in Florida and around the Gulf of Mexico, then the English northward, about Virginia, where his folks and hers had been neighbors; and he could see it all as plain as though he had been there. Some of what she said he stored to remember. Some he missed, watching her sweet seriousness as she spoke. She was sweet—sweet as sugar—for all she was so full of learning. A smart, able, proud young woman, and sweet—a warm, loving, tender armful. And his. His own. He knew now.

She didn't do all the talking. Their quiet time came after supper, when Pokey was rolled in her comforter in the lean-to and, if they weren't pestered by other company, they knew they were alone. It began usually with a settling of the day's accounts. Sarah had a ledger in which she wrote down everything. Her daybook, she called it. It was bound in gray cloth over stiff boards and the pages were ruled in blue lines, with red ones up and down for keeping dollars and cents in order. Didn't he think it would help to know exactly what they had, where they gained and where they lost, she wanted to know. A person, she said, could not rightly keep everything straight in his head. She was dead right. And the funny thing was that, with the beginning of that accounting, everything mostly was gain. He had no mind to spoil all that writing with clumsy blundering.

Then, with the book put away, the talk. She might know more out of books than he did, but he had been more places and seen more than she had. He had more to tell, really, than she did, talked longer, laying out before her what he had kept locked up in the dark all before this. He told her stuff he thought he'd never tell a mortal soul besides himself. Sometimes she would listen quietly all the way through, a knowing smile or a sigh being all her remarks. Oftener she would cut him off with a sorrowing cry.

"Hush now, please, Mr. Cockrell. I cannot bear the hurt of it."

Her eyes would be wet, like that day at the courthouse when she made a blot on his mark. She would put her hand over his mouth to hush him. He'd have to pull her down on his knee or into the chair beside him and rock her in his arms to take away her sorrowing; and they would be young and foolish together, making up for the time when they had lived apart. She would call him Alec then, straight from the heart. Other times it was Mr. Cockrell, properly respectful. She was strong for minding the proprieties; and he humored in that, doing for her what he would never have done for another or for himself alone.

Like wearing a black cloth coat and breeches to match. He didn't take to sober dressing all at once and forever. Being married, having headrights, owning property did not make him over completely, inside or out. Time and again he would have spells of wishing he was alone on the trail, riding from nowhere to nowhere else, with one pair of pants and maybe two shirts to his name. He kept an outfit like that he'd worn the day he first met up with Sarah Horton, suitable for the road; and he wore it—some —when he went off with the wagons for one reason or another. Years slipped from his back when he shucked broadcloth and laid on buckskins and calico. Other things slipped away, too, however; and when he came near home and Sarah, he changed back willingly enough.

He threatened to bolt right at the beginning, when he was getting things in order before he and Sarah were wedded, after she had given him her promise. There was a time of sweat, truly. Proud as he was, and full of ideas, he could feel a rope dropping over him and being drawn too tight for comfort. If he forgot, others reminded him.

"What will you wear to be married in?" Wes Cockrell asked one day.

"Goda'mighty, must I have a special outfit?"

"Most folks do," Wes told him. "The Horton girls are stitching from daylight to dark on Sarah's things."

Texas had come to that. He balked. He declared that, if the clothes he had worn a-courting weren't good enough for the wedding, just let somebody say so! Then he laughed. Of course, he had other clothes, he told Wes, laughed again, and left Wes looking more bothered than ever. With good reason. What Alec had in reserve was a *caballero* suit he had bought down in Saltillo. Why? He couldn't say now. Too much tequila, maybe. At the moment he had fancied the black velvet pants, slashed to the boot tops, with their silver lace and silver tassels, the short velvet jacket, the red sash, and the sombrero with more silver lace and silver dangles. How would it be if he wore that to his wedding? What would the Methody woman—and her kin—say to that?

His spirits lifted mightily. That was how it would be, he swore —a Ranger or a *caballero*—the Methody woman could take her pick. Then, with the wedding one week off, he fell into the worst sweat of all. He came out of it, storming and bellowing again, this time hounding the soul out of all and sundry, especially storekeepers, to find him something decent to put on his back.

"Can't stand up before a parson in such a rig," he said. "Got to find me a gentleman's breeches and a white shirt somewheres. Well, what have you got?"

Finally he had to ride hell for leather all the way to Austin to find something near suitable. At that, the breeches were too short, kept sliding up and out of his boots. The white shirt was too big, but he took a hitch in the sleeves and drew his belt a notch tighter to master the wasted length and fullness of the tails; and that had to do. The coat, made for the same man as the shirt, he wore as he wore fine coats to this day when the weather turned from warm to hot—folded and across his saddle bow. Riding into the Horton clearing to his wedding, by God, folks took him for the parson, who was delayed.

But Sarah held steady; and her voice, when she said her part of the service, was clear as a bell; and the day was got through somehow. Now, like that shut door of their first meeting, it was another cause for laughing and groaning in their quiet times together.

The quiet time ended often with Sarah pulling a sweet potato out of the hot ash and breaking it open and sharing its sugar mellowness with him. Nothing in life afterward ever tasted better than those yams she roasted so.

"Don't ever buy me a cookstove, Mr. Cockrell," she told him, "until you can build me an outside kitchen. I was brought up at an open fire and I wouldn't fancy one of those black iron things poking out into the room."

Lonesome? She might be, but she never said so. After what her father said, Alec gave thought to not leaving her too long alone at the ranch. When he was away on a long haul, he would have her sister Polly or Ennerine to stay with her. They were no great defense if she needed defending, as useless that way, either one, as Pokey; but they were company and kept her occupied and she would have bit her tongue off rather than admit that life at Whitehouse Ranch was less than perfect.

Because there were a few things she was afraid of. One was wolves. Theirs was the first house that far from town in that direction, and the wild creatures had hardly been given notice to move on. On moonlight nights especially, the wolves and the coyotes raised quite a chorus; and during a cold snap they'd come right close. Alec reasoned with her, told her they were hungry and otherwise miserable and liked to get together and raise a tune about it; and she quieted some. Then one night he awoke, to see her sitting up straight and stiff in bed, staring at nothing. He knew she was all drawn together inside.

"What ails you now?" he asked, in the way of a man with his sleep spoiled.

"It's so still," she said. "I don't hear a living thing."

That struck him as funny. He laughed till the bed shook. And that made her mad. She flopped down on her pillow with her back high; and that seemed to him funnier than ever. And he laughed some more.

"What's funny now?" she asked finally in a small, woe-begone way.

"Just heard a door bang shut," he told her.

"You!" she said, but turned and crept close.

She didn't cure so easy about snakes. To tell the truth, he didn't like the idea of them near her himself, especially rattlers. He cleaned out the brush close to the house and brought in some hogs, because they were good at rooting out reptiles. He showed Sarah the difference between a king snake and a rattler, and she knew about black snakes.

"Mr. Cockrell, I do not like snakes. Any of them will get into a henhouse. I have baby chicks coming off. I'll thank you to show me how to fire a gun."

He'd heard that women could handle a musket but he didn't like the idea.

"The recoil will knock you into a heap," he warned.

"I'll rest it on something solid."

As if reptile or varmint would wait on all that. But she was in earnest; so he showed her how to load and take aim and fire. She was quick to pick it up, having lived with hunting men all her days; but Pokey had stronger arms and steadier hands and more heart for killing. And there was a situation. But he slung the gun on pegs over the fire and bound Pokey over not to take it down unless the mistress said so, if they saw something that needed killing, or if they needed a mess of squirrels or rabbit for their dinner. By the way Sarah looked at it, he knew she felt safer. But he set a jug of whiskey in the dish cupboard, besides. If, while he was away, somebody should get snakebit, Sarah or whoever it was must drink all she could swallow, though it rendered her insensible, while the other one got aboard a mule and lit out for help.

Sarah's horror at the picture of herself in a state of intoxication all but passed her fear of snakes. A Methodist to the core, she had a time marshaling her principles against the ways of dusty, rowdy, thirsty Texas. Including Alec, her dearly loved husband—but the less said about that, the better.

Finally there were Indians. Beginning, and, maybe, ending, with Charley John, who paid them a visit the spring after they settled in at the ranch. Sarah, following Alec's lead, spoke kindly to Charley John and saw to his comfort, but plainly was relieved that he didn't want to eat or sleep in the house. Her manner was so strained and mistrustful that Alec, who had told her of his life with the Cherokee, especially Charley John, went all over it again at bedtime that evening.

"There is good in them, maybe," Sarah allowed, putting away a basket of sewing. "They were good to you; but still, they're Indians. They fight the white man and each other and their ways of fighting are cruel and savage. Burning, scalping."

He couldn't picture Charley John with a scalping knife, but . . .

"They fight the best they know how," he defended. "God-a'mighty, girl, Injuns have their troubles, and bad ones."

"Fighting is no way out of trouble," she said. "There is room on God's earth for all his creatures, if they'd only settle down peaceable."

Didn't a good woman beat all? Given her way, she would redd up the world each morning and set it to rights like her house.

"Goda'mighty, Sarah, the Cherokee tried it—over and over again."

Did they know about God Almighty, she inquired. Well, sure they did. From the missionaries. Trouble was, the missionaries were white men; and when you've been swindled out of most of what you own and care about, you don't listen well to messengers from the same people. Anyhow, Indians had their own notions about such matters. They believed in a Great Spirit.

"It isn't the same," she argued.

"Sure it is."

"Prove it," she challenged.

And he was fool enough to try. He told her of the priest leaders of the tribe, whose title was shaman. He told her of the *asi*, the council house, and, as well as he could remember, the tales he had heard there. Of the Little People of the forest and the mountains, who played mischievous tricks on travelers, but also liked to help poor folk who had lost their way, of the beginning of the world and of man and of animals and birds and other winged creatures.

"Fairy tales," she said. "Pretty, but fairy tales."

No more so than Noah's Ark, he thought, but didn't say, watching her busy fingers.

"That's a pretty fancy about the redbird."

A redbird was the spirit of the sun's daughter, slain by a demon in the shape of a rattlesnake, who danced so brightly with the poor ghosts in the Darkening Land of Death that she was allowed to return in the shape of a bird to her beloved earth, to make things brighter for folks there.

"But I can't abide that one about the blackbirds, the ravens. It makes my hair stand on end."

"It's supposed to." Alec laughed. "That's the one young'uns like best."

"But do you believe it?"

He was not sure. He tried to put her off.

"Have you ever watched a blackbird on the ground? he asked. "Seen how, instead of hopping, he walks?"

"Oh, that," she said. "I mean, do you believe they are evil spirits who wait about the house of a man about to die, so that they can eat his heart and live the years taken away from him? Do you believe a word of that?"

Again he put her off.

"Tell you what I do believe. I believe in you, and I believe in Charley John. A truer friend I'll never know."

And that was all of that evening's argument. He had never told Sarah about the old shaman's prophecy concerning him, and now he thought he never would. It would have warmed him some to hear her cry out, argue the tale down with cool reasonableness, shoo it away from him lovingly, protectingly. The spell of the *asi* still was strong in him and the cry of the shaman could chill him to the bone if he was feeling low; but, no, it wouldn't do to tell Sarah. She would never have any use for Charley John if she heard that tale. She accepted his presence unwillingly enough as it was.

"Why does he come visiting now?" she fussed the next day. "April—the busiest time of the year almost."

"Thinks he's doing us a favor," Alec told her, "chasing our crows."

She studied that.

"But you said he had a farm place. Must be plowing time there as well as here. Who does his plowing?"

"His wives," Alec said.

"Wives?"

"Three of them," he told her, "and a bunch of sons. Charley John is a man of consequence at home. Don't have to turn a hand if he don't feel like it."

Might as well shock her as try to persuade her, he reasoned. She plain didn't like Indians. At the foot of the hill where the house stood, a ford crossed Mountain Creek. It was part of an old north-south trail that Indians still used some. Friendly Indians, from government lands to the north mostly, hunting or going out restlessly to see what they could see. Sometimes, if they ran out of food, they would beg some from the nearest ranch house. Fortunately the first time such a party stopped at Whitehouse, he happened to be at home. He went out to talk to the Indians, traded them a sack of corn for a washtub near full of wild honey, and, after the hunters had gone on, came back to the house to find Sarah as pale as a bleached pillow sham.

"You speak their language," she said, as if it was some taint in his blood.

Fact was these were Choctaws, and he didn't. Using Cherokee and signs, he had made himself understood. He might have lost patience with Sarah a little that day, except that she wasn't feeling very good just then and he knew it. Maybe this added to his worry. Suppose a party of Indians came by when he was away? He might have known she'd behave sensibly whatever her feeling, but he felt now he must tell her how to act. If he wasn't around where she could tell him, she must go out and talk to the Indians, find out what they wanted, offer them any food she could spare and take trade for it if she could get it. They would respect her for that. Keep them away from the house, yes, but act as if that, too, was just the proper thing to do. She mustn't show fright. Above all, she must not show the gun . . . he wound up with her looking three shades whiter than before. Didn't dare tell her that he had given this bunch permission to camp near the ford that night.

As it happened, these very Indians . . . but there a door slammed hard in Alec Cockrell's face again. The echo still rang in his ears. He had heard it said that for a man and a woman to go through deepest trouble and come out still holding fast to each other would bind them as nothing else could; but he wished it need not have happened just that way. That was what he meant when he said to John Neely Bryan.

"I want to move Sarah into town as soon as I can. . . ."

And John had answered, "I know."

He didn't need Wake Latimer to tell him there were others to consider. He sat there on Sinful, taking in the picture—Sarah as straight as a scantling securely nailed and braced, the Indian facing her, the pony, the bridge, the house; and everything that had ever happened before, good and bad, everything that was now, everything that would happen tomorrow or after that crowded itself into a hard ball in his breast until he would have burst if he couldn't have let go somewhere.

So he did. He stood up in the stirrups and hailed the house. "Hi-ya!"

Then laughed to see the picture break and the pieces scatter. Sinful reared. Sarah whirled about. The Indian stared. His black boy George came running down from the smithy.

"Hi-ya, everybody! I'm home."

chapter seven

When a Raven Mocker comes to a house...

PURE RELIEF was Sarah's first sensation when, at Alec's shout, she turned and saw him there in the road on his black horse. Relief, though Charley John had said he would be coming.

Earlier, when she had recognized the man on the droop-headed pony as Alec's Cherokee friend, it had been almost beyond her, over her disappointment, to give the Indian her welcome.

"Mr. Cockrell is not at home," she had said, grudgingly, as Charley John turned into the yard and stopped a few feet away from where she stood.

"He comes," Charley John had answered, his eyes intent upon her, neither friendly nor unfriendly—but that was how it always was. "He is not far. ．I will wait here for Little Older Brother."

That curious name, but Alec liked it. The Indian was asking her for leave to stay. Respectfully enough. The Cherokee, Alec had told her, had high regard for their women. Three wives, she thought, well! But . . .

"Yes," she said. "Make yourself at home. Are you hungry?"

"I will wait," he said. "He is not far now." He was so sure of that, she thought he must have seen Alec somewhere on the way; but his next remark stole away assurance from her.

"It is the month of birds," he said, and looked away from her to the house.

That gruesome story! She had decided long before this that it was the reason for Charley John's April visits. There was some added meaning to it that concerned Alec, but he would always turn aside any attempt she made to learn from him what it could be, and she never had enough speech with Charley John to ask him. Come to think of it, this was the first time she had ever been alone with Charley John. By the time Alec appeared, realization of this had her near ready to fly.

Then it seemed that Alec had a word for everybody else before he came to her. First there was the Indian. Cherokee gibberish passed between him and Alec, a look, a touching of hands—the sort of thing that always left her outside, feeling small and of no importance. Jealous? Could be.

Then it was the black servant, come to take charge of Sinful. "You, George . . ."

For him, too, Alec had something to say in low tones that Sarah could not hear. George nodded, said, "Yessir," and laid hold of Sinful's reins.

At last, Alec turned to her. His eyes, hard and bright, held hers as he came toward her. Foolishly she began to tremble.

"I looked for you sooner," she faltered, when he was near enough to hear what others could not.

"Five days?" he questioned, but huskily, in tones meant only for her ears. And his eyes still held hers. "Anything wrong?"

"No," she answered. "Nothing much." If I could only touch him, she thought, but knew she must not. She had not been raised to show her heart in public. The Indian would have lost respect for her. Alec, too, maybe—a little. She must be content with his nearness, the sound of his breathing, the strong, heady man-smell of him, seasoned with saddle leather, horse and—she thought—Adam Haught's whiskey. She reached out suddenly and took a burr from his coat.

"You camped out last night," she said, still tremulously. "Mr. Cockrell, you know it isn't safe. Not for you."

A man known to carry money . . .

"Shucks!" he said, making small of her fears. "One night? Sinful and I made an early start yesterday, left camp before breakfast; but, try as we would, we couldn't make the whole distance in one day. Sinful said stop, so I had to."

Yes, she could tell he had ridden hard. Sinful, after rearing once, was almost as droop-headed now as the Indian pony. The wagons, she thought. Could a man lose himself so in business that he would forget all else? Smelling the whiskey she knew he had ridden through the heart of town and wondered whom he had seen, besides Adam Haught, to talk to? Who, Mr. Cockrell? Did they say anything about—you know what?

His eyes were still hard and bright on hers, but something in her wistful regard turned up the corner of his mouth in that secret smile she was never sure she read aright. He won't tell me, she thought, and turned away in despair.

"I'll see about breakfast," she said. "Only the boys have had anything to eat here so far."

She went on toward the house, but at the door stopped, to turn back and look at the scene in the yard, wishing now passionately that the tall, dark man in black frock coat and boots and broad-brimmed hat might fade away from her sight and a graceless vagabond take his place, a handkerchief tied below his black hair to keep the sweat out of his eyes, a calico shirt, tail out over his jeans, Indian moccasins on his feet, an ox-goad in his hand, bellowing defiance of her and heaven and hell.

Oh, God, she thought, what did we do that was wrong? What comes over a man and woman when they wed that they must make the world all over again, and claim it for their own? Was it for me that he bought this town? Then, if it had not been for me, this day of trouble might never have come. I never thought such a thing could happen to us. Rather than have it happen, I would choose to go back to the way life was before. Did she mean—go back to the ranch? Now? Maybe so. Maybe so.

She had not wanted to leave Whitehouse Ranch, to begin with. Or ever. When the greatest joy a woman has known in living is set, like a picture in its frame, inside the walls of one house— no matter what kind of house—she doesn't close the door on that house and turn away lightly or easily, knowing she will never come back. And sorrow can take even a firmer hold on her. When a part of a woman's own body lies buried on a lonely hillock under a weight of stone and earth, does a man think going away will make her forget? Well, maybe that works for a man. . . .

Logan Cockrell, born 1848 . . .

Late in 1848, the second year of their marriage. For a while it had looked as if they might not have a child, and Sarah wanted one more than anything. Not for herself, not to keep her company. Though often alone at the ranch place, she was never too lonely. She, who had lived twenty-eight years in maiden aloneness, could not feel that way when she had a house to keep and a man to love and do for—and dream about when he was not with her.

Not that she thought Alec would think small of her if no child came. She knew better than that. But she wanted a child, a son, if she could choose. Not to make her proud among women, though it always seemed to do that. She wanted to give Alec this son because . . . well, for something of the same reason she had for marrying him. It was a thing he had a right to expect of life and she wanted him to have it—through her.

When at last she knew her prayer had been granted, she wasn't afraid, though everyone else, including Alec, was.

"You are twenty-eight years old," her mother said, "going on twenty-nine. It won't be easy."

It wasn't easy. For the first half of the way, Sarah, who had never known what it was to be ailing, was pretty sick. Couldn't stomach her food, looked like a sick cat, was cross, cantankerous. That day the Indians came through and stopped to trade honey for corn was a sample.

When that droopy time wore off finally, came a feeling of burden. It was as if every day a fresh weight was hung on her somewhere. Then she did know fear. There was a deadness about the weight that frightened her—until, for the first time, the baby stirred and moved. Then, for all the relief, there was that added discomfort.

"A boy," everyone said. "Only a boy kicks like that—before and ever after."

But, in spite of the growing heaviness and the soreness, she felt better and better. Just a matter of waiting now, she thought, and counted off the months. Soon it would be weeks. Except that she was as big and clumsy as a penned cow, she got along pretty well. Finally there came a day—according to her counting, she had a month still to go—when all the spring and push she had ever known came back to her. She wanted to be at everything all at once, and felt she must be at something.

She looked around her house and decided it was filthy. In the spring, when she should have cleaned it, she hadn't cared. Then had come summer and hot weather. Now it was autumn. Alec was away most of the daylight hours, working with Wes Cockrell and other ranchers, rounding up their cattle, separating the herds, branding, counting, trading, selling. He came in late at night dead tired and was off early every morning. Sarah called Pokey to her.

"We'll sweep down the cobwebs first," she said. "We'll shake out all the pieces of carpet, air the bedding. Take all the dishes down from the cupboards, wash them . . ."

"Ev'y one?" Pokey moaned. "F'om de ve'y top shelf? Miss Sally, you feelin' awright?"

"I feel wonderful. Pokey, don't fool now. Get a broom and all the wiping and scrubbing rags you can lay hold of. I hope we've got soap laid by."

They toiled all morning. They had dinner of sweet potatoes and eggs, which had baked in the ashes while they labored. They went at the dishes now, Pokey doing the climbing, to take down and put away—at fearful risk to the china, Sarah watching. And then it came—an earthquake, all inside her own body. A wrenching, a twisting. What did it mean? What was it?

Pokey was on a stool at the dish cupboard, putting away. With great effort Sarah waited until she was on the floor again, her hands empty. Then she spoke.

"Pokey!"

Pokey turned, and her mouth fell open.

"Miss Sally . . . you . . . ooh, I might a knowed!"

"No," Sarah said. "It isn't time."

"Nobuddy," Pokey answered, "evah kin be suah 'bout dat. Miss Sally, yere we is, alone. I don' know much."

She surely didn't; and Sarah, this being her own self, didn't know much more. They must have help.

"Pokey, catch a mule. Ride as fast as you dare to the nearest house. Fetch somebody, anybody that you can find. Just—help me over to the bed. There, I'm better. No, don't wait to turn down the covers. I'll do that—just in case." Miraculously the pain was gone. "Maybe I'm just foolish."

No. She turned down the bed, began to unfasten her dress and the pain came back. Fortunately the bed was near. She sat down on it; and, when the spasm passed, she put on her nightgown and got under the covers. She was determined not to be caught on her feet again—in the middle of the floor, maybe, not able to reach the bed or even a chair.

Warm and comfortable in the bed, she dozed, but wakened with sharp suddenness. The pain again? No. Pokey was back—with an Indian woman. A shapeless creature in a calico wrapper over the bulk of a man's britches. Strings of beads hung all over the front of the grotesque dress. Her black hair was in pigtails, braided and tied with strips of cloth. A man's hat roosted on her head. An Indian in this house? Her house? Alec had said never in the house.

"Dey campin' on de crick agin," Pokey explained. "Miss Sally, ef I has to go too far to fin' somebuddy else, I cain' leave you so long alone. Miss Sally, dis 'oman talk ouah talk—some. She got babies—fine, fat babies. She say she kin holp us. She will stay twell I git some o' yore folks."

Stay? Nobody could have driven her off. She took off her hat, threw it on the floor in a far corner, and came over to the bed. Her eyes were bright as glass beads in her dark, broad face. She looked Sarah over and put out one brown hand.

"Stand," she ordered.

Did she mean Sarah was to get up? Now?

"Stand!" the creature said again, and laid hold of the covers.

"Don't you . . ." Sarah said. "Don't you dare touch me!"

She could have saved her breath. The squaw took her by the arms, raised her up and just naturally pulled her out of the bed to the floor.

"Pokey!" Sarah screamed. "Hurry! Go find Mr. Alec. Find somebody, but hurry!"

Pokey looked as scared as Sarah felt. She wobbled uncertainly, then turned and ran. And the pain was there again. Sarah reached out blindly. Only one support was handy. The squaw. She gripped the creature's arms and held on. When the spasm passed, the two of them were face to face, and very close. The squaw grinned.

"Walk!" she said now.

All told, she did not speak a half dozen words all evening, and those one at a time. "Stand." "Walk." To her own amazement, Sarah walked. Together, she and the squaw walked up and down the room and around the four sides of it—over and over. When pain came, Sarah clutched the Indian's arms and held fast. When it passed, they would walk some more. This went on, it seemed to Sarah, for hours. She wondered if the day would never end. Finally in trembling weakness, she went down on her knees.

"Good," the squaw said then.

After that, she let Sarah rest each time on a chair; and, at last, when it seemed the very floor must give way under her, she found herself again on the edge of her bed.

"Now," the squaw said. "Now."

Did she mean . . . Sarah fell back on the pillows. When she came to, darkness had come and with it Pokey—and Mrs. Wesley Cockrell and Sarah's mother and Ennerine. The house was full of people, but . . .

"Where is she?" Sarah cried out; and it was the Indian squaw she wanted.

In the nightmare that followed, it was the squaw who held her and the squaw she clung to. That was all Sarah could be sure of. It seemed to her the squaw prayed some—Indian style, chanting in her own tongue. It seemed once she drank something warm that tasted—well, more like dog fennel than anything else she could think of. There was a time of unbearable pain and she thought she heard a thin wail somewhere in the room and then she really went away into deep sleep.

This time, when she awoke, Alec sat by the bed, looking at her as if he'd lost her in deep water and fished her out again but didn't know whether he'd come in time.

"Mr. Cockrell," she said, and tears sprang from her eyes. "I'm sorry and shamed. I just can't seem to . . ."

"Can't seem to what?" he said. "We got the finest boy baby in all Texas."

Little Logan was a sweet baby; and, so far as Sarah could ever tell, he seemed as strong as any other child she had. Through the long autumn and most of the winter—a Texas winter, now warm, now cold—he lived and thrived. Then with February about gone, during a rainy spell that followed a blue norther, Sarah awoke in the middle of the night, hearing him in his cradle gasping over every breath he drew. A black word to mothers in wilderness homes rang in her ears. Croup. It might be membranous croup. She slipped from the bed and knelt beside the child. Sure enough, one touch of her hand told her that he was burning with fever. She turned back to her own bed, to speak a word to Alec; but he was already pulling on his clothes.

In the black of night, through pouring rain and rising waters and over boggy roads he went for the doctor. At home, while Pokey built up the fire, Sarah melted goose grease, burned feathers, warmed flannels, walked the floor with the baby in her arms, soothing him, crooning, praying; but all of it was no use. Just before dawn, a half hour before Alec came back with the doctor, both of them coated with mud and drenched with rain, the baby died.

Afterward and at the time, Sarah was sure she had spoken no word of reproach, because never once did she blame anyone for what had happened; but, with Alec Cockrell, nobody needed to speak of blame. He stayed with Sarah through the burying, selected the grave site himself and saw that the mound was packed and covered, then, with no leave-taking, threw himself on a horse and rode off. It was the stillness of the house he couldn't bear, he said later, and knowing how Sarah cried when he wasn't there to see or hear her.

Sarah had no word of blame for him even then, but she was the only one. Even Wes Cockrell swore and made threats of what he would do did he ever lay hands on the good-for-nothing again.

"And you with another young one on the way," Sarah's mother said. "Does he know?"

"No," Sarah said, "and nobody is to tell him. Nobody is to go looking for him now. He will come back for his own sake and mine, if he comes."

He was gone better than a month—nobody knew where, and he never said. Just the bottom of the pit, that was all; and a person had to believe it, seeing him. One day, shortly before noon, there he was, sliding off a weary horse; but the horse was fatter and sounder than the man. Hollow-eyed, whiter than Sarah waiting at the door for him. His very bones seemed to have lost their marrow. Maybe it was that which made him fall to his knees when he made it into the house, and bury his face in Sarah's lap like a grieving young one, asking, not forgiveness, just understanding. And she asked only one thing in return—a promise, which he gave her.

"I'll never leave you again. Never in this world."

And he never did—to stay. But it was from that time that something grew in his mind and heart that he wanted to do. Something big and mighty. He worked at the ranch and at his hauling as had never worked before, but he was thinking all the while of something else. When the second baby came and was a girl, whatever was in his mind took such shape that nobody could have persuaded him against it. As soon as he could, as soon as he had the money, he crossed the Trinity River and bought the town of Dallas. Bought it outright.

And it was the last thing Sarah would have asked for. How could she leave the ranch now? But, again, she didn't say what she felt, or tried not to. Still, it showed. It must have. She acted, Alec said afterward, as if he'd thrown a scorpion into her lap; and, when he was expecting praise for his proud accomplishment, she had only a question:

"You haven't gone and sold Whitehouse Ranch, have you?"

No, he had not, not an acre; and he gave her another promise.

"Never, while I live, will I part with any of the ranch."

So, he felt as she did about the place; then why? Why, dear Lord, why? Part of his reason, of course, was plain. The death of little Logan had afflicted him finally with a sense of wrongdoing —keeping a wife and child in a home so far from neighbors and help in time of need, separated from town by bottom land that had no proper roads and those not usable in wet weather. He had no mind to let the same sort of thing happen again to him and Sarah.

Then, too, he knew how Sarah grieved for the boy; and he really thought the move to town, the advantages of neighbors and new people and new things to see, school later for the children, would make her forget. Of course, they had to move at once. Alec couldn't begin on any of his plans for Dallas and live or pretend to live at the ranch.

He thought Sarah would forget. Sometimes she almost did. It was only occasionally that a sadness possessed her, thinking of all that had come and gone and what now was here, wondering which was best, after all, what they had left behind or what they had—as if a body could ever make over the past, and no telling whether he'd do any better if he could. It was this kind of doubt, uncertainty and foolish regret, clouded by a real and deep concern over the Moore situation, that afflicted Sarah as she turned into the house to see about breakfast. A kind of mental running away instead of a true wish that she might have the past back in exchange for the anxious present.

Five minutes later the wild hullabaloo of the children's greeting to their father called her out into the yard again to see what the new noise was about. Fun ran high and why that should add to her wistfulness, she could not say. Alec seemed in high spirits, though he could have been pretending. He joked with the boys about the molasses on their faces. All of them were smeared with it, Baby Alec from the tail of his bib to his hair.

"What's the matter? Water scarce around here?" big Alec demanded of Hannah, who was all agrin to see him home again and safe. "Take the lot of them down to the river and wash them before the bees swarm. Your Willie, too. And next time don't be so free with the sweetening. It counts up. Throw this one," he pulled the baby's hair, "in bodily. You'll never get him unglued any other way."

Off they went, shouting and laughing and cuffing each other, and Hannah threatening what she would do if they didn't behave. Little Frank, the second boy, only four, turned around suddenly.

"Don't go, please," he said to Charley John. "We'll be back soon."

This tickled the Indian. He looked with shining eyes at Alec, who slapped him on the back, and whooped his delight. Proud he was of his three sons, and they such small shavers still that nobody could tell what they would grow to be. Proud, but nothing like as proud of them as he was of his one daughter.

Aurelia—he'd named her himself, and where he got the name Sarah had often wondered and finally she had asked him, but he couldn't say. Heard it somewhere, and fancied it. Miss Aurelia, he called her this morning; and, in truth, she put on a pretty show for him. Came down to breakfast, holding Sister Polly's hand, sweet and shy as an angel. If Sarah had told Alec how wicked she had been ten minutes before, snatching Polly's ruffles, he wouldn't have believed it; so she didn't bother.

"How old is she?" he asked, when breakfast was over and he and Sarah were alone in the plain bareness of the room they called the "office." "Eight? I'd like a picture to keep. What's the name of that Frenchman with the picture machine up on Main Street? Gonant? Let's see what he can do."

Gonant was what folks called the poor man, but that wasn't right.

"I've got the name in the trunk," Sarah said. "He had Mr. Latimer print him some handbills." *M. Gouhenant, Art Salon.* But Gonant was what it came to. "He's got his place all fixed up now. Hirsch and Shirek let him have domestic to cover the walls —on credit. Looks nice. He offers to rent it to select patrons for balls."

"That's an idea," Cockrell said. "Done any business?"

"Not yet," Sarah said.

"Well. First thing next week, you arrange with him to take 'Relie's picture. It's bound to be a pretty one. Folks will see it and want some made like it of their young ladies. None of them as pretty as our 'Relie, but their folks will want pictures, just the same. And if he can rent his place for parties . . ."

"He owes Mr. Latimer for the handbills now, and Hirsch and Shirek for the domestic," Sarah pointed out. "Top of the rent he can't pay."

"He can charge 'Relie's picture against what he owes us."

"He'll want to do it for nothing—for you," Sarah said.

"Comes to the same thing, don't it?" To coax a smile to Sarah's mouth if he could, and she obliged.

M. Gouhenant, Art Salon. They were both looking at the same day, Sarah knew. April, 1855—what a month April was for things happening! Three years after the Alec Cockrells had moved from the ranch into Dallas, living at first in the Bryan house, but now just settled in this one down close to the river and the bridge, newly opened to travel. But never before or after did the bridge carry such a troop as it did today. Three hundred footsore, wondering, dismayed, but not yet disheartened settlers from Switzerland, Belgium, France, come all that way to find a new home in America. *La Compagnie Franco-Texienne*—that was how Wake Latimer printed it in the *Herald.* They dreamed of laying out a colony where everybody would live together in peace and equality, all sharing in the toil of building, baking, farming—and then the profits.

They marched over the bridge and up into the town, looking for a Mr. Considerant, the agent who was to have bought land for them in Dallas County. So he had, in the chalk hills on the west side of the river, the poorest land anywhere near, hard as a rock in dry weather and lifeless chalk at best. They were counting on raising grapes, but the most they ever raised was trouble and some of that had begun for them already—when they found out how far Galveston, where their ship had set them ashore, was from Dallas County. At Houston they had bought a few ox-carts, to carry their heavy belongings and children too young to walk and old people and the weaker women; and they had a few pack horses and some to ride, but mostly they traveled on their own feet.

They were a sight to see. The first wooden shoes anybody in Dallas had ever laid eyes on. Some wore smocks, some were in good cloth and linen. All had something of the same look on their faces—a little desperate, but still sure heaven was somewhere. They sang—strange, outlandish songs that made shivers run up and down one's back. They tramped into town, looking for Mr. Considerant; and, when they found him, they turned and followed him back across the river to the barren land he had bought for them. If they had turned on him there and murdered him, nobody hardly could have blamed them, but they didn't. They sighed, maybe; but they shrugged off then what was past and went to work.

They were thrifty folk. If thrift had been all it took, they might have prospered some; but bad luck attended them. It took them most of the first year to get organized and to put up their buildings. The next year they went to work on the land. Only a few understood how. Most were gentlemen or tradespeople—watchmakers, artists, musicians, poets, shoemakers, milliners, jewelers, tailors. Hardly a one had ever farmed. But they worked the land and sowed crops. And, just when everything was up and growing—some things, like peas, ready for gathering—a blizzard struck.

A regular, sure enough, old-fashioned prairie blizzard; and it was May. Nobody in Texas could remember the like. As for the foreigners, they felt betrayed now by God as well as man. This land, which, if it was not all they had been led to expect, had seemed at least warm. Some of them gave up right then and went back home. While they still could. The braver and the more foolish and those who couldn't buy passage to Europe stayed on. They planted more vines and more seed and lost all of that in the autumn.

The coldest winter Texas ever knew—that one of 1856 into 1857. Nobody bothered to cross a river at bridge or ferry. Every run of water was frozen solid from bank to bank. It was a lean time for everybody, even those with stores laid by; and the people at La Réunion had nothing like that. Starvation would have been the end of the colony, if older, more established, more practical settlers had not lent a hand. And that's what they did, sharing their little or their much, without anybody holding back. Especially Alec Cockrell helped, though he claimed it was only good business. He cut logs and siding and set up little houses on vacant land in town and invited those people to move in. The rent was small, if they could pay it. If they could not, he trusted them.

Just business. In some cases it paid well enough. There was M. Gouffe, the tailor, who paid his first rent with the very suit Alec wore today—a better suit, Alec vowed, than any he could buy in Houston. There were the Nussbaumers from Switzerland, who were butchers. They did a thriving business now on Main Street, opposite the square and handy to the Crutchfield House. There were the Frichots, who worked at the brickyard. But with some, like the Reverchons and the Chrétiens, who stayed on the land, stubbornly determined to succeed at farming, it was harder. Or Mr. Gouhenant, with his Art Salon. Or Professor Gernand, who could offer only piano or dancing lessons. Alec helped the farmers on condition that they bring their produce to Dallas to sell. With the artist photographer and the music teacher he could only be patient and wait. Both still owed him for rent. They would pay when they could, but when would that be?

And there were others. There was a watchmaker, a milliner— little Louise Dusseau, married now to a young Texan named Jones, ready to start a family.

"I like them," was the most Alec would say in explanation of his kindness. "They're good folks to have in any town."

Yes, perhaps. But of what use were they to him now? They couldn't even vote to keep Andrew Moore from being elected Town Marshal. How, then could Alec stop to think of them in his present difficulties? How could he stop today to think of offering a helping hand to M. Gouhenant, to give him a start in his business of photography?

Sadness returned, and again that vain regret over a life that had been hard enough, but simple, their only enemies varmints and snakes and lonesomeness. Here they sat, alone now, in this simple room, which of all the house reminded Sarah most of the ranch, because its crude furnishings had been brought from there. She studied each piece lovingly—the rawhide chairs, the cupboard with the pierced tin doors, called a safe, the pine table. She studied the tall, lean man across the table from her, his sharp features, the hollow cheeks, the tight mouth, the eyes with lights in them she could never be sure she read aright. How, she wondered, could anybody bear him a grudge, especially someone he had been willing to help, as he had these other strays?

And now the dark, sullen hatefulness of Andrew Moore was in this room, where it had no right to be.

"He could have come to be my building boss," Alec had said to her once when they talked of him, "if he'd worked for it and played square."

The job Will Toomy held now? No, Sarah thought, never. There was always something lacking in Andrew Moore that had nothing to do with the way he handled a hammer. Some weakness that turned him mean. Not worthy of being trusted. She had felt it before they had any way of knowing the truth. She looked past and through the intrusion, across the table at Alec, and found that he was studying her more intently than she had studied him—her hands, brown strong hands, but not pretty, resting on the table, her dress, the pin at her throat, her face, her hair—and there was on his strong features a hungering and a wishing and devotion and, yes, an anger of his own. She thought, Dear Lord, he hasn't forgotten for a minute. He does know something that I don't know, but he don't let on—not to me.

Before she could shape her fear into question: Who did you see in town besides Adam Haught? What did they have to say?— a screech of metal tore the words out of her mouth and scattered even the thought behind them. It broke the spell for Alec Cockrell, too, apparently. He turned his head to listen, as if anybody could be deaf enough not to hear; and, when he looked back at Sarah, his expression was purely blissful.

"Mill's going," he said joyfully, as if he'd had doubts of hearing that awful saw again.

And Sarah thought, I won't question him. I won't mention what I'm afraid of unless he leads up to it. He's got it on his mind and he's going to meet it his own way. I couldn't stop any of it now, if I wanted to. I don't know what I would do in his place, I'm sure.

"The morning's going," she said, as naturally as she could, "and we haven't talked business at all."

The special, important business that had taken him away at such a time!

"No," he said dryly, his eyes brightly watching her again. "Want to hear?"

"Well, yes," she answered, "if you don't mind telling me."

He laughed, but cut it off, it seemed to her, a little short.

"Have to tell you, I reckon, sooner or later, so that you can figure what it all comes to. It will busy you and your inkwell the rest of the day, I'm thinking. Let me see now. There's several cases of stuff for the drugstore, the same for Hirsch and Shirek. Some stock in trade for Adam Haught. Printing paper for Wake

Latimer. His subscribers had better pay up, so he can settle for that. Lumber. Finish lumber mostly."

"And what else?" Sarah prompted.

"What else? That's several drayloads already, woman."

But she knew there was more.

"You wouldn't ride to Black Jack to oversee those items," she charged.

"I might." Yes, but he hadn't. On the point of telling her, he changed his mind. His eyes widened and his mouth turned up at the corner. "You'll never guess."

"I'll bet I can guess. The hotel? Something for the hotel, wasn't it?"

He pretended anger.

"Who told you?" he roared.

"Nobody. I know you."

It was the hotel now, but there was always something. The bridge, this house, a house for the mill hands, new stores up town, the brick building for Hirsch and Shirek, the new courthouse. Now it was the hotel. He'd laid out to climb a golden staircase of dreams before he was through. This was only a piece of the way up. He loves this town, she thought. He loves building it. He may have bought the town because of me, but now it's gone past that. He loves the town—not ahead of me and the young ones, but right alongside of us. He loves the town, the building of it. And the thought eased a burden on her, but it did not alter her belief that, because of the town and his work there, he had made enemies, grudging folks—did he know? Yes, she thought he did.

"What did you buy for the hotel, Mr. Cockrell?"

"Crockery?" he said, teasing her; then he decided to say. "Remember that man in Shreveport I told to watch out for fixtures? Well, he found them. First steamboat up the Mississippi this year hit ice near Memphis and ran aground, to keep from foundering. Owner was aboard. Got so scared that he sold out on the spot. Had one of the finest saloons on the river, my man says. We bought in the chandelier and . . ."

He left the "and" in midair and so, for the time, did Sarah. The chandelier, she supposed, was for the hotel ballroom; and both were as real to Alec Cockrell as if the building were finished and the roof on and the fiddlers tuning up for the opening.

"Man says it's a beauty. Row upon row of spangles and dangles. When it's lit up, it looks like a diamond merchant's show window."

"I can just see it," Sarah said faintly, "hanging from a cross beam."

In that hollow brick shell up the street. Alec looked at her in question, then he saw how funny it all was, and he laughed with her. When he laughed like that, it was pure pleasure to hear him. More than pure pleasure today.

"How will you haul a thing like that?" Sarah asked finally, to hush him. A wagon coming off the bridge stopped, the driver, no doubt, hearing Alec's shouts and wondering what was going on.

"Wait till you see," Alec said. "You just wait. Nested in comforters, in a wooden box half the size of a lean-to, and that not a circumstance, compared to the piano crate."

No. Not a piano! Surely not . . . and yet, how could she be sure? With his picture of a grand ballroom, taking up most of the first floor of this hotel, Alec Cockrell would never be content with a country fiddler and a jug player—not for the opening, as he dreamed it. Where did he get his ideas, people were always asking. Aye, where? But there was the big, wide difference between him and other folk.

"Right pleased with yourself, aren't you, Mr. Cockrell?"

"No'm. Not exactly. My man didn't get to the auction in time to bid in the bar, and he said that was the best of all. Mahogany wood, and a looking-glass as big as the side of a room to set behind it. Well, we'll keep trying."

He would, and he'd have the bar finally. No use for her to protest, brought up by Methody rules, baptized in that faith, married by a Methodist preacher. No use to protest now and she did not; but something of what she felt might have showed.

"Methody woman," he said, one eyebrow up, the other down, "you can't have a hotel without a bar—not in Texas. That's where we'll get our first money back—from that and the livery stable."

He would be correct in his estimate, she knew. He always was.

Strange that a man without schooling, who did all his sums in his head by rules never printed in a book, should be so unerringly right in figuring what he could do with men and material and money. And seeing visions. Never forget those.

And then he spoke more seriously, as he was feeling, really, right along.

"I'm right disappointed about the bar, Sarah. I wanted all the business of the hotel finished and done. I've been told too often that it can't be done the way I see it. I want to show folks."

"Well, you will and you know it," she said, hoping he could not see her tremble. "And now, if that is all, Mr. Cockrell, I'll thank you for these new bills—so that I can master them and see how near we are to ruin."

"Left them in the saddlebags outside," he said, laughing again. "I'll get them, and you can figure the damage, but never call it ruin."

She watched him walk out of the room. As straight and slender and lightfooted—or almost—as the day she had first seen him. Coming into the house earlier, they had stopped in the bedroom, for him to lay aside the belt with his knife and gun, and to wash up. He took that way out now. She heard his quick, restless footfalls cross the room. Halfway, and then he stopped. Why, she wondered.

I'm still as nervous as a cat, she thought. Then he called to her.

"May take a minute. Got to find out what George did with the saddlebags and I want to see how Charley John is doing."

He went on then through the room to the hall and the outside door. The door closed behind him. From where she sat she could see a small piece of the bedroom, the lower part of the bed, with Alec's gun belt hanging over the footrail. The weapons, the belt, thrown so carelessly on the counterpane, gave her a start. All her fears and forebodings came back with a rush. She bowed her head on her hands and prayed: "God, help me through this day. Help him, too, though he won't ask for it. Keep him safe if You anyways can."

...he finds others of his kind waiting.

OPENING THE FRONT DOOR of his house, Alec Cockrell let in a draught of warm air that seemed to come at him with a rush. Nothing that he knew could warm up as fast as a Texas morning. Going to be a shirt-sleeve day, that was sure. The saddlebags lay on the step against the door, where George had placed them before taking the horses away. Sensible boy, that George. Knew his master would be wanting them.

A short distance from the house, beyond the litter that passed for a yard, Charley John sat on a stump, his shotgun across his knees, his face toward the river, patiently watching nothing whatever. The old fool, Alec thought, but fondly, and wondered how far he could move without being heard.

Not far. He stooped to pick up the saddlebags and the Indian raised his head at the very instant. Alec laughed, abandoned the idea of taking up the bags, raised his hand in a friendly gesture, and walked over to speak to the Indian. Charley John stood up, his gun easy in his hand.

"How're you coming on?" Alec asked. "Have enough breakfast?"

"Plenty," the Indian answered. "You got good woman."

He meant Sarah, not Hannah, the cook.

"So I hear," Alec said. And then, "Listen, will you?"

Down the river his sawmill was screeching. Up the rise toward town a Negro raised a rhythmic chant, which went off suddenly

111

into a chorus. Bricklayers at work on the hotel. The man who mixed the mortar had his first batch ready, and the hod carriers were moving up to the wall with it. A wagon rattled on the bridge. Beautiful uproar.

"Don't tell me you don't hear," Alec said as the Indian watched only him.

"I hear," Charley John said. "Every year I hear more noises. Too many."

"Don't you believe it," Alec said. "I live by them. Where are the young'uns?"

The Indian motioned up the river.

"Gone to the spring for drinking water," he said.

Good. And to see what they could see, going and coming, hunt a few crawdads, maybe. That would account for their morning, but there remained Charley John. Every time Sarah looked out a window, she would see him keeping watch over the place with his gun ready.

"You'd have better hunting in open country," Alec suggested.

Charley John looked at him and did not answer. His Little Older Brother knew why he was there. It was to shoot crows, yes, but only about this house.

"Well, make yourself comfortable," Alec said, more shortly. "You know you are welcome."

But he was not welcome, not today. Alec felt more like swearing than smiling as he turned back to the house. Hell and damn, the best of the early morning was gone now.

And when, in the hall, he opened a saddlebag and rediscovered the Bryan letter, he swore again. It had slipped his mind temporarily, and he wished now that Crutchfield had not pulled it out of the mail and given it back to him. Whatever the letter said, coming today, it seemed another warning. What happened to me, Alec Cockrell, can come to you. Or worse. Why not?

But there was the letter. He took it in to Sarah, and she felt about it, it looked like, just the way he did. She turned it over and over more times than Old Man Crutchfield had, wanting even worse to know what was inside, without facing up to whatever it was.

"It is Margaret Bryan," she said finally, "who will want to hear. Why don't we just give her the letter?"

"It's addressed to me," Alec pointed out. "We'd best see what he has to say."

Though he knew, generally, what that would be. The same sad, sort of dog-tired letter as the other two, only a little more hopeless. Heart weary. Almost beaten now. Jamestown, California—it seemed a million miles away.

I received a letter from you which was written in June last and I answered it at the time of reception, but I have not heard from you since. I received one from my wife at the same time and have not received any since. What can be the cause. I do not write to anyone in Dallas except you, for I cannot place any confidence in any of the rest. I am not able to come home yet. I sometimes get out of heart and conclude I will never see my wife and children again. The gold mines are so worked out that men can make but little now. You could hardly believe that there was in this country hundreds of men that are almost on the starve, but such is the case. There are few but what eats up at night what he makes in the day. It is the hardest country, I think, on earth. I shall be on my way out as soon as I can make the money. Tell my wife what I have written and say to her it is not my fault I don't come home. Give my love to my wife and children. My respect to your lady and any others that you know to be my friends, if I have any about. If I have any friends in Dallas, I want you to write and tell me who they are. I remain your friend. I shall depend on you to act for me as well as you can. I hope to live to thank you and pay you for it. Give my love . . .

Sarah stopped reading, to wipe her eyes. Alec swore.

"Over and over," Sarah sniffed, "he says to give his love to his wife and children." But it wasn't only his family he meant that Alec was to take care of. There was the town. Once it had been his town. He yearned as much for that as anything or anyone else.

"If it had not been for that shooting," Sarah said.

"Look," Alec blustered. "What can a man do but shoot a feller that insults his woman?"

"He could have turned his back," Sarah reasoned, "and stood by

Margaret. That would have been a better way to show what he thought."

"Wouldn't have looked like that to anybody," Alec answered, "not even to Margaret. And you'd as well know. He didn't run off just because of the shooting. He'd been fixing to leave for some time—ever since I took his town."

"Alec Cockrell! You talk as if you had swindled him out of it."

"Feel that way sometimes."

"You paid him more than he'll ever find in the gold diggings."

That was, no doubt, true; but . . . a wanderer, from California to Colorado and back again. Round and round, gathering no dust but that of the road, living where he could—a proud man, with a family, and schooling. . . .

"Reckon it looked like a sight of money," Alec said moodily, "until he found out that was all it amounted to. There it was, in his hand; and he couldn't buy with it a single thing he'd ever thought to want."

"Except whiskey," Sarah said, with meaning.

Alec made out to smile at her. How to reason with an unreasonable woman?

"Trying to forget," he defended. "It hurt to look back and more to look ahead. Trying . . . what's the difference how the money went or for what? It did go; and there he was—town long gone, money gone now, no prospects. . . ."

"Mr. Cockrell," Sarah said, "you are a true friend."

"His only one, he says." Alec slammed to his feet again. "And that's a hell of a note, ain't it? Big, strong, husky, kindly man, with schooling and pride. Do all he did for the sake of a piece of ground and an idea, never stopping to figure on the pure o'neriness of humankind, and winds up with one friend only." His outrage cooled before a sudden chill. "Makes a man stop and think of his own self," he said, his mouth twisting. "Ain't safe, I reckon, to count friends."

But he was counting. Aside from Sarah, there was Charley John, Wes Cockrell . . . and who else? In a hard spot, your luck gone, trouble upon you? A man, it seemed, found his strength and his way through everything in himself, or he went under. That was the hard truth about it.

"I'm off to the mill now," he said, "or wherever I catch hold of Will Toomy. Will you carry the letter to Margaret?"

"I will," Sarah promised, "sometime today, but with a heavy heart. She will take comfort to hear that John is not lying sick somewhere or in want, and that he misses her and his young ones, though he does nothing to prove it."

"Nothing?" Alec snorted, fanning back some good, hot anger if he could do so. "Working himself to the bone, to bring them back a fortune?"

"And all Margaret wants," Sarah said, "is him—himself. If he was to come to the door in the dead of night, in rags, she would open to him with a cry of thankfulness. Don't you see? If she lost him in death, that would be cruel hard, but more natural. There's a shame to the way things are that can just about kill a woman—somebody proud, like Margaret Bryan."

"You mean," Alec said, "she'd rather have John dead than missing?"

"I don't know." And she didn't, putting it hard and quick like that. She, too, got to her feet. "I don't know."

She looked so lone, standing there at the far side of the table, lost in strange uncertainty, that the sight of her went through and through Alec Cockrell. He wanted to go to her, throw his arms around her, wrap her in his own sureness and strength as with a cloak, close her wide gray eyes on the thing that frighted her, comfort her like a fearing child. What held him where he was— away from her? It had happened before. Maybe it was because they had come to know each other too late, when each was full grown, with look and habits fixed. Loving each other well and truly, he was still himself and she was herself and this was what held them apart more than it drew them together. Take the day they met—shucks, take the first time he put his arms around her and kissed her, she having given him her promise and the right. He refused to remember how boldly he had taken hold, but recalled well enough how alarm had seized and paralyzed him then, until it was her lips, warm and inviting, on his cheek that reminded him of his purpose.

So, now, when he finally crossed the space between them and dropped his hands on her shoulders, it was a relief to find warm flesh and firm bone under his fingers. He shook her gently, then rested his chin, whiskers and all, on the smoothness of her hair, roughing it some. She gave a sigh and leaned against him.

"Miss Sally," he said, "how do we come to be talking like this, anyhow? You and me? Get on to your papers. You still got a surprise coming."

"Mr. Cockrell?" She stiffened again, but that was what he wanted.

"Forgot to mention that a wagon mired just this side of the Loosianna line. Had to shoot a steer, and buy a new span."

"Mr. Cockrell—on top of other extravagance?"

He laughed. Felt damn good to do so.

"Miss Sally, if I could figure like you can, I'd be scared to spend a dollar . . . whoa-up!"

A blast from a gun rattled the west window. It was followed by a whoop that was pure aborigine.

"That damfool Indian!" Alec said. "I hope it ain't a young one. Miss Sally, stay where you are."

Sarah had no idea of staying where she was. And she knew Charley John had not shot at a child. She knew what he had hit. As Alec Cockrell stamped out the front door, she slipped out the back way; and, sure enough, when the two of them reached the corners of the house, the Cherokee came through the scrub on the riverbank, holding at arm's length a large black bird. It hung limp and dead from his hand, and one wing fell away from the body, so that she saw again what she had seen early that morning against her windowpane. She cried out at that, but nobody heard her, Charley John swelling up with satisfaction over what he had done and Alec so out of sorts with his friend that he had to hunt around for a respectful way to say so. Finally he pointed with scorn at the dead bird.

"Winged him!" he taunted.

The Indian shook his head.

"No," he said. "The wing he broke before I shoot."

Sure enough, when he brought the bird to Alec, the head and neck feathers were spotted with blood, but the dangling wing was clean.

"Poor thing!" Sarah sighed, hardly knowing she did so.

The Indian turned to her, his eyes glittering.

"No," he said. "It is good he is dead. A raven dies or you do, maybe. Or," he turned again to Alec, "you. Who knows?"

For a measurable minute Alec did not answer. When he did, he spoke angrily.

"Still think it was no shot to brag about—if the wing was broke before you got him."

The Indian's eyes lost none of their glitter for the jeer. He stared fixedly at Alec. Sarah shivered.

"Because the wing is broke," Charley John said finally, "I hear the bird in the brush. I do not hear the others. A raven does not fly alone."

He still stared fixedly at Alec.

"You damn, superstitious old fool!" Alec said, and Sarah could have said "Amen" even to the profanity. "Wonder how he came by the hurt wing?"

Should she say? No, Sarah decided. I will have no part in this moony tale of birds. We have real worries enough. I'll save myself for them.

And now the young ones came trooping from the spring up Elm Street way. If they had been sent for water, the sound of shooting had made them forget. They hadn't a sign of pail with them. Sarah counted her four—the two older boys, Bob and Frank, little Alec, hot and cross from doing more than he was equal to, but being coaxed along and cared for by Aurelia. Sarah hoped Alec would notice that the girl could get as dirty as any of her brothers and seemed to enjoy it. Willie Winn, Hannah's boy, older than any of the Cockrells and supposed to act also as a sort of protector, though usually he followed where the others led. Added to these were two Nussbaumer boys, a Petersen, a Peak. All of them closed in around Charley John, back at his stump now, emptying the spent shell from his gun.

What the children said to the Indian or he to them Sarah couldn't hear. A wagon was coming down Commerce now from the direction of town, coming at a great rate, its iron-shod wheels rattling. This time of day, especially a Saturday, one was usually passing, going one way or the other. The wagon stopped and the driver swung himself to the ground.

"Hi-yah, Will!" Alec called—Sarah could have sworn it was with relief. "I was just starting out to look you up."

Will Toomy, Alec's building boss, his general superintendent when Alec had to be away. Sarah, too, was glad to see him. Glad to have this queer spell broken, if it could be, and glad always to see Mr. Toomy.

Will Toomy. Irish born—you can't beat an Irishman at laying brick, Alec said—headed indefinitely for California, he had strayed this way, had taken time to do a job of work for Alec Cockrell; and now here he was. Still talking California, but making no move to leave Texas. If Mr. Cockrell had a mind to count his friends, here was one surely.

Will Toomy. Medium tall compared to the man he called "Boss," but still sizable. Young—maybe ten years or so younger than Alec—but full grown. Long-armed, with huge hands, hardened by use, that could double into hammer-head fists or swing a tool with equal ease. Sandy-haired, blue-eyed, generally good-humored, but not a man to be trifled with, he fitted exactly into Alec's need for a stay-at-home boss, who could safely be left in charge.

Sarah sensed his worth as much as anyone. His butternut-dyed jeans had always splotches of mud or mortar on them, but they were basically clean; and she liked that. Changed them twice a week if need be, Alec had told her. His homely face wore always a stubble of beard but it wasn't heavy enough to hide his friendliness. Swinging down from the wagon seat this morning, nimble as a monkey, he covered the group of people in the yard with a general greeting, added a "Hi-yah, Charley John" for the Indian, a "Morning, Boss," to Alec, and finished with the same word to Sarah but spoken with a respectfulness that amounted to a bow.

"Good morning, Mr. Toomy," Sarah answered, then excused herself and turned back to the house.

I'm as useless here, she thought, as I ever want to be anywhere.

Charley John, bird in hand again, sat there on the stump, the children clustered around him, their questions still unanswered. Will Toomy and Alec Cockrell stood beside the wagon, a thing passing between them which she could not read clearly, any more than she knew what passed ever between Alec and the Indian.

"Sister," Polly Thompson said to her at the door of the house, "you're real pale. Is something wrong?"

"No," she said firmly. "Everything's all right—the same as always."

chapter nine

A Mocker may take the shape of a man.

UP IN TOWN, life if not exactly seething, was now beginning to stir. One wagon and team and two saddled horses were already tied to the courthouse rail, their owners lost to view among such places as were open to business on the streets adjacent to the square, which at this hour, shortly before nine o'clock, could not have looked more peaceful and been alive. The horses stamped at flies, a hound dog under the one wagon thumped a foot, scratching at fleas; and that was the most movement there was. Andrew Moore, coming out of the Crutchfield House after a leisurely breakfast, on a first reconnaissance of his field of operations, surveyed the picture, spat ostentatiously, then leaned his weight against the doorjamb and stood there a full five minutes. Not that it took him that long to estimate or identify these early additions to the town's resident population. His idea of reconnoitering was not so much to keep an eye on what was going on as to show himself and his authority in various prominent places.

And yet, he was furtively watchful. When he concluded that he had given a proper measure of time to his present position, and let go of the tavern door to saunter across Main Street and down the first block of Houston, opposite the square, his careless pace was a mite too careless to be real. A broad-brimmed hat of a light felt, sunburned from much wear, shadowed his pale eyes; but they were never still. They looked ahead, to the left, to the

120

right, mistrusting the very lack of people to accost him or be accosted by him.

A fine figure of a man, still in his early thirties. Strong, supple, in the way of one who rode a roof beam as easily as another might ride a horse. Strong enough, anyone would have said, to handle any situation without the help of firearms; but obviously Andrew Moore did not think so. Two army revolvers hung from his belt and in his right hand he carried a black, serviceable, well-oiled double-barreled shotgun.

He covered the short block with its three stores—the *Weekly Herald*, W. W. Peak, Drugs and Sundries, and John W. Smith, General Merchandise—without interruption. Before the drug-store, on his own impulse, he did stop a minute to look up at the second story windows; but when those seemed as blank as the rest of the square, he gave an extra swing to his broad shoulders and went on to the corner. He had a sort of appointment to see the Mayor "first thing this morning" in the room above the drug-store and there was always the possibility that the Justice of the Peace might have a summons or two for him to deliver; but plainly neither official had shown up so far.

In the store on the corner, Uncle Jack Smith was busy—or so he would have said—setting his place in order. Since it was the original log building and acutely limited as to space, the process consisted chiefly of moving miscellaneous boxes from here to there on the single counter and making a general survey of an even greater miscellany on the shelves that ran the length of the longest wall. Even so, Uncle Jack, to his own mind, anyhow, was busy and he had his back turned to the door and the one small window. His first warning of a visitor was the dimming of the chief source of light, which was the door. He turned, and there stood the Marshal—in full armor.

Now, Uncle Jack Smith was also a man with a grievance. If the three or four hundred people who, all counted, made up the present population of Dallas could be said to be divided into two parties, he belonged to and voted with those who found progress discomforting. Business was not too flourishing in his store these days. It earned him his vittles and a little over, his bachelor needs being modest; but it looked, like his store, danged mean and small, compared to the business that went on at Hirsch and Shirek's Mercantile Emporium on the corner diagonally opposite. All the fancy trade went to those two Jews who had moved in on Texas from Hopkins County, Kentucky; and who had brought them in? Well, Alec Cockrell, to be sure. Who was behind most of the changes, some good, some bad and all open to question, that kept a feller guessing these days?

So, John W. Smith was one of the forty-five who had voted Andrew Moore into the job of Marshal; but that didn't mean necessarily that he was Moore's friend. He found his bulk in the doorway not nearly as welcome as the light and air he shut out, and the three guns something worse than ridiculous. And he as much as said so.

"Hunting?" he inquired. "Goda'mighty, you could blow a squirrel inside out with that thing in your hand."

Moore looked the storekeeper—and his store—over sourly. If the question was meant for a joke, he didn't find it funny. Crutchfield earlier had remarked on the shotgun when he stood it in the corner of the hotel dining room at breakfast time. Which only went to show that in this state a revolver wasn't worth mentioning but a Sharp's rifle or a shotgun was. His choice was a shotgun. It could be just as deadly as rifle or revolver; and, generally speaking, it was surer.

"Not bothering squirrels none today," he said, his voice rich, sulky, slightly defiant. "Just making the rounds. Might pick up some powder, if you have any handy."

Thoughtfully Uncle Jack moved a box of thread down the counter, turned to reach with sure aim for a canister, marked *FFFg Gun Powder*, and hesitated. Andy Moore, he recollected, owed him still for the last he had bought. Being town Marshal hardly entitled a man to free ammunition. Now, did it?

Moore saw him hesitate and knew the reason. Black anger welled up in him, not directed exclusively at Uncle Jack. Nobody —well, hardly anybody—trusted him for money these days. Flushing darkly, he pulled a minted silver dollar out of his pocket and made it ring on the counter.

"Will that cover?" he asked.

Smith looked squint-eyed at the coin and at Andy.

"Just about," he said, and set the canister, open, on the counter. "Help yourself."

Which the Marshal did, amply, filling his powder flask, and turned out of the store. The silver dollar lay where he had left it; and, for once, Uncle Jack Smith had no wish to pick up a piece of money. Something hot and hateful was reflected from the shining coin. Unbidden, the little town in North Carolina, where he had lived as a boy, spread out before him. Not a pretty town. Poor. But peaceful. You heard of violence outside but it didn't happen, not in the town. Nothing else happened there. That was why he had left it; but . . . gingerly, at last, he picked up the money, and laid it down again.

He guessed the source of it. Sourly, for him, he reflected on the obvious benefit of holding a marshal's badge. Two days—three drunks and a cockfight—and Andy Moore had hard money in his pocket. Wished he knew how much. Did the Marshal pocket all the proceeds of a fine or just a share, the Justice of the Peace and others coming in on the profits? It might pay a man—no! Years gone, he had held a clerkship—just one year. Gained more enemies then than he had made friends the rest of his life. Cured him of ambition. All he asked was a living, without too danged much rustle and bustle about getting on. So now, this dollar. His hand dropped over it. He squinted toward the door, to make sure no other visitor was near, then went stiffly down on his knees to put it in a strong box under the counter.

Leaving the store, Andrew Moore carried the warmth of his violence back toward Peak's drugstore and up the outside stairway that led to the dusty room which served the city of Dallas for the Justice of the Peace Court and a town hall, when such was needed. The screech of the sawmill operations down the river and the chanting of the dusky bricklayers and hod carriers now at work on the new hotel did nothing to sweeten his temper. Scowling, he forced open the door and stepped inside. Justice Smith, he noted, hadn't appeared yet. Well, he'd serve his office later in the day. The Mayor, on the other hand, had arrived. Not to keep the Justice from the use of his bar, the Mayor sat at a side table, a small stack of papers before him. Looking worried, and not alone. Behind him stood the Honorable James M. Patterson, Esquire, Uncle Jack Smith's former partner in business.

The Mayor was not an impressive man. He looked as near like nobody in particular as a man could. Brownish hair, scant. A scraggly beard to match. Features mostly hidden by the beard and large, steel-rimmed spectacles. His black coat and vest, well worn, even a little greenish, indicated a man of no great wealth but conscious of position. A large Masonic charm hung from his watch chain. Still he looked like nobody in particular, but his worried expression and the presence of Judge Patterson stopped Andy temporarily at the door.

"Ah, Marshal?" the Mayor said uncertainly as Andy appeared, and then, "Andy, for the Lord's sake!"

That, of course, was for the shotgun. Recovering some of his swagger, Moore crossed the room and stood it beside the cold chimney. He had entered the room, still angry, but with confidence, feeling sure that here he was among friends. Now, vaguely, he was not so sure. Consequently, his swagger was even more pronounced as he turned again and came back to the mayor's table.

"Good morning, Judge," he said to Patterson and sneered faintly. It looked like Patterson and the Mayor had been weighing up something to say to him. The Mayor, however, was still worrying about the gun.

"Andy, must you carry a thing like that?" he asked.

"Marshal," Andy said shortly, "is permitted and duty bound to equip himself to enforce order. That's the law." And then, because the distress on the Mayor's face deepened, "What's the trouble?"

Patterson answered for the Mayor. He was a man more used to authority. As Judge, he had even let his beard grow long, to add to his dignity.

"No trouble yet," he said, "and we don't want any."

"I'm a man of peace," the Mayor said then, picking up spirit. "I will not support or defend violence in executing the prerogatives of office."

Big words. Andy looked down at the small stack of papers.

"No?" he said. "What's the matter? You been hearing complaints? Already?"

"A few," the Mayor said. "Some have gone to the trouble to write their questions."

"Can't imagine what their complaints could be," Moore sneered. "We campaigned on a reform platform, didn't we? Strict enforcement of the laws as written. So far as I know, we've been doing just that, enforcing the laws."

"Andrew," Patterson interrupted, "you know as well as we do what the complaining is about. People—and they are some who voted you into office—are asking now if it can be true that you sought the office of Marshal in order to work off a personal grudge."

So-o-o? Maybe they should have asked sooner.

"Andrew, in two days you have made five arrests—all of them Cockrell men."

Moore's mouth drooped now in an exaggerated sneer.

"You don't say. A little hard to distinguish one drunk from another sometimes. And who in this town has any money in his jeans if he don't work for Alick Cockrell? He owns the place and every going business in it. And folks don't like it. I thought you were some of them. Opposed to one man having the say-so about everything. Seems to me I remember you saying—loud as any— 'If we don't stop Alick Cockrell soon, he'll own us as well as the town.' Talked it over after lodge meeting, a bunch of us. I was there and so were you, both of you. 'Look at the vagroms,' one of you said, 'hunters, trappers, plain tramps, that he hires at his wood lots and his mill. Look at the furriners he's planted all over the town. Do those folks ever claim rights as citizens, old-timers like us won't be one, two, three. We can maybe handle things this election. It's our one chance, maybe, to put a check on this upstart.'"

The Mayor looked at Patterson. Moore waited. He'd given them back their words pretty neatly, hadn't he? Patterson coughed behind his solemn beard.

"See here," he said finally. "I've known Alick Cockrell a sight longer than you have, young man. And better. I'm the one who called him an upstart. Knew him for that from the beginning and I'll stand by my words; but the law is the law, remember; and it's never one-sided."

"Oh, ain't it?" Moore sneered. "Well, I happen not to agree with you. The law, to my thinking, is strictly on the side of the feller with the upper hand." Then he rested his fists on the mayor's table and leaned over, glowering at the Mayor and his little pile of papers. "Know what's the matter with you?" he sneered. "You're scared. Cockrell's been gone most of the week; but now you've heard, I suppose, that he's back in town? Sure you have— that's what's scared you."

"No, Andy, no," the Mayor protested, coloring up. "I don't happen to like Alick Cockrell. He aggravates me as much as anybody, but . . ."

"Scared," Moore blustered. "Well, I'm not."

Nobody answering right away this time, the words hung on the air a minute; and the Mayor seemed to gather a measure of force finally.

"No, Andy," he said quietly. "I've got no reason to be afraid. Except for one thing—public opinion. As I was coming down the street just now, Wake Latimer called me into the *Herald* office. Putting out a newspaper, he prides himself on not taking sides. . . ."

Andy swore.

"Like hell, he don't take sides. With Cockrell advertising regular—both the brickyard and the sawmill? You couldn't name a stouter Cockrell man, however he prints it or says it. What did he have to say to you?"

"He wanted me," the Mayor said, still with dignity and force, "to write a piece for the paper, saying what my ideas are for the future of Dallas; and I told him I'd be proud to, being as fond of the town as he is and having known it like him from its small beginnings."

"Hell!" Moore said again, in utter exasperation.

"He spoke of the rivalry still going between Dallas and other towns roundabout—Hord's Ridge, Cedar Springs, and others. We haven't got such a start on them that any one couldn't catch up if we should stall now. You wouldn't want to see that happen, Andy?"

"Look," Moore said, almost black with fury now, "I don't give a hoot in hell what happens to this town or any other. I'm looking out for Andy Moore—same as you are looking out for you and the Judge for himself—and Alick Cockrell for Alick Cockrell, if all of us tell the truth. I been duly elected and sworn in as Marshal of the city of Dallas. I know my duties and my rights and I'll not be bluffed out of executing them. Not by any smooth-spoken printer man or anybody else. Anybody I see breaking a town ordinance gets jailed and booked for the same. Law is law, like you say, Judge. Them drunks I collared at Haught's place night before last were drunks, guilty of unseemly behavior in a public place and generally disturbing the peace. One of them flang a bottle at me. If I'd a known which one it was, I'd have had him for assault, because if he hadn't missed me, he'd have laid me out cold."

"Hmmm!" the Judge said meditatively. "And what about that cockfight near the sawmill that same evening? Some of our more respected citizens were there."

He winked at the Marshal now, but Andy was too furious to be softened up by that.

"Didn't touch a holy spectator," he said. "Pulled just the two men outside, writing bets and taking money."

"You didn't have in mind starting a sort of riot, stopping work at the mill and on the hotel, the men packing their tools and making ready to move out, saying they wouldn't stay in a town where a man couldn't take his liquor or have a bit of fun after hours? Only that Irish superintendent of Alick Cockrell's talked them out of it, telling them to wait till the boss got back before starting anything."

"No," Moore said, but his swagger was back. "Just doing my duty as I saw it. A handful of drunks and two men caught red-handed promoting an illegal sport, involving gambling. I arrested 'em and I'll do the same by anybody else that breaks a town ordinance—if it's Alick Cockrell his own self. And there you have it."

The Mayor paled and Judge Patterson chewed at his whiskered lower lip.

"I don't believe you'll have much luck that way," he said finally. "There was a time when Alick Cockrell would have fallen into such a trap; but it's been several years now since he's had one of his typical, hair-raising sprees."

"I'm not saying he will or he won't break the law," Moore said, his temper improving steadily. "I'm just saying . . . if he does . . ."

The Mayor was on his feet, clutching his papers.

"I don't like the tone of this conversation," he faltered. "It wasn't what I had in mind when I called this meeting. Andy, will you do me at least one special favor? Lay aside two of your three guns? The law, I suppose, allows you one revolver, but surely not a whole arsenal."

"I'd like to oblige you, Mayor, but I won't. First place, it's Saturday. Second place, Cockrell's back; and the word is his wagons should be along some time this evening. A long train, I hear, and in charge, like always, of that big red bull, Rudy Horst. If a marshal is as unpopular as you two are making out, he'd better fix himself some protection. Anything else you want? If not, I'm moving on. Should you see our Justice of the Peace for the city of Dallas, and he should ask for me, tell him I'm out making the rounds. And he might as well set up his court machinery. Looks like we might have a busy Saturday—and a right interesting one, too."

chapter **ten**

Then a friend, if he has the right medicine...

"AND THAT'S HOW it is, boss. Five of our men in that lousy calaboose overnight, and me asleep in my bed, knowing nothing about it till morning. I bought 'em free, but that didn't stop the growlin'. Theirs or others'. I had a near riot on my hands amongst the work gang most of yestidday. Nobody liked the idea of a man being locked up for a bit of fun. And it's truth, that's all it came to."

Will Toomy leaned easy against a wagon wheel in the Cockrell yard, and cocked an eye at his employer. Alec snorted.

"Stone drunk if I know 'em—the lot," he said.

"No," Toomy declared. "The three uptown were well soaked, or they would not have missed with that bottle. The other two were sober enough, just arrangin' a bit of entertainment. Had a nice crowd gathered. You'd be surprised."

Alec said he would not have been surprised. He knew the town as well as Toomy, better.

"Fight on the square?" he asked.

"Now, how do I know?" Toomy countered. "Never got started. A black and a Mex' were handlin' the birds. Boss, it would not a-made a particle of difference how the fight was run. A cockfight, Marshal said, was against the law—along with all other gamblin'; so, he run the boys in. Boss, what sticks in my mind is that about 'all other gamblin'.' Was he right about that?"

129

"Afraid he was, Will. That's how the good people in town want it."

"Boss, right now you could knock me over with a feather. Who are these good people? Can you name them to me?"

"I can," Alec said, "but I don't need to. You know. And they are right in a way. If you want to have a town fit for homes and families, you've got to keep things decent. So . . . no free whiskey, no gambling, no rowdyism."

Toomy's perplexity deepened. He shifted a chew of tobacco from one cheek to the other. He took off his hat and rubbed his right ear.

"I see what you mean," he said slowly. "Think I do. Boss, you can't draw the rein that tight. The good people, like you call 'em, don't work for us. They're above swingin' an axe or handlin' logs at a sawmill or mindin' a brick kiln. Hirin' out a nigger or two is the closest they come to toil. We got to take what we can catch as it drifts by. Rough customers, most of 'em; but, if their luck's been bad enough and they're starved to it, they'll do a day's work or several for the sake of a bed and grub and a dollar or two in their pockets at the end of a week or, maybe, a month—some are steadier than they look at first sight —but, when the work is done and they've got their pay, they want their fun. What's more, they will have it. One way or another. If it ain't allowed here, they will pack up and move on. Boss, if this keeps on, it's liable to ruin your town."

He couldn't have been more in earnest if he had been a preacher arguing on the side of virtue. Alec hooted at him, not so much at what he was saying.

"I heard the same talk when free whiskey was outlawed a while back," he said.

"Free whiskey, gamblin', gun-totin'?" Toomy said thoughtfully. "Laws against all of 'em, that's right. But shucks nobody ever took 'em serious until . . ." light dawned on him like the sun coming through clouds. He stood away from the wagon. He set his hat back on his head. Squarely and firmly. "So, that's what the skunk's after. By God, he as much as told me so. When I paid the fines. 'Don't think, because you are in Alick Cockrell's pay, that you can do as you please around here,' he said. 'I'd as soon arrest him as anybody else if he don't keep to the law. Maybe sooner.' I thought he was just talkin' loud, but now— Boss, the scoundrel's up to somethin'.'"

It could be that Toomy was right, though it seemed ridiculous. To work off a spite by enforcing the law. Blue laws, passed when the town was incorporated, to protect the weak—meaning women and children.

"Boss, I'm tellin' you," Toomy said, "I had a time yesterday gettin' the men to stack a board or lay a brick. They were about evenly divided between wanting to kill the Marshal or quit the job or leave town for good and all."

"I counted what they hadn't done," Alec informed him, "when I passed the hotel this morning. Don't think I didn't notice." He stopped, to let his ears drink in once more the hum of the singing Negroes, the screech of his great saw. "Things are moving now," he said.

"You're back," Toomy told him. "That's the difference. They are saying to themselves and each other, 'Boss will fix that man now. You wait and see.' "

"No!" Protest was suddenly like a stomach cramp in Alec. "No. I won't play into his hands so. I raised hell plenty in my day but it was a time ago."

"Boss," Toomy said softly, "you wouldn't be sidin' with the Marshal against your own men, would you now? Say this afternoon, when the wagons come in . . . and Rudy."

Both men were looking at the same picture then. Rudy Horst, a red-bearded giant of a man, loud-mouthed, vehement, boisterous, everything that Alec had renounced when he turned respectable and a few qualities besides that he had never laid claim to. An A-number-one wagoner, an equally good driver of mules or oxen, knowing just what he could get in the way of pull from either, a good boss to all sorts of men, because he knew all sorts. He had a thirst as deep as his barrel chest; and nobody had ever plumbed the depth of that. On the road he kept the thirst in check, rationing whiskey to himself by the cup as he did to his drivers, a moistening of his throat at the end of a dusty day, but never enough to fuddle his senses. But, let him hit town at the end of a long pull and look out! Saloonkeepers reached for their bung-starters and men locked up their wives and daughters. Not that women were the first aim with Rudy, but there was something splendid about him when he let go that turned women silly. Like cats in a beam of light, they stood still to be caught.

"Might be a good idea," Alec said thoughtfully, "for me to ride back over the road a piece to meet the wagons."

Toomy sighed.

"Speaking of wagons," Alec went on, not noticing, "where were you thinking of going in that one?"

"Nowhere at all," Toomy said. "Short of feed down at the mill. Thought maybe you could spare George for a short haul from over the river. Didn't want to take a man off the work anywhere."

"I'll go for the feed myself," Alec offered, as unexpectedly to himself as to Toomy. "Overton's, I'd say. Perry's got sheaf oats, I know."

He didn't know why he made the offer. A vagrant desire to be away from pestering. Could be that Sarah would enjoy a visit to friends over the river.

"Boss . . ."

"Don't tell me any more," he said roughly. "Talked myself dry long ago. Got anything under the wagon seat?"

"The usual inspiration." Toomy reached for and produced a brown jug with a corncob stopper.

"Carry a cup?" Alec asked; and, when Toomy cocked an eye in question, "Not that I'm finicky, but it shows less from the road." As he spoke, he raised his hand in greeting to a passing buggy. "Friends of Sarah's," he explained. "From Hord's Ridge. Want them to spread the word uptown: 'Passed Cockrell's place just now. Alick's home. Started his drinking early today'?"

Then the whiskey was fiery and, at the same time, soothing to his throat. Toomy laughed and stoppered the jug.

"Boss, what will I tell the boys?"

"Nothing," Alec snapped. "Say you've seen me if you want and that I'll be around myself this afternoon with the pay."

Toomy waited. Boss was feeling good now, very good about something. Couldn't be the whiskey. One swallow?

"Enjoyed a few rounds of poker at Black Jack," Alec said casually.

"Now, then!" Toomy's tone was all admiration. "And they not knowing any better than to ask you? Now, there's a town," he finished wistfully, "Black Jack."

"It's a hog wallow." Alec turned to face his house. "It would take more than lawmaking to clean it up. Have to tear it down and start over. Well, so long. See you when I get back. Noon— or maybe a little after."

He wished now that he hadn't asked for the whiskey, though its warmth lingered gratefully along his gullet. His house, he thought. Sarah in there, wrinkling her smooth face over his expenditures. The Indian and the young ones, he noticed, had left the stump where they had huddled together. Crow hunting? Well, Charley John, anyhow. His house, his wife, his young ones—that's what being respectable came to. But savagery, like that raw stump of one of the trees that had gone toward building the house, and the Indian with his gun, bent on keeping bad luck off by shooting blackbirds, believing an old dark prophecy—things like that—together with plain human cussedness on the part of some claiming to be more civilized than the Indians, hung around too close for a man to be sure, tightly sure, of being respectable for long.

...can drive the witches away.

He opened the door and stepped into the hall. After the rising warmth outside, the house seemed cooler than ever; and, after the litter of the yard, the orderliness was awesome. Sarah would say, if he spoke his mind about the house, that it wouldn't bear examining the corners; but that was how it looked to him—clean and quiet, good to come into out of the brash daylight.

Not altogether quiet. He heard now a murmur of talk. He listened, and it was just one person—Sarah. Talking in a steady flow, which she did but rarely. Hadn't heard her go on like that in years—not since their evenings at the ranch, when she would be telling him a tale he had missed reading out of a book because he had never been strait-jacketed in a schoolhouse. Talking to Hannah or Sister Polly? No, not Polly. She would be interrupting. A fidgety woman. Couldn't ever keep still for long.

He catfooted it into the bedroom. The peace and virtue of the house was more noticeable there than in the bareness of the hall. Everything had been set to rights now—the blue and white crockery gleaming clean on the washstand, towels hanging just so on the rack to one side, the baby's trundle bed out of sight under the big bed, the big bed made up smooth under its patchwork counterpane. His belt, with his revolver and his knife, lay straight across the lower end, in a kind of touch-me-not primness foreign to such gear, certainly not careless as he had dropped it. He moved to pick up the belt, but something held his hand.

Leave it where it is, Alec Cockrell. Leave it be.

He could hear Sarah more plainly now, almost make out what

134

she was saying. The door stood open into the office, and that was where she was. He stepped noiselessly now in that direction, but at the door he stopped again.

What he saw was a picture. Sarah had brought in all four of her young ones and washed and slicked them up like a mother cat going over her kittens and company expected. She had finished with the three older ones and had little Alec up on the table in front of her, combing and fingering his curls. The two older boys, Bob and Frank, sat on straight chairs against one wall. It wasn't often they sat that still and proper, but their mother had a tone of voice that they respected when she had a mind to use it. They were behaving well now. Six-year-old Robert, built sturdy and solid . . .

"He has your mouth, Mr. Cockrell; and he's a wild one and stubborn, too, as hard to handle as you could ever have been."

Four-year-old Frank, skinny as a grasshopper . . .

"A sweet and loving child," his mother said, "but into everything."

Eight-year-old Aurelia, in a fresh white dimity pinafore trimmed with some of the thread lace her Aunt Polly was forever crocheting, sat at the end of the table, her dimpled chin in her hands, her elbows on the table top, smiling at her baby brother. Who she looked like nobody could say.

"Must be somebody on your side, Mr. Cockrell. Your ma, maybe, that you can't remember." Sarah would say this with a sigh, thinking what his ma had missed—and so she had.

Then the youngest, with his sunshiny curls and his way of rolling his blue eyes, especially at Sarah, who loved him best of all right now because he was still helpless in many ways and depended on her care. But she treasured every one of the four, good, bad or middlin'; and they knew it or she could never have held them as she did.

None of them saw Alec in the open door. Sarah had her back directly toward him. There she stood, her hands quick and sure with the comb, her voice steady and smooth. Here was a thing she could handle and found peace doing so.

"I felt possessed," she said afterward, "to scrub them all up, myself included. I was never more glad of anything than that I did so."

She was talking to the children about Charley John. Must have been telling them all the Cherokee had done for their father when he was a boy and needed help. She finished off the tale something like this:

"Because he was good to your pa then, and ever since, we call him a friend. Your pa thinks much of him and he of your pa. The Cherokee, according to your pa, are more like white folk than most Indians; but," she sighed lightly, "they still are Indian, with Indian ways."

Now, bless her pure and righteous heart! Stretched it to take in all those she knew and cared about, and did her best to open it to others; but, to save her life, she couldn't help having a shut door ready.

"They don't know about our God and the Lord Jesus, or else they don't believe. They have their own ideas about such things. They make up fairy tales about people and creatures. Especially creatures. All creatures, birds and animals, they say, are really spirits, some good, some bad, who take on the shapes they do, so that they can be around among people, to do good or harm. Crows and ravens are evil spirits, the Indians think. They are robber birds, as you know. Maybe that is how they got a bad name. They follow a farmer when he is planting and eat the grain he sows. Sometimes they do worse. They wait until it sprouts, then pull it out and eat it, young leaf and all. Until the farmer has little left for his work of plowing and planting. The Cherokee, your pa says, are farming folk and so have known the trouble crows make."

"They eat dead things, too," the boy Robert said.

Alec saw Sarah stiffen.

"Dead fish, dead cats, dead cows—" Confound the boy! "I seen 'em."

"You . . . what?" Sarah said. "You mean, 'I have seen,' or 'I saw.' "

"Yes'm," the boy said sulkily. "I have saw 'em."

Aurelia, with two years of schooling behind her, giggled; and the rest, not knowing why, followed her example. Bob thought possibly he had said something smart instead of foolish, and perked up. Alec, still unnoticed, let the picture soak into him, every bit of it; and it made him proud on the one hand, and mad on the other. He thought, this is what I've come to, and I never thought I would. This I have; and it's more than all else besides—four fine children, and a loving wife and mother to bring them up right. These were his own. Let nobody try to take them from him. That was where being proud edged over into being mad. Anger came up hot in his throat, as if Toomy's whiskey wouldn't stay down in his stomach. Who threatened him, threatened these; and he'd do murder before he let them come to harm.

"Well, maybe they do eat dead things," Sarah granted. Had to get herself out of the brush somehow. "Maybe it's crawdads they're after hereabouts. What I started to say was, it's not because the blackbirds have a spite on us that we see so many. It is because we live close to the river. All creatures need water; and birds, most of them, like to roost in trees. Could be that . . ."

"Mamma," Aurelia said pertly and unexpectedly, "why does Charley John call some of them 'Mockers'?"

It was time, Alec thought, for him to move. He did so, and little Alec spied him, squirmed free of his mother's hands and pointed at the door. Sarah turned.

"Well, I never!" she said. "I thought you'd gone off with Mr. Toomy."

Alec shook his head.

"What is this?" he asked. "You all going to a fish fry or other such sociable? Surely, ma'am, you don't expect them to keep for meeting time tomorrow?"

"It's that old river," Sarah explained. "They were mud all over."

That could well be.

"Where's Charley John?" Alec asked.

He had gone downriver now, the boys said, with his gun. Still hunting crows. And Alec thought, why not take them all with me this morning. Haven't had fun like that in a long while.

"Now that you're slicked up so fine," he said, "wouldn't you like to go somewhere?" Sarah's eyes asked where. "Crossing the river after a load of feed," he answered. "Thought of Overton's, it being closest."

A chorus of yelps told him what the young ones thought. Like so many pups smelling dinner. Sarah's eyes warmed. Could be that Martha Ann Overton was her closest friend in Texas, outside of kinfolk; and he thought as much of Martha Ann and her husband, Perry, as anybody did.

A funny thing—friendship. The Overtons were already in Texas before Alec Cockrell came. That is, Perry's folks were there, moved down from Missouri. The old man had a gristmill at Cedar Springs. Later on, when Perry married, going back to Saline County, Missouri, for a girl he remembered, he set up a mill of his own on high ground west of the Trinity a few miles south of Dallas. And prospered. Had a good farm, a good house and a young family now coming on. Called his place Honey Springs, because the bees abounded.

The women found each other first, being brides the same year and living not too far apart; and so, the men, Perry Overton and Alec Cockrell, came together. Should have done so sooner, having every natural reason for being friends. Perry Overton even had a grandmother who was part Cherokee Indian.

"Of course," Alec said now, "if I take all of you, you'll have to stay till somebody fetches you home. Can't bring you back myself. Need the full wagon bed for feed.

Nobody objected to that. Uncle Perry and Aunt Martha were popular in this house. Ten minutes later Alec was loading the boys and Aurelia into the back of his wagon, while Sarah waited with their youngest to mount the seat with him. He set a stool for Aurelia, to remind her, he said, that she was a young lady, and kissed her pretty face under a new pink sunbonnet. Then, for a joke, he kissed the boys, too. Wanted to, suddenly; but made out he was joking.

"My, you smell nice," he told them. "Your ma must a-used her scented soap on you."

"She did, she did!" they hollered gleefully.

So, then he must kiss Sarah; and the boys hollered some more. They loved a joke on their ma, when they had support for it. And Sarah blushed—to think she would, after ten years!

Sister Polly Thompson and Hannah watched them off. Sister Polly was sewing on a sacque that she wanted to have ready for Sunday. Said she might have to walk uptown for more of the braid she had planned for trimming though Sarah had an idea she had other schemes in mind. Some surprise for the family dinner it might be—her favorite spoon bread or some such. Hannah had a wash kettle on; and Willie Winn, she said, needn't beg to go along with his white folks. Who'd fetch chips for her fire? Any time that day, Alec Cockrell could close his eyes and see that picture, too.

They stopped at the bridge for a word with Barry Derritt, their slave man who took the tolls. Alec so far had not managed time for him since his return that early morning.

"Hi-ya, Barry!" he said. "How're things going?"

Barry was another stalwart, almost as tall as Alec, and more solidly built. His stature and a faint saffron stain to his skin were the most that remained visible of his African ancestry. Between that origin and now there had been intermingling of other blood. And good blood, or else he just happened to inherit what was good in it. His features were a white man's, and his manners had the courtliness of a gentleman born and reared. When Alec had bought the town and the ferry that went with it, he had hired Barry to run the ferry. Then, finding him both able and trustworthy, he had bought him outright, and, with Sarah's willing approval, had told him he could call himself a free man whenever he had worked off his purchase price, the terms being generous. This was more to satisfy himself and Sarah than to please Barry, who accepted the offer conditionally.

"You all fix it up how you like," he said. "However it is, I will work for you whilst I live and you have use for me."

They had plenty of use for him. When Alec was away, it gave him and Sarah, too, comfort to know that Barry Derritt stood guard only a few yards down the road. Barry's coming to the house each evening with the tolls was a ceremony that officially closed the day. The meeting now between master and man was on even terms of liking and respect.

"Business about like always," Barry reported, "except it's Saturday. Come afternoon, folks'll be tramplin' each other down up yonder."

They turned their heads toward the town, and for a bit the murmur and the hum and the clatter filled their ears.

"Well, we'll know all about it by evening," Alec said finally. "All right, you in back there. Got your bridge toll ready?"

Three gaping young faces looked at him. The young ones knew he was joking, but how to answer? Looked so much like hungry nestlings that he snorted.

"Pay your fare, or get out," he said sternly.

"Papa," Aurelia said, "you know—" she glanced at her mother—"we don't have any money."

"Sure enough?" he inquired. "You poor folks? Too bad. Reckon I'll have to make you a loan."

He dived into a jingling pocket and located three silver ten-cent pieces. He gave one to each of the children in the wagon.

"Now you can pay," he told them. "Get your money, Barry. Don't let a one of them ride free."

"Oh, Papa!"

This time, repeating his order, he winked at Barry, who reached for the money solemnly enough, but managed to palm each coin back into the hand that offered it.

"Now, where did you learn that, I wonder?" Alec reproved. He was feeling so good right then that he was about to choke. "You'll never get a penny out of any of them from now on. They'll think they own the bridge." Maybe they thought so now. "Cockrell young'uns," he could hear folks saying. "Sit tight, you!" he said more sharply, worry nagging again at the fullness in his throat. And to the mules, "Giddap, you o'nery sons of darkness. Think you've been turned out to graze? See you later, Barry. You keep an eye on deadheads, hear me? We will count up on you, now that we know how you are that way."

The mules stepped into the harness. The wagon creaked, then rattled on the boarding of the bridge. The young ones said, "Ooooh!" coming into the dark, though if you stood outside at one end, you could see daylight at the other. Even the boards above were not too close. A hard rain would drip through. But it was a good steady bridge. The rumbling rattle under the wagon sounded strong.

The next minute the children were cheering the brightness on the far side of the river. The near mule twitched nervous ears at the racket, but the far one put his ears forward, seeming to say, "Shucks! Just our folks. Come along"; and the two of them pulled smartly, considering how the day was warming toward noon, over a road which Alec himself had traced across the bottoms to the ridge of high land south and west of the Trinity. An aggravating task, keeping a road marked through the flood basin, but part of maintaining the bridge. Without the road he might have lost considerable travel to some upstart ferries below the town.

The wagon creaked and rattled. Now and again it gave a lurch, going into or coming out of a dried-up mudhole. The young ones hollered at that, but mostly they twittered and tee-heed to themselves back yonder. The boy in Sarah's arms drowsed against her. She bent over him, so that the curtain of her sunbonnet gave him, too, some shade. Alec studied the picture they made and that full feeling returned to his throat. Sarah felt his eyes upon her and, still hovering over the child, turned her head to face him.

"The same bonnet?" Alec asked, countering the question in her eyes.

"No," she said. "I wore out that one and two more before we left the ranch."

"That so? Make 'em all of the same stuff—all black?"

"No," she said again. "I had me out a light one for today, but I put it back and got out this one, instead. It's cooler. Seems to keep out more heat . . . and light." She was still a minute, then said, violently for her, "If I live to be a hundred, I'll never get used to Texas sun. Some days I can smell things scorching."

Impatient about something, Alec could tell. Not the sun. They rolled along a quarter of a mile or so.

"A hundred years," he said then, "is a piece of time. Think you will live that long?"

"No. It was just a way of speaking. Who knows how long he's got to live?"

Who, to be sure?

"What I was thinking—" Alec said, "some days time lays out ahead of you like these bottoms, till you can't see the end of it. Other days it crowds in on you and you feel pushed every minute. And you call yourself all kinds of a fool for not getting things done sooner. And you know you'll never get to start even a lot of things you've got in your mind to do."

Worry puckered Sarah's lips.

"Most anybody would say to that," she told him, "get done what you have started before you take up something more."

"Sounds sensible," he agreed, "but it don't seem to work out that way."

The wagon bumped along.

"Reminds me," Sarah said, going back to what they'd been saying about time. "Washing up the young ones took me a while this morning. I didn't get to look at those papers you gave me. Just put them in the trunk the way they were. And . . . so many other things seemed to be happening while we were at breakfast and after that, I forgot to tell you I rented that new little house on Lamar Street. Just yesterday."

"That so?" Alec said, "Stranger?"

"Yes. A young lawyer from North Carolina."

"Don't tell me. Another one? What is it about Texas that draws them?"

"It isn't Texas," Sarah answered. "You'd better ask what makes every other young man in the land take up law for a living. . . . Their horse was stove in. Their buggy broke down right off the bridge."

Alec studied this information.

"Family man?" he asked now.

"Just about. His wife's expecting her first. Soon, I'd say."

"Hm! Well, you did right to rent the house. Just standing there. Think they'll be good for the rent?"

"At least as good as Mr. Gonant, the picture-taking man," Sarah said smartly.

"Ha, I should have said—are they gentlefolk?"

"Yes," Sarah answered. "Especially the man. George Guess, he said his name was. Wife's a young thing, and fretful; but they are gentlefolk."

"Especially the man," Alec repeated.

Sarah turned again and gave him a look that meant: Don't be more of a fool than you must be—at your age, and he chuckled.

"All right," she said sniffily. "You know how it is. I've got a weakness for those who look hungry or—or disappointed. Always will have, I reckon."

What he might have answered to that Alec didn't get to say. Right then the wagon dipped into a real hole; and Aurelia upset with her stool and bumped her head, and cried first about the hurt, then harder and louder because the boys laughed. Alec wanted to whale the two of them and might have felt better had he done so; but somehow he couldn't. Something bound his arms, holding him where he sat.

"Shut up, you two, will you now?" he stormed, and that was all of it. "All right, pretty. Don't cry. We're almost there. A little cold spring water will fix that bump. This danged road! And I wasn't looking, leaving too much to the mules. Get along now, you sons of everlasting . . ."

"Mr. Cockrell!" Sarah warned, and he hushed.

But there was still a thing he had to say to her.

"About raven mockers," he began lamely, and wished again that Charley John had stayed at home. He had laughed off his visits before, but maybe that had been afterward. Maybe he always felt uneasy, in spite of good sense, until he saw the pony's dust rolling northward. " 'Relie's a little mixed up about them and I can't wonder. Mockers is what the Cherokees call the birds themselves. Why? I don't know. Could be because they can learn to speak words. Like humans. It's a fact. Take a crow—and ravens are the same—when it's a fledgling, make a pet of it, and it'll learn all sorts of tricks. Words are part of it."

"Who," Sarah asked harshly—a way he'd never heard her speak before—"would make a pet of a crow?"

"Well, I wouldn't, for sure. I've just heard tell. I saw a tame crow once. Right comical it was, to see him walking around, making free with people like he was one of them. Comical, but it didn't seem natural. Looked sure enough as if he'd took flight from Injun hell or anybody's."

"Mr. Cockrell," Sarah said, for the hundredth time maybe, "do you believe that story?"

"No, of course not."

And he didn't really. It was just something got stored in his mind the way a woman in the fall of the year will put away a packet of seed and forget she's got it until past planting time the next year. Then suddenly one day it falls off a top shelf into her hand. And she'll remember.

Remember . . .

"What do you believe?"

Was it Sarah speaking or his own self? It was Sarah. She had turned her face full toward him.

"Don't know," he said, then made a joke of that, or tried to. What did he believe? A man whose life up to the past ten years had been made of hit-and-miss patches had no sort of belief as Sarah Horton meant it.

"Left all that to you," he said. "You're better at it than I am."

"No!" Her steady eyes were wide and troubled. Her face was pale. "Mr. Cockrell," she said, "I've taken fright. I don't know why. Yes, I do know; and it's a fool thing, the way being afraid is, mostly; but I can't talk it down. I am still afraid."

She was, too. And now her fear reached out and laid hold of him.

"Hell and damn, woman!" he roared; and the child in her arms awoke at the noise and roared—but a different tune, one the mules weren't used to. The near one, the one with the twitchy ears, shied, throwing his teammate out of stride. Both of them plunged. A forewheel of the wagon caught on a stump, but, fortunately, rolled up and over without breaking. This lifted the wagon lopsided and overturned Aurelia again. She screamed. The boys yelled, partly to cover their own fright. Little Alec bawled. Alec drew back on the lines, braced himself and roared at the mules; and, by God, it felt good to let go altogether. Only Sarah sat stiffly quiet, but the uproar and the careening of the wagon shook the nonsense out of her, too. Temporarily she forgot other frights.

As it happened, the stump which had all but upset the wagon marked the beginning of the woods that surrounded the Overton house, which, as was the choice of a rancher when he had a choice, stood on its own small rise. Presently the mules found themselves galloping uphill and it was that fact more than Alec's blasphemy that finally slowed them. Alec basted their ears with a few unused epithets, eased his position cautiously, and turned on Sarah.

"Hell and damn, woman," he shouted, "don't ever do me like that again when I'm driving mules."

"Well, I never!" Sarah said, perfectly outraged.

Which, against the dwindling noises behind him and the now sober gait of the mules, struck Alec as funny. He leaned back and roared his laughter. The young ones uncertainly, then happily, came in on the chorus.

"I never did!" Sarah said and pulled away farther. Then her mouth twitched and she shook a little, but recovered ahead of the rest.

"Be quiet now, all of you," she said. "What will the Overtons think?" In a lower tone she added to Alec, "We could have been killed."

"Wonder we weren't," he agreed. "But here we are."

Sarah nodded. Afterward, in the hour she spent at the Overton ranch, all she said in explanation of the uproar that had heralded their approach was "Something started the mules." Alec said much the same. "That off mule, Jerry, is steady as a rock, usually, and a good thing, considering his teammate. Takes fright at a hoptoad. We could have been killed, but weren't."

The Overtons—man, wife and young—were all out in front of their house, waiting to see who was coming at such a gait; and it was good to see them, as it is always good to see the far end of a journey, however short. Theirs was the familiar double-log house, but clapboarded, with a sleeping loft and extra rooms, besides, so that it seemed to spread out wider than ordinary. The passageway had been left open front and rear. Cured sidemeat and hams and some venison hung from the roof beams. Gave the place a smell of plenty and a look of welcome. The Overtons, like their house, were open-handed and friendly.

"Whaw!" Alec commanded the sweating mules. "Stand now, you black sinners. Hi-ya, Perry. Brought you some company. Want I should set it down here or take it back where I found it?"

"Set down!" Perry called back.

Another tall man, but more lightly built than Alec. A light step, a lithe grace when he moved, and his eyes showed his Indian heritage.

"Come down, all of you," he said. "Sarah, let me give you a hand with that big boy." When young Alec held back, scowling, he took him by his waistband, hung him out at the end of his arm until the child squealed with excitement, then set him down with a spank and told him to git.

"Touch-me-not, ain't he?" he said with a twinkle to Sarah. "Like his pa, most of it pretending."

The other young Cockrells were out of the wagon now, all mixed up with young Overtons, puppy dogs and squawking chickens. A person had a time making himself heard above the noise.

"Came for a load of feed," Alec explained at top voice. "Got any to spare?"

"Plenty," Overton shouted back. "What do you want—corn or oats?"

"Oats. Sheaf oats will do fine."

"Glad to oblige. Glad to take your money for a change instead of you taking mine. It's a fact. Every time I take a notion for town, it costs me upwards of fifty cents to cross that fancy bridge. Want to drive to the barn while you're set for it? Wait till I get aboard then. Scatter, you tykes, if you don't want to be trampled."

The whole place echoed with welcome. Just safely outside the tangle Martha Overton waited, plump, smiling, squinting a little in the bright sun.

"I can't stay now I'm here," Sarah said to her. "Only just while Mr. Cockrell loads the wagon."

"But we can stay, can't we, Mamma? Mamma, can't we?"

She didn't know which one of her three cried out at her, they all speaking at once and singing the same tune.

"You haven't been asked that I've heard of," she informed them.

"Sarah, shame on you," Martha Overton said. "They know they are welcome. You know it, too. We can bring them home this evening or tomorrow."

None of this had been planned in Sarah's mind when she had washed and dressed the children.

"You come whenever you want and can," Martha said now to Aurelia, "and stay as long as you like." To Sarah she said aside, "She's a beauty, your oldest one."

From Sarah's heart rose, unbidden, the old lament.

Not my oldest. I buried him at Whitehouse Ranch. Lies there all alone.

Did a mother heart ever forget? Aloud she spoke a warning to Aurelia.

"If you stay, remember you are the young lady of the family. Help your Aunt Martha all you can. Keep an eye on your brothers and don't tear your clothes. They're next to the best you have."

Then she followed Martha into the house. The family sitting room seemed cool and dark as a root cellar, compared to the brightness outside.

"I'll just lay aside my bonnet," she said, resisting Martha's repeated urging that she change her mind and spend the afternoon where she was. "I can't stay, Martha Ann, truly. I left everything to do at home." She thought contritely of papers stuffed hastily into the small trunk, and the key turned on them. Of the letter she kept for Margaret Bryan. "Some days," she said, "the only way you can manage is to close the door on all of it and go off somewhere." She tied the bonnet on the arm of the chair and gave it an impatient, scornful slap. "Mr. Cockrell pokes fun at my black bonnets. I wish," she sighed, "I could think of something prettier that would do the same good."

"Alec Cockrell," Martha said with vigor, "is so busting proud of you and his family that it wouldn't matter to him what you wore."

"You think so?" Sarah asked anxiously.

"Oh, Sarah, Sarah!"

And they both laughed—sheepishly.

"Women are awful fools, I reckon," Sarah said. "Never seem to outgrow some of it."

"Aren't we, though?" Martha agreed, and, "No, we don't, I reckon."

The Overtons' house girl, Nellie, came in then with a jug of fresh buttermilk and a plate of ginger cake; and Sarah wished she could stay the day out, clear into tomorrow. Wished it more than ever. Nellie was a big brown girl, whose first aim was to take care of Martha, her mistress; and she did so ably. She smelled pleasantly of strong soapsuds and wood smoke and, just a mite, of Ethiopia.

"You all ain' been aroun' to see us in a long time," she said reproachfully to Sarah, feeling privileged to add her welcome.

"You haven't been on our side of the river in just as long," Sarah answered. "Hannah was saying so just the other day, wondering if you weren't about ready to make soap again. She hoped you were, because she's about out."

"I'd like to do that," Nellie said shyly; and shyness looked funny, but respectful, on a woman her size. "Maybe someday, when I kin be spared, I'll manage a ride ovah the river. Chillun growin' fine, Miss Sarah. Look good."

"Yes," Sarah agreed, "but don't let them be a bother. Right now, if you can pick out my youngest among them all, you might fetch him to me. It won't take the men long to load those oats. When Mr. Cockrell is ready to start for home, we don't want to keep him waiting. No, Martha. I'll leave the others, but not the baby. He still needs too much care. Probably needs some now."

"You ain' stayin'?" Nellie mourned.

"Not this time, Nellie. Not today."

"Sarah," Martha Overton accused, when Nellie had gone off in flattering dejection, "you've got something on your mind."

"I've got everything on my mind," Sarah said crisply. "Haven't you?"

Not for anything would she tell her best friend what worried her most. She was sorry now that she had mentioned fear to Alec. It would not stop him from anything he thought he had to do. Nor would it save her from any consequence. It only made her seem smaller—to herself, and, possibly, to him.

"I suppose I have," Martha admitted in response to Sarah's question, then changed the talk to other matters.

Out at the barn, while a couple of his hands loaded the Cockrell wagon and fed and watered the mules, Perry Overton dispensed a hospitality more immediately inspiring than buttermilk; and Alec Cockrell sighed appreciatively, then frowned at his tin cup.

"I've got a thirst on me today," he said, "that I'm going to have to watch out for."

"Dusty," Overton suggested. "We're spoiling for rain. Alick, you've got a fine family."

"Yep," Alec agreed. "When it comes to that, so have you."

"Yep. Good thing, a family, don't you think? Keeps a man hustling, but it keeps him sober, too—mostly. A worry sometimes, though. You ever feel that way?"

"Sometimes," Alec said. "The young'uns all being helpless and uncertain as yearling calves. Man gets to wondering. Say something should happen to him before they get their growth. Who will keep a hand on them then?"

"The woman that mothered them, I reckon. Rough on her, maybe, and some on the young'uns, too; but yours, at least, are well provided for. So are mine."

"More to it," Alec said, "than just having enough to eat."

Perry Overton studied him, sitting there with the empty cup in his hand.

"I'm stoppering this jug right now," he said finally, "if it turns you melancholy. Look. If anything happens that you're not around to look after your young'uns, I'll stand by them—and you can do the same by mine."

Later, when the Cockrell wagon, loaded to the rim, was a mere creaking, diminishing finally to an echo, down the wooded slope, when Perry Overton was washing up for dinner and Nellie was rounding up the children, to take their turn after him at the washbench and the towel, Martha Overton wrinkled her round, pleasant face into as near an anxious look as she could manage and pestered some.

"Sarah Horton," she said, coming at her husband sideways, "don't look one day older than when she married Alec Cockrell. So, maybe, she made a better choice than anybody gave her credit for. But I wonder. Is anything wrong over in town?"

"No," Overton sputtered through dripping hands, groping for the towel. "Not that I know of."

"Is Alec drinking again?"

"No. We had a little taste of something while the wagon was loading. Call that drinking?"

"No. You know what I mean. He used to—something awful."

"Not regular. Just when he was feeling low or, maybe, too good about something. Got roaring drunk the day he first saw Sarah and she slammed a door in his face. Did the same the night after she gave him her promise. He told me about both times a while back. He's an odd customer, I'll grant you—all up or all down—but what's it to you or me? If Sarah can stand it, you should be able to."

"I was thinking of Sarah," Martha said virtuously.

"Well, don't," Overton advised. "I mean, don't fret over her. Whatever comes, she'll be equal to it. If Alec Cockrell should die today . . ." He took his face out of the towel in time to catch his wife's expression: half, "I told you so!" and half, "Oh, dear!"

"Now, what did I say?" he demanded. But he knew. The truth was that he was as anxious about Alec Cockrell as any other of Alec's friends, and the truth had come through.

"Poor Sarah!" Martha sighed.

"Poor nothing!" her husband said. "Dinner ready? I'm hungry."

chapter twelve

Still, watch must be kept.

SHORTLY BEFORE NOON, a man of sober costume, black, well-cut, of the best broadcloth, of definite elegance but recognizable as Texan because of the trousers tucked into Wellington boots and the broad-brimmed felt hat, rode across the Cockrell bridge and stopped on the east side to pay his toll and to size up his surroundings. Which gave Barry Derritt ample time to take his measure, too. He was a man on the down slope of middle age, with graying hair, mild brown eyes, a round and genial-seeming face; but he was no softy. Forward on his saddle was the usual coil of rope and behind him the roll of blanket. The rope ended in a cavalry picket pin.

"So, I knew he lived here," Barry reported later. "Here" being all the breadth of Texas.

"This, I take it," the stranger said, looking up the rutted rise of Commerce Street, "is the city of Dallas."

Barry rushed to the town's defense.

"Yassah. Can't see much from down here."

"I can hear—plenty." The mild brown eyes twinkled.

"Yassah." Barry risked a smile. "Boss been away a few days and work kinda slackened off. Hummin' now, though. Boss's home again."

"Boss? May I know the name?"

"Mr. Cockrell, sah. He's the main boss 'round here."

"Alexander Cockrell? I've heard of him."

"Yassah. He's right well known in this part of Texas."

"He is known in my part, too. Austin at present."

Barry claimed he should have guessed it. Lawmaker. That's exactly what the man looked like.

The stranger was now looking back and down at the Trinity River.

"That the stream they claim they can make navigable to the ocean?" he wanted to know.

The sluggish little stream seemed to shrink as he looked at it.

"Mr. Cockrell never did think so," Barry said quickly.

"Then I am on the side of Mr. Cockrell," the stranger agreed.

But Barry couldn't let the river be scorned entirely.

"It's low right now," he defended, "but it riz considerable a coupla weeks back—when it rained."

"I can see," the stranger said. "Got to the bridge, didn't it?"

Now, between the bridge and the Trinity River, Barry was in a dilemma of loyalties.

"Touched the floorboards," he admitted finally. "Didn't do any harm. It don't usually rise much higher, and it goes down fast. On the other hand, like Mr. Cockrell says, high or low, it's too deep to wade. Still—" honesty triumphed—"it won't ever take a big boat, and that's a fact. I know, because I used to run the ferry before Mr. Cockrell built the bridge."

"You work for Mr. Cockrell, I take it."

"I belong to Mr. Cockrell—and Miss Sarah."

The dignity of the answer made the good-humored face of the stranger soften even more.

"Fine!" he said heartily. "Then, perhaps you will direct me to their place of residence. I've come quite a way to speak to Mr. Cockrell. On a matter of business."

"Yassah. That's their house yonder." He pointed to the clapboard cottage. "But they ain't either one at home right now. They're not far. Just went over to the West Side a little piece. Mr. Cockrell said he'd be back by noontime, so it won't be much after that. Miss Sarah's sister, Miss Polly, is home. You'd be welcome to rest in the house if you want."

"Thank you. I think, rather than disturb Miss Polly, I'll go on up into town. There's another man I want to see—a lawyer. McCoy? Know where I can find him?"

"Judge McCoy? Yassah. He's on Jefferson Street, just beyond the square."

"The square?" Never had a townsite given less promise of this dignity.

"Yassah. Do you see that building they're working on—up this same street? Just can make out a piece of it."

"I see it. Been wondering about it. Quite a structure."

"Yassah. That's Mr. Cockrell's hotel. He's building it."

"Oh? Yes, I've heard about that, too. Fact is . . ." he did not finish.

"Yassah," Barry said, affecting not to notice the omission. "Well, this road you are on is Commerce Street. You stay on Commerce past the new hotel. It's on the corner of Broadway and Commerce. The next street that comes across is Houston. Then comes the square, then Jefferson. Lawyer's Row is on Jefferson, looking across the street at the back door of the court-house. Judge McCoy's got his name on a sign out front."

"Well, thank you," the stranger said heartily, studied the matter of showing his gratitude, then said thank you again. "You have been very helpful. Now I have one more favor to ask. Will you tell your . . . Mr. Cockrell that I am in town and am most anxious to see him? I will wait at Judge McCoy's office."

"Yassah?" So far the stranger was nameless.

"Darnell, tell him. Nicholas Darnell. Wait, I'll leave a card with you."

Barry Derritt in his obscure past had learned to read. The card said, "The Honorable Nicholas Darnell, Esquire. Speaker, House of Representatives, Austin, Texas."

"Yassah." Barry in his turn studied the niceties of comparative rank and station. "Yassah, Colonel!"

"That's right," Darnell said. "How . . ." before he could complete his question, a shotgun went off close enough for the noise to obliterate temporarily all other sound. "What was that?"

"Just a harmless old Indian shooting crows," Barry said.

Darnell's round face squared into something harder.

"There's no such thing as a harmless Indian. I know."

"Cherokee," Barry began.

"Cherokee is what I mean. As treacherous as any."

So, it was fighting the Cherokee where Mr. Darnell had risen to the rank of Colonel, and was prouder now of that than all else that had come to him. Fighting did that to folks. 'Way back yonder it must have been, when Texas was a republic all to itself.

"Farming Indian," Barry said softly, "from the Indian Nation. Mr. Cockrell lived with him long time ago when he was a boy and didn't have no other home."

"Oh," Darnell said, a little mollified. "Like old Sam Houston."

"Yassah. I reckon. Pretty much like General Houston, yassah. So now, every year in the springtime, this Cherokee—calls himself Charley John—comes down to pay Mr. Cockrell a visit. Spends most of his time shooting crows—he's got a powerful hate on blackbirds—then goes back north again. Everybody round here knows him. They don't mind how many crows he shoots."

"No. I suppose not. Well, I'll be off. Don't forget to tell Mr. Cockrell I'm waiting for him uptown."

"I won't." All the time Barry knew this man was not fooling around just to talk to him. He was looking things over, studying everything he saw—the bridge, the house, what he could see and hear of the town. "If you like to put up your horse, maybe, there's a blacksmith shop just up the street, very next block after the Cockrell house and on the same side of the street, before you come to the hotel. Henry works for Mr. Cockrell, too. He'll give the horse a feed and rubdown, too, if you say so."

"Thanks. I may stop there. If I don't have too far to go on foot afterwards. Not much on walking—when it's warm. Well, thank you again. . . ."

"Barry," the Negro supplied. "Barry Derritt's the name, sah."

"Thank you, Barry," Darnell said again, resisted an impulse to touch his hat, and rode on up the rise of Commerce Street, Dallas, Texas; the day, the third of April; the year, 1858.

A quarter of an hour later, when the dinner bell at the Crutch-field House and the steam whistle at the mill had signaled the noon hour, bringing a hush devoted to eating and resting, the Cockrell wagon rattled over the wooden bridge; and Barry stepped out of the cool shade of his doorway to hand his master the legislator's card and deliver his message.

"Whoopee!" Cockrell jubilated. "Nicholas Darnell himself, eh? I've been hoping . . . Mrs. Cockrell, look at this." He handed the pasteboard to Sarah. "Read what it says," he said impatiently.

Sarah did so, studying the neat printing. Never, she thought, had she seen Alec Cockrell in higher spirits. All the way home it had been like that. Singing—that old dance tune: "Dinah's got a meatskin laid away . . ." Winking at her, beating his foot on the floor of the wagon. It made no difference to the mules how much noise he made, so long as he made it. So long as she and little Alec did not screech out. Well, they hadn't. Little Alec was fascinated by the entertainment. He bounced in her arms when she held him. He rolled his eyes at her, grinned; and, when she put him on the wagon seat, to rest herself, he concentrated his attention on the beating foot in its now dusty boot. Maybe some day this was a thing he would remember out of the haze of childhood. Funny what would stick in a person's mind. Of course, he was full young. . . .

"You know who Darnell is," Alec crowed, "but you don't know what he's here for."

"Do you?" she asked.

"I do. Think I do. Tell you later. Right or wrong, I'll tell you at suppertime."

He wouldn't stop for dinner at the house. He had to catch up with that man and right away. Had to rid himself of that damned wagonload of oats—where was George hiding, did she suppose?— and get uptown. Sarah couldn't hold him.

"Polly will be so disappointed," she said. "That's why she wouldn't go with us. She's probably spent the time whipping up spoon bread."

"Tell her I couldn't wait."

Fact was, he couldn't abide spoon bread. He had tried to explain that to Sarah. A man got his growth eating cornpone and fat back and then couldn't tolerate light vittles. He'd get a bite of something uptown, he promised.

"You won't stop," Sarah said. "You never do when you're excited." She wanted to add, "You're lightheaded now," but did not. "You don't eat enough," she told him, "to put meat on your bones."

He laughed at her earnestness. If she only knew it, he was lightheaded and aware of it, but thought he had good reason.

"You favor solid men?" he inquired, and named her several.

"No!" She was surprised herself at her emphasis. "I can't abide folks who fill up a room before they step over the doorsill."

He laughed some more; and then abruptly a change came over him. He stepped forward, reached out his hands and put them to either side of her face, pushing back her bonnet.

"Sobersides," he said, looking deep into her eyes. "Sobersides, but mighty sweet." She wondered that she didn't sag to the ground. When he took a notion to talk like that, it always turned her faint. If he touched her in the bargain, she had no more body than a cornshuck doll. "Mighty, mighty sweet," he said again. "I'll snatch a bite of something at the Crutchfield House. Maybe. See you later."

He kissed her on the mouth—hard—let her go, and, laughing again, ran for the wagon. Reaching it, he thought of something else, snapped his fingers impatiently and turned back.

"Forgot about Charley John. Take care of him, but don't send him after me. Better if he stays down here. See you all this evening."

Evening being anywhere from two o'clock on. Sarah raised her hand in a helpless gesture of good-bye.

chapter thirteen

The evil ones still hover...

MOUNTING TO THE WAGON SEAT, Alec cast a practised eye over the sky in all directions. He was looking for a thundercloud. The air felt that way to him—not just hot, but sort of heavy. Mules thought so, too. They had no wish to pull that wagon one foot farther; and, if they had only known it, he would be as glad now to be rid of it as they could be. Other and bigger things waited on him. He might have known— But, well, here was the wagon. He'd have to take it at least as far as the blacksmith's yard.

"Hup!" he said to the mules.

The big off mule raised his head with deliberation. The near one's ears twitched. Might have balked, but the big off mule knew better.

"Hup!" The wheels creaked. The wagon rolled.

Two minutes later Alec turned it into the blacksmith's yard and bawled for Henry, who came finally from somewhere behind his forge. He came, wiping something off his face with a piece of rag. It couldn't have been soot. Soot would not have showed.

"Did I wake you up?" Alec asked. "What's the matter around here? Whole town gone to sleep again?"

"Reckon I did drop off," Henry said sheepishly. Black as soot, powerful as a gorilla and as trustworthy as that big off mule. "Gemmun stopped by a lil bit ago, lef' his hoss fo' a feed an' a rubdown. Give me a dollah right then, so I went to wuk on de hoss. Nice an' shady behind the shop. I must a-drop off."

"Sure did," Alec agreed. "Where's George, do you know?"

"Ain' he come home yit?" Henry asked, surprised. "Missus set

157

him a job yestiddy, fixin' somethin' down at de mill house." This was a boarding house the Cockrells maintained for the transients who worked for them. "He went back to finish it this mawnin' whilst you all was over de river. Reckon he's ketchin' his dinnah down yondah."

"Shouldn't wonder," Alec said. "What about Toomy? Seen him?"

"He was at de hotel mos' o' de mawnin'," the smith said. "Truein' up co'ners fo' de bricklayers. Ain' seen him right lately."

"Did he get this wagon here or bring it from the mill this morning?"

"Brought it wid him, boss. Ain' mine."

"Then he's wanting feed down at the mill. You got anybody around can drive these mules? I've got people to see in town."

"Yassah, I know. Dat gemmun say he here on business. I . . ." Henry smiled suddenly, like the sun coming up. He was awake fully now. "I take de wagon to de mill myself. Jes lemme call de boy I got watchin' my fiah." With that he cupped his hands around his mouth and let go a bellow that Alec could not have equaled. "Joab! You Jo-ab!" There was no answer. He turned his trumpet to the other three points of the compass. "Jo-ab!" Still no answer, and no Joab. "I know wha' he is. Down at de river, watchin' dat Injun man shoot crows. Jes befo' dat gemmun come wid he hoss, we heared de gun go off; and whilst my back was turned, dat o'nery Joab must a lit out. Nummine. I'll skeer up somebody. You jes leave dat wagon."

"Going to do just that," Alec said. "You find Toomy somewhere."

"I'll fin' him ef I kin."

"You plain find him. No 'if' about it. Good-bye, mules. I'm gone."

It was not to be supposed, however, that, with his hotel directly in his path, he would make a beeline for Judge McCoy's office. From the smith's yard he could see the progress made that morning by his chanting bricklayers. Only went to show what steady work would do. The courses of brick were now climbing up the second story window frames, with Will Toomy's corners rearing up like peaks to guide them and pull them on. The building

looked so good from the outside that he was possessed now by a
desire to view the inside. With that in mind, he crossed Commerce Street and the intersecting dirt road named Broadway and
ceremoniously entered the hotel by way of the main door.

Once there, however, he stopped, checked by the rubble of
boards and lime and sand and brick dust and scrap that covered
everything. Even he could hardly make splendor out of that.
Worse than that, where the rising walls provided shade, every man
on the working crew had found a board his own length and laid
it down for a *lit d'repos*, as they called it eastward in Louisiana.
Alec had no idea how the name was shaped or spelled, but he
could think of no other term now for these makeshift beds. God,
they were a tattered, dusty, slovenly lot, his bricklayers! White,
brown and ebony. Some had chunks of lumber for pillows, some
did without. Their vocalizing was everything from a sighing purr
to bugling. He was tempted to kick the shin nearest him, raised
his foot to do so, and put it down without disturbing the weary
sleeper. Hell and damn! It was a hot day, the first of the summer. If he had been a shirt-tail bum still, he'd have hunted out a
plank for himself and joined them. He would tell Toomy—when
he saw him—to keep them at their work, if he could, until they
reached the level of the neat corners, then turn them free for
over Sunday—with maybe an extra half-measure of whiskey.

He turned his back on the sleeping men and walked away, his
footsteps brisk and rapid against the rough floor—or lack of it—
then slowing, then once more stopping altogether as he stepped
through a skeleton partition. He was now in his grand ballroom.
Dismay hit him hard in the chest—as if half a wall had fallen in
on him. Goda'mighty, there was a lot of work to be done here
before anybody else saw what he pretended he could. A man
said, I'll build this or that. And it went fast in the planning but
crawled in the making. Life was never long enough. It couldn't
be. He looked up through a lattice of beams and a twisted grin
creased his flushed face. Hell and damn! Away, he could think
of chandeliers and pianos and bars with mirrors better than on the
spot. A man had to close his eyes even to remember.

He did so; and, to his amazement, here in this empty shell his
dream came back whole. The brightness of the sun was the glit-

ter of a hundred candles caught in the glasswork of his chandelier. More candles shone from brackets along the walls. Candles?
No. Lamps. Real lamps, coal oil or camphine. They could be
just as pretty, and they gave more light. The discordant sounds
behind him became the music of strings, the twitter of light talk,
the swish of slippered feet and gauzy skirts. A hundred times he
had pictured the ball that would celebrate the opening of the
hotel. Maybe the Governor would come, maybe old General
Houston himself, if he lived that long. And now there was another. The Honorable Nicholas Darnell—wake up, Alec Cockrell.
The Honorable is waiting uptown right now.

By the time Alec reached the corner of the square, all that remained of dreaming was a chandelier and a piano, which were
realities and now a problem. So, he crossed Commerce again
and Houston Street to the Hirsch and Shirek store, having in
mind storage room in the merchants' warehouse. Hyman Hirsch
met him at the door. He was a German Jew, more German than
Jew in appearance, well-fed, sleek in his store clothes, showing
only in the apprehensive watchfulness of his eyes and an exaggerated desire to please the mark of age-old difficulties and perse-
cutions and the way that had evolved for survival.

Abe Shirek, he said, was out to his dinner; and what could they
do for Mr. Cockrell? Room in the warehouse? Why, certainly.
Even if they had to push some of their things tighter into corners
or stack a few boxes. Could Mr. Cockrell say how much space he
needed? Time? Time did not matter.

"Does to me," Alec said with sharp impatience.

Ah, so? Well, naturally. It was only a manner of speaking.
Could Mr. Cockrell say . . . a chandelier? And a piano? For the
hotel? Well, to be sure. The finest was not too good for that;
and, if an opportunity had presented itself to buy what was
wanted, Mr. Cockrell had shown his usual wisdom in seizing it.

"The warehouse is yours, Mr. Cockrell."

"You pay rent for it."

Ah, the rent. Now, Hyman Hirsch would not go so far as to
say that the rent was nothing. Some months, with their small and
unstable profits, and people on their books, too, who were slow to
pay, twenty-five dollars was a lot of money and hard for him and

his partner to get together. Still, they counted themselves fortunate to have so fine a store.

"Nothing wonderful," Alec said, but referred chiefly to the contents, not having to look far to go from bolts of calico through shoes and overcoats to rakes and hoes and milk pails. "Someday I'll build you a real store—when I get a few other plans going."

"But for the present," Hirsch suggested, with a gentle smile, "this is very fine, considering the size of the town, and all."

"Town won't stay this size, either," Alec told him.

Afterward Hyman Hirsch remembered the two promises and how Alec looked when he made them, his face lighted up with pride and confidence and, at the same time, drawn, intense, with wanting.

Out on the street, Alec looked again at the brazen emptiness of the noon sky. It ain't so all-fired hot, he thought, as I've got too many clothes on. In honor of the Honorable Nicholas Darnell, he had even put back his coat. A shirt, a vest, a coat—at least two of them were too many. But he needed the vest to carry his watch and chain. And, once you went that far, you might as well go a step farther, and be pure miserable.

Once more he crossed Commerce Street, walked eastward along the square, and crossed Jefferson. Ahead of him now on Commerce was the Marshal's holdout—the jailhouse. The thought of it pricked him, but amusingly. Years back, he would have taken another minute to walk up there and see if the Marshal was at home. If a fight had followed, why, so much the better. Get it over and done with. He hesitated, then turned north on Jefferson. He had other matters to settle first.

John McCoy's office in Lawyers' Row was a refuge from the dust and glare outside. What we need here, Alec thought, as he laid hold of the door latch, is a shed roof over the sidewalk— only, there's no sidewalk. Then, as he stepped inside, he thought the place was deserted until, as his eyes adjusted themselves to the comparative dimness, he made out a man, tall and a stranger, who stood up from a table at the rear of the room.

"Would you possibly be Mr. Cockrell?"

Pleasant spoken. Gentleman's breed. Not Nicholas Darnell. Too young. Tried to hide how young he was. Had let his beard grow, and it was a real one. Full, black, it reached clear to his vest. Hair thick, wavy, and, of course, also black. Hair and beard met near his ears, so that all of his face that showed was his eyes, a stretch of forehead, his nose and cheekbones. Forehead had no wrinkles. Eyes were young. Much too young for the beard or, it might be, Texas. But not afraid. At least, not so it showed.

"That's who I am," Alec told him, and thought, Who the hell are you? but said only, "Where's McCoy? Do you know?"

"Yes, sir. I was to tell you. He and Mr. Darnell of Austin have stepped over to the Crutchfield House for a bite to eat. They would like for you to join them there, if that is your pleasure. Or, would you prefer to wait here? They will return after dinner."

Said it all in one stretch, smooth and easy. Educated feller. But young. Distressfully young, somehow.

"I'll follow them in a minute," Alec said. "Soon as I catch my breath." He let the comfort of indoors take hold. "Done more walking the last half hour than in a month before this," he said roughly, not knowing why he bothered to explain. "Mostly a man rides a horse hereabouts."

"Yes, sir. Would you like to lay aside your coat?"

He would like, but he wouldn't do it. The respect the young man showed him put him beyond the reach of a little discomfort.

"I can just bear it in here," he said wryly. "Notice you are wearing a coat."

"Yes, sir, but I have been sitting quiet most of the morning. May I, then, for the Judge, offer you some refreshment?"

The fragrance of McCoy's Monongahela hung on the still air.

"Surely may," Alec said. "Join me?"

Now why, he wondered, am I fooling around like this? But, maybe, he wasn't fooling. You met a person for the first time and how did you know what it might come to? Without scouting a bit? That was how he'd got on to Will Toomy. And there were others. Some misfortunate encounters, too, he reflected.

The young man bowed and went for glasses and the whiskey. Glasses marked McCoy's social elevation—two notches above the best tinware and four above a gourd. The glasses were clean. The young man, Alec knew, had washed them. He poured Alec a generous measure, himself a small one.

"Your good health, sir, if I may presume."

"Same!" Alec raised his glass, and drank. The young man tasted his. Gentleman through and through. Mannerly. Restrained. Hell and . . .

"You're new here," Alec said, again roughly.

"Yes, sir. I arrived only yesterday. I count myself fortunate that I find myself well placed so soon."

Plainly he was not fortunate generally. His decent black clothes hadn't been made for him. He wasn't old enough to have worn the green shine on them. Besides, now that he moved around, they didn't fit too close. Must have been cut to the measure of his father or some older man who had built out breadth to fill the shoulders of the coat. He saw Alec studying him. That, rather than one mouthful of whiskey, brought color to his cheekbones.

"I hope to prove of some use to the Judge," he said. "I have read law in North Carolina, where my home was originally, also in Kentucky."

Some law, maybe. Surely not all of it.

"Couldn't have hitched on to a better man than McCoy," Alec assured him. "And he wouldn't have taken you in if he couldn't use you. He's a smart man all the way around, you'll discover. How did you come to choose Dallas for a stopping place?"

The flush on the young man's cheeks deepened.

"I didn't," he confessed. "I . . . we were on our way elsewhere, but had a small misfortune on the road. Our horse went lame. That slowed us—some. Just short of your bridge, a buggy wheel gave way and my wife fainted."

Wife. Hell! Hardly old enough to shuck corn on his own, and he had a wife. Restrained? What chance had he to be anything else? While the young man talked in his pleasant, mannerly way, Alec was trying to remember. It seemed to him he had heard a piece of this before.

"Honey—my wife, sir—is not very strong at present."

He had it! The young lawyer with the busted buggy, and the ailing wife.

"Mrs. Cockrell told me about you," he said. "Said she gave you a hand."

"Mrs. Cockrell," the young man said devoutly, "was an angel, sir. There was this house—your home. I had to find shelter, and she took us right in. She put Honey—my wife—to rest on her own bed. She told me where to go with our lame horse and the crippled buggy, and suggested I take a little time to look around the town. That was how I happened on this office. I read the sign and turned in; and Mr. McCoy, fortunately, was present. He, too, was kind. He said he'd been keeping his eye open for a young man—well, like me, sir. So, here I am; but if it had not been for Mrs. Cockrell . . ."

"Shucks!" Alec said. "You'd have lit somewheres. Mrs. Cockrell said she found a house for you."

"She did, indeed. On Lamar Street, east of here. Most convenient. I . . . I could not put down much for rent."

Alec grinned. As good a risk as Mr. Gonant, the picture-taker, Sarah had said. Well, just about.

"What did you do for furniture?" He could see Sarah flying about.

"Mrs. Cockrell supplied us with bedding and a few staples."

"Crockery?" Alec suggested.

The flush on the young man's face deepened.

"The necessaries, sir."

"How's your wife now?"

"She is . . . some better, sir."

"She satisfied with the house?"

A good house, small, but stoutly built.

"She is . . . thankful, sir. Everyone has been most kind to us—strangers."

The hesitation, followed by polite insistence on the kindness of others, meant he was having trouble still. His wife was not thankful. She was ailing, full of fret. He was apologizing for her and for himself, being so poor and shabby-clothed. He was, maybe, not as young as he had seemed at first. Might be he was almost as old as Alec Cockrell had been when he first rode into Dallas. That was young enough—and poor enough. The man reminded Cockrell of himself that way. Could be that Sarah had felt the same.

Now, hell and damn! He set down his whiskey glass, and took his leave.

It took the half round of the courthouse square, back to Houston and Main, to bring him out of his boil. Crossing Main Street to the Crutchfield House, he stumbled and all but fell into the creek that ran down one side of the thoroughfare—and mighty convenient the ditch was, except in a freshet. You old fool, he thought, drawing back and making ready to step over properly. That proper young man is no more like that shirt-tail bum you were than you are like a moolie cow. Sarah Horton would have to draw on more imagination than she's got to picture things that way. Is that what you're mad about? Could be.

No, but still the young man reminded him of someone. Someone he knew or had heard about. Safely across the ditch now, and most of the road, he had it. A young half-brother he had left behind in Missouri. A troublesome toddler then, he had grown to manhood since and was, by all accounts, quite a person. After considerable schooling, he, too, had read law and was a practising lawyer now in a town called Warrensburg. Warrensburg, Missouri. At the time of her wedding with Alec Cockrell, Sarah had insisted on writing the news back to Missouri; and this brother had replied for the family. Claimed he could remember Alec— dimly. Since then, he wrote every once in a while, giving the family news, wishing the Texas branch well, and wanting to hear how they got on. If he could be of any service, please to command him. Same kind of mannerliness—that was his likeness to this new young man in Dallas, who had an odd name—Guess. George Guess. He would be now close to the same age as the Missouri half-brother, Francis Marion Cockrell. Both being lawyers and fancying themselves gentlemen, they would dress the same; only the one would be shabby and the other not. Sarah might have thought of the similarity. She had taken a great liking to Alec's younger brother. That was where their second youngest boy, Frank, got his name.

Francis Marion Cockrell. Alec could have been that kind of man, too. If he had stayed on in Missouri and taken his schooling, however bitter. Might have. Might not. Might be the Cherokee were right in believing that these things were all writ-

ten out for you when you were born, if you could only read the
signs. Shucks! Here he was in Dallas, Texas, and doing all right.
Just all right. Wouldn't trade with anybody anywhere.

He went into the dining room of the Crutchfield House, head
high, and stamping. Face a little redder than sometimes, but it
was a warm day. There was some scraping of chairs as he entered,
folks finishing their meal and going on about their business. A
dozen people hailed him, "Hi-ya, Alick!" Others bobbed their
heads or didn't, but all were aware of him, making his way to the
end of the long table, where Judge McCoy had staked out elbow-
room for himself and a stranger, who, from his appearance, could
be no less than what he was.

"Alick, how are you?"

The greeting was friendly, welcoming, but watchful. John Mc-
Coy, the smartest lawyer in town—Cockrell would have no other
on his business—was just that—a lawyer, slow to commit himself
to a positive statement, liking to save a way of escape, if he needed
it. Added to that, in spite of a benevolent manner, he had
another sort of reserve. For all the years he had spent in the un-
developed West, helping to develop it—he had taken part in laying out Kansas City on the Missouri frontier before coming to
Texas—he was still a Down Easterner—shrewd, calculating, cool.
Pinned to the wall, Alec Cockrell could not have sworn he liked
the man with all his heart but he had meant every word of his
recommendation of John McCoy to young George Guess as a
lawyer.

"We were about to give you up," he said now to Cockrell.
"Where've you been? Never mind. Alick, I am sure you know the
name, Nicholas Darnell, our representative in the legislature at
Austin. Alick Cockrell, meet Nick Darnell. Mr. Darnell, Mr.
Cockrell."

Alec and the stranger shook hands, and the grip of the lawmaker was, Alec thought, the grip of a man. They measured each
other with their eyes and liked what they saw. After that, the dark
room with its one long, now untidy table, with its smell of cold
grease and chewing tobacco and man's sweat on a warm day did
not matter.

"Been wanting to get up this way for some time," Darnell said.

"Wanting to make your acquaintance. I've several matters . . ."

"One in particular," McCoy warned. "Watch yourself, Alick!"

One of Crutchfield's girls set a plate of meat and gravy before Cockrell, then a dish of cornbread and a syrup pitcher. Finally a cup of coffee that smelled like a brush fire, and he let it be. If it had all been ambrosia, he still would not have tasted it. The Honorable Nicholas Darnell, Speaker . . .

"I'm watching," Cockrell said to McCoy. "Also listening, Mr. Lawmaker."

"I stopped for a look at your hotel on the way up from the river," Darnell began. Unavoidably, perhaps, his eyes swept the table, which was hardly fair to Old Man Crutchfield, who did right well, considering all.

"Get on with it, Nick," McCoy prompted. "Alick here is liable to recall some business he didn't see to on the way up here and light out as suddenly as he came. In short, Alick . . ."

"You will allow me, sir," Darnell said softly, but firmly, "to proceed in my own fashion . . . I hope? I am sure you are aware, Cockrell, that you have here a very enterprising small city."

"Should be aware," McCoy persisted. "He's behind most of the enterprise."

This was beautiful talk—back and forth, quick as a whip, smooth, unstudied. A man could enjoy listening, but . . .

"We do all right," Alec said.

McCoy laughed.

"Tell him, Alick," he said, "how the population doubles every two years, going from thirty-five to sixty-five, from that to one hundred and fifty—men, women and children of both colors— and we've passed that now, thanks to the demise of La Réunion. You've heard of La Réunion, sir?"

"I have," Darnell said. "A great asset, I am sure, the acquisition of those good citizens of many skills. And so, Mr. Cockrell, to the point. Are you interested in connecting with a railroad?"

"Which one?" Alec said. What a day this had turned out to be! He, and others, had thought it might be a bad one. Couldn't be now—not all bad, surely.

McCoy laughed and called to Crutchfield's waitress.

"Set another glass," he said, "and take these other dishes away. Mr. Cockrell is not hungry."

He wasn't, either. And yet, not lightheaded. Not now. His head had never been clearer or steadier, his wits never sharper.

"I've had some dealings with the Southern Pacific and Western," he explained.

"Still at the stage of survey," Darnell said, not exactly contemptuously; but that, plainly, was not his railroad.

"Yep," Alec granted. "Setting poles and drawing a bead on them, then pulling up poles and line and setting it all somewhere else. Got it surveyed now as far as the military establishment at Fort Worth, west of here."

"Passing through Dallas?" Darnell asked sharply.

"No. Who wants a railroad laying tracks right through a townsite?"

"All you want, of course, is connection," Darnell agreed, not too positively.

"That's all," Alec agreed.

It helped, too, to own the land that the railroad might want to use. Watching the advancing survey, he had seen to it that he did. Now in Sarah's trunk were papers giving the Southern Pacific right of way through land near his millsite east of the Trinity, and a record of sale of three hundred or so acres on Mountain Creek. Not from Whitehouse Ranch. This side, nearer Dallas.

McCoy sighed and pushed a filled glass toward him. Alec flicked a look at him, no more. McCoy was sitting in on this game, but the stranger was dealing.

"Own a few shares of the Galveston and Red River," Alec said carelessly.

"Do you, indeed?" Darnell seemed surprised.

"First railroad to run in Texas," Alec said. "First one to get anywhere."

As far as Houston, even a little beyond.

"From Houston," Darnell said, "we call it the Houston and Texas Central."

"You don't say?" As if he, Alec, didn't know. Wake Latimer, who found news where there was any, kept him informed. Particularly about railroads, which they both believed in.

"Progress is still slow," Darnell allowed.

Thirty miles out of Houston was slow, real slow. The stage line north from Dallas to the Red River still seemed a profitable undertaking—for years to come.

"What we need," Darnell said, "is the push of a man like you behind the undertaking. Could I interest you, sir, in the purchase of some shares in the Houston and Texas Central?"

"Yep." Alec sampled his whiskey. Kentucky. Very good. "Always interested. I might make a deal with you. Own quite a bit of land on the west side of the Trinity."

"Owns most of it," McCoy put in.

"A stretch," Alec admitted, and could hear how he sounded—steady and sure. "Bought it for timber. I could trade you an option—after I get the timber—outright sale in prospect or just the right of way, in return for shares in the railroad."

He waited for an answer. None came immediately. Darnell frowned at his glass. McCoy laughed.

"And I collect my bets now," he said gleefully. "I told you, Nick. I told you he'd sell you more than you sold him. I knew it, knew it, knew it."

Darnell looked up from his whiskey and his eyes were full of light.

"I am still interested in your proposition, sir. I want to hear more."

So they adjourned the meeting to McCoy's office. Coming out of the Crutchfield House, Alec thought again of his promising young Missouri half-brother, but now with a distant condescension. Boy was probably doing all right, but did he deal with high-ranking members of the state's legislature? Did he own shares in Missouri's railroads? Hardly . . . not just yet.

They crossed Main Street and its little creek, Darnell remarking only that the town should be well supplied with water. Were there springs about? All around, both McCoy and Alec informed him. A fine spring at the foot of Elm Street, the next street north from Main, had been the main reason for pitching camp once upon a time on what came to be the townsite, the man camping being the first to see the advantages of the location.

The dinner hour being over, people moved again or gathered in knots on the streets surrounding the square. On Houston, near Main, Andrew Moore leaned carelessly against the rail fence. In full armor, he made quite a picture.

"Who's that, for the Lord's sake?" Darnell asked.

"Town Marshal," McCoy said shortly.

"Is he afraid of trouble or does he want some?"

And that, Alec thought, about sized up Andy Moore truthfully, then put him out of his mind. Easily, other and larger matters crowding the space more agreeably.

They finished up the railroad business in McCoy's office, as well as business could be finished that looked far ahead at what was coming instead of what was right now; and, while young Mr. Guess set their agreement down on paper, they drank a toast to Texas, each saying in his own fashion what Texas meant to him.

Their second toast was to the city of Dallas and McCoy made that speech.

"The second such metropolis, which I have been privileged to help shape. Both, I can safely say, I think, are now going concerns."

"If Kansas City, Missouri, has the prospects of Dallas, Texas," Darnell agreed, "you are right, sir. I see only the fairest future. I see . . ." he paused, not for lack of words. "If I were not firmly implanted in another part of this imperial state, I should move— I may, anyhow. I have a son just coming to manhood, bears my name. I want him to see your city, gentlemen. Cockrell, I want him to see the hotel you are building. His youth would take fire . . ."

So, they drank a toast to the new hotel on the other side of the square.

"A noble hostelry," Darnell pronounced it—Sarah should have heard him. "Fit to welcome visitors to this thriving city. May it become known far and wide for its hospitality, its comfort, its elegance!"

Hell and damn, Alec thought, that was speechmaking by a master.

And then the papers were ready—three of them—one for the Cockrell trunk, one for McCoy's safe and one for Nicholas Darnell to carry back south with him. Mr. Guess read out what the papers said. A power of words, to make the transaction lawful, stating that, in consideration of an option granted to the Houston and Texas Central Railway, either for outright purchase of the land or the purchase or lease of a right of way through lands— and so forth and so on and so forth. Everything clear and precise and complete. Young Guess had copied from McCoy's records township and section and description of the land in question. Wait till Sarah sees this paper, Alec thought. He had a clear picture of her studying it. Finally she would nod her approval, not just of what the paper said but of the young man who had set the words down.

"I knew he had character, Mr. Cockrell. I could tell."

And now it was time for him to set his mark at the foot of the page. He took the pen firmly in hand and made a broad X, Mc-Coy writing in his name. Either the office was still beyond ordinary as he did so, or the pen scratched loudly; but, when he looked up, young Guess was busy assembling more paper at his table in the rear and the Honorable Nicholas Darnell merely held out his hand gravely for the pen. Alec twisted his lips into a smile.

"No blot," he said to McCoy, calling to mind Sarah's teardrop.

John McCoy shook his head. He, too, remembered.

And that, except for a final stout drink to seal the contract, was all there was to the meeting. While it went on, a message had been sent to the blacksmith, asking him to saddle up Sinful and Darnell's horse and have them both at McCoy's office by two o'clock or thereabouts. Darnell was not staying overnight in Dallas. He wanted to be back in Lancaster, at least, that evening on his way home; and Alec had more to show him of the town before he left. While the papers were being signed, the shadow of the horses showed outside, Alec's George riding Sinful and the blacksmith's Joab on the other. Alec stepped out to speak to George.

"Go on home," he said. "Tell Mrs. Cockrell not to look for me before evening. I'm listening for sign of the wagons from now on. You might tell Henry that. Make yourself useful there or elsewhere, hear me."

He took Sinful as Darnell came out to take his horse from Joab, who, the next minute, went prancing down the road, closing his fist over a piece of silver money, Alec's George good-humoredly urging him on with the flat of his foot and the flat of his hands. Alec and Darnell mounted, laughing; and then . . .

"Our friend the Marshal—" Darnell said quietly, calling Alec's attention to Andrew Moore, now perched on the fence on the Jefferson Street side of the courthouse—"seems to have followed us."

Alec nodded. Except for Darnell's remark, he might not have noticed. Now that he had noticed, he felt impelled to wave an arm in offhand greeting, and received, as might have been expected, a scowl and a blink for response.

"Man doesn't like you," Darnell observed.

"No."

"Why?"

"Owes me money."

"And he hates you for that?"

There was no other reason. If there had been, it could hardly have penetrated Alec Cockrell's present frame of mind.

chapter **fourteen**

...*watching, waiting*...

ABOUT THE TIME when Alec Cockrell and Nicholas Darnell rode away from the square to look at brickyard, sawmill and other points of interest, Sarah Cockrell was ready to give up trying to reduce the bunch of papers before her to sense and order.

I don't know what ails me, she thought. I'm like a woman distracted, have been all day. I've handled harder business than this without getting myself tangled. It's all down here in writing, clear as can be. Goods bought and what we owe for it. All I have to do is enter it in the book and, when we send the drafts, mark it paid. Goods bought on consignment. Those made a separate entry, the sum paid out by Mr. Cockrell to be balanced against sums received in payment. No trouble about that. Wake Latimer, Hirsch and Shirek, the Peaks, Adam Haught—they never gave trouble or left a debt unpaid for long. Decent folk don't, unless calamity strikes.

Before actually adding any sums, she could see how it would all figure out. What Alec received from his friends on the square would cover any extravagance, even to paying off his wagon drivers. Somehow, without his doing any close figuring himself, it always worked out that way. He had a sense that told him, a sense sharper than book learning, which might to him have been even a hindrance, when to step forward and when to hold back. He just took one cool look at what he had in mind to do, then went ahead and did it.

A large sum invested in pine lumber. Pshaw! He had orders waiting for finishing wood that would earn him a handsome profit.

Other orders for lumber. Hardly anybody cut up his own trees now or trimmed his own logs. Folks were glad to bargain with Alec Cockrell to come on to their places and take down a stand of trees for them, just saying what they wanted in logs and boards and he could take the balance for pay. He could say on the spot what he could afford to let them claim and how much he must have for himself. Always turned a profit. As he would now on the pine lumber. Just get out the book and set everything down, Sarah Horton, and stop this foolishness.

She got out the book, but did not open it. A new book in clean board and canvas covers. A new book now for each year, and she didn't know but what she ought to have a separate book for each business. It would come to that some day. The hotel, the mill, the brickyard, property for rent, the bridge. What they paid out for church and charity. One of these days she'd make ready to set things up that way.

But not right now. What frets me, she thought, is that one paper I can't find. The scrap Alec had tossed on the table before he left the house to see what Charley John was shooting at—the first shot, the one that killed the crippled raven. A scrap of brown paper. She could see it as plain as anything. The record, Alec said, of that span of oxen he had bought at Black Jack. All paid for but it had to be figured with the cost of the haul. She was certain that she had put the paper with the others before she went out the back door, and then into the trunk before she called in the children; and now she couldn't find it. Mischievous the way it escaped her. Fretted her to pieces.

Pshaw! It must be in the trunk, had probably slipped down behind one of the other bundles. The trunk, carefully closed, rested on the floor beside her. She reached down to open it; and, as she did so, Charley John fired off his gun again. The first time since Hannah had called him back to the house for a bite of dinner.

"I think," Sarah said to her sister Polly, in sharp exasperation, "he's shooting at stumps now. If blackbirds have any sense at all, they are far from our trees by this time."

Polly Thompson sat with her sewing near the south window of the office, Sarah taking her light from the east window.

"Do you mind?" Sister Polly had asked before she placed her chair. "I've got the fidgets today." Polly, too? Must be something in the air. "Home alone most of the morning. After you'd left, I wished I had put on my bonnet and gone with you."

"It was hot driving over the prairie," Sarah had answered. "Summer trying to see what it's going to be able to do to us, I think. And we didn't stay long enough at the Overtons' to make the trip worth while."

She thought, I am glad you didn't go. Unworthily, I am glad. I hardly ever get a time alone with Alec Cockrell lately. Not enough time, surely. Then she was sorry to have such mean thoughts and spoke kindly to Polly.

"Come in here, if you want," she said. "Long as we don't get to chattering. I've a sight of bookkeeping to do."

And then she hadn't done the bookkeeping.

Poor Sister Polly! A widow woman, Sarah thought now, without chick or child, is the lonest person on earth. Lonelier than if she had lived and died an old maid. Sister Polly, clinging so to her pretties, and nobody to indulge her for doing so. Sewing herself now that sacque, silk, to wear to church on Sunday. A fashionable do-thing she copied from a picture. Looking with each new piece of finery more shrunken and frail . . .

Sister Polly, feeling Sarah's eyes on her, looked up from her sewing, blinked at the light, and blinked again.

"That Indian's an odd person," she said in her prim way, not meaning to sound affected. It came natural for her to speak that way. It was how she had practised speaking when she was young. "Comes for a visit and Brother Alec says howdy and he says howdy back. When he's ready to leave, it's good-bye the same way, and that's all until next year."

"Sometimes," Sarah said, "they chin together for an hour or so—come evening."

"Don't say much even then," Polly sniffed. "I listened once— to find out." She giggled.

"Now, that was a sneaking thing to do," Sarah said.

"Yes, wasn't it? But I had to know. Not that I got much satisfaction. When they had anything to say, they talked Cherokee. Mostly they just sat."

"Never mind," Sarah said. "Either way, they understood each other. Men are queer creatures."

"I know," Polly sighed, and stared out the window.

What did she know? Sarah thought, I never gave much notice to Brother Thompson. Never knew him, really. He died too soon. Were Polly's memories sweet or sour? Couldn't tell by looking at her. She seemed always just lonesome, kind of lost; but now she looked . . .

"Polly," Sarah asked in quick alarm, "what ails you? Is something wrong?"

"No, course not," Polly declared; but she rubbed her eyes, and, when she took her hands away, her eyes were red. She shook out the sacque she was sewing, and made a face at it. "Piece of foolishness," she said. "Like everything else I try to do."

"Why, Polly Thompson!"

"Look at that spoon bread. Messing around in Hannah's way all morning and she does despise to have me in her kitchen. I wanted to do something. I used to make spoon bread real good back in Virginia—and later, out here."

When she kept her own house, she meant.

"It was good today," Sarah comforted. "I know, Sister Polly. Nobody but us to eat it. I'm sorry about the children, but they do have good times at the Overton farm and they hadn't been visiting in a long while. As for Mr. Cockrell, with that Mr. Darnell in town, he wouldn't know what he was eating."

"He don't like spoon bread, anyhow," Polly said.

"No," Sarah granted. "He says himself that, when a man has lived rough all his days, his tastes set themselves to rough ways. We must excuse it."

"How come, then," Polly asked pertly, "he took a fancy to you? He never knew anybody like you in his rough days." She looked sadly out of the window—at nothing. "It must be wonderful," she sighed, "to have a man so set on you. It would make up—for everything else."

"What do you mean?" Sarah began, ready to claw her sister if she was working around to mention a fault in Alec Cockrell; but then her heart failed her. Maybe Polly was thinking of Brother Thompson, not Alec. Maybe she had never been any happier

as a wife than she was now, as a widow. "Sister," she said, "you've
sewed too long. You'll bring on one of your headaches if you don't
stop."

"I've already brought it," Polly told her. "I'm near blind with
it." She folded her sewing and got up, stiffly. "Think I'll go lie
down somewheres."

"Try the parlor sofa," Sarah suggested. "It ought to be cool in
there."

"The new sofa?" Polly tittered. "I'd feel like I was laid out.
Not that I'd mind," she finished, doleful again, "if my time had
come. But, since it hasn't, I'll thank you but take my proper bed."
At the door of the room, she turned back wistfully. "What are
you going to do now?"

Sarah told her about the missing paper. When she found it,
she said, she thought she would walk up to the Bryan house. She
hadn't been to see Margaret for some time.

"Why do you want to go now?" Polly asked.

Unwillingly Sarah mentioned the letter that had come. Unwillingly, because she was afraid Polly might want to go with her,
to hear the contents of the letter; but Polly only said, as Sarah
often did:

"Wouldn't you think he'd write to his own wife instead of
Brother Alec?"

"I wish he had done that," Sarah said.

"Well, I wish you a pleasant visit," Polly said now, "but you
won't have it. If you want to carry something with you, there's
the rest of that spoon bread. Of course, Margaret won't thank
you for it—you know that."

"I'll take it, anyhow," Sarah said. "How she feeds her family
nobody knows."

As a matter of fact, most people did know or guessed, though
Alec Cockrell would have been the last one to make public the
liberality of his guardianship. Margaret Bryan continued to live
in what she was sure was her own house and took each month
from John McCoy, who had been sworn to secrecy, what he said
was due her from her husband's properties, though Alec gave most
of it out of his own pocket. John Bryan could well say he depended on Alec to act for him.

It was all right for Margaret to pretend like that, but the airs she put on with Alec Cockrell in return for his kindness were wicked. She never called him anything but Alick in public or private, and never got done telling him—Sarah, too—what he looked like when he first drifted into town and how wild he was for some time after.

"Nobody thought you'd ever amount to a hill of beans," she declared, suggesting, somehow, that all might still not be as good as it looked, which was what those believed who grudged Alec what he had attained to.

Sometimes Sarah wanted to shake her; but, if she could go off and cool down, she could come around almost to proper forgiveness. Goodness knows, she thought, in her place I might act worse; and she felt then, thinking of Margaret, the way Alec felt about John Bryan, kind of guilty, as if her good fortune came from the other's misfortune.

Sure enough, when Margaret Bryan opened her door to Sarah that afternoon, and saw the covered dish in Sarah's hands, she looked for a minute as if she would close the door again and leave Sarah out on the step. She didn't like Sarah any too well, anyhow, Sarah being now what she could only pretend to be.

"It is good of you to take the trouble to come," she said, finally deciding to let Sarah in, "when you have so much to do. All Alick's business to attend to, over everything else. Mr. Bryan has said over and over that, without you, Alick would never even have made a start."

As if Mr. Bryan were just at the other end of the house, napping. She accepted the spoon bread charily.

"I made some sweet biscuit myself today," she said. "The children fancy them. Especially Coffee." Then, as if to justify such lavish fare, "Coffee is helping Uncle Jack Smith at his store now—Saturdays."

Coffee Bryan—nobody knew exactly why he was called so. Mr. Bryan must have known somebody somewhere by that name—back in Tennessee probably, where he had come from. Neither he nor Margaret would have called their child Coffee for a joke, though that was how it sounded. Coffee, the oldest of five Bryan

children, aged fourteen and not generally accounted of much promise; but at fourteen how could you be sure?

"I am glad," Sarah said. "Be sure you tell him that was how
Mr. Cockrell got his start. He did his first hauling for Smith
and Patterson."

"Don't I remember?" Margaret said, intimating that many of
her memories Sarah wouldn't care to share.

Sarah thought, she is younger than I am. She told me once,
before all this happened, that she was seventeen years old when
she married John Bryan. That was in 1843. I married Mr. Cockrell four years later and I was twenty-seven. She's half a dozen
years younger than I am. All that younger, and look at her. No
gray in her hair, but not a mite of shine in it, either, like brown ash.

She must have been a pretty girl, with big blue eyes and hair
curling like our Aurelia's. Wrinkles all around her eyes now and
her mouth pulled tight from all she's been through. She's had a
hard life from the beginning. Though she will have it that they
had plenty back yonder, never knew the meaning of want. Mr.
Bryan, she tells me every chance she gets, was an educated man,
knew his law, and was a good trader. Also a great hunter. They
had turkey and venison and partridge on their table, besides their
own pork they raised. Wild honey for sweetening. This house
now, which isn't even hers, is clean as a pin, though picked bare;
but back yonder, when there was nobody around to see, when
there were only two or three families in the whole town, when
home was a small, single room log cabin, they had everything—
so she says.

Back yonder, in that little old cabin, when life and the world
were new . . . My stars, Sarah thought, I near forgot what brings
me here. And she produced the letter.

"Well, thank you," Margaret said, her head a notch higher.
"When I saw Alick ride by this morning, I wondered if he
wouldn't have brought the mail with him. I've been looking,
rather, for a letter."

And she took it and put it away in a cupboard.

"I'll read it later," she said.

Then she proposed to Sarah that they have a taste of her sweet
biscuit and a cup of tea. Sarah thought, I don't want to drink her

tea but how can I say no? Oh, Margaret, Margaret, come down off your high horse and talk to me. You are the only woman I know who could help me now—you who claim to know my Alec better than I do because you knew him when he was still starving poor. You who have had a man and lost him—what is our great lack that we must always be stopped by a high fence when we would have them do what they won't—or the contrary?

"Unless you think it is too warm for tea," Margaret said.

It was now midafternoon, or past. Trees and houses threw some shade; but it was warmer than ever, with a queer feeling to the air. Walking up to the Bryan house, Sarah, too, had looked to the sky for a cloud, but saw none. A light breeze blew, but fitfully, stirring up dust devils on the road, then dying away. And everything would be calm as before, too calm.

"It is warm for early April," she agreed, not wanting the tea.

So, they tasted the sugar biscuit; and Sarah thought, there are four besides Coffee, one girl, younger than our 'Relia, and three boys, the least one the age of my Frank. She could feel them, rather than hear them, out in the passageway, watching her eat their food; but she finished her biscuit, then took a second, rather than offend Margaret. Later, when she had gone, Margaret might set the spoon bread before the children, saying, "Eat it up if you like. I don't crave any myself." But the lean stomachs of the young ones wouldn't be as proud as hers.

She and Margaret talked like anything but two women who had known each other for ten years and once had been friendly. It was as if they had only just met and neither was sure of the other. Across the way the Negro bricklayers, who had taken up their work slackly following the noon hour, worked now in a frenzy, as if they saw a mark they must reach if they wanted to be free of toil.

"It's curious," Sarah said, watching them through the window, "how one layer of brick makes a wall climb."

"I had no idea when Alick begun to build there that he would run the hotel up that high," Margaret fretted. "Used to be that I could look right across to the square. Now I can't see a thing that goes on."

"There will be plenty to see when the hotel opens," Sarah told her. "People coming and going."

"Do you think they will come just because of the hotel?" Margaret asked.

Talks the way I do to Mr. Cockrell sometimes, Sarah thought, but I'm trying to hold him down to this earth if I can. She is envious.

"They might, if the hotel is fine enough," she said. "At least, they'll be more likely to stay overnight if they've a decent place to sleep."

"Who, for instance?" Margaret insisted.

As if to answer her and to point the truth of Sarah's remark, a gentleman rode down the street on a sleek bay horse. That he was someone out of the ordinary was evident from the fine felt of his hat and the cut and cloth of his coat. That man from the state legislature at Austin, Sarah was sure, Mr. Nicholas Darnell, who had come to see Mr. Cockrell on a matter of business. If Margaret Bryan had been Martha Overton, she would have said so. As it was, she thought she had better not. She thought, too, the business was not too important or Mr. Cockrell would have brought the man down to the house, so that she could hear all about it. He sometimes did. But not always. Not always.

Ten minutes later—the stranger could not have ridden a mile beyond the bridge—she heard from up the street, nearer the square, a wild shouting. It sounded for all the world . . . no, it couldn't be . . . he wouldn't. Margaret heard, too, and had, it looked like, the same thought. She looked at Sarah in startled question. And, while they still stared at each other, Coffee Bryan came pelting down the street. Neither doors nor young ones could stop him. He pelted through the passageway and into the room.

"Ma!" Then he saw Sarah.

A gangling fourteen-year-old, nowhere near grown up to the size of his feet, his hands, too, hanging what seemed a good arm's length below the sleeves of his faded shirt. At some time that day he had broken a strap to his galluses, and tied it up the best he could with binder twine; but his pants sagged perilously still in that quarter. A face that might someday come to be fair-looking on a man but was now all nose and teeth, as he stood there, gawping.

"Coffee Bryan," his mother said, moving between Sarah and the boy, "what on earth? Don't stand there like that. Speak up!"

"Ma," he looked past his mother at Sarah and stuck again, "I . . . can't."

So, Sarah knew at least a piece of the truth. She didn't say a word. She didn't make a sound. But the moan in her heart was the one with which she had wakened in the early morning—that searching, restless, anxious cry:

"Alec?"

chapter **fifteen**

...until the hour is right.

TAKEN ALL IN ALL, that day, Alec Cockrell himself would have said, if he had been called upon to testify, was the very top of his life. Taken all in all, leaving out no part of it. Some promise, as well as warning, not to be recognized for what it was—but there—had been behind all that remembering he had done, riding into town that early morning. Adding things up, like Sarah in her ledgers. Charley John with his spook birds—that was part of it. Charley John should be present that day. He belonged. But the top of everything was the coming of that lawmaker from Austin, Nicholas Darnell. Had he come just to interest Alec Cockrell in a struggling, slow-moving railroad venture? No. We know about you at the capital, his coming meant. We want to know more. We aim to keep an eye on you—and Dallas. Texas is a big state, made for big men. You are one.

Coming out of the Crutchfield House after dinner, that was how he had felt—big. The Honorable Nick Darnell on one side of him, John McCoy on the other. Afterward the shining eyes of that bearded young man in McCoy's office paid him tribute. Now I am seeing Texas for sure, those eyes said. This is the promised land I've heard about. Bursting with promise.

Mounting their horses later at McCoy's door, turning their backs on the square and that bird of bad omen on the fence rail, picking their way through the now plentiful scattering of horses and rigs and folks, Alec touching his hat and hailing his friends, including those he wasn't too sure about, a question did occur to him. Suppose his luck should turn? Right now? But he was sure it would

183

not. He knew that feeling of masterful bigness. It was part of winning. My town, he thought. Hell and damn, I'm glad I grew a set of whiskers. Feel like a pa-tri-arch out of Sarah's Testament.

Riding free of the press, away from the square, out where new growth began to show, the feeling of bigness swelled until he didn't know whether it was inside or outside. It carried him along like a chip on a millrace. It was a bright light, apart from the light of the sun. It warmed, without burning. It put a touch of gold paint on everything, even the homeliness of the brickyard; and anybody knows a brickyard is not often gilt-edged like that.

The yard had been set to rights, it seemed like, for his satisfaction. No firing going on at the kiln, only neat stacks of finished brick, layered with straw, stood about. Only three men were at work—Pierre Frichot, his new superintendent, Pierre's brother Christophe, and his son-in-law, Jean Priot. They were working over a new mold. They were always working at something but they stood up at once to offer Alec respectful greeting. Three more good men saved from the wreck of the La Réunion colony, but anything they owed their rescuer they had long ago paid with interest. Knew more about making brick than Alec would ever learn, and they talked to him, cap in hand, their faces serious and devoted.

It felt good to see them. It looked good. The Honorable Mr. Darnell was thoughtful as they rode away. No speech, just a little more sweat popping out on his face. Maybe, for the time, he had run out of speeches. How many toasts had they drunk in McCoy's office? Alec had lost count. Not that it mattered.

In this balloon-like lightness and brightness they rode on— finally into the screech and whine of the sawmill. Alec looked sideways at Darnell to see what he thought of the uproar, but met only a manly, challenging grin for answer. Doggone, the lawmaker was feeling as good as he did! It was the horses, Alec's black Sinful, and Darnell's bay, that objected most. A quarter of a mile from the mill, they balked at going closer and had to be pulled up.

Ahead now was a stretch of dusty road ending at the mill, the mill boardinghouse on one side, the lumberyard on the other, all touched by that bright, white light. A man appeared on the road, walking toward them. The light touched him, too. Alec thought it was Toomy. Knew it was. Hopping peat bogs in Ireland had given Toomy a quick, high step Alec had known in no other. He stood up in his stirrups and bellowed:

"Turn off that blasted noise."

Toomy stopped. Alec waved his arms in a cutting motion. Toomy turned toward the mill and repeated the movement. There was a last high screech and whine, then silence; and Toomy turned again and came toward the men on the horses, his long, homely face, as he approached, lit up with friendliness. Trying to seem offhand, Alec presented him to Darnell, then gave him a set of new orders.

"Set the men to cleaning up now, Will. Put things in order to start cutting and trimming pine boards first thing Monday morning. Then turn them off. Don't cut any more posts. Got enough now to set a stockade around the town."

Toomy lifted his hat to air his head, shifted his chew and grinned as if he had taken in some prize money.

"Had to keep 'em busy, boss, till you got back with the pine." He turned once more and walked toward the mill, the bright light all around him.

"Good man," Alec said, gloating a bit.

"Tough?" Darnell suggested.

"Better be."

As they rode on, down toward the mill, the boardinghouse threw its shadow across the road. By accident or plan, as they passed the house, a black girl, her head tied up in a red bandanna, opened the front door to sweep a broomful of trash over a small entrance porch into the brush beside the steps.

"Hi-ya, Pokey!" Alec called.

A grin divided her face horizontally.

"Evenin', Mist' Cockrell."

"How you getting along down here, Pokey?"

"Doin' all right, Mist' Cockrell. Menfolk—jes' menfolk—is awful dirty, though, seems like."

"Ain't we just?" he called back; and Pokey fled into the house, shrieking happy laughter over his notice.

Alec held that bit in his hands for a spell, knowing its worth in love and good will. Then:

"Boardinghouse I put up for the men," he said, trying to appear offhand about that, too.

"Been looking at it," Darnell said. "It's bigger and better than you own house."

Surely it was bigger, and, in some ways, better. A full two stories in height, frame, built plumb and square, with this entrance porch. Alec started to say that it held more people but didn't get the words out, a whimsy interfering.

"Just what Sarah—Mrs. Cockrell—says every time she sees it. I threatened once to put it on rollers and move it uptown for her." Whimsy tugged at him still. "Going to build her a fair house of her own someday. I promised."

"When?" Darnell jibed.

"Soon."

It seemed to Alec now that the light was not so bright. Fading because Sarah wasn't there? And she wasn't. That wasn't right. Without her he'd have no cause for being proud. No cause at all.

"I hope," Darnell said, "to have the pleasure of meeting Mrs. Cockrell on my next visit to town."

So, he was coming back. Up came the light again.

"Make it soon," Alec said; and they dismounted to look at the mill.

Proud as he was of other and fancier accomplishments in the busy, thriving town, now at their backs, he kept a special glow for the sawmill. Why? Sometimes he thought it was the noise the mill made. The first screech of the great circular saw had seemed to match his own yell of defiance at any who doubted him or his undertakings. Sometimes he thought it was the power of the saw to turn out boards and posts that put a spell on him. Always it was a challenge. You started me going, feller. Make something out of it now. Sometimes . . .

Hell, there the mill was! A stout shedlike building. No niceties like windows or flooring. Dirt, beaten hard by many feet, absorbed a carpeting of sawdust. Wide doorways opposite each other let in light, men or timber, and, without sills, made the disposal of surplus shavings simple. The odor inside, whatever its other parts, carried uppermost the fragrance of new-cut cedar. A man crossed before Alec and Darnell as they went in—with surprising swiftness, considering his bulk. Grease-stiffened overalls may have made him seem wider than he was, but he was wide enough. Pale hair made a narrow fringe below a soiled cotton cap.

"Hi-ya, Axel!" Alec hailed; and the man turned a round, grimy face and flashed a smile, waving a handful of greasy cotton waste to emphasize it, and disappeared into the shadows.

"Swede," Alec said. "Knows machinery, but not much else."

Other eyes, black or blue or gray or no color in particular, looked from round or long faces, old or old-young, at the two men, measuring them. Shifty eyes, some of them. Evil faces or such as had learned the ways of evil. Out in the wood lot, among the piles of cut timber and untrimmed logs, Darnell wiped his forehead, and blew out his breath.

"Your boss, Will Toomy, carries neither gun nor knife," he observed.

"No," Alec said. "There've been times when he would have used one or the other if he'd had either on him. But a scantling in Will's hands works as well—better, nobody dying in consequence. Generally he gets along with even the meanest. They know how far they can go. Besides . . ."

"They know," Darnell finished for him, "that, after Toomy, they would have to reckon with you."

Alec grinned.

"A man out to do murder," he said, "don't usually do that much thinking."

"Right." The friendly eyes of the lawmaker measured him coolly. "Right. So long as you remember . . ."

A good deal of a man, the lawmaker.

They went back through the mill then to look at the ford Alec had made safe across the river, with stones to steady the quaking, muddy bottom. Am I showing this to Nicholas Darnell, he wondered, or just pleasuring myself with looking?

"To draw trade from the West Side," he explained. "Used to be considerable feeling between West Siders and East Siders. Still is some. Funny thing—I took up land myself over yonder, but the town drew me. Did from the start."

"And now," Darnell said quietly, "you hold it and its future in your hands."

Alec did not answer. It wasn't a thing a man ventured to say exactly about himself. Even if he thought it.

They turned from the ford, went through the mill again and out to the road, where the dust devils were doing their dance. Will Toomy waited near the horses with a bit of refreshment. The usual.

"Breeze springing up," he said. "Just enough to lift the sand and blow it down a man's goozle."

Maybe it was the blowing dust or the refreshment, or both, that put now a mellow haze over all, dimming the picture of Toomy standing in the road, watching them ride away, and the mill and the other buildings. Spreading a veil, still shot with gold, over what lay ahead. Going back, they skirted the town, riding out where houses made a scattered pattern, surrounded by farmlands—and not many houses, either. By unspoken common consent, they reined in their horses on a swell of ground rising above the prairie.

"Magnificent view," Darnell said.

"Nothing to see," Alec challenged.

"Not if your view is limited to what actually stands there now, but I'm seeing what you are seeing—houses in close order, thousands of them, homes, church spires, schools—a hundred years from now we'd have to ride much farther than this to view the open prairie."

Alec studied the picture. It was, as the lawmaker had guessed, what he was seeing out this way, what he had seen often before, only never, perhaps, quite so surely. But . . . a shadow fell over the view.

"A hundred years," he said thickly, unwillingly, "is a sight of time."

"It is," Darnell agreed, "one way you look at it. On the other hand, time, in the larger sense, is only relative—no, I'm damned if it is." He yanked out his watch. "Getting on toward four o'clock," he said. "I meant to be on the road before this."

That was time, of course, in the smaller sense. They turned abruptly and headed for town, but the friendliness, the sharing of understanding, rode with them. Half of the warmth was that—

friendliness—though Alec vowed to himself that, once Darnell was safely beyond the river, he'd have off that damned long coat he was wearing.

And the dust haze, shot with gold, followed them into town, glorifying the ugly cabins, the wagons, the horses, the people, the hound dogs, the flies. Adam Haught's dramshop on Commerce Street off the square cast a blob of shade over the road. It seemed only fitting—hell, you couldn't wave a good friend like the law-maker away and call it good-bye. Two boys came up out of the dust with outstretched hands.

"Joab," Alec said, "what're you hanging around here for?"

"Want we'uns to hold yore hosses, Mist' Cockrell?"

Laughing, the two men dismounted.

"I am, or should be," Darnell protested, "near to being saturated with overflowing hospitality."

"You'll slake your thirst once more before crossing the bot-toms," Alec insisted, waving off the idea of too much. "Liable to be dustier on the West Side than it is over here."

The lawmaker's face seemed to him only pleasantly flushed, like a harvest sun going down, as they entered the dramshop. Inside, a few others had retreated from the heat of the sun into this moister darkness. Afterward, Alec could not have named any of them. Two cavalry officers—bright yellow stripes up their light blue pants—leaned against the bar. They turned their faces toward the door as Alec and Darnell came in, and discreetly retreated to the far end of the rough counter. Which wasn't far in this small, tight cabin. Their uniforms made still a blob of color almost as good as a light in the murk. With the help of that light, Alec made his way to the bar. Hell-raisers, military men could be when on leave; but these seemed extraordinarily quiet.

"Adam!" he called. His hail bounced against the log walls and came back like a blow on his own ears. He grinned, then straight-ened his face, the grin, somehow, feeling foolish; and here was Adam's homely face staring at him over the bar. "There you are," he said, could hear himself saying it—the damnedest thing. "Dark-est hole this side of eternity, but that's all right. Adam, my old friend, want to make you acquainted with my newest friend, Mr.

Nicholas Darnell of Austin and other points south. Adam Haught, meet Mr. Darnell."

They shook hands ceremoniously over the bar. It was a thing to see. That was how a man came to be elected to high office— he knew how to meet folks.

"Adam," Alec asked solemnly, "how is the state of your deep well now?"

"I can draw from it," Adam answered just as solemnly, "till about four o'clock. By then them wagons o' your'n had better be whoopin' it into town."

"Is it four o'clock?" Darnell asked anxiously.

"Not yit," Adam told him.

Of course not. Couldn't be. Day couldn't be going that fast.

"Adam," Alec ordered, "set out your best. For all."

He took in the indefinite acquaintance behind him with a backward wave and faced the soldiers.

"Strangers here," he said, "but . . ."

The soldiers, instantly alert at the prospect of a drink that would not come out of their lean pay, spoke up. They were a lieutenant and a captain. Their names—shucks, it didn't matter. Just this murky pool of friendliness and himself and Darnell and Adam mattered really.

"From Fort Worth," Alec said. "Then you have a dusty ride home, too. You will join us, I hope, in drinking—" he paused. "What day is this?" he asked. "It's slipped me, right this minute."

"Saturday, April third." Seemed to come in pieces, the information, again bouncing off the walls.

"We will drink to this day," Alec said. "May it be one we will always remember. Fill 'em up, Adam, old friend."

The demijohn was on the bar, handy to a row of tin cups. More cups came from the rear, held fast by disembodied hands. All were filled and emptied.

"To this day," Darnell said.

"And confusion to our enemies," a soldier added.

"You got enemies?" Alec asked, the whiskey flowing smoothly down his throat, and general kindliness taking a fresh increase.

"There's always the Provost Marshal," the soldier answered.

Marshal . . . Marshal? Oh, yes. Ha!

"Fill 'em again, Adam," Alec commanded. "Confusion to marshals. Everybody's marshal!"

Five minutes later—or was it more—Nicholas Darnell was bidding Adam Haught to fill the cups again.

"To the prosperity of this city," he said, "and its promoters."

"Hear, hear!" the soldiers cried.

Then, after a short consultation, it was their turn.

"For the honor of the service!" the Captain said. "We insist."

By then the murky darkness was soft and thick, almost like a featherbed. Adam's seamed face was a moon shining through the fog. The lawmaker's was even more like a harvest sun setting.

"All good things must end finally," the setting sun said. "I must be gone now. Riding on to Lancaster. Would like to be there before dark."

That was right. On to Lancaster—before dark. Someday—not too far off—nobody would ride out of Dallas this late in the evening. Alec found the lawmaker's arm, and together they worked their way out of the cabin. The heat and the bright light of late afternoon pushed against them. They grunted, but went on.

"Steady him now," Alec said to the boy holding the lawmaker's bay horse; and he himself steadied the lawmaker as he let go of the ground and mounted.

Looked big up there suddenly, like a bronze statue; then came back to his proper size, raised his hat, and rode away in good style, back straight, head up, coat-tails spread. The image blurred as it drew off into the distance, but was still a purple blob, edged with gold. Finally he was gone.

Alec stood a while, staring at the spot where Darnell had disappeared. And people gathered about, but not too close, to stare at him. Why? He was only looking down the street, thinking of all that had happened since he had ridden the length of it that early morning. Finally the foolish faces of the people and the heat and the bright light and the warmth and joy inside him ran together and touched him with madness. He took off his hat, spread his arms, and yelled.

A woman, standing too close—and what was she doing there, anyhow?—covered her ears. He saw her, opened his mouth and turned loose a second yell, and heard a coat-seam rip. His coat? Well, damn! He was still wearing that thing? He jerked at the sleeves. They seemed glued to him by their tightness and his sweat. Then he saw that Joab, holding his horse, was having trouble; and he gave a mighty jerk. That did it. The coat split right down the back, but he got out of it.

He laughed, and Sinful quieted. He walked that way—right steadily—and laid the coat over the saddle. The little breeze that had come up fanned his shirt-sleeves pleasantly. He thought, for only that reason, of woods and shade and a cool stream. Damn, he thought of Charley John. In his calico shirt. Shirt, with the tails out, that was the thing. He began to unbutton his vest, met his heavy watch chain halfway up, and knew he was trapped. He laughed at himself for a fool, fumbled for the buttons he had freed, but couldn't find them. A shadow fell across the road, between him and his horse.

"Alick Cockrell, you're drunk!"

The Marshall? Andy Moore? No. He wouldn't dare. But then, maybe, he just would, all strung over with guns like he was.

"Drunk on the public square. Disturbing the peace."

Yep, it was Andy. His voice thick and loud, making bluster take the place of true bravery. A heavy hand seemed to fall on Alec's shoulder. It wasn't there, really; but he shook it off, anyhow. He stiffened and turned.

"You skunk!" he said, and made sure folks heard that, too. His fists closed. He would have taken on the Marshal then and there; and it might have been better so, but he made the mistake of thinking. Better sift this out, he thought. See what it comes to. He turned again, drew Joab's scared attention, held it, and pointed to his coat.

"Watch it!" he said. "I'll be back."

chapter sixteen

Then, though it may be too late...

IT TOOK SEVERAL SHAKINGS from his mother and more sharp words before Coffee Bryan got the story out.

"Last I seen," he stammered, "they were heading up Houston Street, people follerin'. Mr. Alick hadn't a gun, but the Marshal did. I come home . . ."

Margaret let go of the boy and turned to Sarah. Her face was as white as Sarah's own. Anybody could see that nonsense had been jarred out of her, and only woman was left.

"Is that the truth?" she asked. "Alick didn't have a gun on him?"

Sarah shook her head. She could see his belt, with the holster, across the counterpane of her bed.

"It's the law," she said. "Only a marshal can wear a gun up-town."

She could have died where she stood. People following—but it wasn't shame that struck hardest. Fright numbed her. Not a new fear, not just of this day, though it clamored harder now than ever before. In the happiest time of her life, through courtship and the sweet madness of early marriage, the least untoward happening had set her a-tremble, showing that she never was sure of what she seemed to hold so securely. But now . . .

Fear numbed her. And, close behind the fear, stood sorrow. It was Alec Cockrell who would feel the bitter shame that Andy Moore had put upon him in the town square, in front of everybody, friends, some not so friendly, strangers. The people following—as Coffee Bryan said.

193

"Was he drunk, Coffee?" Margaret asked, taking the sour word from Andy Moore's slack mouth.

Coffee thought over what he knew of such matters, and it was considerable.

"No'm," he said finally. "Not specially. He hollered some. A couple of times. You know how he does."

The way he had shouted that early morning, riding down to his house. High spirits? No. Tell it true, Sarah Cockrell. This is a wild, rough land you call home now. It was a wild, rough young man, not broken to yoke or bridle, who came striding out of a cedar copse a dozen years ago and rooted you here. In love and service. For you he put on the clothing and the ways of decency, but the wildness and the roughness burned their brand deep into him before you ever saw him. You knew that when you took his name. You trembled when you took it, but your heart beat so that you gave no heed.

Methody woman, what are you saying?

I love him, Lord. I was a poor, lone creature in my purity and righteousness before he came storming through those trees. I have known the very depth of trouble since; but I have known, too, the tiptop of joy. I have known sorrow. Often enough, others would say, I have known shame. It was never that altogether. Pity would not let me look at things that way. It would be Alec who felt torment afterward, and the spells have been few and far between of late. Almost I hoped that they would never come again.

I had pity for his torment. I never knew what brought on the wildness—whether he was furiously angry because things went against him or just as crazy because all went his way. I don't know today how wild he was uptown. That man from Austin, Mr. Darnell. He rode his horse down the road, sitting straight enough. But a man, a Texas man, can do that, no matter what.

Methody woman . . .

Lord, I am afraid. I've been afraid before, but never just like this.

And now, through the clamor inside and the numbness outside, Margaret Bryan was saying something to her again. Insistently, like as if she were shaking Sarah as she had shaken Coffee, to get him to talking.

"Do you know where his guns are?"

"Yes, of course."

She spoke strongly, scornful of the question. She was surprised to hear herself.

"All of them?" Margaret said.

All. The revolver in its holster on his belt, the shotgun above the mantel in the best room the other side of the hall—her parlor.

"Then go home," Margaret said, "and hide them. Bury them somewhere. Throw them in the river. Put them where he can't lay hold of them."

"I couldn't," Sarah told her. "I wouldn't."

"Don't be a fool, Sarah Cockrell. If my man had not had a gun in his hand that night three years ago, and enough liquor in him to make him feel like God Almighty, I would not be as I am now and he would not be traipsing all over, hunting what he knows he will never find, growing old all alone, eating his heart out with wanting what he's too proud to come back to. I say, don't be a fool. Hide those guns, and don't dawdle. Alick Cockrell won't take peaceably this public shame Andy Moore has put on him. He's madder than a nest of hornets this minute. He'll win free, somehow; and then, look out! Sarah, do you hear me?"

Hear her? There was no reason why Sarah should not hear. Everything, after the wild shouting, had gone deadly still. The sawmill had stopped screeching some time before. Now, across the way, the chanting and the shuffling of the bricklayers had stopped.

"Listen," Sarah said. "They've quit work—on the hotel."

"Sarah, in the name of common sense, will you move?"

"Yes. Yes, I will. I . . . must."

Her feet, which had seemed grown fast to the floor, loosed themselves finally. She drew one long, shuddering breath of unwillingness, and ran.

...*to save the one marked for death*...

THERE MAY HAVE BEEN a sight of people on Houston Street that evening, as Coffee Bryan reported, probably were. They meant little to Alec Cockrell. He walked apart from them in the white heat of his anger. From Adam Haught's place to the drugstore, and the Justice of the Peace Court above it, Andy Moore following with his naked gun. Who else followed did not matter.

His anger grew, rather than lessened; but he was never bereft of reason. When it finally was clear to him that Andy Moore meant just what he said, that he was taking Alec Cockrell into custody on a low-down charge of disturbing the peace, when he realized that Moore had bided his time all day, meaning to do some such thing, that he had waited not just till it seemed he had grounds for the charge, but until there were the most people looking on, anger blazed in Alec Cockrell, but he still knew what to do. He remembered what Will Toomy had told him that morning. On a charge like that, if you paid a fine, you went free. He meant to set himself free in short order. Then he could settle the other score, the personal one. He breathed hard a couple of times, and he was ready.

"Come on," he said hoarsely. "What are you waiting for?" And stepped out into the street.

It might be that the bravest thing he did that day was to turn his back on the Marshal. Put a star on the chest of a man like that, give him the right to carry a loaded gun, and there was no telling what could happen. On the other hand, if Moore had been going to shoot him out of pure spite, he'd have done so before this. However it was, they set out, Alec ahead, the Marshal following, his face, too, set in a scowl. This thing was not going just as he had planned it, not exactly. And the crowd followed, but not too close. Finally only Joab, holding Sinful, was left at Adam Haught's corner, until the two cavalrymen came out of the dramshop and spoke to him.

"His horse?" one of them asked.

"Yassah, an' I dunno . . ." Joab faltered, looking wistfully after the crowd.

"Hold it," the military man said, and winked at his friend. "You hold that horse."

"Yassah." But now Joab looked the other way, down Commerce, toward the blacksmith's yard. Where was Henry? Or George? Where was anybody?

Moving down the west side of Houston, turning off the street at Peak's pharmacy to the outside staircase at the rear, Alec Cockrell still led the procession. He was the first to climb the rough steps. He opened the door to the room above. And there he was halted—first by the stagnant heat inside, the low roof seeming to press down what air there was and hold it like a bake oven, secondly and mostly, by the smell and the taste of dust. The flavor of it was dry on his lips, his tongue. Unbelievably he was thirsty again. He shut his mouth tight, and there it was, tickling his nose. Dust . . .

By God, he thought, here I am again, back where it all started; then threw the door wider open and stamped into the room.

No lawyers this time; at least, not so far. No counsel, no feeling of having the upper hand if he could just sit tight and outstubborn the other fellow. He did not have the upper hand. Temporarily he, Alec Cockrell, was in trouble. The law couldn't help him. He had to figure his own way out. All right, he would do that.

No lawyers. Only Justice Smith sitting behind the counter over which he handed out his decisions. Angrily, Alec strode up to the bar.

"I've been arrested, Justice," he said. "Don't wish to waste time arguing the right or wrong of it. What does the fine come to?"

The door behind him closed. Moore coming in, he supposed, but did not trouble himself to look.

"Not your place to open proceedings," Justice said. "Marshal, did you make the arrest?"

It was Moore who had come in. He took two steps forward now and Alec took two to one side. Didn't aim to stand any closer than need be to a skunk.

"State the charge," Justice said.

"Drunk and disorderly." Moore was defiant, but uneasy. Now, why? Natural born coward, like most bullies. Didn't know just when he did have the advantage. "He come out of Haught's place into the street, whooping and hollering. Scaring womenfolk and children. Then he begun to tear off his clothes."

The door opened again and closed. This time it was John McCoy. Lord, news traveled fast. McCoy shook his head at Alec. He looked damned serious, so serious that Alec grinned, his dry lips cracking, and McCoy shook his head again.

"Ripped off his coat," Moore said, "and begun on his vest. That was when I stepped in."

"Mr. Justice," McCoy said hastily, "it is a warm day."

Justice looked at him sourly. Sitting here, he knew that much.

"Did you," he asked Alec, "engage counsel?"

"No," Alec said. "You know I never. When would I?"

"Do you wish advice of counsel?"

"No." It came over him like that. He'd fight this out alone. He had to.

"Then we will proceed. Marshal, was the prisoner abusive? Did he speak any obscenities?"

No, but he could have. Could make up for it right now.

"Pardon?" Moore said.

"Did he resist arrest? Using foul language?"

"Called me a name or two."

"One," Alec corrected. "All I could think of at the time."

"Alick!" McCoy warned.

"Keep out of this, John."

"Prisoner," Justice said, "don't want the advice of counsel."

Prisoner—now there was a word. "Marshal, I take it, then, the charge is just drunk and disorderly."

"Generally disturbing the peace," the skunk added, to show how much he knew.

"Alick Cockrell, do you plead guilty to the charge as stated?"

By now the door had opened several more times, to let in other people. Alec could hear them behind him, shifting their weight, breathing hard.

"Not pleading anything," he said, tired of palaver. "How much does the fine come to—that's what I want to know. Hell and damn! Got other things on hand this evening." The wagons. Might be right up to town now. "How much?"

Justice squinted, studying something. Not the amount of the fine, hardly. He must know that. It was fines mostly that kept the town government—and its officials—going.

"Fifteen dollars," Justice said at last.

"Sure?" Foolish to twit the man, but he couldn't forbear.

"Certainly I'm sure."

Alec dug into his pants pocket and came up with two gold pieces, ten and five dollars. Only then he remembered his wallet in a deep inside pocket of the coat he had thrown off. Most of his poker winnings at Black Jack. Now, if Joab loosed his hold on Sinful . . . but, shucks, Joab wouldn't.

"Big sum," he growled, slapping the bright coins down on the counter, "to make all this stink about."

"Fines are set by law," Justice said. "You'd do well to pay the law more respect."

Ha! He, Alec Cockrell, was the most law-abiding citizen in the whole of Texas, compared to some not an arm's reach away. An arm's reach . . .

"I'm all square now?" he asked.

"For the present," Justice said, but cautiously.

"I'm my own man again?"

"Yes, but . . ." he didn't finish, but Alec got his meaning. Another offense would bring stiffer punishment. Ha!

At that John McCoy must step forward, in spite of all. As he did so, young Mr. Guess of North Carolina showed up behind him. Must have been one of those who had come into the room later. The young man's eyes, Alec noted, had that same shine that had brightened them earlier that afternoon in McCoy's office. Alec favored him with a slow wink.

"Your Honor," McCoy said, "I will go this man's bond, guaranteeing good behavior."

"Better not," Alec warned.

With that, he began once more to undo the buttons on his vest. This time, when he reached the watch chain, he unfastened it carefully, took his silver watch from its pocket and handed both, on a whim, to the young man from North Carolina, who hadn't a word to say as he took the watch, but his eyes went on shining.

"Now!" The last button free, his vest hanging open, Alec turned on Andrew Moore.

"Now!" He took a half-step forward. Moore wavered, his eyes dilating, as if he didn't believe what he saw and wished not to believe it. Then he gripped his gun hard, and stood where he was; but his jaw dropped, to go with his frighted eyes.

"Peel!" Alec said, not loud, just cold and hard, his eyes cold and hard on Moore, as if he had cornered a diamondback and had to pin the reptile where he had him, and the truth was he had Moore so pinned. Fellow would have liked to move, but he couldn't. Nailed to the floor.

"Drop that gun," Alec said, pressing his advantage. "You heard what the Justice said. I'm a free man again. Ain't a question now of marshal and unarmed prisoner. We're just two men, with a bone to pick; and nary one of us will know peace in this town until we've picked it—clean."

And now Moore moved—the least bit he could. His eyes went toward the Justice who was halfway to his feet, ready to take a hand if needed; but he never did—just stood that way, behind the barrier of the counter.

"Peel!" Alec said again, snaking out his bullwhip. "Drop all your guns and peel to your shirt. Take off that badge you're not fit to wear; and, for fear we'll show disrespect to this place, step outside with me—man to man."

But Andy Moore had no idea of doing any such thing. He did not move, nor did anyone else in the hot and dusty room. John

McCoy, too, looked ready to spring into the battle, but something held even him where he stood.

"You don't dare," Alec taunted. "Do you?"

"I don't . . . have to," Moore managed finally.

"Oh, hell! Say it the way it is. You don't dare. Hold to guns, don't you? You heard him, folks. That's how he wants it. Well, I've got guns, Andy, as you know. Happens they're at home, where a man with true respect for the law and not afraid to go unarmed keeps them. But now I'm going after them. Take me about ten—fifteen minutes, maybe; and I'll be back. Sure as death, I'll be back, Andy."

For the second time that afternoon, he turned his back on Andy Moore's loaded gun. He shouldn't have done it, for only one reason. Moore wasn't a skunk, he was a snake, full of venom, and cornered. It wasn't safe to give him time to hunt cover. He should have gone for him bare-handed, knocked the gun out of his hands, got him by the throat, and finished him off then and there, where they stood. He could have done it. He lacked some pounds of matching Andy's weight, but in every other way he was the better man.

Why didn't he do it? Did he think the others would interfere? Might have; but the truth was he didn't think at all, except, this here is a fight to the finish and we are going to finish it—odds even. For the time it took him to go for his guns he forgot that you can't fight a reptile that way.

He strode to the door. Through a very press of people, it seemed to him now, all of them slack-jawed except one. The young man from North Carolina stood there holding his watch, reading the face of it as if he was counting time—second by second, minute by minute. Alec tore the door open and clattered down the steps.

chapter **eighteen**

...still one must strive...

IF ONLY A WOMAN would not shake so when she had a fiercely hard thing to do!

Sarah left the Bryan house by the back way, then cut across the blacksmith's yard stealthily to Commerce Street again, and went into her house from the front—but quickly, not wanting to be seen from the road, say someone should pass who knew her. When she had left home earlier, little Alec was with Hannah behind the house, he and Willie Winn, making a show of gathering chips for Hannah's wash kettle, though no fire could have been kept going with what fuel those two provided; and Hannah said so loudly and repeatedly, her glasses flashing in the strong afternoon light. She could have seen better without them, but Sarah doubted that she removed them even while she slept. The young ones, Sarah hoped, were still there with Hannah, though she heard neither their laughter now nor Hannah's scolding. But Hannah might have them with her in the kitchen. It was getting on toward time for starting supper.

The house, when Sarah entered, seemed unearthly quiet. That was probably because all the disturbing elements were outside. A wistful smile touched her pale face, flickered and went away. No time now for reflection. Margaret Bryan had been most urgent about that. *Sarah, will you move? . . . Hide those guns and don't dawdle.*

The parlor first, where Alec's shotgun hung above the mantel and the cold fireplace with its elegant brass screen. The parlor with its braided rag rug—a woman had no dearth of rags, with

202

three growing boys and one overactive man in the household. With its marble-topped center table and the painted-china lamp standing on it. Most folks still made do with candles, homemade or store-bought, coal oil being hard to come by except in port cities, and, some thought, dangerous. But Mr. Cockrell would have lamps for his house, plain and fancy. This one was a beauty. As pretty as it was prideful. As prideful as the couch and chairs of walnut upholstered in tufted red rep.

Not a chair in the room, Sarah thought now, good for standing on; and she needed to climb. Well, there was no help for it. She took off her shoes and did what she would have switched a young one for doing, mounted an elegant, curved-back chair, so that she could reach the gun over the mantel. When she had it, it was a wonder she did not drop it, she shook so, taking it off its pegs. It was cold and heavy in her hands then; and she hugged it to her with her elbows, not trusting her unsteady grip, as she sank to her knees on the chair cushion, then stepped to the floor. All carefully done, because she could not say whether the gun was loaded or not. She could not recall Alec's rule about that. She tried to remember how her brothers did. It seemed to her that it was thought preferable to hang a gun away clean and oiled and empty, that a fresh charge was best for hunting or any other kind of shooting. On the other hand, if a man needed a gun all of a sudden, he might not have time to load it.

She sat on the pretty chair, with the ugly, heavy gun across her lap, trying to think, trying to remember. But she could do neither, it seemed like. She wished now that she hadn't touched the gun. Maybe she ought to climb up and put it back on the wall. If she was able.

Methody woman . . .

Oh, yes, that was it. She was to hide the gun, to save Mr. Cockrell from doing hurt with it. In his great anger. But what right had she . . . she shook her head, to clear it, sighed, and stood up. She laid the gun on the marble-topped center table, while she set the chair in place and put on her shoes. Then, turning to pick it up again—to take it, she didn't know where—she looked at the wall opposite the mantel; and there was Columbus. On his knees, holding a cross, with a flag waving over him, asking God's blessing on this new land he had discovered and was claiming for the King and Queen of Spain.

"Furriners." She heard Alec Cockrell's high and scornful laughing. "So, that's where the trouble begun."

Oh, the dear, foolish, happy days! Who would have thought they would lead up to this one?

Well, no use standing around, mooning over what was long gone. She was through in the parlor now. Carrying the gun as far from her as possible, she left the room, closed the door carefully, and walked swiftly across the hall to the bedroom. She either was going to do this thing, or she wasn't, and that right now, before too late.

But, as she stood beside the bed, resolution wavered again. A man, she thought, had a right to his guns if he needed them. Alec Cockrell's gun belt lying there, kept, it seemed to her, the shape of his lean hips, till it looked almost part of him. She touched the belt gingerly, then took firmer hold, impatient afresh with shilly-shallying.

Hide his guns, Margaret Bryan had said, out of bitter experience. All right, but where? Bury them? Throw them in the river? No. If she set foot outside of the house either front or back, with a shotgun in one hand and a gun belt in the other, somebody must see her and raise a fuss. It had to be right here, in the house. Dear Lord, where?

She took the first place that came to her. And it might be, if she'd had all day to plan, she couldn't have done any better. The guns were there on the bed. The bed was made up with a mattress foundation on the cords, then a thick featherbed on top of the mattress, then sheets, blankets and so on. Carefully she turned back the coverings, doubled the featherbed and thrust belt and shotgun between it and the mattress. Her movements were swift. By now she either had all the time in the world, because nothing was going to happen, or she had none at all. In a frenzy of haste, but still carefully, she replaced finally sheets, coverings, pillows and shams.

The whole process couldn't have taken but a few minutes. She could have sworn that, when she began, the house had been as still as it was when she had first stepped into it, coming from the

Bryan place; but, the instant she gave the final pull to the counterpane, a complaining cry came from the hall.

"Sarah? Is that you banging around down here? Sarah?"

Polly, Sarah thought. Sister Polly. I forgot all about her. She
stood now in the bedroom door, rubbing her eyes, looking pitiful,
as always, one side of her face pinked up where she had slept on
it, the other pale and drawn.

"I thought you were asleep—upstairs," Sarah said sharply, because it gave her such a start to have Polly standing there looking
at her. "I thought you had a headache."

"Headache's some better," the sly creature fretted. "But it's
awful hot up there under the roof. I came down for a drink of
water."

"You came down," Sarah said, and knew she spoke truly, "to
see what I was doing—to spy on me. You're always spying on
folks. How long have you been there in the hall? What did you
see?"

"Sarah Cockrell, don't you speak like that to me. I didn't see
anything. I heard somebody moving around downstairs. Maybe
that's what woke me up; but I didn't know who it was until just
now. What makes you think . . . ?"

Her face crumpled suddenly like that of a child unjustly and
cruelly slapped. Sarah was ashamed, but only in a measure. She
still had her suspicions.

"Well, all right," she said impatiently. "It's no matter. I'm
sorry I spoke so. Only—" suspicion laid tighter hold on her, "whatever you saw or didn't see, you're not to breathe a word or let on—
not to anybody, no matter who or what. If you do, I'll haunt you
to your dying day."

"Sarah Horton," Polly whimpered, "if Mamma could hear you!"

"Well, she can't," Sarah said, and almost added, "Thank God!"
but was spared that blasphemy. Again she heard, or thought she
heard, her stirred-up imagination being 'way ahead of any thinking, some sort of outcry from the direction of the square. It set
a thousand needles to pricking her.

"Sister Polly," she said, and her voice sounded thin and strained
to her own ears, "go back upstairs. Go upstairs, and stay. Don't
you come down, no matter what you think you hear."

All the time she might have known—she might have known.

"Where are you going?" Polly fretted.

"Never mind," Sarah said. The pricking needles said run; and she knew she would, but had no idea how far or in what direction. "Don't you follow me."

That was her mistake. All might have turned out differently, if she had taken Polly with her; but she didn't. As she ran blindly out the back door, Polly stood halfway up the stairs, but with her neck stretched and her head thrust out, so that she could see through the house. Still watching, missing nothing that went on.

chapter **nineteen**

...however vainly...

THE FIRST THING Alec Cockrell saw when he flung open the parlor door was the empty gun space over the mantel; and he knew, without stopping to think, who had taken the shotgun.

Leaving the Justice of the Peace Court, he had less sense than before of who or how many watched him go striding down Houston Street, cut the corner at Commerce, and make for home. He had no idea of the figure he made, in his shirt-sleeves, with his vest hanging open, his watch and chain in that Carolina young man's keeping; but he had never felt so tall, so free, so unconquerable, not since the madness of early manhood. Mad was what people said who saw him then, striding toward his house between four and five o'clock that evening. Said he had a look of madness in his eyes. Didn't see anybody or anything, not even Joab, holding his horse.

Didn't care about trifling things like that. Not right then. Mad was what he was, but not crazy mad, the way those folks meant. Angry mad, through and through and through. That damn, o'nery, low-down no-account! Talk about thieving Indians. They aren't a circumstance. Looks like he is a piece of the old rough life that I can't shake loose. Long as he's around to spite me, I'll never win through to what I'm aiming to be. Who would have thought it would come to this? But there it is. A man can break his neck falling over the littlest tree stump if he trips over it in the dark. Got to settle with Andy Moore today—or lose my life trying.

Or lose my life. He had no intention of doing that. He was as

207

good a shot as Andy any day in the week at any range. Might be a little out of practice; but, unless a man went blind or palsied, he never lost the way of that once he had mastered it.

Or lose my life . . . he shook his head angrily. Seemed something buzzed around his ears and he didn't want to hear it. Passing the half-finished hotel, he thought he heard behind him somebody call out his name—or maybe it was across the way. Didn't matter. He didn't stop. His boots stamped the hard ground and kicked the clods aside and he went right on. And now he was inside his own house, in Sarah's prideful parlor—staring at an empty wall.

He knew, as surely as if he had seen it in her hands, that Sarah had taken the gun. The Methody woman who had stolen his heart out of his body and made it over to suit her own ideas. The Methody woman who had taken his heart, his manhood, the labor of his hands, the stuff of his dreams, and, with a witchcraft that good people called by a different name, had put a spell on him. And what had it all come to? This.

At that, the spell broke. All in one second the lessons of control that he had willingly and unwillingly learned were lost. Passion and fury, pent these many years, broke over the barrier of decency. Anger as unreasoning as that which had ruled him on the day he first laid eyes on Sarah Horton and she had taken fright and run from him and slammed the door in his face swept over him again. Wild Alec Cockrell, the shirt-tailed ne'er-do-well, was back.

"Sarah!" he bellowed. He had no goad in his hand today, but the crack of a whip was in his cry. "You, Sarah!"

The house gave back an empty echo. Hell and damn, she had to be here! Who else—he stamped across the hall into the bedroom. Then it wasn't just that his belt with his revolver was gone. The smug tidiness and the emptiness of the room infuriated him. Fury was the agony of pain not to be borne, but he didn't recognize it as such.

"Sarah!" he let out another roar; and, when there was again no answer, he snatched a small flowery pitcher off her washstand and dashed it on the floor, breaking it to bits. For a second, even he was awed. Sarah's crockery . . . and then he heard somewhere in the house a whimper.

It wasn't Sarah. No. She might in fright or other misery drop dead in a faint, but she wouldn't whine. It wasn't Sarah, but it was somebody. He crunched the bits of crockery under foot and went to the rear of the house. Hannah, the cook, opened the door and looked in, her mouth spreading in horror.

"Mist' Alick," she said, "wha' fo' you go on lak dat? Fo' Gawd's sake, what ails you? You look . . ."

And he roared at her.

"Never mind what I look like. Where's Miss Sally?"

"I . . . don' . . . know," she said. "I ain' seed her since right after dinnahtime."

"You bespectacled old witch!" he said. "If you're lying to me . . ."

Then she took fire.

"I ain' lyin'," she said, "to you or nobuddy!"

But she shook like a long, skinny limb in a windstorm. Shook the spectacles right off her nose. There was the tinkling sound now of brittle glass going to pieces. With a shrill cry she swooped down, snatched up the frames, with such parts of glass as still clung to them, turned a look of complete horror upon her master, and fled.

The door banged to behind her. At that, emptiness was inside Alec Cockrell as well as outside. An empty, betrayed man inside his empty house. No, the house was not empty. The stairway to the second floor went up from front to back in the central hall or passageway. He stood now almost under the head of it. From there he heard movement, a light, scuffing step. Mice could have made the sound, but it wasn't mice. It was a person, the same person who had whimpered.

Now, generally speaking, he held no spite against Mrs. Polly Horton Thompson, his sister-in-law. It bothered him only now and then that she lived in his and Sarah's house. Widowed soon after they moved to Dallas, she had been part of the family ever since. Sarah being a woman bound to care for anybody in need of her help, her own folks or not. He knew Polly Thompson's short-comings—a poor thing, compared to Sarah, and a Meddlesome

Mattie, besides; but he had no real grudge against her. Most of the time he forgot all about her. He didn't think now that she could help him; but there he stood, his hands, as well as the rest of him, empty, and he had the day still to finish. She was just one whit better than nothing—maybe. And time was passing.

He walked forward to the foot of the stairs.

"Polly! Polly Thompson!" he called. "Is that you?"

There was, of course, no answer.

"Sister Polly?" He set one foot—loudly—on the first step. "I'm coming up," he warned.

Ha! The light scuffle of movement again.

"Sister Polly!" He went up another step, stamping his foot to make her hear. "Show yourself."

She cried out at that.

"Don't you dare come up here!" he thought she said. Anyhow, that was what she meant.

"Show yourself," he said again, "or I sure as hell will come up."

Then he saw her, pale against the shadows above him, and shaking worse than Hannah. What came over women? You would have thought he was in the habit of using a whip on them, and he'd never lifted his hand against one.

"Don't you . . ." if she had finished, if she had said, "Don't you dare!" and stood her ground, he couldn't have done a thing about it. But she didn't. She just stood there and shook, and he despised her for it. He had to.

"Where's Sarah?" he roared at her. "Tell me!"

"I don't . . . know," she said; and somehow he knew she didn't.

"What do you know?" he roared. "Where are my guns?"

"I don't . . ." but the lie stuck in her throat. She did know.

"Did she take them away with her?"

"No." She clapped a hand over her mouth then, horrified at what she had said.

So, the guns were somewhere in the house. Now he'd get them.

"Are they upstairs?" he demanded, still roaring.

She shook her head and began to cry. He stamped a foot on the next step higher, and saw her shrink away.

"Come down here!" he bellowed. He could have torn the house to pieces and found the guns for himself, but that would take time. "You know where she hid them. I can see that. Come down, and show me or . . ."

She dropped her hand from her mouth, but couldn't seem to move—one way or the other.

"Go away," she whimpered. "Go away!"

Ha!

"I'll back down, step at a time," he offered. "One step for every step you take this way. Well?"

Hell, he could have torn up the house almost by now, but maybe not. He drew her by inches, it seemed to him; but she came. He backed away from the steps and watched to see where she would turn at the foot of them. It was left, toward the bedroom. Ha! If he had to begin ripping and tearing . . . sure enough, she backed across the hall, right through the door.

"She said I wasn't to tell," she cried finally, desperate with fright, the poor fool. "Said she'd haunt me to my dying day."

"This is your dying day if you don't tell me," he told her.

She drew herself together in a final spasm of terror, and then something came over her. She straightened her thin little body and stood up to him.

"I don't care," she said. "I don't care what happens now."

And she pointed to the bed.

chapter **twenty**

...against the forces of evil.

IN THE DUSTY ROOM over the drugstore, opposite the square, after Alec Cockrell had stormed out, there was a time of heavy silence. One of those times when hearing and seeing are not enough, when all the smells come out—dust, paper, mice tracks, stale tobacco, sweat—so mixed, that a body couldn't say what it was that stopped his nose, but knew poison was in the blend. Justice Smith rubbed his chin, opened his mouth to speak, closed it and said nothing. Wasn't necessary to order the room cleared. By ones and twos those who had drifted in were now drifting out—a mite faster than they had come. Finally only the Justice of the Peace, the Marshal, and the two lawyers, McCoy and young Guess, were left. Justice coughed.

"Andy Moore . . ." he said uncertainly.

Moore, braver now, threw back his shoulders and stuck out his jaw.

"Only did my duty," he said, sullenly.

True. So had the Justice done his. All according to law, but . . .

"Question is," he said, "what will you do now?"

"Me?" Moore said, then found an answer that wasn't one, really. "You heard him threaten me. All of you here heard him threaten me."

John McCoy released his breath—gustily.

"That is what concerns us," he said. "Andy, would you do yourself and everybody else the favor of making yourself scarce for a while?"

"You mean—hide?"

"Well, yes. Give anger time to cool."

"Don't have to hide," Moore said. "Ain't done a thing wrong."

McCoy considered that, and sighed again.

"In a way, you haven't," he said. Then, in baffled exasperation, he turned on the bearded young man behind and beside him. "What are you doing here, anyhow?" he demanded.

George Guess, lately of North Carolina, looked down at the watch and chain in his right hand. With some wonder, he moved the watch to the palm of his left hand, and covered it. To muffle the ticking? Perhaps. It was a small sound, but steady, like heartbeat.

"I don't know," he said to McCoy's question. "Hardly my place, of course."

"Nor mine now," McCoy agreed. "So, let's get out—pronto."

"Something's got John worried," Justice Smith said, as the door closed behind the two lawyers. "As Alick's lawyer, he's bound to take his side, but . . ."

Moore licked his dry lips.

"Don't make no difference, whose lawyer he is," he said. "We got two good witnesses. Swear them to tell the truth and they know they'll have to do it."

"Yes," the Justice agreed, "if you're alive to benefit. Alick left here awful mad. I still think McCoy's advice was best. Hide—if it's not too late."

It was late. And getting to be later. The fear that had wakened with Andrew Moore that morning returned to haunt him again.

"Where?" he demanded.

"Jailhouse?" the Justice suggested. "It's a stout building. Andy, you ain't got much time."

No time at all, maybe. When Alec Cockrell moved, he moved fast. Always had. Andrew Moore had no way of knowing that time would stand still for him while Alec hunted for his guns. But he didn't like the thought of the jail. He'd heard tell of mobs . . . hell, Alick Cockrell was no mob.

"Don't have to hide," he maintained.

"No," the Justice agreed, "but I still think it's a good idee."

Near him, on the bar of justice, lay the fifteen dollars that Alec had laid down. He studied the bright coins with a wry expression on his face, then picked them up and pocketed them.

"Maybe I'll hold on to these for a while," he said thoughtfully. "If there is some sort of inquiry."

He didn't know when he'd been more in a quandary at the end of a hearing. A misdemeanor was a misdemeanor, surely; but it seemed like this time the afternoon's activities were more to the credit of the accused than to that of the accuser. Truth was, he hadn't much use for the town Marshal, hadn't liked him ever since he'd carried that bad debt case to a higher court.

"Andrew," he said abruptly, as one solution finally occurred to him, "I am adjourning this court temporarily. You can lock the door after me, if you want, and stay right here."

He had already snatched up his hat and was on his way to the door. The air in the courtroom was now almost unbreathable, but that could have been due to a change shaping up outside. As he opened the door at the head of the steps, a gust of wind drove him back a step. It was only a gust. He went on out then, but stopped again, just beyond the threshold, to study the sky. A few small clouds showed now. Not many; but they were moving fast, as if a stronger wind blew high above the earth than down near the ground. Going to have weather, he forecast, and hoped it wouldn't drown his garden. He had a good one started.

Left alone in the courtroom, Andy Moore had no notion of locking the door and staying there. For the minute or two that the door stood open he listened intently, but it was only for noises from the square or the street below that would say Alec Cockrell was in sight, with his guns. He thought in that case the justice would come back faster than he had left. When that didn't happen and there was no noise, he, too, opened the door and, cautiously, stepped outside.

The Justice of the Peace had disappeared; and it seemed to him that the town was quieter than it had been since early morning. Still cautiously, he went down the steps and out to the street. Dust was beginning to blow there; and he, too, thought briefly of weather. Not much. Not for long. He looked across Houston to the hitch rail about the courthouse green. A good many people had left, he noted; and most of those who hadn't gone were now untying their horses and making ready to go—and that with as little commotion as possible.

Hell, what was he afraid of? One man, and he plainly not yet in sight. He took one step boldly out into the street, then drew back. Only sensible to have a wall between him and Commerce Street. He must play his hand carefully now, though the odds again seemed to be changing in his favor. Just one store was now between him and the corner—Uncle Jack Smith's.

He reached the corner. Nobody tried to stop him, nobody hailed him. He saw nobody. Diagonally across from him, Hirsch and Shirek's store was as deserted, or looked so, as any other place near the square. He looked with a certain longing at the roof, two stories above the street, with a low coping. If he could have taken up his position there, nothing on the ground could escape him. But it was too late to try for that, even if nobody over there ventured to stop him. He had to make the best of where he was. He placed himself tight against the logs of the small building, waited until he was again breathing easily, then turned and rested his gun on the jutting joint of two logs at the corner, pulled his hat low over his eyes against the western sun, and waited.

A minute or two later he heard movement behind him and turned his head a quarter of the way around; but it was only Uncle Jack himself, turned anxious.

"Andy?"

"Go on back where you came from," Moore growled. "Mind your own business."

Directly across from him on Commerce, there were no loungers now before Adam Haught's dramshop. The two cavalry officers had gone—inside, he had no doubt. Either one was a likelier candidate for lodging in the calaboose than Alec Cockrell had been, but a marshal had questionable authority over a soldier in uniform. Cockrell's horse had disappeared. The boy must have led it off somewhere. More likely somebody had come for it while Cockrell was at the courthouse. Cockrell's boy George, or the blacksmith, either one.

He looked down Commerce Street now to the river, scanning each short block. The Bryan house across the way was quiet. So was the shell of the hotel, though he had a sneaking suspicion that some of the bricklayers might still be there. In the next block he saw Henry come out of his shed, then go back in. Below, there was only the Cockrell place and the last stretch of road leading to the bridge, with Barry Derritt's cabin huddled alongside. No movement down there that he could see.

But that was a far way to look. Somewhere between where he stood and the river—a little over six hundred feet, counting crossings—was Alec Cockrell. He hadn't run off, and he would take no other way but Commerce in coming back to the square. There! What was that? Sounded like a door slammed. Down yonder at the house.

The Marshal drew back, shifted his shoulders, moved his feet, then tensed himself against the wall. He sighted along the gun barrels, moved the gun slightly, making sure it covered the one short block between that corner and the next, which was all he needed to cover, and waited.

chapter **twenty-one**

And finally...

Eᴠᴇɴ ᴀꜰᴛᴇʀ the toll bridge over the Trinity was finished and operating, the Cockrells kept the ferryboat which Alec had bought from John Bryan along with the townsite. It was no great shakes of a boat—a length of puncheon floor, floated on two pontoons dug out of cottonwood logs and pulled across the river by a cable which was still the original rope, hard-twisted from buffalo hair. Short as the crossing was, the ferry in the days before the bridge had done good business. Fords on this muddy river were treacherous. Let a team lose its footing in midstream, and the wagon it pulled, with all it carried, could be lost. Even now, should anything happen to make the bridge unsafe, the little mudscow had its value.

It was Barry Derritt's idea that the ferry should be kept in order. He had for it a brooding affection such as parents feel for a child not particularly well-favored, but still one's own. He kept the boat, half in the water, half out, at its original landing below the bridge, almost on a direct line with Hannah's kitchen and cabin behind the Cockrell house. The Cockrell children, under scorching threat of punishment if they whittled or otherwise defaced the craft, and worse, if they untied it or tried to, were allowed to play on it. Periodically, Barry himself went over the raft for leaks or rotting timbers, and put it across the river and back, to make sure that it was always ready for use.

It was toward this boat that Sarah ran as she fled from the house that afternoon after hiding Alec Cockrell's guns in her bed. It was the only refuge that occurred to her, and not a good one.

217

Instinctively she gathered up her skirts and tried to hold them close, to keep them away from the brush of the overgrown path that led through a patch of cut-over timber to the water. Anyone who happened to be looking that way could have seen her, but nobody did, or so she thought.

With the ferryboat clearly in sight, she stopped—to gather her skirts still more tightly about her, and held them higher. It was mud she wanted to avoid now. Near the water you could step into a spot of it without trying. She picked her steps carefully for a short way, then stopped again. She thought, it is a fool thing I'm doing—running like this, hiding. Then she thought, no, it isn't. If I were back there and he asked for his guns, I'd give them to him. I could almost take one in my own hands and go after that good-for-nothing who's making all this trouble. I've a notion to go back and put the guns where I found them.

But she did not go back. Panic swept her again, like a sickness. Dread of man's violence, which could smash ahead to accomplishments beyond the reach of woman's puny strength and shrinking timidity, but could just as surely, and for the same reason, invite destruction. She took a few more steps, putting her farther from sight and sound of the house and nearer the boat; and, when she stopped again, it was for an entirely different reason, but one equally foolish. A coil of rope lay on the rough deck, forward. A coil of dark rope, more of the buffalo hair twist; and some motion of the water or play of light through the thin branches of the willows made it seem to move; and her stomach went into the special knot reserved for reptiles. Even when she saw she was mistaken, the knot remained. It could have been a snake coiled there. The children were warned to watch for them, never to take hold of a branch or a root until sure it was a branch or a root—or a coil of rope.

The knot in her stomach tightened. The children. If they were only near enough for her to put her arms around them— something warm and alive and tender to hold to. Pshaw! Aurelia might stand still and accept such handling, but not the boys. Once a boy left the toddling stage, a woman had her arms around him mighty seldom, unless he was ailing. She drew a long, sad breath, and looked away from the coil of rope, beyond it, toward the river, and so became aware for the first time of the Indian, Charley John.

Partly hidden by the rope, he lay stretched out on the rough boards; and he lay so still that in his drab clothing he seemed fairly all of a piece with the raft. She rubbed her eyes and looked again, to make sure now that he was really there. He was—and his stillness was not sleep. His eyes were wide open, studying the sky, particularly the western sky, where the small clouds that had been whipping across in solitary flight seemed to gather now in a fleecy pile. Dirty fleece from dusty sheep, blotched with shadow. With a start she thought again of the children. This could be warning of a storm. Then she sighed, wearily. A storm wouldn't matter. Not now. Nothing in the world of nature mattered. Only man's evil intentions had to be reckoned with. Then, why did this Indian, Alec Cockrell's sworn friend, after banging away furiously most of the day at harmless birds, lie there on his back, dreaming . . . now, when he could possibly be of some use? Alec might listen to Charley John—she knew he would not, but oh, for the grace of a little more time! She must try for it. She tightened her hold on her skirts and hurried to the boat.

Charley John heard her coming. He turned, looked at her dully for a second, then in a single, easy motion got to his feet, picking up his hat and his gun from the floor of the boat as he did so. Slowly then he made his way toward her. They met at the edge of the boat.

"Charley John?" she said, not knowing how to shape her appeal.

"Woman of my brother," he said respectfully, but left what she must say to her.

"What are you doing—down here?"

Words, she thought, are like small stones, thrown to get someone's attention. They merely give notice, they mean nothing in themselves. Fear was bitter and full in her throat. Could Charley John hear that? He gave no sign.

"Like you," he said, "I wait."

"You wait?" she cried. "For what?"

"For the hour." He looked back halfway toward the gathering

clouds. And he mumbled something that sounded like, "Later, when the sky is dark all over."

"No," she said, crying out at her own fears, not at his mutterings, "No. What about the birds? I've not heard your gun in a long while. Have you given up fighting the birds?"

"The birds have gone," he told her. "They, too, wait for the dark."

"Charley John, stop it!"

The Indian in his homely, unsuitable clothing, stared at her without moving. Their eyes are queer, she thought, not like other folks' eyes. They fasten their eyes upon you and . . . what did they know more than other people?

"The birds," Charley John said, "are spirits of evil. They are not the evil itself. I can shoot them. I can drive them away. I can keep watch, but that is all. Can you do more?"

No. No, she could not, she knew; but she would not say so.

"I can try," she cried. "Charley John, there is still time."

"No time now," he said.

"Yes. A little time. If we don't waste it. I hid his guns."

"That was a foolish thing to do."

"No," she said. "He will find them, but it will take a while. That is our time." Did she or did she not hear a door slam to? "Charley John, come," she said. "Hurry! There is trouble in town. There is a man . . . take your gun and follow Mr. Cockrell. Catch him if you can. Stop him . . . do what you will, only go! Don't stand there. Don't wait on me. Go!"

He turned toward the house. He moved, but she had never seen such deliberation. With all the entanglements of her skirts she could have gone through the brush faster. What had him by the heels? What dragged him backward?

But she was wrong about her own ability to move quickly. Vines, sharp ends of branches, obstacles that she had cleared safely going down to the water, reached out and caught her now. She had no breath, no strength. She . . .

She stopped short. She dropped her skirts. Her hands flew to cover her ears—against a burst of sound which, if not crashing loud, was still the voice of destruction. She recognized the sound. It was the report of a heavily loaded, double-barreled shotgun.

chapter twenty-two

...*when death strikes*...

THE NEAT BEDROOM, after Alec had recovered his guns, looked as if a tornado had swept it. Tumbled, torn, ruined. Counterpane, blanket and sheets in one heap, pillows in another. The feather pad hung halfway off the bed. The shards of the broken pitcher made their own litter on the floor. It gave him bitter, savage satisfaction to see the wreck he had made of it all. To recall how Sister Polly Thompson had screeched and skedaddled as he lunged at the bed, both hands reaching out.

The rack and ruin did more. It filled him inside with hate and unappeasable anger clear to the neck of the bottle. The mess around him hardly matched the spoiling of this big, fine day, the threat that would becloud every day for him now unless he rubbed out the man who held this ugly spite against him. He buckled his gun belt around him with steady hands, feeling the drag of his Colt in its holster a familiar weight, and part of him. He had no notion that he would need either the revolver or his knife; but, if he did, both were ready.

He took up his shotgun now, hurriedly checked hammers, triggers and the percussion lock, found all free and clean, nodded his satisfaction, and carried the gun to the safe in the office to load it. Powder flask, shot pouch, a box of wads, felt and paper, and a smaller one of caps were all in their proper places. He set the butt of the gun against the inside of his right instep and blew sharply down each barrel. Then, working with the same haste but more care, he measured powder into each barrel, settled a felt wad over each charge, rammed it home, poured a measure of shot on top of that, settled it with a heavy paper wad; and he was ready. He pocketed the box of caps and, balancing the gun in his hand, went back through the tumbled bedroom, through the hall, and out of the house without a backward look.

He was on his way to kill Andrew Moore. As surely as if Hannah had said, "Dey's a varmint hidin' in de smokehouse somewheres, Mist' Alec. He's aftah ouah meat."

A varmint. Hiding. It would have helped if he could have known whereabouts. But, not knowing, he did not hang back, wondering. Hardly nearer than the square, he calculated. He walked with purposeful stride, leaning forward a little, past the full length of Henry's smithy, and slowed only a little in crossing the next street, Broadway. That brought him to the Bryan house opposite his hotel building.

He stopped there perhaps a half-minute. His thought was that he would find Moore finally, forted up in the calaboose. Still he knew it was possible that the varmint was closer. He could be most anywhere now, hiding around the corner of a building, or, maybe, inside one, squatting by a window, his eyes, his gun just above the sill. He thought, I don't want to give him the upper hand now, exposing myself too much. I'll cross over here and follow the hotel wall as far as it goes. Then we'll see.

He, too, in that same half-minute noticed the emptiness of the street. His sight was as clear now as his hands were steady. He saw that the cavalrymen had disappeared from before Haught's cabin, that Joab and his horse were gone. He hoped Joab would be just around the corner, hunting shade. It would be handy to mount Sinful there—when he had his business done uptown. Wagons must be near now. Time was going by. Shade fell over the street. Not that late. Must be clouding over out west. But he didn't turn to look. He set his feet to cross the street.

He made a quarter-turn; and for him, too, the world crashed in a blast of sound. But for him there was more to it than that. It was as if the unfinished wall of the hotel had fallen on him. The ground heaved under him. Caught between the two, he could not cry out, he could not breathe. But, oddly, he could still think. This is death, he thought. I'm dying. I . . . I lost this throw. Sarah . . .

And darkness came.

chapter twenty-three

...and darkness gathers...

SARAH COULD NEVER remember how she reached the house after the burst of gunfire. She didn't see Charley John disappear, could not say where he went. Suddenly she was at the back door, then inside, in the hall. She heard a whimper. That was Sister Polly, in the door of the bedroom, wringing her hands. She heard a moan. That was Hannah, stumbling in from her quarters. Then Margaret Bryan came running, as if blown by the wind.

"Sarah?" she cried. "Oh, Sarah, be thankful you didn't see. Shot him down in the road right in front of our place. He didn't have a chance. They . . . they're bringing him here now."

"Here?" Polly Thompson stiffened and laid hold of the bedroom doorknob. "Not in here, Sister. Not in here."

She closed the door so quickly that even Sarah had no more than one short look at the turmoil in that room. No matter how weak or foolish Polly had been before, and no matter how she took on afterward, Sarah forgave her for the sake of that one movement, closing the bedroom door before anyone else saw the state that room was in. Then she heard movement in the road and went to the front door, to open it.

So calm, people said afterward, so quiet, in perfect command of herself and everything else. No. She was as hollow as a cornstalk in the wintertime, with the pith all dried out inside.

Three men came from the road through the gray twilight, carrying Alec Cockrell on a folded horse blanket. They were Will Toomy and the servant George and Henry, the blacksmith. Behind them walked a fourth man, white, square-set, with a black

223

satchel. Dr. McDermitt from uptown, though at first she did not know him. She just saw him.

"Is he . . ." she heard herself say, with no breath behind the words.

Nobody answered her. The panting men carrying the litter stared at her, but now she could hear Alec breathing. Roughly, but he was still alive.

"Take him into the parlor," she said. "Put him on the sofa."

"A bed will do better," the square-set Doctor said.

"The bed," she explained, "is not just ready."

So the three men carried Alec into her pretty parlor and laid him on the tufted sofa, Dr. McDermitt still grumbling about a bed. Then he asked for towels and water and she went with George to fetch them, telling herself she must not stumble, and trying to forget how Alec looked there on the couch, knowing she never would. Breathing hard—it was almost snoring—and his eyes closed in false sleep. His shirt under the open vest soaked with blood. Dust and little sticks in his hair. His face unearthly pale. Oh, Alec, Alec!

Later, back in the parlor, when the Doctor asked for a light, she herself turned up the wick in the painted lamp on the center table and lit it; and it was in the soft glow that came as she put the shade back in place that she saw the Indian. He was standing near the north window, just standing, in his way of being motionless.

But the Doctor grumbled now about the lamp.

"More shadow than light," he said. "Have you got a lantern?"

So she sent George for a tin lamp they kept in the office, the first coal-oil lamp they had ever owned; and when he came back with it, she begged to be allowed to hold it, or to help the Doctor in some other way; but the Doctor looked her over and shook his head.

"Better not try it, ma'am," he said. "Best let George hold the lamp; and Henry here can give me a hand when I need it. It calls for a man, ma'am. Toomy, you might set a chair for Mrs. Cockrell in the hall."

So, that was the picture she walked away from, unwillingly: George holding the tin lamp, the whites of his eyes glistening,

Henry in a sweat, but standing ready with his big blacksmith's arms and hands, Dr. McDermitt opening his satchel on scissors and lancets, and rolling up his sleeves, and the Indian standing beside the window. Alec still breathing, but . . .

"He is hurt bad, ma'am," the Doctor said. "I'll do what I can."

He had not much hope, she could tell; but she must hold hers in every way she knew. Will Toomy, his face inches longer than she had ever seen it, set a chair for her in the hall and she took it, thanking him.

"Mr. Toomy, I'm thankful, too, that you were there—to pick him up."

Toomy groaned.

"I wasn't, ma'am. Damn it, I wasn't. Henry was first. He got the blanket. He sent his boy for the Doctor and was looking around for another pair of hands when I happened along. Coming from the mill, ma'am. Boss had said something earlier about paying off the men himself and I thought he'd maybe forgot. So I started uptown—now, if I'd only started five or ten minutes sooner!"

"Don't blame yourself, Mr. Toomy," she said faintly.

Looking down, she saw that her hands were wrapped tightly around each other in her lap. The tightness was a cramp almost, but it felt good. She didn't care about Mr. Toomy or the mill or the men, but she felt she must pretend.

"It is Saturday, isn't it?" she said.

"Hell," Toomy growled, "it don't matter now."

No, it didn't matter—to her, or to Will Toomy, it seemed. It might matter to the mill hands.

"We must see about the pay," she said. "Later."

"Yes, ma'am. I . . . there's just one thing. The boss had the money on him. Quite a lot of it. There was a poker game at Black Jack. You wouldn't know . . ."

But she did know. She knew all the places where Alec Cockrell went, all the things good and bad, he ever did. Even when she closed her eyes or turned her back or shut a door, she knew. She thought—never again? Not even the gaudy haunts of sin? Oh, Alec, my husband, rise up from that couch and stand where I can see you.

Lightning flashed suddenly, and thunder growled.

"Tomorrow," Toomy said, "will be all right—or the day after."

Tomorrow? The day after? There was more thunder.

"I'll be getting on back to the mill now," Toomy said, "and the men." He listened to the thunder. "Maybe I'd best close the shutters before I go."

A minute or two later she heard him at them, and then Dr. Mc-Dermitt opened the parlor door.

Opening her hands, she stood up so suddenly that she all but toppled, and was glad of the Doctor's arm steadying her. He still had his sleeves rolled up; and, in the parlor, on one of her best towels on the center table were spread out his instruments. More towels had been laid over Alec on the couch. Against their bleached whiteness bright spots of blood stood out here and there. She closed her eyes, gave way to another touch of giddiness, then rallied. She must not behave so, she must not. This was Alec, her dear husband, lying there in bloody anguish. His eyes were open now, but stared vacantly at the ceiling. Some color had returned to his face, but not enough. Spasms of pain lined his forehead and drew his mouth, then passed. He breathed perhaps not quite so noisily.

"Speak to him," Dr. McDermitt said. "He may know you."

Speak to him? She wanted to bend over him, gather him and his wounds into her arms, hold him, mother him like a young one; but how could she without doing him more hurt?

Another spasm crossed his features. She touched his forehead with her finger-tips, then, on impulse, laid her whole hand there. Instantly the grimace of pain was gone. The vacant stare left his eyes. He looked up at her, knowing who she was. He smiled; but, when he tried to speak, he coughed. Foam bubbled on his lips. The Doctor wiped it away, and the cloth in his hands was stained red.

"Eight slugs in him that I know of," he said. "Riddled his guts."

He was dying. It seemed to Sarah that the slight warmth under her hand was already less. He was dying, but he had known her. No one else in the room had heard the word he had tried to say. No one but her would have known what Alec Cockrell meant.

Methody, she thought. Methody woman. It was a name he had for me sometimes. Usually when he was out of patience with something I wanted him to do or not to do. Methody woman, why did you hide my guns? You shouldn't have done that. If I forgive you, it is only because you are you. . . .

How long have I, she wondered. Time enough to say what I never took time or thought to say when I could have done so? No. There was never time enough for that. Never for anybody.

The lamp George had held was now on the mantel and George was busy gathering towels and clothes up from the floor. There was light enough in the room to see everything and everybody in it. Not too sharply, but plain enough. Henry, the blacksmith, had disappeared. The Indian stood like a statue beside the now darkened north window. Dr. McDermitt had settled back in a chair—to wait.

"Mr. Cockrell? Alec?" Sarah murmured. "Don't you try to talk any more. Just you rest now. Rest, and listen to me. I . . . Alec, do you hear me? What are you looking at now? Charley John?" No, it was not the Indian, but something above his head—that old picture—Columbus. Once he had asked her. . . . The change came. She felt it.

Dr. McDermitt heaved himself up out of his chair, but he was too late. Alec Cockrell was gone.

chapter **twenty-four**

...and storm clouds cover the sky...

GONE. He'd not come back from this journeying. Never, never again. A hush settled down on the house. A hush seemed to fall over the world, as the gathering storm lulled for a spell. Indoors, in the parlor, where the lamps were suddenly too bright, Sarah could have sworn that nobody moved; but she was wrong about that. When Dr. McDermitt spoke to her again, his voice seemed to come from over her head:

"Come now . . . come."

And she was kneeling beside the couch, clinging to Alec's hand, imploring him not to leave her. Hope still would not give way. Dr. McDermitt loosened her fingers and lifted her to her feet. His touch was kindly in its strength; and he wasted no effort on idle pity or comfort. He just told her what to do.

"Call your women."

Her women. That would be Hannah and, she supposed, Sister Polly. On feet that dragged she left the parlor, crossed the hall, and opened the bedroom door. Polly and Hannah had just finished their work there. The room was spotless, its order too perfect. If there could only have been a boot track of dust on the floor, a rug kicked up, a belt with a holster thrown carelessly over the foot of the bed. Oddly, then, at the sight of her white face, it was Hannah who threw her apron over her head and moaned, and Polly Thompson who straightened up, then came forward with outstretched arms and a cry of pity:

228

"Sister, dear! Oh, my poor darling!"

She rocked Sarah in her arms, murmuring endearments, kissing her gently. Not in years had Sarah experienced such tenderness from another woman. When she had lost her first baby, her mother, who had been living then, had fondled her so. She thought now of that time and how she had leaned on her frail mother. She tried to lean so on Sister Polly, but found at once that she could not. It was part of the delirium of that black night, during which she passed from numbness to the agony of realization, through that into refusal and wild protest, and finally with the dawn found her sure answer, that always something outside herself, some little thing, pricked her and gave her direction.

Now, if you please, it was Polly Thompson's bones. Gratefully, she dropped her head on her sister's shoulder and the next instant jerked it away. The skinniest shoulder that a stricken woman had ever tried to nestle against. That this should come to her now! Forbidding her to trust the support to which she wanted to cling! But there it was. Holding Polly up more surely than Polly held her, she raised her head, then fumbled for a decent reason and found it.

"So much to do," she said. "You must help me, Sister. You and Hannah."

Hannah turned promptly toward the rear of the house.

"Wash 'um," she muttered. "Put on all clean cloes."

"Hannah," Sarah said, the habit of concern for those around her asserting itself, "let somebody else carry water for you—and wood. George or Henry—whoever is around. Hannah . . . Hannah, where are your spectacles?"

Surely that was not important, but it seemed so.

"Broke 'um," Hannah said unwillingly. " 'S afternoon. No time to talk now. Got to poke up my fiah—dis minute."

She shuffled away.

"They fell off," Polly explained. "At the kitchen door. Then she stepped on them, smashed them good. She's got the frames in her apron pocket now, maybe the glass, too. She swept it all up, every scrap."

Sarah shivered, not knowing exactly why.

"Polly, how . . ."

"Never mind," Polly said. "Never mind now. Sister, you will want Brother Alec dressed in his best. Will you show me where to find everything?"

Sarah closed her eyes. The shiver had been the mere beginning of chill. Polly's words took her back into the parlor. That shattered body, she thought—so strong, so abounding in health an hour or two ago. Dusty now, draggled, stained with blood. That Hannah should see him so—and Sister Polly.

"Polly," she said, "he had nothing better than what he wore today." He had never looked taller or finer than he had that morning, riding home. She felt her face go now into a thousand wrinkles of perplexity as she tried to think. "But when it turned real warm this afternoon, he must have taken off his coat. When they brought him in just now, it seems to me he didn't have it. Do you remember, Polly? Did you see?"

Polly's face, too, crumpled now; but, before she could say what she knew or didn't know, George was at the door of the bedroom, his arms full of clothing. Seeing Sarah, he ducked his head over the bundle and clutched it to him, as if he also had something to hide.

"George," Sarah said, "are those . . ."

"Ee . . . yas'm."

"Have you got everything?"

"Yas'm." Then he hesitated. "I . . . de coat turned up missin', but Henry had it. He brung it in jes' now. Miss Sally, de coat's tore—kinda bad."

"Let me see."

Shamefacedly, as if he were to blame, he showed her. The back breadth was split from tail to collar. She could not hold back a cry of dismay. Not in rags, dear Lord! Not now, after all these years. I couldn't bear it.

She took the coat into her hands and felt as torn apart as it was. Pity, anger, fear shook her.

"Sister," Polly said, "maybe I can mend it."

Maybe she could. More than likely she could not.

"Nobody will see."

But she, Sarah, would know. Alec knew. He must know. Those

who dressed him would know. She would not have it said that Alec Cockrell was laid out in a torn coat.

It was then, she knew later, that she began to fight. Desperately, with all the odds against her. Feebly, because strength was not easily come by. She laid the coat on the bundle in George's arms.

"It's more than a mending job," she said, forcing quiet into her voice. "Brush and clean everything the best you can, George; but, before you begin, send somebody to find Mr. Gouffe, the French tailor. Tell him I want to see him here as soon as he can come. Tell him to hurry, please."

"Miss Sally, it's startin' to rain."

"The weather doesn't matter. Go on. Do as I say."

chapter **twenty-five**

...*when lightning glitters and thunder rolls*...

BUT IT WAS BLACK Pokey finally, who put the proper words to chaos.

After George had gone away with the bedraggled clothing, there was a minute of nothing to do. So alone, Sarah thought, so all alone; and then, as if they had been watching for the opening, the children again rushed into her mind. For one thing, there was the storm. George had said it was beginning to rain; and she could hear for herself the tapping of it against the shutters. A gentle rain, for Texas. It would not go on like that. It would stop, the clouds would ride past and be gone, or there would be a downpour. A gust of wind hurled a hatful of water against the north shutters. Lightning flashed and thunder growled.

The young ones—three of them at Honey Springs. Safe there as anywhere; but, if it rained hard and the river rose and spread out over the prairie, nobody could say when she would see them again. She was thankful to have the baby with her, but where was he? Tucked away somewhere with his black playmate and guardian, Willie Winn. But where? Who watched the two of them while Hannah was busy in the house? She fretted like that.

"Pokey came from the mill," Polly said. "Ran every step of the way. Couldn't talk when she got here. Hannah threw some cold water on her, to quiet her, then set her to watch the young'uns. Shes' all right now, but she was in a state."

Pokey—yes, she would be in a state. She adored Mr. . . . . Sarah shivered again, everything in her drawing into a tight knot of rejection.

"How did Pokey know?" she asked.

"How?" Polly said shrilly. "Everybody knew as soon as it happened. Everybody this side of the river, and by now the word's all through the West Side. People going home, to be ahead of the storm. Sister, do you realize it's going on two hours now since they brought Brother Alec home?"

No. No, she didn't realize. Two hours. Would they have the word at Honey Springs? They might. Hord's Ridge folk might stop or even go out of their way to carry the news. What would the Overtons do then? Well, probably nothing. Night coming on and the storm. Wherever you crossed the river, you had low ground to cover.

Just the same, she took time to listen. For the sound of wheels if they should come by wagon, for the snort and scuffle of a horse if Perry came alone. She heard nothing—only the rain, harder now and an almost unbroken roll of thunder that drowned all other sound.

She did not hear the Overtons when they came. The first warning was a pounding on the front door. When she opened it, there they were—Martha in a big shawl, and, behind her, Nellie Johnson—the two of them pushing into the house Sarah's three lost ones, so blanketed that she could hardly tell one from another, and they couldn't see where they were going. Outside, in the dark and the wet, Perry Overton called from the wagon.

"I'll drive around to the back, Sarah. Got a few things to unload."

Before he could start the mules, Henry was there.

"Don't turn the wagon, Mr. Overton. Kind of mucky roun' de house awready. I'll unload fo' you. I knows where to step better'n I kin show you."

It was clear dark now, the air still warm, the wind blowing in gusty puffs. A forked streak of lightning tore through the blackness. Nellie Johnson closed the door and bolted it.

"No use gettin' de house wet, too," she apologized. "Men'll make out."

Another minute—it seemed no more—and Nellie was going

through the house to the back, to find Hannah, because that was what she had come for, to help with the laying out; and the rest of them were in the bedroom, Sarah on her knees, unwrapping little Frank while the others shucked their blankets. And saying over and over words that poured from a tortured heart.

"I was never so glad to see anybody in my life." For the first time, tears filled her eyes. "Never so glad ..."

And Martha Overton, taking off her shawl, and with Polly's help picking up after the others, was almost as bad, talking around and around.

"Well, I didn't know whether to bring them back or not. Mr. Toomy sent us word; and Perry said right off, 'We're needed, Mother. Get your bonnet and come on!' I didn't bother about a bonnet. And about the young ones, I said to myself, 'Shall I or shan't I?' But I figured, if they were mine I'd want them with me. So I told Perry what else to put in the wagon—oh, just some things we had on hand. Buttermilk, butter, a smoked ham and some bread. We baked this afternoon. A crock of honey, a sack of meal—time like this, you never know how many you'll have to feed."

"Never so glad ..." the words slipped from Sarah, speech as uncontrollable as her tears. Little Frank put his hand to her face.

"Don't cry, Mama. Don't cry."

She kissed his fingers, caught him to her, and looked her love at the other two. Only that morning she had thought, how fast they grow. Now, they were no more than babies in their young helplessness—Aurelia, rumpled from the blanket and the ride, robbed, somehow, of her prettiness, Robert, solemn-faced, big-eyed, showing for the first time a haunting resemblance to his father, which, she had declared, none of the boys had.

"Martha, do they know?"

"We told them—best we could," Martha said. "On the way over. I don't think they realize."

No, how could they? Oh, it was too much—too much for a woman to bear. She did not need Pokey's cry of distress to tell her that, though Pokey said it better than anyone else. With the other three close beside her, Sarah had a craving now for her youngest, and sent Polly to find out where Hannah had tucked

him away, and said, bring him to her. Black Pokey came, carrying
him into the house and the bedroom, in a temper at being waked
out of deep sleep on the pallet Hannah had made for him in the
kitchen. Pokey was glad to set him on his feet, where he scowled
and blinked, and scowled again, so that the others, changing mood
faster than a butterfly can light and be gone, laughed at him, as
usual.

But not Sarah. The black scowl on the round pink face, framed
by flaxen hair, was too familiar. Even more so was the clearing
of the scowl into a furtive, half-shamed, wistful, mischievous smile.
Sarah caught her breath—not once, but twice—for it was then that
Pokey released a howl of her own.

Poor Pokey! She had until that minute been as quiet and good
as could be; but, seeing her mistress standing there, so white and
sad, with the young ones close around her, she could bear no more.
Her howl was a cry of pure, primitive agony. She fell to her knees.
She dropped her head to the floor and beat it and her hands
against the boards, and howled again. The sound cut through
Sarah like a knife.

"Pokey," she said, and then no more.

Lightning so bright, so fierce, that even closed shutters could
not keep out its unearthly brilliance, burst all around the house.
Thunder crashed, and the skies opened. Rain beat upon the
house with a roar. Even Pokey sat back on her heels, her mouth
open in awe.

"I thought sho'," she said afterward, "it war de en' o' de worl'."

When she knew it was not that, when everything, except for
the beat of the rain, was just as it had been, she crawled on her
knees to Sarah's feet, then raised her arms, clasped her hands and
made her cry:

"Miss Sally, Miss Sally, wot is to come o' we all now?"

chapter **twenty-six**

...*beware the Raven Mockers,*
who ride the storm...

"**W**ot is to come o' we all now?"

Among the many, in Dallas and roundabout, who had reason
that stormy night to echo black Pokey's lament, the first, oddly
enough, was Alec Cockrell's wagon boss—big Rudy Horst.

The wagons were late. By midafternoon, Rudy knew that he'd
not make the town much, if any, before dark. It was a long train—
two ordinary box wagons and three oversize freighters. Mules
drew the wagons, but double spans of oxen were hitched to the
freighters; and there was a span to spare following behind, in case
it was needed. Every wagon was loaded to the guards. You didn't
take a wagon over rough road that distance if you didn't expect
to fill it. The mules stepped right along, but it was hard to tell
about a mule. They pulled till they dropped and you had no warning. It was the oxen that had Rudy worried. They had about all
they could drag, even on level road like this one.

The first freighter, uncovered, carried a towering load of raw
pine lumber, and it was, maybe, the heaviest; but Rudy, riding
back to look things over a half-dozen times that afternoon, swept
the lumber rig with his eyes and passed on, but gave close inspec-
tion to the two canvas-covered loads that followed. If a load of
lumber got stalled, you had work to do; but, if anything happened to those other two, he was ruined. Because, centered in the
first covered wagon, crated and padded and lashed to the wagon
bed, was a piano almost as long as the freighter, and in the second,
even more carefully padded and tied down, was a crystal chande-

236

lier. A hundred times on the way Rudy had cursed those two objects and finished each swear with a grin.

There was a man and a boss—Alick Cockrell! Thousands of dollars' worth of merchandisable stuff on the five wagons, but he cared more for that pianna and that chandelier than all the rest of it. Why? It was hard to say. The way Rudy heard it, the boss was in some trouble back in town. Some son-of-a-gun with a grudge was threatening him with his life; so, what did the boss do? To show how little he minded, he went out and bought fancy furniture for a hotel he hadn't half finished building. It could just be bluff, but maybe not. Maybe he was just that sure he would finish the hotel and anything else he started. All that concerned Rudy now was that he'd better make it the rest of the way to town without busting a single wire on that pianna or a bob on the chandelier, if he valued his job or his own life. And he'd better make town this evening, like he'd promised, and, if possible, before a storm broke. He didn't like the looks of those clouds piling up now in the southwest, though he'd been looking for them all afternoon.

It was the heat. At the noon rest, in a spot of shade and deep grass beside clear water, if it hadn't been Saturday and he hadn't given his word and there hadn't been the promise of storm in a brassy sky, he'd have pitched camp and made a fresh start the next morning. As it was, he'd rested men and animals all he could take time for, then had sent them on. Now, with the afternoon moving faster than the wagons, all had taken more punishment than they could stand up to. As he turned to ride back past the train again, his horse, walking, was all in a sweat. So was he, for that matter, though he might look as big and almighty as ever, his red beard glinting in the sun.

The mule wagons rolled by, the mules stepping, the drivers spitting carelessly into the dust. They were all right. In a pinch they could break and run for it. But now the freighters. Barely moving. He stopped to speak to the driver in charge of the lumber load. A Frenchman. The boss favored Frenchies now with oxen. They had fool ways—called the beasts by pet names, sang to them, used a goad mighty little—but they got the most out of the animals, Rudy had to admit.

"How're you coming, Pierre?"

The driver smiled halfway, and shrugged his shoulders.

"We do what we can."

Heads down. Crawling.

"Think you'll make it?"

"How far?" the Frenchman countered, and held up three fingers, guessing.

Rudy nodded. It was all of that and more, but not too much, maybe. If their luck held. The load of lumber rolled by, the pianna, the chandelier. A dozen oxen with their heads way down, three drivers smiling in faint apology. Here came the extra span, a boy of sixteen in charge. By God, the fellow had made a wreath of yellow flowers and hung it on the neck of the near ox! Outrage flared in Rudy. Take a time like this . . . he got control of himself before too late. Just worry boiling up, and he knew better than to show it. He contented himself with an explosive, "Hell!" which the boy took for a cheer. He laughed, white teeth shining against a beardless, sun-browned face. A kid—a high-spirited, happy-go-lucky kid!

And, as suddenly as if a bolt of lightning had shot out from that bank of clouds yonder, it came over Rudy Horst that a kid was exactly what he was not—not any more. Twice this wreath-making boy's years were his and what did he have to show for them? His strength, his job, a record of sin, and that was all. At the peak of his strength now, maybe; but how much longer could he go on like this? Who could say? He'd seen giants crumble before. A man got pinned under a wagon, setting a wheel, and broke a leg that never mended just right. Or he finished a barroom brawl at the bottom of the heap instead of on top. Things like that did something to a man's spirit even if he got well of his bruises. Cock of the walk Rudy Horst was now but . . . maybe he'd have done better to listen to the boss when he hinted something about taking up ranch land and putting part of his pay into cattle.

He never had listened. Wouldn't. Take up land, and you had to live on it—part time, anyhow. That meant you built a house. What good was a house without a woman? So you married. But who? Great sizzling fires of hell, amongst all the women he knew from here to Shreveport, wasn't there one? No. Not one—worth keeping. Oh, maybe, he had seen one once or twice—from a distance. And maybe she had seen him, but turned her back fast and gone away. With good reason.

And that's how it stands, big, red Rudy. You get pinned under a wagon today and what have you to get up to? Nothing, you good-for-nothing bruiser. On the other hand, take the boss. Say . . . he just might take the boss at his word now. What was that about ranch land? I'm in the notion sort of.

The afternoon wore along. The wagons rolled, wheel by wheel. The clouds crawled not much faster up the sky. Four miles were three, then two, then one. But the clouds were piling up faster now. The sun was gone. A queer light, not yet darkness, though that would come soon, fell over the land. A chimney, a house, more houses. The head driver raised a whoop and Rudy pushed his horse to the front to see. What he saw was a man riding fast toward the train. Took it to be the boss. It was the boss's horse. Then the man pulled up and he knew it wasn't the boss.

It was the boss's Irish bricklayer, Will Toomy. He let Rudy ride close, then said, maybe, six words; but they knocked Rudy's narrow world into a heap.

"No," he said. "I don't believe you. The boss?"

It was true. Where, then, was the blackguard who had shot him? In jail. Well, it had better be a stout one.

"None of that," Toomy said. "We've work ahead. Follow me into town. I'll show you where to unload."

In Rudy's great chest something crumbled.

"I've got a pianna on one of the wagons," he said brokenly, "and a chandelier."

That had been taken care of, too. So Rudy again rode back along the train.

"Follow that man," he ordered his drivers, "and stow your noise. It's a funeral waiting for us in town—not a celebration."

Whose funeral? His own, maybe. What was this about taking up land, settling down? Hell, he didn't even have a job now that he could be sure of.

"*Wot is to come o' we all now?*"

In Dallas, in their store on the southeast corner of Houston and Commerce, Abraham Shirek and Hyman Hirsch sat on opposite stools and faced each other in the gathering gloom, little Abraham looking woefully like the peddler who had moaned his discouragement a few years back on the Cockrell doorstep.

"And to think," he said, "I wrote to my brothers, Samuel and Saul, to sell all they had in Berlin and come here. It was only January. Of this year. They could be on the ocean now. I said, you can clerk in our store until you learn the way of business in America. Then you may want to set up for yourselves somewhere; or maybe you will choose to stay with us—the way business is expanding. That is what I said, Hyman—the way business is expanding."

"Um-huh," Hirsch said in dirgelike response. "Um-huh."

"And you, Hyman," Abraham went on, "you had a good business in Frankfort, Kentucky. You sold it to come in with me here. It was a good business, Hyman?"

"It would be a fine business," Hyman said, "if I had it now to go back to." He drummed a while, thoughtfully, on his knees with his fingers. "Abraham," he said then, softly pleading, "maybe it is not as bad as it looks right now? We have the store, the merchandise. We are here. We could talk to Mrs. Cockrell a little later, maybe?"

"Mrs. Cockrell," Abraham Shirek said with finality, "is now a widow—or she soon will be. While her husband lived, she was his bookkeeper, and that is all. Will she, a widow, run his businesses like he did? Alone? Will she operate a sawmill, a brickyard? Will she build houses? And rent them? Will she build a hotel?"

No. Such goings on for a woman seemed most improbable, but Hyman Hirsch had still one hope.

"Abraham, could we, maybe, buy the store building?"

"With what?" Shirek demanded.

"Our prospects," Hirsch suggested. "Look, Abraham."

"I am looking, Hyman. And I don't like what I see. Hyman, I have told you what it was like in this town when I came here. I tell you now, if Mr. Cockrell dies of his wounds tonight, by this time next week, you will see ruin coming back on us. Next year this time we have again a dirty little village clinging to a riverbank; and the next year? Maybe nothing. Well, Hyman, shall we take inventory now? We advertised in Mr. Latimer's paper a sale for next week. So, it will be a closing-out sale. That's all."

"Um-huh," Hirsch said slowly. Unwillingly. He still preferred Dallas to Frankfort, Kentucky, and even more to what he had known of Prussia. "We take inventory. God send that your brothers arrive in time for the sale. Then, what is left we can divide into four packs instead of two, and start out on the road again. Shall we draw lots to see who goes where?"

"You can joke?" Shirek said bitterly.

"I am not joking," Hirsch assured him. "I never felt less like making fun. I . . . listen, Abraham. Do you hear something—like somebody calling?"

Shirek listened. It was Rudy Horst's wagoners saluting the town. Hear them? Through closed shutters the sound came; and Abraham Shirek drew himself together in a knot of misery.

"Abe, my friend," Hirsch said in alarm, getting down off his stool. "What is it now?"

"Hyman," Shirek moaned, "it is the wagons. Mr. Cockrell's wagons, with three, four cases of goods for us, bought on credit, still to be paid for. Well, Hyman, shall we purchase the building now, besides?"

Mr. Hirsch drew his shoulders high about his ears and lowered his head again. He was beaten now. Then down went the shoulders and up came his head. He listened once more, this time to the whipping of rain against the shutters. And nothing else. The shouting had stopped.

"Abe," he said, "are you sure?"

"Of course, I am sure," Shirek said impatiently, but wondered a little himself. "The wagons are late. They should have been here before this, but . . . what else could those wild yells mean?"

"And now it is raining," Hirsch meditated. "Put on a light, Abraham. I will get a lantern. It is our goods out there, getting wet, maybe. Not only that. Out there is a fine piano, and a crystal chandelier. We made a contract to store them, remember? All day we have been making room for them."

"Oy!" Shirek moaned, remembering. "Oy! That poor Mrs. Cockrell. Merchandise is merchandise, which we can hope to sell to somebody for something finally; but what will she do with a piano and a chandelier and a hotel half built?"

"Wot is to come o' we-all now?"
This was the fear that haunted many that long night through. Pokey's wail found its echo on every muddy street or road, wherever people lived or gathered who, by some chain of circumstance, had attached themselves and their hopes to the brave, indomitable, and—so they thought—unconquerable man who now lay dead in his home at the foot of Commerce Street, though few outside that house knew until later just when life departed.

Down at the sawmill, men sat on stools or waste ends of logs or upturned pails—whatever came handy—bunched about a hooded lantern, and talked of the day's doings—why things had happened the way they had and, the men being human, what effect the turn of events would have on each one of their lives from now on. When they talked. The meeting was from the first strangely solemn. The lantern light was weak. The shadows of the silent mill loomed big around them. Maybe it was that which put a hush on rough speech; or it might have been the admonishment that Toomy left with them when he rode off to catch Rudy Horst and give him the news, then hold him, if he could, from tearing the town apart.

"You will oblige me," Toomy said to the mill hands, "by behaving as decent as you know how this night. Actin' rough will only bring more trouble on all. Be thinkin', not of your no-account selves, but of the brave, small woman who will be a widow before mornin', and four small ones lookin' to her for care. She will not be forgettin' you when she gets around to rememberin'; so do you not be forgettin' her. If there be one o' you who knows the way of it, a prayer would do no harm."

Nobody offered a prayer, though some might have listened if anyone had been bold enough to try praying. As it was, they were all hard put to apply words to what they were thinking.

"I'd-a never believed it," the boss of the lumberyard said, out of the silence. "I still don't believe it halfway. I'd put my money on Alick Cockrell coming out on top of any fight, no matter what the odds."

"Been a fair fight," someone growled from the shadows, "you'd a won and so would he. Andy Moore knowed that, sure as you do. Figgered to lose if he fit fair, so he fit foul. Can't much blame him, one way you look at it." A growl welled up beyond the lantern. "I mean—if he wanted to go on living."

The question was should Moore be allowed to live. In their several ways the men meditated on that, and put it to Toomy sharply when he came back to tell them that Alick Cockrell was dead. When he tried to hush them, saying that others had raised the same question and that a meeting had been called in the courthouse of those in authority, to which other citizens had invited themselves, and that Andy Moore was now locked up in his own calaboose, growls turned into open threat.

"That I want to look at for myself," a shifty-eyed ne'er-do-well said. "Who's for going to town with me, to have fun with the Marshal?"

Toomy reached for a scantling, which even in the dark he found ready to his hand.

"Stow it," he said. "Or will I crack a head or so, to let sense come through to you? I said, no rough actin', and that's what I mean. Will it bring your friend and mine back to us? It will not. There are some in this town who held it against Alec Cockrell that he brought in the likes of us to work for him. Do you want to prove they are right? I know, I know. You're achin' to work your spite on him that hurt us, and you're wonderin' where you will turn now for a livin' if the mill shuts down. So am I wonderin', and so is Rudy Horst, up there in Shirek's yard, unloadin' what needs to be unloaded from the wagons, and coverin' the rest, and stablin' his tired animals at Henry, the blacksmith's. Swearin' and sweatin' and strainin' to keep from bawlin'—that's Rudy right now. And I'll tell you again, like I did him, that there's one worse off than we are—and that's Alec Cockrell's widow, with them four helpless young ones dependin' on her, remindin' her every time she looks at one of them that their pa, her man, the one she looked to for everything, is gone. Think of her now, and take shame to yourselves, and show yourselves men, if you are men."

"I don't know whether it was that that held them," Toomy said afterward, "or was it the weather. About midnight it come on to rain awful hard, you'll recall. Or whether it was that I gave them work to do. I set them to layin' out boards for a coffin, and them as were not handy with tools I invited to lend a shoulder and a bit of choice cussin' to Rudy; and somehow, the best in them had the better of the worst in them, and finally the night was gone. Ah, do not be thankin' me, ma'am. It was yourself and Gawd Almighty and the respect we all of us had for the one we were proud to call Boss."

"Wot is to come o' we all now?"

In the gloom of the sawmill, where itinerant sons of misfortune faced what might well be a friendless tomorrow, in the forge of Henry, the blacksmith, where a banked fire warmed but did not cheer a gathering of hands from the brickyard and Mr. Toomy's building gang, blacks chiefly, making moan in the way of their kind, seeking, needing, as always, someone to lead them out of darkness into the light, to feed and clothe them and give them work to do, in every quarter of the rain-drowned, storm-battered village, distress ruled.

Distress, anxiety, uneasiness was behind the restless movement of feet and the hither and thither direction of talk in a gathering of citizens in a vacated trial room of the Dallas County courthouse. There, because now the tragedy seemed to concern a wider area than this one small town. The meeting was well attended, given increase by quite a scattering of outsiders, men who had been caught by the storm and were now compelled to spend the night at the Crutchfield House or with friends in Dallas.

Wake Latimer, as editor and publisher of the *Weekly Herald*, attended the meeting in the courthouse. In a far corner of the room he tilted his chair back against the wall and, in the way of those who must always be thinking how to shape and preserve events with words, listened and did not listen to all that was said, hearing the sense of it, whittling that down to stark fact, tossing in words to make the story tingle, tossing them out again. This week, he thought, I printed a paper that hummed like bees swarming— from advertising to politics. Full of promise. Next week I'd as well run a black border around the sheet. I will border the story

in black, for that is how it looks to me. The whole town is dead—
or dying. The story—that is all most people will see in the paper,
all anyone will remember; and how shall I tell it? At that moment
of search, he heard Nat Burford, the highly respected District
Judge, say clearly, "Our regret for the fatal *rencontre* . . ." The
words were not his own; but, strictly speaking, they were not
Judge Burford's, either, words belonging to any who found them
and turned them to good use. Silently he dropped the legs of his
chair, picked up his hat from the floor, and slipped out of the
room. He must get to where he had pen and paper, to set this
much down before he lost it.

Another at that meeting, one whom everyone but himself would
have called an outsider, was young Mr. Guess, lately of North
Carolina. He, too, left the meeting early. Honey, his wife, was
alone in the raw little house on Lamar Street; and Honey was
afraid of storms. He followed Wake Latimer out into the night,
and bravely enough made his way to the corner of the square and
turned east on Commerce. But bravery was not enough to keep
him dry. Before leaving the courthouse door, he turned down
the brim of his hat and rolled his trousers boot-top high; but the
water ran off his hat like from the eaves of a house and his
breeches were soaked through in no time. So were his boots. Too
thin, both the broadcloth breeches and the fine leather boots.
Too much worn.

He could not hurry. The footing outside was too uncertain, and
he not familiar with any of it. No pavement. Holes where this
afternoon there had been dust. Rivulets where there had been
ruts. Even when his eyes adjusted to the gloom, it was best to
take bearings with each flash of lightning. Especially at crossings,
and he had no sooner let go of the courthouse fence than he had
to make one. However, in the next block, he had the protection
of a few buildings. He rested against the stoutest of these briefly
and didn't realize until he left it that it was the jail that had given
him anchorage. He laughed, but ruefully, thinking of Andy Moore
a prisoner in his own stout, peeled-log calaboose, and probably
the only thoroughly dry citizen in town. Then the slow burn of
outrage warmed him and he went on.

His next stop was the doorstep of the sturdy little house on

Lamar Street. Strategically located right now on the west side of the street, it protected him from the worst of the rain, which drove hardest from that direction; and he could stand in the doorway and shed some of his wetness. He took off his hat, poured all the water off, shook it, then turned down his trousers and let the rain run off them before he raised his hand and pounded on the door.

"Honey," he called, knowing she had to be there. "Honey? It's me, George. Open the door, sweetheart."

She opened it finally, after a struggle with bolts, and let him in, but held him at arm's length.

"You're wet as a dog," she told him. "Don't touch me."

Poor Honey. Only the bright gold of her hair seemed to be left of the pretty sixteen-year-old he had married less than a year ago. But she was right about his being too wet to touch her. He took off his coat, hung it on the back of their one chair and busied himself with the fire, scolding her gently for letting it die down and why hadn't she made a light? He would have liked then to take off his boots and change to dry socks but he wasn't sure he had dry socks. Poor Honey, indeed! Warmed now by working with the fire, which blazed up brightly against the gloom, he sat down on the chair, from which his coat hung, and disregarding her protests, took his wife on his knee, hoping to cheer her a little. He hadn't much luck at that.

"You didn't come home to your supper," she fretted. "Why?"

So much happening in town, he said. He couldn't pull away. He tried to tell her, taking her through the long, warm afternoon, then the scene in the dusty courtroom, followed so soon by the tragic shooting, and the commotion that followed after that, the arrest of Moore and the citizens' meeting in the courthouse, which he had left to come home to her, all being still in a state of confusion, nobody seeming to know what to do next. He stopped talking, realizing suddenly that Honey was sitting up, a new light on her tear-stained face. Out of the whole account just one thing was clear to her.

"Mr. Cockrell," she said, "is dead. Your wonderful hero—dead."

"Honey!" he said, shocked at her tone. "He . . . well, yes, he was a wonderful man and . . . yes, dear, he is dead."

"Dead," Honey repeated; and she was standing now, head up for the first time in weeks or even months, it seemed to him. "Well! Other people may not know what they are going to do, but I know about us. George Guess, tomorrow morning you will go and see about our buggy. You will buy a new horse and we will leave this horrible town. Right off—tomorrow. I will not spend one more night in this miserable settler's cabin. You never lived in such a place in your life before and surely I haven't. We're leaving tomorrow, do you hear me? Tomorrow?"

Leaving? The thought had not occurred to him. He put it aside now. He had no intention of leaving Dallas. But he temporized.

"Honey," he said again, "we can't leave—not tomorrow, at any rate. I've tried to tell you how it is storming. In this tight house you can't realize it. The roads are deep in mud and water. Nobody will be leaving Dallas for a day or two. Anyhow, where would we go?"

"Back to Kentucky," Honey said passionately, "where we at least have folks."

Frankfort, Kentucky, to which he had brought Honey as a bride? Discovering, too late, that every other gentleman's son there read law and they were setting up universities to turn out lawyers even faster?

"I did more legal work in Judge McCoy's office this afternoon," he said, "than I found to do in a month in Kentucky."

"Then we'll go home," Honey said. "Back to North Carolina."

North Carolina? He could hear folks talking. George Guess, Squire Guess's youngest, is back. Did you hear? With Honey and their baby. They're living with her folks now. Didn't do so well out west, seems like. Suddenly he realized it was no use temporizing with Honey or himself.

"Honey," he said, "we are not leaving tomorrow for either Kentucky or North Carolina. We are not leaving for anywhere any time soon. We are staying right here. For a time, at least. Until I see."

Honey gasped. Her eyes were wide and unbelieving in her small, tear-stained face. Mighty few people ever had said no to her tears —but now he must.

"Honey, it was my privilege this afternoon to meet a man. I don't suppose that, according to any classical definition, he was a hero. But he was heroic—in everything he did. Big, bold, grandly sure of himself and what he was doing. Unafraid . . . I thought, this is the measure of what I would like to be, if I can make it. Honey, I like Texas. I liked what I heard of it before we came and I like it now I am here. I can reach and grow in Texas."

"You talk," Honey said, "like a man bewitched."

"Maybe I am," he agreed. "My acquaintance with Mr. Cockrell was brief, but I treasure every minute of it. It was a privilege to give legal form to one of his undertakings. I was proud to do that. I was proud . . . you know, he seemed to approve of me. At least . . . it was up in that courtroom, Honey, when he offered to fight out the differences between him and that scoundrel who later murdered him. He gave me his watch to hold. A dozen others stood by, but he chose me."

"George Guess!" Honey said, but could not continue.

"I still have it—here." In the pocket of his vest, the chain crossing to another pocket, into which he had dropped the winding key. "I had no opportunity to return it, but I must do so now. I thought of going to the house directly after I left the meeting uptown, but I came here first to see how you were. Now . . ." He reached for his coat, steaming before the fire.

"Now?" Honey said. "You're not going all the way back there now surely."

"I must," he told her. "Mrs. Cockrell will have missed the watch and she will wonder what has become of it."

"But at this time of night? Everybody in bed—asleep?"

He looked at her in amazement.

"Haven't you heard a word I've said?" he asked. "Nobody in this town is sleeping like that this night. Just nobody. Least of all, Mrs. Cockrell." A memory picture flashed before his eyes. A woman, starched, straight, able, and yet, so thoughtfully kind. Now so alone. "I think she will appreciate my coming." He took another step toward his coat, but again Honey stopped him.

"Show me that watch you are making such a fuss about."

Sighing, he loosened it from his vest and handed it to her.

"Silver," she sniffed. "Papa wears a gold watch and chain."

He took the watch away from her then and put it back in his vest pocket.

"Silver," he granted, "but still, something special, I believe. I tried this afternoon to read the lettering on the face, but I couldn't. Much too fine. Foreign make, I'm sure. Swiss, perhaps."

"Where would a man like that get a fine, foreign watch?" Honey asked.

"There are many possibilities. Bought it, perhaps. Or he may have taken it in payment for a debt. We are not the only ones the Cockrells have helped. Well, I'll be off now, before it gets any later."

This time he took his coat from the chair and put it on. It was still wet, but warm, at least. Then he turned once more to his wife.

"Honey," he coaxed, "you will go to bed now? I won't be long."

She had her back to him and kept it so. He thought she was crying. Poor Honey! And yet, she could not be nearly so desolate as that brave little woman who lived in that house by the river. All evening he had wondered how he could offer her sympathy and help, if she required it. It might be that a word from a stranger, who was a friend, would be most welcome. At any rate, there was the watch. He must take it to her; and in that way, perhaps, he could have a word or two with her.

"I'm sorry, dear," he said to his wife. "I must go."

Outside, the cold rain felt good now, and there was a new freshness to the wind. Not bothering to pull down his hat, he faced both wind and water, and turned his steps back toward Commerce Street and the river.

A black night, with a wind that alternately moaned and howled, and hushed only to gather force to drive gusts of rain ahead of it, quickening the steps of those who were caught out in it, filling ditches and branches, beating against windows, lifting the covering of roofs where it could seize a loose shingle or a thin board, so that inside there was a scurrying for tubs and pails to catch the drip. It tossed bucketfuls down some chimneys, enough to douse low fires or make a great hissing where they burned brightly. Such a hissing went on in the chimney place of M. Gouhenant's Art Salon out on Main Street; and M. Gouhenant considered the sound and the way the flames leaped up to lick at the descending water and died down, to leap again, and shrugged his shoulders finally, committing the issue to the good God.

"Ah, well!" he said. "The roof will not catch fire from the sparks, that is certain."

That is how things went generally in the Art Salon of M. Gouhenant that evening, where his compatriots and fellow fugitives from the crumbling colony of La Réunion gathered, by invitation and on impulse, to discuss this new misfortune and borrow cheer, if there was any, from one another. A special fear added itself to their distress—the lost feeling of people who have not yet put down good roots in a new land, to whom home is still a place thousands of miles away, across a turbulent ocean. A horse and buggy would hardly carry them there. Moreover, in the hearts of most there was no strong inclination to move in that direction. Hunger and want and cold are hard to endure, but oppression and injustice and tyranny are even harder. They had here in Texas, in America, what is called freedom. But little, besides. In some cases, nothing. In others even less, debt haunting many. Tonight they had again, and strongly, that feeling of being lost. God's forgotten children—this handful of men and women who had just lately gathered up the scraps of one set of blighted hopes and, largely on the assurances of one man, Monsieur Alexander Cockrell, come to live in Dallas.

That fearless one, that madman, perhaps, who had marched, in the heat of a great anger, just as blindly and bravely to his own destruction as he had to any of his successes, was gone; and what was to become of them in consequence? What was to become of this town called Dallas, in Texas of the United States of America? Would it crumble now, like La Réunion?

"I do not think so," Maxim Guillot, the carriage-maker said, with the air of one who has studied the matter.

But Maxim Guillot was a special person. He had a trade and a good one. He had built a business and had a following. He was prosperous and known. If trade slackened or disappeared in Dallas, there were dozens of other Texas towns—well, quite a few, at any rate, where he could set up his wagon shop and prosper.

The same thing was true, in a measure, of Père Frichot, the

maker of brick. Nobody present had been more shaken by the death of Mr. Cockrell than he. Mr. Cockrell had been most appreciative of Père Frichot's skill, had even paid him for the use of a little invention he made for the pulverizing of clay so that brick molded from it came out smoother and more resistant to weather. And now? Well, it was possible that Père Frichot and his brother and his son-in-law could arrange to purchase the brickyard. If that did not come to pass, they could surely start another somewhere else. The great Mr. Cockrell had, at least, made building with brick popular in this part of Texas. And yet, the Frichots were not too hopeful. It was easier when Mr. Cockrell assumed the risks of contracts.

Still, they would survive. So would Athanase Chrétien, who was of those who had bought the community land when La Réunion fell apart. A good farmer, that one, as was the man who sat beside him, Jules Reverchon, formerly of Lyons, France. With Reverchon tonight was his son, Julien, long and awkward and only nineteen, who fancied himself a naturalist and was more interested in strange animals and birds and flowers than in plowing. Still he was good help to his father between times. Good farmers, all. If at first they had not understood Texas land and Texas weather, they were learning. They were even experimenting now in new crops for the money market, such as *tabac* and cotton. The loss of Mr. Cockrell's patronage would go hard with these men, too. Still, they would survive.

And so would fat, round, jolly Jacob Nussbaumer, whose people had been butchers in Switzerland since ages ago. Poised now on his feet, like a balloon not too securely tied, he tried to share with his friends something of his own surety.

"I promise you all," he said, and he was as earnest as such a jolly man could be, "that nobody here shall starve. Not while pork runs wild in the brakes, and deer and buffalo and partridges abound on the prairies."

Those who heard him cheered his words and even laughed a little; but it was like the flames springing up the chimney, only to fall back the next minute under a deluge of more rain. There were too many in this room who had no profitable trade, no land and now no prospects.

There was M. Gouffe who, for making one suit of black broadcloth, had been given a house by Mr. Cockrell, rent free for six months, in which he might set up a tailoring shop. How much business could he count on now? There was a watchmaker from Zurich. There was M. Gernand, who could teach the piano—if he only had such a thing as a piano. There was François Santerre, a scholar. Who here had much need of learning? There was—himself. Why go farther? How many months' rent did he owe now? How much to the Jewish merchants for the wall covering that served to reflect light as well as to cover rough logs? What did he have to pay on his debts? A suit of clothing? A silver watch and chain? No—he had, if you please, a *camera obscura* and a supply, a small supply of thin plates, metal and glass, for making pictures, together with bottles and jars of evil-smelling, but rare chemicals, all of which he had brought, with only he could say what difficulty, across the ocean and overland to this place.

He had one thing more. It was a bottle of wine. A large bottle, but not large enough for the many people in this room. Each could have only a sip, if it was to reach. He had saved it for the day that must come to mark a turn in his fortunes. Well? Could anyone look to see a sharper turn than had now come? No. It was time, he thought, to pour the wine and serve the little cakes Mme. Ettienne had brought with her. Good Mme. Ettienne—who would provide for her now that small *pâtisserie*, which would be a credit to the town and a living for her and her children? Or build the gristmill, which would grind wheat into the fine white flour she needed to do justice to her *finesse* in baking?

"Madame Ettienne," he said, tasting a sugary *pouf* from her basket, "the cakes are, as always, perfect."

Then, not to notice the tears spilling over on her round, rosy cheeks, he turned quickly to the young woman who sat beside her.

"Madame Jones!" he bowed elaborately.

This caused those close by to laugh, as it was meant to do. It even brought a small smile to the dark, pointed face of the young lady. Mme. Jones, born Louise Dusseau, daughter of another colonist. The first to marry from the colony, her choice of husbands had been a young American, named Samuel Jones. For all anyone knew to the contrary, Mr. Jones was a young man of character and promise, but, well, just not quite so remarkable as the girl he married, who, besides being pretty in a dark, witching way, had certain gifts with the needle, inherited from her mother and enhanced by teaching at a convent in France. Her fingers were busy even now; and, when M. Gouhenant asked her what she was making, she held up for him to see a baby's cap of white Swiss muslin, embroidered with a myriad delicate stitches, all of her designing and setting.

Well, to be sure! As anyone could see, Mme. Jones was expecting a child. But was this a cause for weeping? Alas, the pretty brown eyes looking up at M. Gouhenant were filled with tears. Could it be that the prospects of Samuel Jones had also suffered an eclipse?

"Madame," M. Gouhenant chose to ignore the tears, "my felicitations. What will you name the child?"

"Guillaume," the young mother-to-be answered sadly. She could not shape her pretty mouth to say William.

"Guillaume," M. Gouhenant repeated. "But what, in case you are disappointed of an heir and should have a daughter, instead? Had you thought of that?"

White teeth flashed again in a brief, unsteady smile.

"Yes, monsieur. In that case—Guillelmine."

Guillelmine? M. Gouhenant waved his wine bottle.

"Hold!" he said with authority. "My friends, when I have filled your glasses—as I can—I wish to propose a toast. To a stranger, a newcomer. I will ask you to drink with me to the safe arrival and good health and prosperity of Mademoiselle Guillelmine Jones!"

Guillelmine Jones—it had a sound. It was meant to make everyone laugh. Alas, no one did; and when M. Gouhenant turned to Mme. Jones, to see if she could offer an explanation, her tears were flowing as freely as Mme. Ettienne's. He put down the wine bottle, as a deluge of rain came down the chimney, all but drowning the fire permanently. A hush settled on the room, broken by a sigh here and a sob there.

And it was in that moment of stillness and despair that a knock sounded on the door. When M. Gouhenant, his feet suddenly as heavy as his heart, went to open it, there stood a black boy, hardly to be distinguished from the stormy darkness that surrounded him.

Water ran from him as from a lead waterspout. His teeth rattled.

"I's lookin' fo' M-mister G-g-guff, de tailorman."

M. Gouffe stood up in surprise.

"Who sends for M. Gouffe, the tailor?"

"But enter first, boy," M. Gouhenant interrupted. "Come at least far enough that I may close the door against the rain. *Ciel*, you are half-drowned."

Joab, the blacksmith's boy, came in—miserably, teeth still rattling.

"Miz' Cockrell sent me," he said. " 'Bout Mist' Cockrell's coat. Hit . . . hit got tore uptown dis' af'noon. She wants to know kin you mend hit? I b-been lookin' fo' you . . . all night."

"I will come at once," M. Gouffe said—with alacrity.

Now, why that? What was there about the summons—to mend the coat of a dead man—to raise hope from wet ashes? But that was how it was. M. Gouffe could not wait to be gone and all present could not do enough to help him.

"Papa Gouffe, wrap up well. Put a shawl around your shoulders. Here! Take mine. It is warmer than yours. Is your hat whole?"

When M. Gouhenant looked now at Mme. Jones, her tears had dried. She had laid aside the baby's cap. Her hands folded and unfolded scraps of nothing that he could see, shaping them, however, into something she saw quite well.

"For Madame," she said shyly, when she saw him looking at her in question.

For Madame? A bonnet, perhaps? Certainly a bonnet. A widow's bonnet, naturally, but . . . well, there you had the source of hope. M. Gouhenant seized his wine bottle and began to pour from it feverishly into all sorts of containers, the least of them too large.

"Hold," he said again as he rushed about, "I have now a new toast to offer." And, when everyone had some wine and he had only the dregs, he once more waved the bottle aloft, and offered the toast.

"To Madame!"

He meant it to ring against the roof. Could he help it if it came out sounding like the whisper of prayer?

To Madame . . .

...*their wings trailing fire, making a rushing sound like the wind.*

Wᴴɪʟᴇ ᴛʜɪs ᴡᴇɴᴛ ᴏɴ about the town, in the snug, clapboarded house close beside the river, time dragged, beginning with a supper that, do what she would, Sarah had not been able to eat.

"Sarah," Martha Overton said, "try to take a little more of something."

Sarah had tried. While the children were still at the table, she had picked at her sweet potato and chewed and chewed on the good, hot, fried pork, to set them an example, hardly needed. They were, as always, healthily hungry. A little quenched in spirit, but hungry. They had gobbled their supper, kissed her good night and gone upstairs, docilely enough, for once, under Sister Polly's care. She and Martha were alone and pretense wasn't needed. She picked up a half of sweet potato, broken on her plate. It was cold, tasted like straw. She laid it down.

"Try," Martha said, met Sarah's eyes, and stopped.

Mr. Cockrell, you don't eat enough. You won't stop . . . you never do when you are excited.

How many times—not just today—had she fussed at him like that? And always he had a quick, turn-aside answer.

You favor solid men?

No, but, maybe, if he had been a hearty eater . . .

"Maybe," Martha persisted, "a little warm milk might slip down. Help you to sleep."

Sleep?

"Sarah, you must get your rest. You will break if you don't."

"I don't feel that I will," Sarah said. "I don't feel that way at all. Martha, I'm not going to bed, if that is what you mean. I couldn't. The bed's all made up fresh. I wish you and Mr. Overton would feel free to use the room."

"Perry's still uptown," Martha reminded her.

Yes. Just as Martha had announced that she had supper on the table in the back room, Perry Overton had come out of the parlor. His swarthy face was pale, his eyes like pits with embers glowing in their deeps.

"I've seen Alec," he said to Sarah and his wife. "I'm going uptown."

That was all. He turned and went right out into the storm.

"Let him go," Martha had said, as if Sarah would or could have stopped him. "He's mad all the way through. He'll speak his mind to a few folks, but he won't do any harm. He's got to find his peace in some man's way. That's all."

That was all. Peace . . .

"You plan to sit up all night?" Martha asked.

Sarah said she might.

"There's really nothing you can do right now."

"I'll find something," Sarah said. "I must. Everything seems quiet upstairs, doesn't it? Later on, if Joab doesn't find Mr. Gouffe, the French tailor, Polly will have to do the best she can on Mr. Cockrell's coat. Nobody else in town can do any better. I do hope, though, Joab finds the tailor."

They listened to the storm for a spell. The rain was coming down harder than ever, pouring off the roof in sheets.

"George must keep the fires going," Sarah said.

"We'll see that he does," Martha promised.

They would see that George kept the fires going. George would be glad of that to do. Nellie and Hannah were still busy, in and out of the parlor, Pokey on the run to wait on both, Polly and Martha doing her, Sarah's, work of superintending. During supper Margaret Bryan had come again, dry-eyed, but haunted. Was there anything in the world she could do? She would scrub, she would take the children—anything. Later, perhaps, Margaret. Later . . .

"I'll turn the bed down," Martha said, persistently kind and mistaken, "so that, if anybody should want to lie down, it will be ready."

"Yes," Sarah said. "You might do that. Now, shall we clear the table? Then, if you will help me carry that trunk from the bedroom out here, I'll be obliged."

"Sarah!" Martha was scandalized. "You don't mean to work—tonight? What will people say?"

For the first time, Sarah felt smiling muscles twitch in her face, though a twitch was all it came to.

"I can imagine—fairly," she answered. "Martha, I must. All day I've been flighty, jumpy. I shouldn't have felt so. Maybe, if I had steadied, if I had said, and believed it, that no harm would come, it might have stayed away."

"You know better," Martha told her. "You had enough to make you jumpy. That Indian didn't help. Sarah, what brought him here—in the first place?"

Martha Overton, with a husband who had Indian blood, still shared Sarah's dark mistrust of savages.

"Birds," Sarah said dully. "He's been coming for several years at this time—to shoot birds. Is he still in the parlor?"

"Still is," Martha said. "Hasn't moved an inch all this time. Standing there, stiff as a post, with his gun beside him, his hand on it, ready. Watching, waiting—but what for now?"

"I don't know," Sarah said, but told her then of the bird on the window that morning.

"For heaven's sake!" Martha said, awed. "But there wouldn't be another. No, just hear it rain. No bird alive would be flying tonight."

No bird, except those Charley John believed in. They flew through wind and storm and fierce lightning—Sarah wished now that she had listened more respectfully to the spooky tale. What was it that Charley John thought he must guard against now? He had said he had known he couldn't save his friend's life. Then, what . . .

"Well!" Martha said finally. "Now I'm jumpy, too. All right. We'll clear the table; but, land's sake, Sarah, you can't settle everything tonight. There will be plenty of tomorrows."

Who knew, ever, about tomorrow?

"I want the trunk," Sarah pleaded. "I want everything of Mr. Cockrell's that he had with him today—money, papers, everything. When Barry Derritt comes with the bridge tolls—hasn't he been here? He usually comes before this."

He had been at the house earlier, Martha said, just to ask about Sarah, was she all right. He had left then to watch the bridge, saying he'd be back later. The river, Sarah thought. All this rain. No, Martha said, he hadn't mentioned the river, didn't seem concerned. No. If he had concern, he wouldn't show it. Even if the river was rising; and it was too soon for that, unless there had been heavy rains earlier on the upper forks.

"You see," Sarah said, "I'm still jumpy. Next time he comes, say I asked for him. Have him bring in the toll box just as always. And now . . . the trunk."

However, when the homely, scarred little chest was there on the table before her, she thought, I can't open it. It's an account that has been closed, sealed. It would be like rifling a tomb. She put her hands on the lid and bowed her head, everything in her dissolving into formless prayer. Alec, I can't! Then a strange thing happened. Through her hands on the scarred lid strength flowed. Sarah, who else is there? She raised her head. She sighed, then reached inside her dress for the key. There! The trunk was open.

Wouldn't you know? The first scrap that met her eyes was the brown paper she hadn't been able to find that afternoon. With tingling fingers she unfolded it, then dropped her head again, tears squeezing out on her cheeks. Alec, Mr. Cockrell, you great torment! A span of oxen, indeed! He had ordered from Maxim Guillot, the carriage- and wagon-maker, a high-wheeled buggy—for her. Of the best wood and strong springs and shafts, with a leather cushion for the seat. "For Madame—" Maxim Guillot had written out the order. "For Madame."

Where would she drive such a buggy? Why, to church on a Sunday morning. Farther, maybe, to a meeting at Farmer's Branch or Cedar Springs. Across the river, to visit the Overtons or other friends, whenever the notion took her. And people, hearing the light roll of the wheels, would say, "It's Mrs. Cockrell, in that buggy her husband had made special for her." Oh, Alec, I never dreamed when first I saw you that you were so proud. Sinfully proud, it could be. No, just proud—a boy, reaching out his hand for the moon.

Tears ran down her cheeks to her mouth, salted her lips. She pressed the fold in the paper, creased it with her fingers until it was a wonder the fold did not split then and there. Of course, she needn't have the buggy. Maxim Guillot would understand. He could hardly have begun work on it. When had Mr. Cockrell given the order? Before the wagons left for Shreveport to pick up their freight? In that case, in any case, the materials needed might have come back with them. During supper she had heard the wagons enter town, without the usual uproar, but had been too weighed down with other anxieties to wonder.

Now she did wonder—a little. All those things Mr. Cockrell had bought—the foolish splendor. What had been done with it now? Compared to a chandelier or a piano, wood for a buggy was very little. Little, but warmly personal, like a piece of jewelry, just for her. She need not have the buggy. She might never have use for it in that dim, shadowed time that was the future; but inescapably she had it now. Here in her hands. For Madame— greedily, passionately, she kissed the scrap of paper and thrust it into the bosom of her dress.

Now, then . . . but it was a night of interruptions. Barry Derritt came, with the tin box in which he kept the day's take at the bridge. Barry in high boots, which he had managed to wipe clean of mud before entering the house. A drop of water showed here and there on his head, but generally he was dry enough. He had, he said, a mackintosh, which, with the mud, he had left out back.

"Miss Sarah?" He stood on the doorsill, hesitating to enter the room, fearing, almost, to look at her.

"Come in," Sarah had to say, and was surprised at the strength of her tone. "I was asking about you. Surely nobody is crossing now."

"No'm. Won't be much crossin' tomorrer, either. Maybe longer. Bottom roads goin' to be bad for a while, I reckon."

"Is the water rising?"

"Not specially. Not just yet."

"It will," she said, to save him from saying it.

"Yas'm. All depends on how much more it rains. Miss Sarah, you ain't frettin' about the bridge, I hope." Meaning that he was, some. "Water can come high over the floor without shakin' it much. I know."

"I'd just as soon it wouldn't rise that high," Sarah said. "Is the ferryboat all right?"

"Yas'm. I took a look at the cable before it got clear dark. She'll do. Miss Sarah, you are all right here, too. House sets good and high. It would take a powerful rise to harm you here. I know that ain't goin' to happen, but don't you worry. I'll keep watch."

"I know you will, Barry. I'm grateful to you and all the rest—who keep watch."

"They's quite a few of us, Miss Sarah," he said, trying to reach her with the assurance. "Humble folk. Don't amount to much, each one—like the bridge fare; but when you add it all up, there it is. All of us wanting to help you."

She studied his fine, clear features, the earnest humility of his pledge; and the shadows behind him were filled with others like him—white, black and in-between—reaching their hands out to her, offering help, and, at the same time, pleading. She brushed her hand across her eyes, not ready to speak to them, or even hear what they might have to say to her.

"Thank you, Barry. You do help; but . . . won't you sit down, while I count the money? Though I know you've kept track."

"Miss Sarah," he asked, "you feelin' right well?"

"No," she said, "not exactly. Of course not. But why do you ask?"

"You always do count the money, Miss Sarah. I make it sixteen dollars and eighty-five cents, in case you don't feel just equal. . . ."

Equal—unequal—that was how she did feel.

"I'm all right," she insisted, opened the box and counted the coins, stacking silver dollars, half-dollars, quarters and dimes, with a few five-cent pieces and copper cents. The sum was as Barry had named it. It always was.

"Miss Sarah, you will put the money away—real careful?"

"Yes, of course. In the safe, where it belongs. What . . . it's quite a lot, isn't it? I can't recall a day when we had this much from the bridge."

"Only a couple," Barry told her. "When we had racing over here."

Racing. Sinful coming down the track at a gallop, a tall rider in the saddle, tall, brown as an Indian, with Indian black hair, claiming he was getting to be too solid, too heavy now to ride a race, even in jeans and a calico shirt; but he and Sinful led the field home, crossed the finish, breathing fire, the two of them.

"Saturday," Barry said, "is most always a good day, makes up for slack time. Goin' to be slack now for a few days, but along will come next Saturday and the bridge will pay off again. It has since the day it was declared open and it will as long as it stands, and that's goin' to be some time yet. Miss Sarah, can I talk free with you?"

"Of course, Barry. What is it?"

"It's about the boss, Miss Sarah. They say he's dead. I know he is. He's dead, but he ain't gone. A man puts his mark on things the way he did can't die like plain folks. As long as the bridge stands, he's here. And longer. As long as there is this town, he's here. A man shooting him does evil but he don't remove him. Time and again, Miss Sarah, Mr. Cockrell said to me, 'Barry, I'm goin' up to the courthouse and make out papers and name you a free man. Goin' to pay you wages like other free men, because you're better than a lot of folks born free.' But I wouldn't allow it. I said, 'I'd rather be your man, Boss, than be free.' And I meant it. Miss Sarah, I'm your man now. Yours and his young-'uns' man. Long as I live, long as the bridge stands, I want to mind it—for him and for you. Goin' to come every evening with the money to count. That's a trust the boss left to me. I couldn't be prouder if I was the President of the United States. I . . . excuse me, Miss Sarah. Standing here preaching. I better go now—back across the road. That's where I'll be whenever you want me for anything. And . . . you will put the money away right soon?"

He was gone then, swallowed by the black of the stormy night.

"If you needs me, Miss Sarah, just let somebody come to the door with a lantern and wave it once. I'll be right over."

How different from Pokey and the others moaning low with the wind, reaching out their pleading hands! They hovered in the shadows all the long night through, giving her no peace for their soft, helpless crying. George, as she had asked, brought her Mr. Cockrell's money—what he had on him when he died and what he carried in the deep pocket in his coat. Poker at Black Jack, she thought. Gambling money? How did a woman of principle handle gambling money?

Methody woman—she heard him say it. Not loud. Nobody else would have heard, but she did. Methody woman, every move a man makes in this world is full of chance. Did you never take pleasure in risk? How about when you married me?

No, she protested. I knew.

Did you, Methody woman?

My heart knew, spite of all. She heard him laugh then, low, teasing, richly happy because he was wedded to such a dear fool. Methody woman, take the money with the rest. Do good with it in your way. So, it may lose what taint you think it carries. Had I left it where I found it, those who had it would not have done as well. With a deep sigh, she set the sum down on paper —better than three hundred dollars altogether. She put it away in the safe with the bridge money, closed the cupboard doors securely, then stood, frowning at the pattern of perforations on the tin. It was too much money to keep in such a flimsy place. While Alec Cockrell lived, nobody dared lift a hand to steal from him or his, but now . . .

She dropped back in her chair by the table, smothering a cry: Mr. Cockrell, I can't. I just can't!

You're doing all right, Methody woman. Get on with the books and papers now. You'll give out most of that money, come Monday. Look at the list of folks we hire.

She opened the ledger at the mill account, and there it was—a list of men hired and fired—and, if they stayed on beyond a few days, a note about each. Good machinist, but mean. Good man, has family somewhere, loves children. This boy is sick, needs doctoring. Things like that until all became real folks and a kind of responsibility. They stood with the others in the shadows—good men, bad men, unfortunates—and looked at her in question: Where now? And when?

Mr. Cockrell, I cannot run a sawmill. Whoever heard of a woman who did? Where would I turn for help? Mr. Toomy? No man, worth his salt, wants to work for a woman boss. He won't stay on here now. I couldn't hope for it.

She turned a few pages, and there was the brickyard. Almost as bad as the sawmill. Worse in a way. These people, such as were not slaves hired out, lived in small houses around the fringe of town. Much of the money due them on payday was owed to storekeepers, so that if you took out rent, besides, there was nothing for a man to ring on a counter anywhere; and no man could be content with that. Of course, there were exceptions. There was that French family—maybe they would take the brickyard off her hands. But would they? Now? Did they have the means? She must be paid and paid well.

I declare, she thought, suddenly weary to death and really frightened, it's like something you pile up and pile up without counting and it looks fine; but, if you try to let go, or if you take out a piece here or there, all falls in a heap. Mr. Cockrell, if I could, I would put on shawl and bonnet and run.

Where, Methody woman? Where? What of the young ones? And Sister Polly? You are not going to be a cowardy coward now, are you?

But I need help, Mr. Cockrell, I need help. Where can I find it?

On the table, beside Cockrell's now empty wallets—one of them a deerskin pouch she had sewed up herself—were a few papers from his pockets. She had shrunk from opening them before. Her fingers still were unwilling; but, there, she had them in her hands now. She moved the lamp nearer to her, because a first glance told her that here was a business new to her.

They were the papers drawn up in Lawyer McCoy's office that afternoon, amounting, when she put everything together, to the purchase of shares in that railroad reaching north from Houston. She had heard tell of that railroad. A dream all this while, now suddenly it was real. A few strokes of a nimble pen—not John McCoy's—and the locomotive was snorting right down Commerce Street. She smelled the smoke, she heard the cars rattling behind the engine, she heard people shouting. There would have to be a depot somewhere, a stronger bridge over the river, iron maybe, built high above flood water.

It was too sudden, too much on top of everything else. She had a fresh spell of shakes. Then she read the papers closely again; and the train of cars was hardly that close, though still a-coming. The shares had been given in return for a right of way through Cockrell land, not an outright sale, just an option. Alec had driven a good bargain, had nothing much in his hand but paper to show, but neither had he yielded much. Wild imagination, working alongside cool, hard thinking. What had Barry said? *"He's dead, but he ain't gone."*

Alexander Cockrell, his mark. Opposite that the name of a stranger. In round, firm writing: *Nicholas Darnell.*

The lawmaker from downstate. So, that was what he had been up to. Come all that way to do business with Mr. Cockrell. Smart, knowing . . . now, just maybe, he was the man she needed. A stranger—she'd have to look sharp.

A stranger. Had she no friends among those she knew who could help her? Yes, she had many friends, though, maybe, not so many as she had dependents. There was Perry Overton, for one. She discounted women, knowing too well what a woman's weakness came to. There was Perry Overton. Quiet, strong, resourceful, and a loyal friend, if there ever was one. He had done well for himself, had made a good farm of his headrights at Honey Springs. His mill was popular, but he had always talked against any important move that Alec Cockrell made, shook his head beforehand and poked fun later, until the thing was done and he was proven wrong. And what did he say then:

"Lucky, that's all! A fool for luck, that's what you are!"

What advice would Perry Overton give Sarah Cockrell, widow? Why, this: "Better sell your holdings, Sarah. You will realize a fair sum, I think. You can buy a place next to us then, if you'd like that. Martha would like it, and I'd help you bring up the boys. Or, if you'd rather, you could take the young ones back to Virginia. Or to Missouri, to Alec's folks."

No. Not Virginia now, homesick as she had often been for the dear place. Homesick, in the way grownups are for the memories of childhood; but she knew well enough that a person who has left childhood behind can never find it again. She had never deeply wanted to go back to Virginia, once she had married and sent roots down into Texas.

Missouri? Mr. Cockrell had hinted several times that someday they might visit the home he had run off from. But he had been in no hurry and she knew why. He would like to see the land, and his folks; but he would want to go proudly, in new clothes on a fine horse alongside her and the children, dressed just as elegantly, riding in the new buggy probably, with a light wagon following, to carry their trunks and Hannah, to wait on her, and George, to wait on him. He would want to go, head up and proud, or never. Would she go now, a widow, sad, bereft, crying out for help? No.

She would have to write to Mr. Cockrell's folks now—as soon as she could get around to it—telling them of his death and how it had happened. To that half-brother probably who wrote to them here occasionally, fancying himself, she sometimes thought, head of the family now and liking to brag a little—about himself and Missouri. Francis Marion Cockrell—he was a lawyer. Land, Missouri, it seemed, like Tennessee or Kentucky—raised more lawyers than anything else. However, if Francis Marion Cockrell, being a lawyer, had a mind to offer her a steadying hand and some advice, she could use both. He might even come to Texas to see how things were with her, out of respect for his brother and moved to anger over the way of his death.

The best help in the world if he should come, but she hardly believed he would. If he was a good lawyer, he had business that he couldn't leave easily. He had a family of his own to care for. And it seemed to her she had heard something about his being in politics. Almost every Missourian of consequence was. Missouri had come into the Union as a state when Texas had only a scattering of settlers. It had had much to do with settling Texas. Something very like Texans, its people. It had come into the Union, the citizens fighting each other and everybody outside fighting it, like two women in a store laying hold of the same bolt of calico; and that had gone on ever since. Paid a man to know his law.

The Honorable Francis Marion Cockrell—he would answer her letter politely, give her cautious advice; but she doubted that he'd take the time or the trouble to come and see for himself how things were.

Nearer, there was Wesley Cockrell, rancher. A family man

himself with a brood now twice the size of hers. Jolly, kind, but what did he know of business, outside of ranching? Nothing. The same was true of her brother Jim. Too lazy, well, maybe, just too easygoing to more than keep his mill turning. It fed him and his family and he asked no more. Dear Jim—good to cry against, but that was all.

The truth was, she had nobody whom she could trust who knew as much as she herself did about running a business—which was a one-sided knowing, to be sure, and yet, better than ignorance—or who, lacking that knowledge, had spirit and gumption to—well, to go out and buy a chandelier and a piano for a hotel not yet half built. She had never known but one man with such spirit. And he was dead. So, forever and ever, she was alone.

She dropped her head on her arms and cried her heart out then —tears of loneliness, of sorrow, of desolation with no foreseeable end. Martha Overton looked in on her once, and drew back.

"Let her cry," she said to Polly Thompson. "It is what she needs most."

The rain—a storm of rain against the house, down the chimney —roused her finally. She raised her head, listened, and shook herself in a kind of impatience. She was, she thought, as soggy wet as any creature caught out in the downpour. And for all that, how had things changed for her?

She shook herself again and stood up, stretching herself straight and tall. That achieved, she marched into the bedroom, poured some water into her washbowl and bathed her face. The cool water felt so good that she wondered she had not tried it before. She risked then a look at herself in her mirror. You poor, sad thing, she thought, caught a sob in her throat, and held it, then took up her brush and smoothed her hair. She would have liked to change to a fresh dress, but decided to wait with that. Tomorrow she would be seeing more people, and would want to be presentable then. The last thing she did before leaving the room was to empty the washbowl, wipe it dry, set the water pitcher back in it, and hang her towel, straight and neat, on the rack. Then at last she was ready to go back to her books.

In the office, she opened the ledger once more, drew her inkwell close, and dipped her pen. She worked busily for the most of two hours, entering the item mentioned on each loose piece of paper where the entry belonged. Again, there were interruptions. Will Toomy came, to report his night's activities.

"The boys at the mill are laying out boards for the coffin, ma'am. I will be going back there now to give them the measure, and set the pattern."

"He was tall, Mr. Toomy. You will remember?"

"I will, indeed, for I know. In his socks he stood four inches over six feet; and he was broader in the shoulders than some might think, too, able to wrassle any drifter that ventured to give him a disrespectful bit of his lip. One or two of the boys will have that measure to remember."

A coffin of boards. He could rest so, but . . .

"You will leave room for a pillow, Mr. Toomy?"

"I will, ma'am, whatever you say. Your friends, the Frenchies, could maybe help out with that, and be glad to be allowed to do so."

It was from Toomy that she learned about the gathering in M. Gouhenant's Art Salon.

"You see, ma'am, they've lost their best friend, and they know it. Their spirits are low."

So are mine, Mr. Toomy, Sarah could have told him. But she felt better now, knowing that Joab would eventually find the tailor.

"Mr. Cockrell's watch is missing too," Sarah told him then. "The watch and chain, with the key for winding it. They could hardly have fallen out, and there was no time for thieving."

"No." Will Toomy settled back on his heels, and tried to shape the picture. "Now, that is a puzzle," he said. "The answer to it will be worth having."

Sarah sighed. A heavy weariness was now upon her.

"Is there anything else, Mr. Toomy? Did the wagons all come in safely?"

"Ow!" Toomy beat his head with a hard fist. "That was what I came to say in the first place. They are in safe, ma'am, and unloaded—the lumber at the mill, the rest in Hirsch and Shirek's warehouse. The boss made the arrangements personally."

"There was a glass chandelier and a piano," Sarah reminded him. "For the hotel."

"Aye. They are housed securely, not a string or a dangle broken, I do believe." He forbore mentioning what effort the unloading had been—a matter of deep cursing and much straining, to say nothing of the care such freight had been on the road. "Though what you will do with them now that they are here, I wonder." He sighed dolefully, and Sarah understood. What of the hotel now, he wanted to ask. What of the mill? What of a dozen other projects? "It is too soon, I suppose, for you to know what all of us naturally ask ourselves," he finished, and raised an eloquent eyebrow.

"Yes," she said. "I don't know, Mr. Toomy. Not just yet." Mr. Cockrell, I don't see how I can. "Do thank the men for me, Mr. Toomy, though I know how much of this is your doing."

"No, ma'am," he declared. "Give the credit where it belongs. There's Rudy Horst, for example. Will you believe it, that big redheaded madman is cold sober? He and one or two more are in Adam Haught's place now. I thought it only right that they warm their insides whilst drying their breeches. And Adam set out the whiskey. But Rudy stood there, his whip still in hand, and said, 'A dram a piece, no more, Adam, and none for me. Not tonight.' Of course, it will not last, ma'am. He'll be himself in a day or two, maybe sooner."

Mr. Cockrell, you know this is all beyond me.

"It is out of respect to my husband, Mr. Toomy. I understand. Tell the men I appreciate this. Tell them, too, that, if they wish to call at the house tomorrow, they will be welcome. There can be no burying very soon at this rate."

"They will track up your house," Toomy warned.

"We will be prepared for that, Mr. Toomy."

Pokey, she thought. Pokey knew the men. She could stand guard—with a mop.

"I'll pass the word, ma'am," Toomy said. "Do you now . . ." He gathered himself together, stretched himself full height, and made her a bow. "My humble respects to you, ma'am. I will be back tomorrow early."

Fierceness, not humility, marched out of the room with him.

He had said what had to be said, and so had she; but neither had said a word of what really burdened their hearts—pain, bewilderment, sorrow, anger. The burden was, perhaps, heavier for their meeting. She sighed and went back to her papers.

Not long after Mr. Toomy had left, M. Gouffe came for the coat and carried it away, promising to have it back early, but very early in the morning.

"He'll work over it the rest of the night," Sarah said to Martha Overton when he had gone. But, Martha had no pity to spend on the tailor.

"Sarah, have you any idea what time it is? Long past midnight, and the rain has stopped. But hear that wind!"

A gust shook the shutters and went away, moaning.

"You said you would rest—some," Martha reminded her.

"Yes," Sarah said. "Did you turn down the bed? I'm almost through here. I think I will lie down for a while. When I get up, Martha, I want to change to a fresh dress, something more suitable. I feel as if I had worn this forever. Now, just one more paper, please."

She knew exactly where to find it, securely tied in its own bundle. It was the deed to the townsite, made over to Alexander Cockrell by John Neely Bryan in 1852.

"Mrs. Cockrell may I present you with a town?"

She had drawn away from the gift then; and, if she had known what the end of it all would be, she would have drawn clear away. Drove one man to drink and exile, she thought. Killed another. And here am I, nowhere near as strong or brave as either. But she spread the old paper on the table before her. Printed by fingers not purely clean and handled much, it was beginning to break at the edges. She passed her fingers lightly over it. You loved the town, didn't you? I know. I wish . . . but how can I? Will you tell me how, Mr. Cockrell?

"Sarah," Martha Overton again, "George is waiting to put more wood on the fire. You know it is getting very cold. The house will be like a barn if we don't keep the fires up. Sarah, I'm sorry, but there is a young man out in the hall who would like to have a word with you. He came in with Perry just now. He says he had something of Alec's . . . Sarah, I'll send him away. He can come tomorrow just as well. You are so tired!"

So tired! Her very jaws seemed unwilling to move when she answered.

"What does he have, Martha?"

"I don't know. Didn't have sense enough to ask him. Shall I now?"

"No," Sarah told her. "Tell George to build up the fire and bring him in. I can hold out that much longer, I reckon."

chapter twenty-eight

Even then, if only one or two friends keep watch...

So TIRED, so deadly tired!

When Perry Overton brought the young man in, she wished she had said she would not see him.

The room was dark, filled with shadow. The logs that George had added to the fire were wet and did not catch at once. From where she stood at the end of the table, Perry's bright black eyes and the other man's dark and heavy beard were all she made note of, and she had no idea who it was that had asked to see her until, in a deep, pleasing voice, he spoke her name.

"Mrs. Cockrell, I have chosen a bad time to call."

She looked at him more closely. Oh, of course! The young man who had come—day before yesterday, it would be now—in the broken buggy, with the lame horse and the poor, sick little wife. Mr. Guess. His name came readily to her lips, and she asked about the wife. How was she now?

"Poorly, ma'am, I am afraid. I must get back to her soon. I . . . may I help you to a chair?"

He had one ready before she could answer and held it respectfully while she sat down. A mannerly young man, if she had ever known one. How fortunate his wife, though possibly she did not know that. No, as Sarah remembered the few hours of their stay in this house, the wife had not inclined toward appreciation.

"So sick, poor child," she said. "How old is she?"

"Seventeen, ma'am."

272 • DESTINY IN DALLAS

"And so far from home? No, you should not leave her alone. But you said you had something belonging to Mr. Cockrell."

"His watch, ma'am. He did me the honor this afternoon of giving it to me, to hold. Then he went off and I had no further opportunity to restore it."

Sarah studied his face, thinking, I hardly noticed him the other day, except that he was big and kind and gentle-spoken.

"Tell me," she said. "How did he come to give you his watch, to hold?"

So he told her about the hot, dusty courtroom and all that had happened there. Told her carefully, repeating each word that was spoken. He told her where each one stood, how each one looked; and she saw it all as clearly as if she had been present. The first true report she had had, and it should have sorrowed her, but it did not. For the short time of the telling, Alexander Cockrell lived again, his warm, vigorous, stormy self. She raised her head proudly.

Methody woman? Hush now. He was my husband, my brave, true love.

"He was very angry," she said to young Mr. Guess. "When folks are angry, they do not choose their words with care."

"Ma'am, there are times when to do so would seem cowardly." His eyes had the strangest light in them. "Would you care to have a report on Andrew Moore at this time? He is in jail. Under heavy bond. He will stand trial on the charge of murder, though I would not venture to promise what the result will be. There are some who believe he will have a case if he pleads self-defense."

Some. Even John McCoy, perhaps. At this point, numb with weariness and shock, Sarah could not care too deeply or even think clearly about the final judgment on Andrew Moore; but the lack of staunch and able friends struck at her afresh.

"But I . . ."

Mr. Guess hesitated, as if he felt his opinion was also of no importance to her. But it was important. He had spoken so truly and feelingly about Alec.

"Please say what is in your mind," Sarah told him. "I am listening."

"Ma'am, I am a great admirer of your husband. I hope you will understand when I say that I had rather be Alexander Cockrell dead than Andrew Moore alive. Who in time to come will remember Andrew Moore except as one who killed a better man than he could ever be?"

There! That was the forthright sort of thing she wanted to hear. He gave her the watch then. It was cold and heavy in her hand, and she held it to her breast, to warm it.

"I am obliged," she said. "He set great store by this watch."

"It is a fine watch, ma'am. May I wind it for you? I have heard that it is well to keep a watch wound and running. The mechanism demands to be used so. It should be wound every day."

He set the key into its hole and turned it. The watch had not run down entirely, but now it seemed to take on new life. Almost two o'clock in the morning, Sarah noticed, and thanked the young man again, wanting him, too, to leave.

"Ma'am," he said, "I would like to be of further service." A champion? It was almost as if Alec had sent him. "If the time should come, for example, to press for the collection of that debt that is still standing, I should count it a privilege to handle the case for you."

"I believe you would," Sarah said, studying his face in wonder. "But why? Surely you can think of a better way to start practice in a new town."

"This is the way I want to start, ma'am. I said I would count it a privilege. I will not trouble you further tonight. I will call again later, if I may. Please do not forget that I asked."

"Such a nice young man." Martha Overton said, when he had gone. "Perry took to him right away. Who is he, Sarah?"

"I'll tell you tomorrow," Sarah said. "It is too late now. He brought me Mr. Cockrell's watch, Martha. That's how I know how late it is. Yes, I will rest now—and sleep, I think. Dear Martha, I am richer in friends than I knew."

chapter **twenty-nine**

...through the night...

SHE SLEPT THE SOUND SLEEP of exhaustion—a whole night crowded into a few hours. She could not have said what wakened her. Perhaps some inward urgency that pricked through her drugged senses. She did not waken with a cry, or any other sound. For minutes she lay as still as everything around her. It was still night, dark beyond the closed shutters, dark in that room, except for the g⁻ntle illumination from the office beyond—a lamp turned low, a fire aglow in the chimney.

The bedroom was as it always was—almost. The fresh clothing she had asked for as she went to bed laid out over a chair. Too quiet, perhaps. Alec was away. He would always be away now. No more doubt. No more uncertainty. A stark fact to be met and dealt with. No trundle bed, no child. Little Alec had moved upstairs yesterday evening. He would sleep with his brothers from now on. No baby in this house ever again. In place of him, Martha Overton rested in an armchair, wrapped in a blanket. The pile of blanket moved up and down as she breathed. Must be cold in the room. Sarah thrust her hand out from under the covers to see, and drew it back quickly. Dear Martha, she thought, and smiled fondly, then was shocked at realizing that she had smiled. Did healing come so soon—and forgetting?

She lay still, but wider and wider awake, perhaps for another quarter of an hour. Someone knocked on the front door. Steps went down the hall. The door opened to a low murmur of voices, then closed; and two sets of steps crossed the hall to another door, which also opened and closed.

274

"Martha! Martha, are you awake?"

The blanket heaved and fell away.

"Land sakes, Sarah! You scared me. You sick?"

"No, Martha. I just woke up. I'm ready to get up now."

"Not yet," Martha protested. "Still the dead o' night."

"Oh, it can't be. I've been asleep a long time. Look at the watch."

It lay on the dresser. Wind it every day, the gentlemanly stranger had advised. Keep it running. She would do that.

"Not five o'clock yet," Martha protested.

"I heard somebody come in just now," Sarah said.

"Expect you did," Martha grumbled. "Been a-going and a-coming all night. I wonder anybody could sleep."

"I slept fine. Martha, this was somebody special. Could it be Mr. Gouffe with Mr. Cockrell's coat?"

"Not yet," Martha protested again.

"I must get up and see," Sarah said.

"Well, all right," Martha yielded. "Wait till I stir that fire, will you? Pokey! Pokey, get up off the floor and fetch another stick of wood. Mrs. Cockrell is getting up. But be quiet, Pokey. No need to rouse the whole house."

But there were others who could not lie abed for long. Before Sarah had finished dressing, Hannah came in, to say that the tailor had delivered the coat.

"Miss Sally, Mist' Alec look jes' beau-ful now. A body might ask what diff'unce it make wid de coat tore or not down de back, but it do. He . . ." she stopped in sudden awe and a new pleasure. "Miss Sally, you look fine, too. Pale, a lil' washed-out, mebbe. Yore eyes kind o' deep in your haid, but handsome. Yore hair shiny smooth . . . Miss Sally, I laid out de church dress. Was dat right?"

"Exactly right, Hannah. Thank you."

"An' you got dat pretty lil' shiny black pin on Mist' Alec brung you. You ain' wo'n it much dat I see. Miss Sally, you goin' to look at him now? Pity he can't see you. You need yore big shawl, honey. Hit's cold in yondah. We got to keep it so."

"Yes, Hannah, I know."

But she didn't know. She had never known just the particular chill which that room laid upon her when she went in, closing the door behind her on the living warmth of the remainder of the house. She had never known such silence. She had said she preferred to go in alone, and she was glad of that. That way she could stand against the door and get hold of herself. Close her eyes, then open them and see.

Daylight was as yet only a dim promise in the eastern sky. The lamp with the painted-china shade glowed softly on the center table. The room had been put in order, except that the couch was still drawn away from the east wall as it had been the evening before while the Doctor worked there. The first of the morning light fell upon it there; but the lamp was between her and the couch and she saw it only in general outline. The Indian still kept watch in the angle of the room between the north and the east window. It was as though he had not twitched a muscle all night, though she knew he must have. The man was human . . . wasn't he?

"Charley John?" The old reluctance, the strangeness still strong upon her. I'll never lose it, never, she thought. "Charley John, you must be tired. I am here now. Will you take some rest?"

The light from the lamp was reflected in his dark eyes.

"Good!" he said, deep in his throat. "I go now. No harm can come to my Little Older Brother, too far now on the trail for evil spirits to catch him. No harm now. You stay. I go."

"Charley John, you are a good friend—to keep watch like this." What he watched for or against, she still did not know clearly and never would. Was he leaving? She hoped so. In some dark way he was forever part of her sorrow. "Ask in the kitchen for something to eat. The women are awake back yonder."

"I take something in my hand for the journey, if it is given," he answered. "It is far to my home."

"Charley John, as long as you live, our door is open to you." There! Did I say that right, Mr. Cockrell?

"You are good woman." That was the Indian's thank you. "I do not come again. I go home to stay, to wait until I am called to follow my brother to the Darkening Land. It will not be long. I have done what I must do. I go. You stay. You good woman.

You live long, long time. You strong. Only woman is strong like that. I go now—for all time."

He raised his hand, whether in a kind of Indian blessing or simply to say good-bye, she did not know, not even seeing clearly for the dim light and the sting of tears again in her eyes.

"Charley John . . ." she turned away; and, when she looked again, he was gone.

Alec? She went around the table. The lamp was at her back now and there was a faint increase of light from the window. How could she look; and yet, how could she not? Then, to her astonishment, reality was less than her dread. Alec!

She saw what Hannah meant by beautiful. She had heard it said that death could work wonders on a body from which the soul had fled. Now she knew it was so. Except for the closed eyes and the too tightly closed mouth, all that she had known to be noble and upward reaching in Alexander Cockrell—the good which he would have incontinently denied—was chiseled on his still features. She studied them with old affection and new wonder—the high, broad forehead, the hollow cheeks, the whole face narrowing to the chin, and that masked by the fringe of black whiskers, which he had grown, she did believe, chiefly to plague her. The noise of him, the waywardness, the quick rise of passion, all were gone; and yet, this was Alexander Cockrell.

I'll never see you again this side of eternity, she thought then in sudden renewal of fright, never. The children will never know their father. Mr. Cockrell, you went away too soon, too fast. So far away. The Indian is right. So far . . . how can I make you hear what I came to say? I must say it; and you, wherever you are, must stop and listen. She drew up a chair.

Mr. Cockrell, the town you gave me six years ago—and I said I didn't want it, and time and again I have said the same—you have given it to me again and forever now. And I want it less than I wanted it before—and more, because it is your town and I will not have it said by anyone that what you built and strove for came to nothing. I will find help—that young lawyer who brought your watch, or Mr. Toomy, or the lawmaker from Austin. Maybe your brother in Missouri. Somewhere I will find help, and all you planned will come to be, I promise.

She raised her head, to look, to listen. The light was some stronger now; but she felt, rather than saw or heard, the hush of the sleeping town about her; and from it, and beyond, from as far as the gold diggings in California, a cry that would never let her off that promise:

"I depend on you . . . depend on you . . . on you now, Sarah Cockrell."

Martha Overton at the first real light opened the door of the parlor softly and stepped inside.

"Sh!" Sarah said. "Oh, it's you, Martha. Martha, will you do something for me? I want you to send George or whoever else is awake and responsible uptown to Mr. Gouhenant's Art Salon on Main Street—Mr. Gonant, the picture man, Martha. I want him to pack his camera machine and all else he needs and come down here right away to make a picture of Mr. Cockrell."

"Sarah, for heaven's sake!"

"Martha, how else will the children know their father in time to come? I can tell them what he was like, and others will tell them, but it won't be the same. Mr. Gonant can make a picture right here. He will know how to do it, and how to fix up the likeness afterwards to seem more lifelike. He will know. I don't, but I am sure he can do it. Martha, I want this now more than anything. People die and are so soon forgotten. Martha, please."

"Well, all right," Martha said unwillingly. "I'll send somebody as soon as it is full day."

"No," Sarah said. "Now. Once the sun rises, the day will go too fast. It will take Mr. Gonant time to fix up things here as he wants them. The clear morning light will be lost. Now, Martha. Don't wait."

"Now," Martha agreed, but doubtfully. What had come over her friend? "Sarah, it's cold as ice in here. Will you come out for a cup of coffee?"

"Later," Sarah said. "After Mr. Gonant has been here. We'll all have coffee together then. I'm not cold, really. I have this shawl. Please, Martha, do as I want."

chapter **thirty**

...with the dawn, the evil spirits flee.

DAWN CAME OVER Dallas County with rare splendor that morning of April 4, 1858. The sun, not yet risen, gathered together the night vapors and flung across the sky gauzy scarves, dyed pale gold and pink and silver. Too delicate to endure, they would perish under the first warm breath of true day; but they had their exquisite moment. Every prairie flower, every blade of grass, every leaf held up a crystal bead, or several, to catch the light. Some, growing lush in basins that now were ponds or too close to the banks of streams, were drowned entirely or lay, limp and mud-plastered, against the earth; but, at the first stir of air, even they lifted heavy heads to the wonder of another day. Waters ran brown and thick, but not now with the foam of rising flood. Already drying mud marked where water had been but now was gone.

Again it was a wide and empty land. In hamlets or scattered houses, wearied by late watching and the mystifying terror of the night's storm, people slept, blanketed now by the peace of a perfect Sunday morning. Here and there a cow lowed, in close harmony with the mourning of doves. A mockingbird awoke and tried a line of song, then rushed into a delirium of melody. A lark soared into the sky, trailing silver sweetness.

In this pure peace of emptiness, only one human being showed —a solitary man on a pony that picked its steps with deliberation and what looked like elaborate caution along the edge of a mired

279

road. Charley John was going home. He, too, seemed to drowse, his legs clamped about the pony's sides, his hand slack on the bridle, his head on his chest; but he was only meditating. Not too mournfully. In the theology of his people, the Tsa-ra-gi, whom white men called Cherokee, death, however it came, was the natural end of living. He whom Charley John had named Little Older Brother was now gone, whether to a happier land or to oblivion did not much matter. What of him was immortal, his extraordinary spirit, was safe. It might have been snatched from him by demons or spoiled by a mortal enemy, but that had not happened. A woman had now taken it into her keeping, a strong, brave woman, with steady eyes and steady hands, who walked erectly and spoke kindly, but never too much. She would guard that spirit as one fed sticks to an altar fire. She would breathe it into his children, and so into his children's children. The work of his hands, the desire of his heart, would grow even beyond his imagining. What was mortal of Little Older Brother was gone; what was immortal could never be lost.

In Dallas, bemired as elsewhere and mostly heavily asleep, M. Gouhenant, who, after finishing the wine his guests had abandoned, bidding himself alternately not to despair and not to hope for too much, had finally dropped off in an armchair in his Art Salon, awoke to a thumping sound, which he could not identify and a dishevelment, which he did not wish to see. So, he closed his eyes again, to hide the shameful state of this elegant room and to see whether the thumping, which might be in his own head, would not go away also.

When this did not happen, he knew the noise was outside. He pulled himself then to his feet, and, with eyes still turned from the room's defilement, went to the door and opened it. There stood the Cockrell's trusted servant boy. Was another such miracle as had befallen Antoine Gouffe about to transpire for him, Jacques Gouhenant? It was.

"Miz' Cockrell say, will you please pack up yore picter-takin' ap'ratus and fetch it down to our house right off? She want a picter made o' Mist' Cockrell befo' dey puts him in a coffin."

M. Gouhenant shook his head, to clear it. In delirium he

could not have conceived that good fortune would come just like this. He had never heard of such a thing, and said so.

"She wish fo' you to try, please," George insisted.

"It's not even daylight," the artist objected.

"Hit will be soon . . . an' sudden," George told him. "Mist' Cockrell on de parlor sofa now. Miz' Cockrell say de light is fine an' I's to holp you tote all you needs an' de expense don' matter."

M. Gouhenant shook his head again, but who was he to look with doubt on the demands of what could be his hour of hours?

"Will you enter, please?" he said.

"No, sah, I cain'. Boots is muddy. I'll wait right yere. You kin han' me out what I kin tote. Shet de do', you better. Hit's right cool dis mawnin'."

In Lancaster, Texas, south and west of Dallas, Nicholas Darnell awoke from a night made restless both by the storm and the astonishing news that had come his way at dusk, took a minute to get his bearings in the visitors' half of a stout double house, then rose, put on his boots and stepped outside to see what was happening to the weather now. He found his host ahead of him, testing the sponginess of ground that looked plenty treacherous.

"Mawnin'." A wide grin in a cheerful, weathered, bearded face. "Sleep good? Me, neither. When the rain let up, come the wind. Nice day overhead, but soft underfoot. Can just about make it to the corncrib—with the help of a couple a boards here and yonder."

"Roads, I suppose, are impossible," Darnell said. "How soon do you think they'll dry?"

"Hard telling," the other said. "Which way you heading?"

"Back to Dallas—as soon as I can get there. Transacted a bit of business with the deceased yesterday afternoon. Important business. Would like to know what's what. Well, nothing to do but wait, I reckon."

If that river only were navigable, he thought. If I had any idea what sort of woman the widow is. Husband spoke respectfully of her. Bound to be one of two kinds. Either hard-faced, able, and mean to deal with, or the reverse, in which case, the sooner I separate that railroad contract from the rest of the confusion, the better. Well, I'll not dry the road by blowing on it. What's for breakfast, I wonder?

Though he knew—corncake, fried hawg, and coffee.

In the jail at Dallas, Andy Moore paced the puncheon floor, beating his arms, to stir up his blood. The floor had been his bed, all he wanted of bed. Vermin traps in a place like this—regular beds. He wouldn't have minded the floor's hardness. Didn't need to sleep soft. But he could have done with a blanket. Cold and damp had kept him awake. Must have been the cold and damp. With the first hint of light he was on his feet, tramping the floor. That helped some. Cup o' hot coffee woulda helped more—or somebody to talk to. Who?

It would be hours, he figured, before anybody showed up. His friends all layin' low now. Couldn't figure to see anybody but those who had to come. Hell, that was who he wanted to see. Old Patterson or the Mayor, to tell him his bail had been raised, and that deputy to let him out of here. Bail had been set at five thousand dollars. Pretty high. Hard to raise on Sunday, maybe.

"Looks like you shot too quick, Andy," somebody had hinted.

No such thing. Wouldn't a been here if he hadn't. Shucks, his friends would raise the money among them. Be scared not to. He'd no notion of spending another night in this stinking jail. Not if he had to lift the roof with outcry that some people wouldn't enjoy hearing. Sunday? It was a poor Sunday that couldn't fill a Texas jail with drunks and assaults and such. Desperate men, some of them. Say, Rudy Horst should be one? Oh, hell, somebody would be along to set him free before that happened. Free—what, then? It had been hinted that he was safer where he was. None of that now. He wanted out. Out, out, out! The place was giving him hants, that was what.

Free. Would they give him back his badge? And his guns? Not likely. Just free—to stand trial. Lawyers would get him off then. Self-defense, the dispute rising out of his trying to enforce a town ordinance. And still folks might not want him for Marshal. Might hold a new election. Pious folk, on his side or against him, would feel it looked better.

Then, what had he gained? By God, satisfaction, that was what.

Andrew Moore stopped pacing, his murky brain pierced by sudden illumination. Had he mentioned hants? A hant in the shape of a woman. A slight woman, but strong, dressed in black. A widow's bonnet and a veil, thrown back to show a pale face with deep, sad eyes that looked him through and through. Sarah Horton had never looked at him any other way, if she saw him at all. Deep eyes, unflinching. Steady mouth and a damnably steady chin. Hell! He could fight a man, kill him if he hated him enough; but how did you fight a woman, without she was your wife and you had the upper hand to start with?

In the parlor of the house at the foot of Commerce Street, Sarah waited for full day and the photographer. Waited in growing calm and peace. She sat still near the foot of the couch, as near to her husband as she would ever be now. Very near, really. Talking to him, talking it all out for all time.

You would look more natural, Mr. Cockrell, with the watch chain across your vest; but that young man said to wind the watch and keep it running, and it seems, when I hear it ticking, like something of you alive. A great comfort and I think I was meant to have it. I will never give it away, not even to one of the boys. It ticked against your heart for so long—I want it now for my own.

Such a fine young man, Mr. Cockrell, that Mr. Guess. I know you took a fancy to him or you wouldn't have given him the watch to hold. His wife's not much, a poor, fretful child. She'll be a drag, but he'll do all right, I think. In my mind I've engaged him to help me with law business. I will need somebody for that. And he is honest, I believe, and devoted.

You died, looking at Columbus, my dear. My dearest dear. I never got to tell you all that story. It was a sad one; and I think you knew, because you always hurried off, not to hear it. He knew prisons and chains and sorrow, though he was set free finally. And after he died, only think. It's near four hundred years and we still are proud to hang a picture of him on the wall. Now don't say, what does that matter to Columbus? If things like that didn't matter, we'd all still root for what we need to eat, and hollow out a place to sleep, and that would be our living. If glory and pride and such didn't matter, I couldn't do what I will do now, and from now on—to honor you, as I promised when we were wed.

Mr. Cockrell—Alec—do you remember . . .

It was so that M. Gouhenant found her, seated close beside the couch, leaning forward, just far enough to have placed her warm, strong hand under one of her husband's, where the women had laid them on his breast. Her head, with its smooth braids of hair, the sweep of the shawl across her shoulders, made the French artist of the camera forget his difficulties about a darkroom and sensitive plates. He paused, his hand on his lips, then motioned to George to give him his magic box, but quietly, quietly. Even so Sarah heard him and lifted her head.

"No," he said. "Please, no. Stay as you are. Yes, madame, I know. It is the picture of him you desire and you shall have it. But, please, do not move. It," he hunted for a reason for his plea, "is a matter of shadow contrast."

A matter of shadow. Changing light moved across Alec Cockrell's face. The harshness softened, he seemed about to speak. If he had spoken, what would he have said? Just this:

Methody woman . . .

AUTHOR'S NOTE

It seems longer than the calendar shows—two years—since Brenda Gieseker, making ready to catalog J. W. Rogers' *Lusty Texans of Dallas* for the library of the Missouri Historical Society at St. Louis, came out to me in the reading room with one finger marking a place in the book, and said, "Here is something you might use."

She laid the book on the table, open at Mr. Rogers' brief account of the life and death of one whom he styled "the first capitalist of Dallas." The story was there, packed with drama, shadowed by tragedy, bursting with true Texas dynamics; but I put it aside. I thanked Mrs. Gieseker, whom I have known through many books, and told her my reasons. In the first place I was no Texan. A Missourian, and so close kin, but yet, not a Texan. In the second place, the man got himself killed. Thirdly, his wife was altogether too wonderful. I always view with alarm a wholly remarkable woman.

So, Mrs. Gieseker took the book away and I went home. To walk the floor, saying over a story that would give me no peace. To lie awake nights, studying it. I took it to church with me, to the supermarket, into the kitchen, wherever I went. And so finally, here it is. My first grateful acknowledgment, therefore, belongs to Mrs. Brenda Gieseker, Librarian of the Missouri Historical Society at St. Louis. And my second must go to Mr. J. W. Rogers of Dallas for setting down so ably the salient facts of the legend. When I wrote to him, he allowed that it was a dramatic story for anyone who wouldn't mind the trouble and risks of running it down and writing it. Well, I minded all right; but I never yet wrote a book that didn't give trouble or have its perilous moments; so his warning did not stop me.

My third acknowledgment, chronologically, is due to Monroe F. Cockrell of Evanston, Illinois, senior grandson of the story hero, who, out of devoted interest in the family history, has amassed over the years a remarkable collection of letters, records, photographs and other mementos, beautifully arranged and filed. Among these is a history of early Dallas, compiled from firsthand

285

reports by Frank Cockrell, Alexander Cockrell's second son, which Monroe Cockrell has edited and published in a limited edition. All these papers and records, on a visit I made to Evanston in the autumn of 1956, Mr. Cockrell opened and painstakingly reviewed with me. And after that, with a patience almost untiring, he wrote out answers to questions that arose continually as I set down the story. "Here you are again," he would say with a sigh and then produce many typed pages of verified information. But even more valuable than recorded evidence, perhaps, were the hours he and I spent in talking over scenes, people and events. Through these I hope I arrived at a true presentation of Alexander Cockrell and Sarah, his wife, and of the town they both served devotedly.

The following spring, with the book taking shape, I went down to Dallas, to look up more records, to visit the story scene, and meet more of the family. As my friends there and I said merrily afterward, I went down to see what the weather was like in Dallas in the spring of the year. I arrived by plane only a few hours ahead of the first of the 1957 Texas tornados. But a few hours is a wide margin of time for dodging a whirlwind. Through the worst of the storm I sat in the library of the Dallas Historical Society, located in the basement of the Dallas Hall of Fame, a handsome building with marble floors and columns, well supported. I could not have found a better cyclone cellar. When I finally lifted my head from old census records and realized from murmurs of talk that a present-day catastrophe was taking place, the storm was already whirling away over West Dallas. I got upstairs and into the open only just in time to see the last of the ugly cloud, the funnel of which had missed my airport by a whisker. The torrential rain and noisy thunderstorm that followed that night I put to good use later.

In the library of the Dallas Historical Society, ably administered by Mrs. Herbert Gambrell, I had, again, unstinted help from Mr. K. L. Gowin, who seems to be the liaison man there for questing authors. He had books and papers laid out for me to study and each day added to them. He produced from a dusty storeroom Sarah Cockrell's trunk, in which she kept her papers, and from a safe her personal effects, among them the silver watch and chain worn by her husband. It is of inestimable value to an author to hold such things in her hand. Later we compared notes and maps and so forth. To Mr. Gowin and his assistants I owe thanks that I find hard to measure.

Outside of the records, I owe much to three women of the Cockrell family—Mrs. Ruth Cockrell Wilson, granddaughter of Robert Cockrell, eldest son of the story hero and of Guillelmine Jones of the French Colony, to Mrs. David Spangler, born Aurelia Cockrell and sister to Monroe Cockrell, both children of "Baby Alec," and to Mrs. Mary Vardaman Cockrell, sister-in-law and cousin respectively of Mrs. Spangler and Monroe Cockrell.

Mrs. Wilson gave me a room in her house during my stay. She did more. She shared with me family portraits, a thousand intimate reminiscences, and gave me the privilege of knowing her family, which, in addition to her husband and children, included a sister and two brothers, all of whom, and Ruth Wilson herself, established and steadied physical images and character traits. On one memorable day, Mrs. Wilson and I visited the Overton farm at Honey Springs, where in an attic I saw a lifelike portrait of Perry Overton. Later that morning we called at the home of Mr. George Santerre, whose book, *White Cliffs of Dallas*, preserves the legend of the French Colony. There in a charming home, almost untouched amid the destruction left by the tornado, in a parlor filled with the atmosphere of the Old World, we talked more about early days. The afternoon of that day was spent then in riding over the "high ground" of the West Side, and included a memorable view of the Mountain Creek Reservoir of the Dallas Light and Power Company, where once Alexander Cockrell owned ranch land.

On other days Mrs. Spangler and Mrs. Vardaman Cockrell were my chauffeurs and guides, showing me, at my request, the "wide prairies," the Trinity River, the old square and many other points. Evenings in their homes were spent in retelling family legends and looking at more old portraits, notably the one that figures in the final pages of the book.

Around and between these adventures, I was still busy asking questions of all and sundry. Here I should mention shotguns. After Monroe Cockrell obtained from Olin-Mathieson and Remington Arms authentic statements about the range and proper ammunition for a shotgun of 1858, my editors obtained from Mr. Jac Weller, Honorary Curator of the West Point Museum, a detailed paragraph on loading such a weapon. All the while I was reading everything I could lay my hands on that would give me the lore, the history, the feel of Texas—everything from the songs of a balladeer and the autobiography of Amelia Barr, who lived exactly the right years in Texas, to reports of the United States Bureau of Ethnology. It was from one of these reports—*Myths of the Cherokee*, by James Mooney—that I took the legend of the Raven Mockers.

Finally, having exhausted the resources of various libraries and worn down uncounted librarians, I got the book done. Finally, too, it is fiction, in that I have embroidered and enlarged upon fact, combined incidents and invented others, to serve a storyteller's needs; but the outline of the tale—the fact pattern and sequence—is true. The characters, I hope, resemble closely people who once lived and are now gone. Only one major character is purely fictional—Charley John, the Indian. I hope, again, that reading the story will justify my creating him. Alexander Cockrell learned and kept much from his years spent among the Cherokee. His toll bridge could have been one thing. The Indians north of the Red River, in what was then called "The Indian Nations" and is now Oklahoma, used them profitably on main lines of travel.

Now the last word is to those who always want to know what happened afterward. Andrew Moore was tried on the charge of murder and was acquitted; but three months after the tragedy, town elections were held and he was one of those put out of office. On the new roster we find young Mr. Guess a member of the Board of Aldermen, to which group he was re-elected a number of times. He represented Sarah Cockrell in her suits to recover the Moore debt, and won judgment and payment. Sarah lived to keep all her promises. The hotel was opened with splendor and fanfare in 1860. It was called the St. Nicholas Hotel, after its first manager, Nicholas Darnell. In later years, when the railroads came, and a new iron bridge was built over the Trinity, Sarah Cockrell's name is first on the roster of the company that built it. She lived until 1892 and died a wealthy woman, respected and loved by all who knew her, especially the poor.